A Case of the Lycans

A Case of the Lycans

Michael Fursdon

Cover Art by Grimsloki Gempiloyi @grimsloki

Illustration on page 78 by Kevovelac @kenetersa

Illustration on page 98 by Keith King @sauelapsey

Illustration on page 288 by Maearc @keckes

Illustration on page 307 by Julianto @lian_00

Illustration on page 385 by Kevovelac @kenetersa

Illustration on page 172 & 524 by Michael Fursdon

Special thank you to Bill C, Bob P, Charles F, and the Wozniaks

Published by Michael Fursdon, A 20/20 Fantasy story

Table of Contents

Introduction

Back during ancient Greek times, tales of lycanthropy were being told. Lycanthropy is derived from a pair of Greek words, which are lykos, meaning wolf, and anthropos, meaning human. Combining these Greek words yields the term wolfman, describing the transformation from a human to a wolf.

Around the 5th century, Greek authors would use the term lycan-trope in their stories to describe humans with the supernatural ability to transform into a wolf. By the 18th century, the word was condensed to lycan. Old European legends would regale of tales of people who change between human and wolf forms calling them lycans.

Across the hills and plains of North America, fanciful fantasy tales of lycans roaming wild and free in the night time became plentiful. By the 20th century, these folktales began to distinguish lycan from werewolf. The first difference is that werewolves can only involuntarily transform during a full moon where lycans can change at will anytime. The next difference is that lycans keep human intellect and reason where a werewolf behaves as a wild feral wolf. Finally, werewolves look like wolves once transformed as opposed to lycans who take a hybrid wolfman form.

Now moving forward to more modern-day tales, the city of Cathedral, known for its abnormal criminal activity, is being terrorized by killers dressed as wolfmen. These villains were becoming infamous for their wolfish personas and brutal butchering. The megamedia in Cathedral dubbed these individuals as the lycan masquerade killers. Fearful citizens flocked to their favorite media outlets for lycan dressed killer news and clamored for the police department to provide some answers. Amidst this turmoil is where this story begins.

Chapter 1

A Case of the Lycans

Lightning lit up the sky and brightened the night for about two seconds. Rain continued to come down hard on the windshield of Detective Emily Goldsmith-Oftenmarch's vehicle. One second the sky was dark and stormy, the next second it was bright and stormy, and then a couple of seconds later it was dark and stormy again. The storm that recently raged in the city of New Carnelian was now here. It was actually 1:47am this stormy morning which was way too early to be responding to a dispatch but that was part of the job of a Cathedral police officer.

Cathedral was a modern American city built to have a retro appearance, with many buildings constructed with historical architecture. One reason this was implemented was because a sizeable segment of Cathedral was built on the ruins of the old city called Arden. From the ashes of Arden, the metropolis of Cathedral was made. A second reason was to give the city a more historic appearance. Unfortunately, a large portion of the city was also not well maintained, which resulted in a deteriorated rundown look, making the city look older than it actually was. Cathedral was also called the Central City because three cities had developed in the surrounding area. Those cities were Chatham, Granthum, and New Carnelian; they were often referred to as the daughter cities. Cathedral sat in the middle of the three daughter cities.

Between the cities of Cathedral and Chatham was a suburb called New Terranceville. New Terranceville was an oblong shaped town located adjacent to Cathedral's southern border. It had a large rundown shabby industrial section which could depress the cheeriest of individuals. This section was in stark contrast to the rich decadent residential and commercial sections on the opposite side of New Terranceville. Emily was heading for the rundown industrial section on this very early hour in the morning.

Emily was named Eighth by her parents, since she was their eighth child. This was the simplistic reason for her name. Her parents and

1

siblings called her E for short. When she turned eighteen years old, she changed her name legally to Emily. Her family and childhood friends still called her E and she would tell people who did not know better that it was short for Emily. When Emily was twenty years old and a junior at the University of Cathedral, she married her college sweetheart Abraham Goldsmith, who she met at an event at Grand Central State University. He was the son of Powercore Unlimited Corporation CEO Jeramiah Goldsmith and nephew of the Vice President of Jaycox Motors, Jared Goldsmith. At the time of their marriage, he had graduated from GCSU as a business major. Abraham had become a financial management advisor for medium level corporations and was a race car enthusiast. It was the latter that tragically got him killed in his twenties. Two years later, Emily remarried. She married a pastor and a part time librarian named David-John Oftenmarch. She kept the Goldsmith name just to infuriate her former father-in-law to become Emily Goldsmith-Oftenmarch.

Driving in the pouring rain at an unpleasant hour in the morning, Detective Emily Goldsmith-Oftenmarch had the radio going to keep her company. She was a sports fan, not a sports talk fan, but her choices were limited given the hour so she was listening to some sports talk highlights. After seven innings with the score tied 2-2, there had been a rain delay for the Cathedral Bishops, and the league planned to finish the game later that afternoon. The Granthum Grey Sox were on the road and their game went fourteen innings. In the top of the 14th inning, the Grey Sox catcher hit an RBI double to take the lead 4 to 3. In the bottom of the 14th inning, the Granthum fastball reliever had a three up and three down inning to record a save. Emily liked baseball, she swam and ran track in college, but her favorite sport was association football, aka soccer. Her favorite team was the New Carnelian Miners and she was a season ticket holder to their games. Wishing she was heading for a game instead of driving to a crime scene in a deluge, Emily sighed. She had reached her dreary early morning destination on the depressing side of New Terranceville.

Frederick Incancennio was well known for his over-the-top massive breweries. However, on this particular dark and raining morning, it was one of his bottling factories which had earned attention. That earned attention came from the New Terranceville police after multiple emergency calls were received regarding an attack in the factory. The first call was received around one o'clock followed by a half a dozen more frantic calls in the next seven minutes. The first New Terranceville patrol car arrived at the somewhat secluded bottling factory at twelve minutes after one. It was joined by a pair of fellow New Terranceville patrol cars two minutes later. Two minutes after that another New Terranceville squad car and a neighboring Bourbon Heights police vehicle arrived at the scene. What these officers found was hysteria and homicide. Their discovery led to the dispatch of detectives, the coroner, and forensics around one twenty-five am on a now darker and more rainy morning.

The town of New Terranceville, which did not have a homicide squad, sent the call to the city of Cathedral. The Cathedral detectives on call that night were the city's most unorthodox law enforcement personal. The chief of police referred to them as mud tusslers. They fought through every case, never failed to get messy, but always trudged to a conclusion, albeit sloppily. If there was a quick and clean solution to a crime, the mud tusslers would not find it. However, there were no detectives more dedicated, diligent, or determined than the mud tusslers. Lt. Eddie Knighton was the most prompt of the mud tusslers to arrive, which was typical. His peers referred to him as Steady Eddie or Silent Knight for his unflappable demeanor and brevity of conversation. Eddie quietly observed the hectic scene at the bottling factory until his partner, you guessed it, Detective Emily Goldsmith-Oftenmarch, arrived on the scene. She was neither quiet nor unemotional by any means of measure. Her passionate drive with a proclivity to burst into a barrage of babbleless conversation complimented Lt. Knighton's style very well.

Before Detective Emily Oftenmarch exited her vehicle, she was still adjusting her holster and revolver. Lightning lit up the early morning sky again and a not too distant rumble of thunder could be heard. During her years as a patrol officer, the department's service semi-automatic had sufficed. However, in her first year as a detective, Detective Oftenmarch decided to switch firearms after three well placed gunshots from her service weapon failed to stop a particularly large and overly motivated drug dealer. Since transitioning to the Maxwell TriAlloy XL-2, she never had that problem again. With her weapon harness adjusted, Emily began to untangle her officer cam charging cable from her cell phone charging cord and the power cord used to connect the video drone to its charging station. Disentangling the spaghetti of cables, Emily freed her officer cam and attached it to her three-fourths-length charcoal grey leather jacket. Flashlight now in hand, Det. Oftenmarch got out of her police vehicle and closed her driver's side car door with a sigh. Moving quickly, Emily opened the back driver's side door to retrieve the robodroid. The robodroid was an automated detective assistant called MADAD, mobile automated detective assistant droid or MPAR, mobile police assistant robot. The police personal called them servicebots.

The MPARs had a cubic design with multiple compartments and were two feet tall, 16 inches wide, and 18 inches deep. They had an array of sensors installed, a top mounted video camera inside a protective dome, and a digital front display. The cubelike servicebot travelled on a series of rotating wheels. In its compartments, a detective could access supplies and store collected crime scene evidence. The droid was supposed to be a convenience but often became a hinderance.

These servicebots were transported in a small case on wheels. She pulled the case out, set it on its wheels, and lifted the case's telescopic handle in one fluid movement. Closing her back driver's side door with another sigh and pocketing her flashlight, she headed for the oversized bottling factory's colossal entrance. Running her free hand through her luxuriant hair, Emily sighed yet again. There was no good time for crime, but this hour of the morning was a particularly terrible time. After a ten-hour day, Emily was so tired she had been asleep dreaming she was sleeping before dispatch woke her. That was the problem with villainy, it had no boundary of time; it never took time to rest.

The early morning was dreary and rainy, which set the mood as somber. The flashing lights of the police cars glistened in the rain and lit up the dark. The coroner's van reflected the lights to double the effect. Oftenmarch could tell from the swirling sea of competing bright police lights that the costumed lycan killers sighting had drawn a lot of police attention. They indicated there was trouble on this damp, dark, and dreary post midnight. Det. Goldsmith-Oftenmarch pulled her charcoal gray jacket collar tighter to herself in preparation to dash in the precipitation. Emily hustled up the front walk to get out of the rain. Emily had two pairs of running shoes from Landers Shoe Company. Both pairs were the SuperFlex X3 Trim athletic running shoes. The pink and white pair, Emily wore for working out and jogging. The black on darker black pair, Emily wore to work on after hours dispatches. With the darker solid color pair she could pass them off as work shoes in the twilight hours and night time. She was currently putting those black running shoes to good work. Emily flashed her detective badge to the police officers standing guard at the door.

"What's the bad news tonight, officer?" Detective Oftenmarch inquired to one of the soggy and unhappy looking uniformed officers.

"Initial reports were burglary. When we arrived on the scene we found a pair of murders." one officer answered.

"Where in the factory were the murders?" Emily asked.

"In the maintenance department located in the lower sections. Coroner's office personal are already there." the other officer informed her as they opened the door for her.

"Thank you." the detective politely replied.

Inside the entranceway stood Lt. Eddie Knighton, her ever reliable partner. My Steady Eddie was her nickname for him. He had a concentrated look on his face, his eyes never stopped scanning the area. Police officers and plant workers were crossing back and forth the main lobby in a cacophony of conversations reviewing the events of the early morning criminal activity at the factory.

"My Steady Eddie, looks like a breaking and entering turned to burglary, escalating into assault, and for the finale crescendo culminated in murder. Sound about right, so far?" Emily greeted.

"Too soon to tell" Eddie replied.

"I hear you and right you are. You can never judge a crime by its dispatch." Emily surveyed the receptionist area of the factory. "What a dreary place and at this time of night it is down right creepy."

"Wait until seeing the basement.", Eddie retorted.

Walking across the lobby, two New Terranceville Police officers were in a loud discussion with a plain clothes police detective. Emily recognized the detective as Jack Kettlemore of the Sycamore Hills police department. The man was large, loud, lazy, and slovenly, but did not seem to care that that was the image he portrayed. Sycamore Hills was one town over from New Terranceville. It was similar to its neighboring town in almost every way, only on a smaller scale.

Jack Kettlemore was declaring himself the lead detective. "Even though the main entrance to the brewery is in New Terranceville, the plant is actually located in Sycamore Hills. I will be the primary investigator on this particular case." he incorrectly reasoned.

"The bottling factory is actually in Cathedral city limits." replied a New Terranceville patrol man inaccurately. "We just assist as friendly neighboring law enforcement."

"Cathedral and New Terranceville can assist all they want; I am in charge." the blowhard detective bellowed.

Detective Emily Oftenmarch and Lt. Eddie Knighton looked at each other with the same quizzical look that expressed they both were wondering the same thing. Why was a Sycamore Hills detective dispatched on this case, and why was that detective already at the scene of the crime? He had no jurisdiction here, period. Furthermore, Emily was not in the mood to watch the husky Sycamore Hills detective mark his territory, but she was also far too tired to argue over something so trivial especially when compared to multiple murders. Besides, the detective suspected that her captain would be throwing his big city weight around and have Lt. Knighton and herself assigned as primary detectives by morning breakfast.

However, Detective Kettlemore was challenged on his self-proclaimed authority far sooner than breakfast. A contradiction to his claim of being in charge came almost immediately from the main entrance to the bottling factory. "You are large but not in charge, fatty." came the voice of Cathedral Lt. Peter Parnes of the 272nd Precinct. He stood in the entrance of the factory with his partner Det. Kenneth Barsons, with a stern no nonsense look on his face.

"No way, Poker Parnes. You and your fellow big city hot shots are not stealing this case from me." Detective Kettlemore challenged.

"You know full well homicides in New Terranceville are handled by the 271th and 272nd Cathedral precincts. Tonight's homicides are no different." Lt. Parnes countered.

"You think this is New Terranceville? Is that what brought Cathedral homicide here?" Kettlemore cackled as he spoke.

"It was not polite conversation and no coffee that brought us out here at this time of the morning." Emily returned.

"Nobody asked you, cupcake." Kettlemore shouted.

"Didn't Eddie tell you that you were supposed to bring the coffee, cupcake? Oh, that's right, Eddie doesn't talk." Det. Barsons joked to Emily.

"Don't be daft, Kettlemore. This is New Terranceville where your wideload is standing." Lt. Parnes proclaimed.

"This is Sycamore Hills where this building stands, you idiots" Kettlemore replied with a red-faced roar.

"What town is this?" Eddie asked the nearest factory employee.

"New Terranceville." answered the local employee. Lt. Knighton looked at the next closest employee and that person responded in agreement, "New Terranceville."

"Eddie speaks intelligently. Maybe that is why some people don't hear him." Emily slyly stated, looking straight at Barsons.

"Go buy a map, Kettlemore, and disappear from my sight before Barsons uses his stunner on you for fun." Lt. Parnes snarled at the Sycamore Hills detective.

"You will be hearing from my captain." Det. Jack Kettlemore yelled before storming off across the lobby towards the factory floor.

"That is a disappointment, I was looking forward to stunning him for fun." Det. Barsons jested with a wide smile on his face.

"Why are you guys here? ", Emily asked baffled.

"We were working another case when we heard this dispatch get broadcast. The breaking and entering homicides sounded similar to the case we were working, so we are here to see if they are connected." Lt. Parnes explained.

"Wow, that sounds like dedication coming from the 272nd precinct. The last time that happened was, well, never. That has never happened." Det. Oftenmarch mocked.

"Hilarious, cupcake. You two suckers must be on call for the 271st precinct. Don't worry, we are not here to hurt your feelings. That is just an added bonus." Lt. Parnes surmised.

"We know you like your beauty sleep and dress-up hour, sugar plum." Det. Barsons ribbed.

"Similar how?" Lt. Knighton asked simply.

"That is for us to look into, detective. You just worry about the homicides." Lt. Parnes declared then motioned for Det. Barsons to follow him.

"Barsons, your fly is undone." Det. Oftenmarch said in her farewell sticking out her tongue. As the two homicide detectives from the Cathedral 272nd precinct crossed the lobby, Emily moved closer to her partner. Quietly she asked, "Am I crazy or does this many homicide detectives seem off or out of the ordinary?"

"Crazy, yes. Wrong, no." Eddie answered simply.

"Could someone please direct us towards the scene of the not Sycamore Hills murders?" Emily asked the room of police officers and idle factory employees.

"Take the stairs to the right and head down a level, detective. The first crime scene is in the second hallway about 20 yards to the left." a helpful New Terranceville officer informed her.

"Thank you." Detective Oftenmarch responded as she opened the case to the MADAD unit to release the robodroid. Switching on her officer camera, Emily followed Lt. Knighton to the stairs as they got to work.

A pair of New Terranceville police officers followed Eddie and Emily down the stairs to the basement level of the factory. The basement had low ceilings lined with utility pipes and its stone slab walls were in need of repair and paint. The below ground level smelled musky and like spoiled fish. It was not hard to find the first crime scene; the coroner's office personnel working the scene made it easy to locate.

Doctor Brahm Brownling was hovering closely over a male victim examining the body. Dr. Brownling wore large thick oval shaped glasses and often had a starring look of concentration on his face. He had that look now. His assistants had set-up a large overhead lamp for the doctor to work in better light. The light was casting long shadows of the doctor down the hallway. The basic medical assistance droid, BMAD, was stationary next to the doctor, buzzing and beeping in continual quiet levels.

"What unfortunate mess do we have tonight, doctor?" Emily inquired.

"Most dreadful, my dear. It appears this poor person was mauled by some sort of wolf. The bite marks around the neck area are of a large canine variety. Furthermore, the claw marks running along the victim's abdomen are more consistent with a wolf. This is peculiar because, despite their fearsome reputation, wolves are in reality quite shy and very unlikely to attack humans. There are more bite marks on the left shoulder similar to the neck bites." the doctor indicated pointing to areas of the deceased as he spoke.

"Wait a minute, doctor. The dispatch was for a pair of intruders entering the factory. Nothing was mentioned about dogs or wolves.", Emily expressed with puzzlement.

"Some of the witnesses said the intruders were wearing wolf masks." one of the New Terranceville officers shared.

The servicebot, MADAD or MPAR, had finally reached the first crime scene. Its bells and whistles were audible as the unit had detected the scene and its BMAD counterpart. From the sounds it was emitting, the slow-moving robot seemed to now be recording the crime scene and the remains of the victim.

"Was this poor person mauled to death by wolves?" Emily asked the doctor.

"It is difficult to tell at this juncture. However, there is one obvious observation which is noteworthy and that is there are a couple of deeper more serious wounds hidden among the canine made injuries. It is very likely that these wounds were the fatal ones." Dr. Brownling explained as he pointed to specific wounds on the victim.

"When you say hidden among the canine made injuries, does that mean the deeper wounds were not inflicted by wolves?" she looked for clarification.

"The more serious wounds are not consistent with the rest of the wounds. They are more likely to have been made with a man-made weapon. Although, it will take more in-depth analysis to confirm this hypothesis." Dr. Brownling replied. The BMAD gave three quick beeps.

At that moment two events simultaneously happened. First, the power to the bottling factory shut off. All the lights went out and the emergency exit lighting came on, leaving the plant in ninety percent darkness. Second, a call for help came over the NTPD's digital portable transceivers, or walkie talkies. An unknown individual had attacked an officer and fled in the basement of the bottling factory. A request for assistance in the pursuit of the attacker was broadcast.

"The night the light went. . . .", began Lt. Eddie Knighton.

"...out in Georgia, does not stop the music for you and me in Tennessee" finished Det. Emily Oftenmarch.

Before the detectives had a chance to identify the first victim, they decided to respond to the distress call from the New Terranceville Police. After thanking the doctor, the pair of Cathedral detectives accompanied by the pair of New Terranceville police officers went to provide assistance. They moved as quickly as they could in the dark as their MPAR struggled to keep pace. A second BMAD unit provided light in the darkness as it was scanning the second crime scene, which was a second murder victim. The group swiftly circumnavigated the second grisly crime scene and began playing hide and seek for a stairway. After several minutes of searching in the dark, they discovered a set of stairs and descended into the depths of the bottling plant. The lieutenant had to help the MPAR navigate the stairs. Once the group of four reached the basement level, their new search for an attacker began.

Emily was first to enter the basement. Eddie was on her right; he had his shoulder searchlight running and his handheld flashlight lit. Emily had her shoulder searchlight going and pulled out her flashlight, a compact MegaLight Plus II, to turn it on as well. To her far left was the mobile police assistant robot, MPAR, which had its pair of spotlights running. The pair of New Terranceville patrol officers were behind her. Both of them had their flashlights shining. Their collection of lights had brightened the immediate area quite effectively.

Anything outside their sector of light quickly faded into a deep darkness down in the dank depressing basement. There was an eerie quiet, like the basement was a noise free zone. The MPAR let out a hum, like its cooling fans had come on, which broke the silence. The noise was actually calming to Emily.

"Let's get this over with so we can get out of this basement." Emily suggested. She took the lead moving forward with her Maxwell TriAlloy XL-2 drawn and ready. The group of them sent off down the first corridor at a steady, ready, and safe pace. At the first set of doors, Emily branched out to take the left door while Eddie swung to his right to take the door on that side. One patrol officer followed Emily for the left door. She smoothly and swiftly opened the door and put as much light into the room as possible without overly exposing herself as a target. Holding her flashlight high above her head revealed a storage room full of old holiday decorations, abandon advertisement standees, a markerless dry erase board with proposed rules dated ten years ago, a half dozen folding chairs, a pair of unused water coolers, and other miscellaneous forgotten treasures. In a dozen balanced steps Emily swept around the room for any hideaways before telling the officer who followed her the room was clear.

Having cleared the room, Detective Oftenmarch moved past her covering police officer and wasted no time in proceeding to the next door on the left side of the corridor. In a half dozen paces Emily was at the next door with one of the officers still following her. With one quick and even motion, she opened the next door and again shone as much light as possible into the room. This room appeared to be a filing room with four filing cabinets lined against the back wall, a stack of boxes filled with papers, a broken swivel chair with an unused copier sitting in it, and unopened boxes of hanging folders listed as its contents.

As Emily carefully inspected this room, Eddie moved to the door and said one word: Clear. He moved from the door to take the lead down the corridor. Emily traversed her steps and exited the room to follow Eddie. The lieutenant had quickened his search moving rapidly to the next door, indicated to one of the police officers to take the next door across the hall, and then without hesitation entered the next room to make an inspection. The group began to swiftly and efficiently conduct a room-to-room search. Making quick work of the first hallway, they turned a corner and began repeating the process in the next hallway.

The MPAR droid had fallen behind again, its spotlights were nowhere to be seen. The New Terranceville police officer opened the second door on the left side of the second hallway. As soon as the door had opened the officer was knocked forcefully backwards. Something big and hairy abruptly pounced the officer and he yelped in pain as he stumbled backwards. A pack of five or six monstrous looking beasts then steamrolled over the unsuspecting officer, crashing him awkwardly to the floor. Landing with a thud the officer was sprawled out on his back as the beastly brutes trampled him.

Detective Emily Oftenmarch sprinted from her position racing past the nearest NTPD officer to get to the downed officer to assist. The overtaken officer was putting out a distress call over the radio as Emily holstered her gun and pulled out her stream stunner to then fire off a pair of pulsating protoelectric projectiles. Rapidly, the pair of shots prompted the unidentifiable creatures to disperse. In an echoing clamor of noise, the beastly pack made a mad dash down the hallway away from the police.

Detective Oftenmarch fired another stream from her stunner to keep the pack of mystery monsters moving as she slid down alongside the prone officer. "They are heading away from the lobby staircase towards the rear of the factory." she called to the trailing NTPD officer. "Are you hurt?" she turned her attention to the officer on the ground.

"Thing bit me on the shoulder. Several stepped on my chest, stomach, and important parts." the officer answered in pain. Emily pulled out a small rag she kept inside her left inside coat pocket and offered it to the officer for his shoulder. The trailing officer, Eddie, and two additional officers were now around the injured officer as Emily aided him. As they congregated around the trampled and rumbled officer, the NTPD mobile radios had chatter rolling nonstop. The hum and buzz of the MPAR could be heard slow rolling down the hall. Multiple flashlight beams shone down on the recovering officer.

"What in the world were those things?" one of the New Terranceville officers cried.

"A problem, that's what they are." answered his partner.

Lt. Eddie Knighton pointed to one officer, "With me." Then he pointed to a second officer, "With Emily" he commanded.

"Understood, lieutenant." the first officer responded.

"Roger that." the second officer replied.

Eddie then instructed a third officer by saying, "Stay with him." pointing downward to the injured patrolman. Promptly Eddie motioned to Emily to head down the hallway toward the departed creatures as he made his way to the nearest T-junction corridor. Detective Oftenmarch sprung to her feet and started a quick march down the remaining section of this mostly dark hallway, skipping several doors to broaden and quicken their search. At the end of the hallway Emily took the right turn which was her only option.

She had made the decision to keep using her Phasepulser IX stunner. The Cathedral Police Department had a strict policy against using deadly force unnecessarily. This stance originated when the state governor began promoting the capture not kill legislation. The more sour of police officers called this policy the catch and release program. In contrast, high ranking members of the Cathedral police were extremely bullish on using stunners and non-deadly force keeping in compliance with state law. The detective did not want to be penalized for killing an animal without justifiable cause. And in the unlikely event these were werewolves, she certainly did not want to be suspended for killing a person with the ludicrous defense of the werewolf transformed back into a human after their death. Neither the disciplinary board nor a judge was going to accept that outlandish argument. Thus, she continued to search with her stunner at the ready.

Emily began repeating the process of sweeping the hallway quickly and only checking some of the doors. Keeping a quick pace, the detective and her accompanying officer made quick work of searching this hallway. Their fruitless exploration brought them to an intersection of hallways. Pausing a moment to listen, Emily was trying to ascertain which was the best direction to proceed. Her fellow searcher also came to a halt as she scrutinized her blackened surroundings. With nothing to go by, Emily picked a direction at random and the duo continue their eerie basement perusal.

A sizeable creature of an undeterminable breed suddenly appeared in the stark dark, charged past Detective Oftenmarch, and knocked the nearby New Terranceville officer off balance. It came out of nowhere, was instantly there, and then was instantly gone. A second creature barreled past them seconds after the first running beast, this one knocking the officer awkwardly down to the floor. Fumbling with her flashlight, Emily fought to get her light onto the dashing animals. Her heartrate had spiked from the jolt of shock and surprise from the dark sprinting creatures. The light briefly displayed a pair of canine looking creatures. Like a pair of oversized hounds evacuating hell, the duo were hurriedly moving down the hallway. Emily fired her service Phasepulser IX stunner twice, striking the rear running animal both times in its rear hind quarters. The fast-paced creature stumbled and came to an abrupt whimpering halt, then wobbled away woundedly. Meanwhile, the lead animal streaked onward, disappearing into the deep dark of the blackened basement.

"A pair of giant dogs just ran by us" Emily reported on her wireless radio as she tried to help the fallen police officer to their feet.

"Roger. Two also passed us." Eddie's response came back over the wireless.

"Where are these beasts going?" Emily wondered as she shone her shoulder light down the hallway to see the injured creature had vanished into the dark.

"Wherever they are going, they are in a hurry to get there." the now standing police officer replied.

Emily picked up the officer's dropped flashlight. "Were those wolves?" she wondered.

"I have no idea. I have never seen a wolf in real life." the officer responded taking back their offered flashlight.

Detective Oftenmarch purposely strode forward to the vicinity where the large creatures, maybe wolves, had last been seen. Moving her flashlight back and forth in a zigzag pattern, Emily was searching the hall for a stunned wolf and then the floor for drops of blood. She continued her search for several feet. Finding nothing, Emily stepped back to repeat the search more slowly. No blood. The stunner did not break the skin, and no blood trail. She widened her torchlight path farther down the hallway. This time she scanned for several yards down the hall still to no success.

"What are you looking for?" the officer inquired.

"Struck one of the poor large wolves, going to go with wolf, in the bum with my stunner. But I see neither a blood trail nor a pacified creature." Emily explained in puzzlement as she continued forward with her search.

"Tough hellhound, going to go with hellhound. With its size your stunner probably felt like a tickle." the officer responded.

"Let's go tickle it some more then." Emily replied as she began a quick march.

They doubled their pace in the enblackened labyrinth basement to track down wolfish creatures or find a hiding assailant, or possibly both. The NTPD officer's flashlight was dimming as its battery power faded. Most of the light was coming from Emily's megalight and shoulder light. There was no ambient light in this area of the dark basement, no windows nearby, no exit lights in the corridor, and still no electricity in the plant. With Emily in the lead, the pair of law enforcement officers made their way uneventfully down the subterranean corridor. They came upon a crossroads of hallways. To their right they could see torchlights. Emily shone her flashlight straight ahead to show empty hallway. Illumining the option to her left, Detective Oftenmarch discovered much the same. Deciding to take the left, Emily resumed their quickened pace. Footsteps of cops echoed in the hallway from behind them or at least that is what it sounded like to Emily. Keeping her flashlight fixed forward hoping to reveal something in the dark, Detective Oftenmarch heard soft splashes. Stopping her progress, she shined the flashlight downward to the floor to discover she was standing in a small pool of water. The patrol officer with her kicked and sent water spraying onto the wall. Moving her torch beam along the ground, Emily illuminated a wet hallway floor for several yards ahead of them.

Emily called out, "We have a water leak ahead."

Her companion officer was on the NTPD radio sending out the aquatic update. Continuing forward into the dark and now wet basement, Emily lengthened her stride and softened her pace hoping to create less splash. Emily could now hear her shoes splooshing with each step. After covering several yards of soggy darkway, they came to another intersection.

Hearing voices to their right, Emily turned her lights in that direction. A pair of torchlights could be seen in the mid-distance. A pair of voices were calling to them to come that way. Inspecting the floor that way by flashlight showed Emily more waterslick ground.

"Wolves, water, and wandering in the dark. Oh what a wonderful morning this has been. Let us go see what is next." Emily decided as she turned to her right. Water trudging toward the new torchlights, Detective Oftenmarch led the way down yet another black corridor.

With her splish splashes intensifying, Emily put away her Phasepulser IX stunner. This section of the basement was no place to get knocked down by a megawolf with a charged stunner. The air in the dank basement was transitioning from dusty smelling to musty smelling. Both corridor edge standing police officers seemed reluctant to leave their current position. Communication on the NTPD radio had diminished.

"We have a large open room here with a lot of water." the first stationary officer greeted them.

"We can hear water running from somewhere in that room." the second stationary officer continued.

Emily then took out her communicator and gave Lt. Knighton a heads up on the waterflow. "There is a shower somewhere in this section of the basement, Eddie."

"Following the water" his reply came over her communicator.

"Follow the shouts of frustration as well." she added then returned her communicator.

Emily noticed the officers' uniforms now that she was standing next to them. "Which Cathedral precinct are you from, officers?" she inquired

"I'm Officer Beddingfellow from the 238th precinct." the first office answered.

"Officer Tannis, also from the 238th. We had chased a speeder into New Terranceville and were finishing writing their ticket when this dispatch was reported. So, we came to help." the second officer explained.

"Detective Oftenmarch from the 271st precinct. They woke me up for this bizarre trip through the midnight carnival funhouse. Let's go find the attacker or the next surprise." Emily returned.

Unholstering her service revolver, Emily led the way into the ground drenched, low visibility, and unknown room. Her gut told her the time for caution was done. The open room was dark, damp, and waterlogged. Judging from what she could see by torchlight, Emily surmised this was a maintenance storage area with all the tools and spare parts being stored on tool racks, work benches, and shelves for stocking parts. Many of the shelving units were tall enough to block her vision of most of the room. They gave the area a mazelike aspect.

As Detective Oftenmarch led the way into the dark maze, her splashing steps were making her socks and pant legs wet. Out of the rain and into the flood, thought Emily. Following close enough behind her for Emily to hear, Officer Beddingfellow was cussing quietly to herself. Also hearing falling water nearby, Emily cautiously moved in the direction she thought was the origin of a possible waterfall. The detective's heart rate quickened as she moved past the first row of shelves. Emily walked around some fallen parts knocked off a shelf. Her torchlight and shoulder light illuminated a new section of the area to reveal more parts and equipment.

Emily began to softly recite Psalm 119:105, *"Your WORD is a lamp for my feet, a light on my path."* As she recited Scripture, the detective moved onward to investigate the next row between the shelving units. The water was deeper in the next row as Emily looked down to see she was standing in an ankle-deep puddle of water. They were making waves with their footfalls, which were slopping water over the bottom shelves of parts. The detective, followed by a trio of police officers, mindfully and methodically walked down the row, searching their surroundings by flashlight. Their beams of light poured into the black of the basement to reveal nothing to relieve the tension of the dark and dank search.

Emily continued to recount Psalms aloud as she examined the plant's dark depths. This time it was Psalm 23. *"The LORD is my shepherd, I lack nothing. HE makes me lie down in green pastures, HE leads me beside quiet waters."* Emily added, "Maybe into less quiet waters today."

She could hear rushing water getting louder upon reaching an opening in the shelves to her right. Pivoting slowly in that direction, Emily hydrostepped through the gap in the shelving. Shining her torchlight and shoulder mounted spotlight in the direction of the noise of the water cascade, the detective continued forward. Each step made a kerplop; each passing moment increased the tension of the basement search. Emily continued to recite Psalm 23, *" HE refreshes my soul. HE guides me along the right paths for HIS Name's sake. Even though I walk through the darkest valley, I will fear no evil, for YOU are with me; Your rod and Your staff, they comfort me."*

As she spoke, Detective Oftenmarch was able to put her torchlight on the origin of the falling water. Past more shelves and benches at the left wall of the room was a broken water pipe. The water pipes were exposed in the basement, probably for maintenance purposes. A section of that exposed pipe had been damaged, allowing water to pour onto the ground. Her megalight displayed the tumbling water adding to the flood waters. It actually was like there was a shower in the basement. While reciting Psalm 23, Emily examined the damaged pipe by torchlight.

"Are you a priest?" an unknown voice came abruptly out of the dark. Officer Beddingfellow screamed in surprise from her position directly behind Emily.

Emily took a long slow breath to gather her composure and collect her heart from wherever it had jumped. "My husband is a priest, does that count?" she responded to the hidden person in the dark.

"Can you make holy water?" asked the voice. A distressed looking man dressed in grubby work overalls stepped into the detective's torchlight.

"First questions first, sir. Why would we be needing holy water?" Detective Oftenmarch redirected.

"The lycans are coming. The lycans are coming." he replied in a shaky voice as his trembling hands held a bucket of water.

"Holy water is used against vampires, I thought, but not werewolves." Officer Tannis interjected.

"Good news, friend. First, the moon is not full. Second, the lycans have run away. My partner Eddie chased them away. And finally, I will protect you." Emily reassured the frightened man as she discreetly holstered her weapon.

"Suspect located, maintenance storage section." the New Terranceville officer reported into their radio.

"What if the other wolves come back around?" Officer Beddingfellow asked having recovered from her shock.

"Do you have your department-issued somnipepper spray with you?" Emily wondered.

"How can you stop the lycans from returning?" the frazzled and soaked suspect asked Emily.

"I have a pair of sealed somnipeper spray canisters." Officer Tannis responded.

"I am smarter than I look. What is your name, mister?" Detective Oftenmarch began to query the basement hider.

"I have one full canister and one partially used canister." Officer Beddingfellow inventoried.

"Zeke Ryerson, Jr. My friends call me ZJ.", the lycanphobic man replied. He had a maintenance uniform with the bottling plant's name printed on it.

"New Terranceville does not issue officers somnipepper. I only have some standard mace." the NTPD office informed everyone.

"Ok if I call you ZJ?" Emily asked and the man nodded vertically. "Let us get out of the water to find a better place to talk, ZJ. Let's also talk as we walk."

"What about the lycans?" Zeke worriedly wondered.

"The detective has a plan for the werewolves." Officer Tannis informed him as he handed Emily one of his canisters of somnipepper spray.

"Leaving the water zone and doubling back from where I entered with a new friend in tow, lieutenant." Emily reported over her communicator.

"Six canines headed your way!" Lt. Knighton's urgent reply came over her communicator.

"We have company coming, unwelcome company." Detective Oftenmarch reported.

"Did your lieutenant say six of them?" the NTPD officer asked after overhearing Emily's incoming communication.

"Please stay with us, ZJ, there is safety in numbers. We should have reinforcements coming to put us on the power play." Emily encouraged as she observed Zeke preparing to run and hide again.

"Meanwhile we play a mean penalty kill with the somnipepper spray." Officer Tannis added.

Emily used her flashlight to quickly search the nearby shelf for anything helpful. Officer Beddingfellow saw her plan quickly and wasting no time rapidly searching the next shelf. Emily passed over fasteners and cables, then grabbed a pair of couplers from an opened box and passed them to Zeke. Splashing from bounding hounds and paws running on a hard surface could be heard echoing down a hallway.

"Move into the next aisle and form a circle." the detective instructed taking charge.

No sooner had Emily and company hustled to hold the chosen aisle, the sounds of displaced water could be heard as megawolves entered the room. Within seconds the first megawolf could be seen in the beam of the flashlight at the top of the aisle.

"Tannis please intercept that one and spray it." Emily directed. She then spun around to shine her torchlight to the other end of the aisle where she illuminated two more megawolves. They had slowed their pace to a stalking approach. "Beddingfellow, you're with me." Putting her Superflex X3 shoes to good use, Detective Oftenmarch charged.

Emily ran straight at the front massive creature. The megawolf leaped into the air launching itself at the detective. Having the canister of somnipepper spray ready in hand, Detective Oftenmarch met the teeth bearing megawolf mid-attack with a face full of somnipepper spray. She gave the big beast a generous helping of the substance and it let out a huge howl of a protest. The now maced mutt reversed in rapid retreat.

Officer Beddingfellow had engaged with the second megawolf. She was trying to get the spray into its face as it tried to find a place to bite her. It made for an unpleasant dance for the duo. Emily kicked some basement floor water at the megawolf to distract it. As it avoided the splashes of water, Officer Beddingfellow was able to successfully give it a snoutful of somnipepper spray.

A loud crash and splash came from Emily's right. A third megawolf had entered the fray by way of the shelving. The brute had leaped onto a shelf, spilling its contents to splash onto the ground. It growled at Emily as it attempted to maintain some footing atop the shelf. Wasting no time, Emily swiftly greeted the beast with a benevolent blast of somnipepper spray. The dosing caused the megawolf to pull back and thus fall backwards off the shelf. It disappeared into the darkness with a whimper.

As law enforcement battled with the megawolves, Zeke was in a panic. He dropped both couplers onto the ground. The pair plopped into the water, both barely missing his feet. The frightened man then threw the water from his bucket at the megawolves. In his unsteady state he missed the brutish wolves and got water on both Emily and Officer Beddingfellow.

Now baptized in basement water, Emily pivoted her position to look for the next megawolf adversary. Juggling both the canister and megalight, Emily positioned her megalight to shine down the aisle. Officer Tannis had put a megawolf to sleep but the New Terranceville police officer was struggling with the next grand canine. Sprinting to the rescue, Emily zipped past the now weeping Zeke Ryerson, took his bucket, and raced up next to the officer. Detective Oftenmarch poked the megawolf with the newly acquired bucket as it tried to attack the officer. The hearty hound pounced at the provoking bucket. Pulling the bucket away like a magic cape, Emily revealed the canister of somnipepper spray and supplied the surprise substantially to the megawolf. She emptied its contents on the back-pedaling brute, and it gave a sleepy whine as it dropped to the ground with a splash.

With one less megawolf on the prowl, Emily took a moment to scan her surroundings by torchlight. Sweeping her search back behind her, she spotted another pair of megawolves approaching Officer Beddingfellow. Quickly Emily was back on the move. Dropping the empty canister and bucket, she darted past the still weeping Zeke again. As she ran splashing all the way, Detective Oftenmarch grabbed a box from one of the shelves. Still on the run, Emily threw the entire contents of the box at the megawolves like confetti of deterrence. Both beasts dodged the incoming debris with little difficulty. Staying with an aggressive defense, the detective charged the right flank megawolf and forcefully dropped the upside-down box on top of the menacing megawolf.

The beast bucked and fought with snarling strength to free itself. Water was being splashed in all directions. Emily pushed down on the box with all her weight but the megawolf might have outweighed her. Next to her, Officer Beddingfellow was struggling to get the last of the weakly spraying dregs of her canister into the snout of the left flank megawolf. The confrontation was sending splashes of water and paths of whirling torchlight everywhere. Despite her best efforts to pin the megawolf under the box, the beast broke free. In desperation, Emily reached out and adeptly pulled both the megawolf's front paws out from under it. The irate hound was tackled to the ground, causing a minor tidal wave. As it scrambled back to its feet to attack Emily, a newcomer to the fray intervened. Lt. Knighton applied copious amounts of somnipepper spray into the face of the feisty megawolf. The oversized creature transformed from combative to docilly demure as it diminished into the dark to doze.

Moments later everything went somewhat silent; there was a sudden calm in the bottling plant basement. The battle was over; the megawolves were sedated. "Compliments of Mrs. Montclaire." Eddie told Emily as he handed her a canister of somnipepper spray.

"Your Christmas gift from your sister. I love that woman." Emily complimented as she looked at the canister, superstrength somnipepper spray. Squatting down but not all the way into the wet, Emily began to pray in thanksgiving. "Thank you, LORD, for your love and protection in times of trouble. When the lights fail and the wolves circle to assail,

Your merciful love endures to prevail. It's your endless love pouring down on us. You relieve our fears with love so wondrous. Thank you, LORD. Amen." Emily prayed.

"Amen" agreed Zeke squatting beside her. He was now calm and less agitated.

Emily took a moment to collect herself. "Let's talk somewhere more suitable, ZJ." the detective suggested.

"Higher and drier." amended Lt. Knighton.

As the New Terranceville police officers attempted to figure out what to do with the slumbering megawolves, Eddie, Emily, and Zeke Ryerson Jr. made their way through the dark corridors of the bottling plant basement. Zeke repeatedly gave them praise for fending off the lycans that were coming to kill him. The mobile police assistant robot, MPAR, had halted at the water and was just waiting in place with a whine of fans and an amber light alerting high water detection. Emily spun the stymied robot around and instructed it to follow her. The MPAR fell behind again as they made their exit from the basement. Once up on the ground level of the factory, Eddie found a small quiet receptionist office to congregate. Emily borrowed a battery operated lightstand from the South Cathedral Valley police, who had joined the collection of law enforcement at the Incancennio's bottling plant.

The pair of detectives had a multitude of questions for Mr. Ryerson, like why he assaulted a police officer, why he thought lycans were coming to kill him, and when did he first feel threatened. While Zeke Ryerson works in New Terranceville for the Incancennio's bottling factory in the maintenance department, he lives in Cathedral. About a month ago he had witnessed a burglary at a convenience store near his apartment. The man was shopping for a few needed items when the store was robbed via armed robbers. Mr. Ryerson indicated that he had given his statement to the Cathedral police at the scene of the crime. Weeks later Zeke returned to the convenience store as a customer to discover from the manager that the arrested robbers accused of the crime had been released due to no eyewitnesses. The potential per-petrators of the burglary were never charged because the police could not find any evidence or viable witnesses to incriminate the suspects according to what the manager told Zeke. Upon hearing this informa-tion, Mr. Ryerson claimed he went to his local police precinct to come forth as an eyewitness. According to Mr. Ryerson, his local precinct sent him to another police precinct that was handling the case. At the 272nd precinct, he stated that he was turned away. Whether they were not interested or felt they now had enough evidence to charge he did not know, but Zeke indicated they neither took his statement nor accepted his offer to help.

The next day a local news reporter for the Cathedral Press came to see him. The convenience store manager had given the reporter Zeke's name. According to Mr. Ryerson, he told this same account to the news reporter. Two days after speaking with the reporter, two masked men came to his apartment and threatened him. The victim believes they came to shut him up. Ever since speaking with the media, he claims to have been harassed.

"When these masked men came to your apartment door, were they wearing wolf masks?" inquired Emily.

"Nothing like that. They wore happy and sad faces like they had on the wall of the old night street theater." Zeke answered.

"Greek theater masks." Eddie inserted reservedly.

"ZJ, when did your lycan harassment begin?" wondered Emily with some confusion.

"After the initial threatening visit, I called the reporter to tell about their warning given to me. The following night I was followed to work by a dark colored car and it was lycans that got out of that car. They came to get me." Zeke explained with increasing distress.

Emily interrupted him, "Did the werewolves approach you in the parking lot at work?"

"Yes, they got out of their vehicle and came over to my car and put their finger to their mouth." Zeke mimed the gesture as he spoke. "Then the lycans smashed my left headlight and dented my hood."

"By hand?" Emily looked for clarification.

"With a tire iron. They used a tire iron with lycan strength." Zeke answered still highly agitated.

"What's the reporter's name?" Eddie redirected the interrogation.

"Beano Benzetti of the Cathedral Press." Mr. Ryerson revealed.

"Beano Benzetti, the reporter who died about three years ago?" Detective Oftenmarch queried with puzzlement.

"The reporter was a ghost?" Zeke gasped.

"An impersonator." Lt. Knighton calmly retorted.

"Why did you think they were lycans and not strongmen in masks or costumes?" Emily circled back to the werewolves.

"Those were not fakers. They were not in full form like the ones in the basement tonight but they were real. They were as real as you are now and really superhuman strong." Zeke professed.

"Why did the lycans come into the plant tonight? What changed to escalate their aggression, ZJ?" Emily wondered.

"I called the office of my councilwoman this afternoon. Got to speak to her personally. Told her my story." Zeke replied proudly. "The lycans must have found out."

"Councilwoman Applegroove or Councilwoman Burnett?" Emily asked patiently.

"Councilwoman Burnett." Zeke responded quickly still somewhat upset.

"What phone number?" Eddie questioned pointedly.

"The phone number listed on her website." Zeke explained as if obvious.

"How would the lycans have known about your phone call?" Emily challenged.

"They must have intercepted my phone signal. The lycans have eyes and ears everywhere. You must be aware at all times." Zeke almost shrieked in panic.

"Thank you, Mr. Ryerson." the lieutenant ended the interview. He held a less than convinced expression on his face that Emily knew all too well.

"Thank you for your time, ZJ. We will be in touch if we have any more questions for you." Emily farewelled as she gave the odd man a friendly smile.

After concluding their interview with Zeke and his uniqueness, Emily convinced the New Terranceville Police not to charge Zeke with assault. Accepting that he was under duress from the factory's unexpected attackers and maniacal megawolves, the New Terranceville police officers extended Zeke much lenience. He was then escorted home by some Cathedral police officers. Before leaving the factory, Eddie and Emily interviewed several factory workers and checked in with Doctor Brownling to get his preliminary assessment on the second victim. He reported his findings to be very similar if not almost identical to the first victim. Mauled by a large canine and killed by a deep stab wound. By the time they had left the plant to head for their cars, the rain had stopped and the power had been restored to the factory.

jasked her lieutenant, looking to compare impressions.

"Possible, very strange circumstances." Lt. Knight surmised, glancing back at the bottling plant, still hosting much law enforcement activity.

"Do you think Zeke is a creditable witness?" Emily posed her second question.

"Nines to aces missing." Eddie commented with a frown.

"Sure, he is not playing with a full deck and top half of the deck is missing, but parts of his story makes some sense of this ridiculousness." Emily concluded.

Eddie just sighed heavily in response and waved farewell to his partner. She could tell he was exhausted and heading back to bed. That was an option for him since he lived in Cathedral. However, for Emily it was too early in the morning to head to her home in Chatham Heights. Her only option was to head to the office and maybe, but probably not, get some sleep at her overcluttered desk.

Chapter 2

Redirected

Detective Oftenmarch found both the city of Cathedral and the 271st Cathedral Police precinct blissfully peaceful before the workday commute and the start of the workday. It was one of the rare times driving within the city limits of Cathedral was unstressful. Her home base precinct was wonderfully calm and quiet in the pre-day shift work hours. The combination made for the optimal time to get some work done. Emily had gone straight to the 271st precinct from the bottling factory. Facing minimal traffic coming into the office and no bottleneck in the precinct parking lot, she made great time. Being the first person into the office gave her a calm and inviting work environment that was almost worth the lack of sleep. Working during the 4am hour did have a few advantages.

Unfortunately, Emily's socks, shoes, and pants were soaked from the manmade basement river in the bottling factory. The detective could not make use of the quiet time until she could rectify her soggy discomfort. She had brought her reserve bag from her car into the office to change. When changing in the staff restroom, Emily discovered she forgot to pack some socks into her reserve bag. It was going to be one of those days. She decided to still take off her wet socks and leave her shoes off and just sit barefoot Indian style at her desk. The rest of the squad took the new ergonomic chairs provided by the department. Eddie and Emily had decided to keep their old cushioned seats. They were broken in nicely. Emily was glad to have her old chair on this occasion; it was comfortable and warm after a few minutes of sitting down to work. After having brewed a pot of coffee from the squad room's coffee maker, Emily began reviewing video footage from the morning's activity. She began scouring multiple video recordings and security recordings at an accelerated speed. The process was tedious and downright difficult when strenuously sleepy. The bottling plant surveillance footage was of poor quality and the video coverage of the plant was sparse, making it difficult to see anything noteworthy. Watching the recording from her copcam was like reliving the events from earlier that morning. The footage from the mobile police assistant robot, MPAR, was completely useless. Video recordings from the droid neither captured the megawolves nor either of the murder scenes while illuminated. As she watched videos, the detective drank several cups of coffee, which were terrible as usual. Emily was missing not having some of her home brewed french pressed coffee when Detective Hedra Shippendarrow came into the squad room to get some coffee.

"What has you at work so early?" he asked.

"Massive wolves attacking, murders at a bottling plant, intruders wearing masks, and the usual pile of paperwork all before sunrise." Emily answered.

"Another day at the office." Shippendarrow quipped. "Which bottling plant?"

"Incanncennio Bottling Plant in New Terranceville." Emily answered.

"That bottling plant had a reputation for bootlegging moonshine. There are rumors it still goes on today." Shippendarrow shared.

"A worker at that bottling plant claims he was being hunted by lycans." Oftenmarch wearily revealed.

"Did he have a gun loaded with silver bullets?" Shippendarrow queried.

"Better than that. He broke a water line and was seeking a priest to bless the water." Emily shared with the coffee seeking detective.

"That is a new one. My former partner and I once responded to a suspicious death at a creepy old building outside a rundown commercial district in the West 48th Street and Bishop Avenue block. The building was a vacant ill maintained one and the deceased was set out in some strange looking pagan ritual display. While investigating the scene we discovered another person on the premise. It was a drug addict high on some combination of crazy chemicals. He was ranting and raving on how aliens were coming to get him. This nutcase had covered himself in the deceased's blood from head to toe to ward off the aliens. It was too bizarre to ever forget." Shippendarrow shared his story from the past.

Long tenured and highly experienced detective Kenneth Murkendale entered the squad room to start his workday. He was neatly dressed and unlike Emily looked as if he had experienced a good night's sleep. He hung his scully cap on the arm of his chair and tossed his suit coat over the back of the chair. The stout man had his necktie tied like a vaudeville comedian on this particular morning.

"Did you see any lycans?" Shippendarrow wondered somewhat sarcastically.

"Good morning. What are you working on this early in the morning, Emily?" Murkendale asked in greeting.

"Still looking at the video footage from this morning's recording off my copcam." the tired detective responded.

"Another after hours dispatch? We have been getting a lot of those dispatches recently." Murkendale observed with a frown.

"Gotta love searching footage from something that might be there." Shippendarrow commented.

"That is part of the joy of our job." Oftenmarch concluded.

"Roger that." the older Murkendale copied.

"Why would a criminal use oversized wolves to break into a bottling plant?" Emily asked out loud in puzzlement.

"The perp is crazy and stupid." offered Shippendarrow.

"Oversized wolves, how big are we talking?" Murkendale curiously asked.

"Ridiculously big, they were so big we could not initially tell they were wolves. These behemoths were bowling over grown officers." Oftenmarch answered with emphasis.

"Bowling for cops." Shippendarrow joked then sipped some coffee.

"Wow, they were that big. Sounds like an exhausting overnight dispatch. Why watch the footage in this dump?" Murkendale questioned still curious.

"Catch you later, Emily. Shilom." Shippendarrow sent his farewell as he made his exit from the squad room.

"Peace." Emily replied.

"Coming in early for peace and quiet, you are dedicated. Eddie is a lucky lieutenant." Murkendale commented.

"I'm the lucky one, Ken. Would you like some fresh fowl coffee? I can make another pot." Emily politely offered.

"No coffee, thank you. I have brought some home brew with me. I have to cut back on coffee, doctor's orders. I have to make the most of what little I am allowed and the home brew is the only type in my digestive and financial zone. The office swill disagrees with me and the coffee house and store brands are too expensive. My darling daughters are at prestigious universities which cost my wife and I prestigious amounts of money. Therefore, I must limit my coffee to home brew. You went to the University of Cathedral, Emily. May I ask how you managed the tuition." Murkendale shared.

"I was lucky, Ken, because Cathedral offered me a full scholarship for athletics. The swimming and track and field programs combined to offer me four free years of studies." Emily explained as she poured herself some more coffee.

"Ah, yes. You look the part of the college athlete." Murkendale replied.

Detective Theo Vallens-Scantling came striding into the office bullpen. He was muttering to himself as he tossed his coat over his chair and slammed a folder of papers on his desk. "Be on the lookout, the captain is in early today and just full of tidings of police bureaucracy. He gave me the rundown of this morning's agenda. We have three new forms to learn, a new time logging program to use, and he will be assigning federal trainees to some of the teams." he ranted in greeting.

"Good morning to you, Theo." Emily counter greeted.

"Well, Lefty, last week it was three new forms, a new procedure for submitting expenses, and the prosecutor's office mandated a 30-minute training video for handling evidence for the whole precinct. It seems like just another week on the job." Murkendale responded casually.

"That may be true, Murk, but it is getting tiresome. You have lucked out this week, none of the trainees are assigned to you. No babysitting young punks in your future. But for Mark and I, we have no suck luck." Vallens-Scantling complained.

"Try to look at it as a compliment. They think so highly of Mark and you, they want more detectives versed in monkey business style investigation." Murkendale mused.

"You want me to look on the bright side, Murk. I have done. They assigned one of the buggers to Eddie and Emily, the good old mud tusslers. The only person Eddie speaks to in this whole city is his partner. He is not going to put up with training anyone. He does not suffer inefficiency well. He wouldn't say more than three words to the trainee all day. Our lovely lady detective here will have to translate grunts, mimes, and dirty stares for the newbie." Vallens-Scantling jested with great amusement.

"You're very funny, Theo. Eddie speaks when there is something to say. However, you are not wrong about the training part. Eddie will not be a fan of that; he finally has me functioning as a useful detective." Emily responded.

"Steady Eddie will just send the Fed trainee my way." Murkendale speculated.

"Captain did not make the assignments, they came from the division. These marching orders came from the higher authorities of the Cathedral police department." Theo revealed. He clicked his heels and saluted, mimicking a German officer.

Murkendale's partner, Detective Darius Cole, entered the room carrying his usual sack full of bacon and egg croissants and a large cup of Talbert's Gas and Go coffee. He was whistling some tune from days of his younger years. "Wow, this place appears popular this morning. Do I detect dedicated civil servants?"

"Innocent." Murkendale professed.

"Guilty." Oftenmarch confessed.

"Disgruntled." Vallens-Scantling pleaded.

"Unanimous in disagreement. Now that that is settled, I can move on to more important things, like breakfast." Detective Cole suggested. He sat down at his desk to begin his morning flavorful feast.

The squad room was beginning to come alive with activity, which meant the day shift was soon to commence. A patrolman came into the squad room with a file for Detective Murkendale. Lt. Knighton walked into the 271th precinct homicide squad room reading a file he held in his right hand and watching his copcam video he held in his left hand. He was neatly dressed; his appearance was as tidy as if he had slept all night. He nodded at Murkendale as he walked to Emily's desk.

"Good morning, lieutenant. Spare three words for me?", Vallens-Scantling welcomed Eddie with a grin.

"Barn door's open." Eddie replied. He set a file on Emily's desk and pointed to a section he had highlighted.

"This morning's copcam video footage has not been helpful, but the bottling factory's security footage was instructive. These costumed clowns waltzed right through the front entrance. The megawolves were received at the loading dock like they were the standard nightly delivery brought by the friendly neighborhood wolfman. Either plant security is tremendously lackadaisical or the intruders had inside help at the facility." Emily reported.

"Leave the bottling plant case, that has been reassigned. I have another assignment for the mud tusslers." the captain was at the door with three young men in tow. Captain Bronzesmith was a sixty-some year-old veteran whose experience far exceeded his peers in other Cathedral precincts. He was small in stature but had a commanding presence emanating from his demeanor, his professional comportment, and his stern look.

"I have ten dollars that says it went to the 272nd precinct." Emily commented.

"I have one hundred." Eddie upped the ante.

"We have one hundred, do we have one-fifty? One-fifty, going once, going twice." Vallens-Scantling began an auctioneer routine meant to be funny.

"Let's get serious everyone." the captain spoke seriously.

"Question for you, Captain. Filling out a requisition form for somni-pepper spray requires a pre-requisition form 23PR-10. To obtain a form 23PR-10 one needs a signed permission to requisition form 9. But to get a signed permission to requisition form 9 signed requires a requisition form, which cannot be received without a pre-req 23PR-10. How does one get off the merry-go-round?" Emily asked her captain a serious question.

"Make a mock requisition, get a permission to req signed, fill out the pre-req form 23PR-10, and then submit the real requisition." Murkendale gave his solution to the paperwork labyrinth.

"Well, that's not more complicated than it needs to be." Darius Cole commented. He then resumed his breakfast consumption.

The captain sighed. "While the department appreciates your hard work and dedication, we need you to reprioritize your efforts. We have three new forms to learn and three new trainees from the Federal Bureau of Law Investigation's new division, the Federal Department of Improved Law Enforcement. These young men are part of the new trainee initiative being implemented by the Federal Department of Improved Law Enforcement. This is part of the state and federal program for next level detective training. Detectives Vallens-Scantling and Maxson are assigned trainee John Paul Tuttle. When Dectectives Joppers and Weibei get here, they will be assigned trainee Patrick Monkhouse. And trainee Jeremy Dean Fairbankers is assigned to Lt. Knighton and Detective Oftenmarch. Please treat them professionally and teach them properly. Scantling and Maxson will continue the bar shooting case. Murkendale and Cole will continue to investigate the Golbennger poisoning. Knighton and Oftenmarch have a new case to investigate, an apartment shooting in midtown that was just dispatched. We will respond with the utmost effort and efficiency. The case of the wolf charades will be handled out of the 272nd precinct. We have a lot of work to do, so let's get to it." Captain Bronzesmith addressed the squad.

Without a word, Eddie had walked out of the room before the captain had finished speaking. It was unusual for the captain to address the squad so early. A pair of detectives had entered the room as the captain was speaking. One of them looked at their watch wondering if they were late. Another entered fifteen seconds later with a bewildered look on his face. The captain exited the bullpen area and headed in the direction Eddie had gone.

Vallens-Scantling threw his arm over the shoulder of his trainee and began asking him how well he typed and texted. The second intern was being given coffee and donut orders. Which left the third trainee standing there on his own, unsure what to do or where to go. The young intern was all disheveled. He looked like an unmade bed with his hair uncombed and his shirt untucked. Emily beckoned him over as she put on her ankle high black boots. She preferred having a pair of dry socks to wear but had to forego the amenity on this chaotic morning. With her charcoal grey trench coat still damp, Emily grabbed her lightweight three-quarter length black coat with burgundy trim and dark burgundy buttons.

She welcomed the young man, "Welcome to Cathedral Police precinct 271, home of hard work and witty co-workers. I'm Detective Emily Oftenmarch. You will meet my partner and boss Lt. Eddie Knighton shortly."

"Hi, I am Jeremy Dean." the unsure newbie quietly greeted her in return.

"You will find that things move rather fast around here, Jeremy." Emily continued. She began to collect the mount of electronic devices from her desk charging surface. As she grabbed her cell phone, work cell phone, portable police tableau, copcam, and digital all in one compulink, the detective added, " Some days circumstances change rapidly and a police detective wants to double their pace without tripling their mistakes. It's better to find a pace and rhythm that works for you, then keep steady through the storm."

"We were taught at the academy to work each case like it was the most important case." trainee detective Fairbankers replied.

"That most important case can be altered on short notice like what just happened this morning. But I digress; we have a new case assigned and the address of the scene has been sent to my portable. Let's go find Lt. Knighton and get enroute." Detective Oftenmarch answered.

"Sounds great." Fairbankers replied enthusiastically.

Detective Oftenmarch found the lieutenant working on his coplink, or police issued complink, outside the larceny division's common room. He seemed to be avoiding Captain Bronzesmith. Emily informed Eddie of their new assignment and they began their preparations for another homicide case in the ever bustling city of Cathedral.

Like many of Cathedral's police precinct, the 271st precinct had one of its borders extend to the city limits. The higher authorities in the Cathedral Police Department call these precincts the border precincts. Many official directives from the Cathedral Chief of Police included Cathedral border precincts co-operating with neighborhood suburbs.

Unlike any other Cathedral border precinct, the 271st precinct had a long winding section of its precinct area which was located in the mid-town region of the city. When seeing the 271st precinct on a city police map, it made for a very odd shape. The Cathedral Police Department would refer to precincts in the midtown region as midtown or middle precincts. Middie precincts had to run three full shifts because, unlike downtown Cathedral and the grand financial district of Cathedral, the midtown regions saw a lot of night life and late-night activity.

The 271st precinct of the Cathedral Police Department was unique because it was the only border middle precinct in the city. Many members of Cathedral law enforcement would refer to the 271st precinct as the whackadoodle precinct. Whackadoodle for both the crazy shape of the precinct and the zany events which occurred within the precinct's territory.

The trio was travelling to a part of the midtown regional portion of the 271st precinct which was known as the Twelves. The Twelves derived its nomenclature from twelve twelve-story apartment buildings all located within blocks of each other. Getting out of the office and away from paperwork usually made for a nice change of pace. However, the rush hour traffic was particularly bad for this morning's commute. Additionally, Lt. Knighton, Emily knew, was already in a bad mood because the captain allowed the lycan masquerade murder case to be reassigned but the poor trainee, Fairbankers, had no clue this was the case. This was the first time he had ever been to the city of Cathedral and he was full of exuberant questions. Jeremy Dean found the television show museum very interesting and had multiple questions about it. Emily and Eddie both knew it was a tacky museum full of inexpensive displays, wax figures, and cheap trinkets to sell tourists but neither wanted to say this to the young enthusiastic visitor. The tourist questions continued to flow as the traffic flow lacked progress for several blocks before Emily changed the subject.

"When you keep working this morning's case unofficially, I am with you lieutenant. I have your six on that cause." Emily declared.

"Without advertisement, please." Eddie replied with his eyes focused intently on the traffic ahead.

"Understood." Detective Oftenmarch confirmed. She could tell Eddie did not care to speak any further on the topic.

Detective Oftenmarch returned to making polite conversation with J.D. Fairbankers. Emily discovered he grew-up in Northern California, graduated from Midwestern State University, had a brother and sister, enjoyed playing golf, and once dated a country music singer. After about fifteen minutes of friendly conversation while stuck in traffic their discussion dwindled down to quiet. Continuing to struggle through the city of the midscrapers, or average sized skyscrapers, their conversation also bottlenecked.

As much as Lt. Knighton wanted to use the PSUV's lights and sirens, detectives in the Cathedral PD were being reprimanded and disciplined for using those apparatuses for non-emergencies. Many officers and detectives had been abusing their lights and sirens for personal convenience or for all trips to crime scenes. The misuse of them was so prevalent that the Cathedral PD created the Lofton-Lincoln rule, named after the Cathedral police chiefs that proposed the rule. Within the police, it was known as the do not cry wolf rule. As part of the Lofton-Lincoln rule, all city police vehicles were equipped with a tamperproof device that recorded every time their lights and sirens were used.

Therefore, the trio travelled in silence the remainder of the trip and they reached their destination without sirens and without any more discussion. They drove, idled, drove, and idled their way through rush hour Cathedral traffic to the scene of the crime. Earlier that morning at the bottling plant there was a sea of police vehicles; here at the Twelves there was a sea of spectators and very few law enforcement personnel to manage the crowd. The crowd control police servicebots, the department called them crime scene preservers or CSPs for short, were losing the battle to contain a perimeter around the apartment building's main entrance. Several robotic voice requests to please stand back and red lights flashing from the CSPs were not enough to keep the crowd dispersed. More CSPs or more officers would be needed if this investigation became time consuming at the crime scene.

Emily took her cell phone, portable police tableau, and work cell phone, a digital all in one called a complink, from the police SUV's charging station. Emily did not bother with preparing the MPAR; it would not be able to navigate the crowd and transporting it physically did not seem necessary for this dispatch. As soon as Eddie found the least obstructive location available to park, Emily was the first one out of the vehicle to get to work. She was followed by Jeremy Dean, who still had an overwhelmed look on his face as he looked at the city surroundings. Across the street was the Shopwell Market Center, full of activity at this time of the morning. Next to the market center was Rumpolle Tower, an extended stay suites facility popular with out of town lawyers, bankers, and business people. Next to Rumpolle Tower was the corporate headquarters of Lipsmackers Chocolate. The popular chocolate maker had several manufacturing plants in the area. Cathedral was proud to be the home of Lipsmackers Chocolate. Behind Rumpolle Tower could be seen Presston Tower, a business office building. Most of its prestigious offices were rented by real estate and insurance companies. Recently the Tower had seen an influx of economic growth companies take occupancy. Neighboring the tower was the old Arden arcade. Four blocks to the north were the midtown offices of Polytech Robotics, Efficient Software, Acme & Acme Technical Services, and Reboot Technologies. Each sixty-story triplex polyglass skyscraper was a scaled down version of each company's downtown building.

As Jeremy Dean took in the city view and Eddie secured the SUV, Detective Oftenmarch spotted a Cathedral police officer she knew working door security for the crime scene, officer Jack Stalk. As Emily had weaved her way through the nearby crowd and held out her badge for a CSP to scan, she called out to Officer Stalk. "Hey Bean, how have you been?"

"Emily Oftenmarch, how is the most beautiful cop in all of Cathedral? As for me, I am doing well, just trying to stay out of trouble." Officer Stalk responded.

"Likewise." Emily answered. "You still pulling extra overtime hours to pay for your children's private school tuition?"

"My captain gave me permission to join a private company doing part time police work. I have been putting in extra hours patrolling riverfront properties for a company called Next Generation Patrol." the friendly Officer Stalk disclosed.

"Good for you, Bean. You are a hard-working man." Emily encouraged him as she pulled out her complink and began remotely downloading video wirelessly from a video camera on the street corner near the apartment's entrance.

Detective Knighton walked up to the entrance with Federal trainee Jeremy Dean in tow. He was adjusting his tie as he approached. With a nod to Officer Stalk, he opened the apartment doors to enter.

"The dispatch said the crime scene was on floor eleven, do you know the apartment number?" Emily asked Jack Stalk.

"Apartment 1127, my partner Jessica is standing guard at the apartment door." the Cathedral officer replied as he held the door for Emily. His gaze and attention was being averted by something in the crowd.

"Thank you, Bean. Stay happy and healthy." Detective Oftenmarch farewelled.

The dispatch was for a single homicide victim inside his apartment. Reports of shots fired had been received prior to the request for homicide. Initial indications were that the deceased was a gunshot victim. Now the mud tusslers had to discern the who and why of the crime.

Emily entered the small apartment lobby mostly occupied by mail slot boxes. Using her complink, she wirelessly downloaded video footage from the building's lobby camera. The floor of the lobby was suitably clean; however, the walls and ceilings were overdue for a good cleaning. The lobby's cleanliness decreased as its altitude increased. Cobwebs surrounded the lobby camera. On the far side of the lobby was a small, narrow, and shabby doored elevator with a Cathedral police officer standing guard by it. Lt. Knighton had shown the officer his credentials and pressed the elevator's up button without preamble. Trainee Fairbankers had a less than impressed look on his face as he examined the elevator's exterior. Detective Oftenmarch showed her badge to the officer on elevator sentry duty; he nodded at her.

"Are you new to the 272nd precinct?" Emily asked the officer.

"I am with the auxiliary Cathedral patrol. We are just filling in for this incident, detective." the officer answered.

"Much appreciated, Officer Barkley." Emily thanked him as she read his name badge. The elevator door opened and the trio filed into the small elevator wordlessly.

The inside of the tiny elevator was shabby, smelly, and severely cramped even with just three people. Riding to the eleventh floor in silence, the trio simply endured the trip on the rickety rank little elevator. Once at the eleventh, they swiftly exited the ensickening elevator. Almost at the end of the dimly lit hall was an officer standing sentry outside one of the apartments. Lt. Knighton wasted no time making his way down the hall to once again show his credentials to the officer on guard duty.

"Smiling Jessica Gerranium, how are you this morning officer?" Emily greeted the patrolwoman cheerily.

"Another day on the job, detective." she answered with an expressionless but stern look on her face.

"This is Detective Fairbankers, he's very pleased to meet you." Emily introduced. J.D. grunted quietly and half waved to the officer.

"The medical examiner is already inside the apartment examining the victim." Officer Gerranium informed them, keeping a stern look.

Eddied nodded and went into the apartment. J.D. Fairbankers quietly followed him closely. Detective Oftenmarch trailed a little as she headed into the apartment. Pausing at the door she whispered, "Your left shoe is untied, Jessica." The officer was tying her shoe as Emily entered the apartment.

Covered in beer cans, takeout food containers, pizza boxes, and half-eaten frozen dinners the room reeked of stale food. In roughly the middle of the living room, the coroner currently on duty, Dr. Hogglestien, was examining the body of the untimely deceased. Dr. Hooglestein was not nearly as friendly or forthcoming as Dr. Brownling. The trio put on byglex latex gloves and applied sealant as they entered. Emily and Eddie turned on their copcams to record the scene.

There was a considerable amount of blood around the victim and Dr. Hogglestien was cautiously attempting to make an examination while disturbing or smearing as little as possible. Briefly looking up from his work, Dr. Hogglestein glanced at the incoming investigators and grunted a grumbled greeting.

J.D. suddenly became very excited as he took a device from his pocket. "Check this out, we got it on our second week of training." he exclaimed eagerly. After beeping several times, the device in his hands shone a light outward to project a holographic image. The image appeared to be a well-dressed portly man with good posture in a tailored suit. He wore a neat flat black waistcoat, a tidy black bowtie, and a black derby hat.

"How may I be of service?" voiced the holographic image.

"Please analysis this crime scene." instructed Fairbankers.

The portly and spectacled holographic detective turned its attention to the victim as the device appeared to be scanning the body. "Setting is an urban dwelling. One victim is detected, no life signs. No weapon has been detected. Coroner is currently onsite to exam deceased. There appears to be a male victim in a reddish substance. The substance is something like ketchup, or red paint, or a cherry syrup." it voiced flatly. Dr. Hogglestein rolled his eyes and returned to his work.

"Try blood." Eddie told the holographic inspector.

As the device scanned again, the hologram requested a moment then robotically replied, "Blood is correct."

"Turn it off, please.", Lt. Knighton ordered.

As J.D. was making the hologram disappear, Emily intervened. "Good morning, doctor. How did the bocci tournament go?" The detective gingerly scanned the corpse for an identification. The fingerprints did not show-up on the database so Emily switched to facial recognition to id. She simultaneously macropulse digiscanned the body with a maxrecorder.

"Not as well as my team had hoped." the doctor answered. Lt. Knighton lifted up a printout that was sitting on a half-height coffee table.

Emily encouraged, "But you had fun none-the-less, right doctor?" The facial recognition succeeded. "Victim is a Dixon Downmore, listed as living at this very address. When would you surmise Mr. Downmore died, doctor?"

"The preliminary findings suggest death occurred around 7:30 this morning. Hypostasis has not yet occurred." the coroner disclosed, not looking up from his work. Meanwhile, Lt. Knighton had put the first sheet of paper into an evidence bag and was currently looking at a second sheet of paper with a puzzled look on his face.

As she knelt down by the victim, Emily took a moment to say a prayer for the departed, "Almighty FATHER, who frees us from sin, grant this man peace and raise him up. Lord JESUS, our redeemer, your love and sacrifice paid for the sins of the world. By Your glorious power give Dixon peace in heaven where you live for ever and ever. Amen."

"Amen." repeated J.D. Fairbankers.

"Did he succumb to gunshot wounds?" Emily ventured a guess.

"Early indications suggest the three gunshot wounds were the cause of death." Dr. Hogglestein tentatively concurred. His attention remained on the wounds.

"Looks as if the shooter or shooters missed one of the shots." Detective Oftenmarch indicated as she pointed to a bullet size hole in the far exterior wall. J.D. walked over to where she had pointed to get a better look. Eddie had put the second sheet of paper into an evidence bag and was now scrutinizing a third sheet of paper.

"These gunshot wounds are atypical in entry size. They are too big for a .22 caliber but too small for a typical .38 caliber." Dr. Hogglestien noted his observation aloud. His basic medical assistance droid, BMAD, had been completely silent until that moment and was now chirping and chiming continually.

47

"How much smaller than a 9mm?" Emily wondered.

"Surprisingly smaller. Somewhere in the neighborhood of a fine tipped .32 caliber." the doctor surmised.

Emily sighed, "Could it possibly be a .29 caliber?"

The doctor looked up at her while the BMAD continued its light and sound show. "It would be possible. Why choose that particular caliber?" he queried.

"There was a Belarusian-Russian-American gang years ago that made their own custom weapons and ammunition. Their custom-made weaponry was .29 caliber." Detective Oftenmarch answered as she watched her lieutenant.

"You think a gang did this shooting?", trainee Fairbankers wondered.

"Not a gang, just one nincompoop." Eddie responded as he bagged the third sheet of paper, which he had been studying.

Emily was typing into her compulink. "Mr. Downmore is the cousin of the person the lieutenant just referenced and according to our records that cousin lives three blocks from here. Too many coincidences not to pursue."

After picking up some gaming equipment from the floor, Eddie headed for the apartment's lone door. "No shame in placing second. Thanks, doc." He made his exit from the crime venue.

With some adjustments to her copcam, Detective Oftenmarch zoomed onto the hole in the far wall. She pulled a pair of pinched-nose precision power pliers from her coat pocket and yanked the embedded bullet from the wall with some struggle. Once freed, the bullet was placed into an evidence bag. With the bullet collected, Emily started checking the living area windows for signs of forced entry to be thorough. As she checked, the rest of the morgue team arrived with a robolift gurney to remove the body. "J.D. please go into the lieutenant's field kit and pull out the numbered markers and digital fine definition camera." she asked politely as she pointed to the bag which Lt. Knighton had left on the short table.

As the federal trainee gathered the needed items and the morgue team prepared to remove the body once the doctor was done, Emily swiftly checked the kitchen windows. With her check recorded, the detective returned to the crime scene room and began locating nickel electroplated brass casings on the apartment floor. Fairbankers handed her the numbered markers for her to place them. Within twenty seconds, the detective had four markers placed and the trainee was taking room view and close-up digital photos. Picture taking in progress, Emily momentarily recorded Dr. Hogglestein at work with the victim then quickly moved into the bedroom for an inspection.

The apartment's lone bedroom was far messier and more cluttered than the living area. Navigating the mess, Detective Oftenmarch recorded a tertiary inspection of the room. She moved to the window to check for forced entry. Once satisfied with the negative detection, Emily turned to leave the room only to spot drug paraphernalia among a pile of clothes and magazines. Having to spend a couple of minutes bagging the contraband, she missed the end of Dr. Hogglestein's examination. Returning to the less messy living area, she observed the morgue team was loading the corpse on the robolift gurney.

"I should have a more in-depth report around 2 o'clock this afternoon." the coroner informed her.

"Thank you, doctor. Please get the bullets to the forensics tech lab as soon as possible. Confirmation on the .29 caliber will be helpful." the detective concluded. J.D. had collected the markers and the lieutenant's bag as he trailed Emily out of the apartment. Emily took the stairs to the lobby, not wanting another ride on the rickety rockety elevator, and met Eddie in the building lobby. He had downloaded the lobby camera's video footage and was watching it on his portable police tableau. When Emily came into the lobby, he showed her a paused frame of the footage which displayed a suspect they both knew, Veedan Downmore, and a time stamp of 7:35am that morning.

"Think he still owns a .29 caliber hand gun?" Emily asked, half-knowing the answer. Eddie nodded affirmatively then led the way out of the building.

Twenty-four minutes and three blocks later, the trio was outside Veedan Downmore's apartment building. Parked illegally in front of the apartment building was a bright lime Cobra Turbo 3 hot rod. Detective Oftenmarch started her copcam as Lt. Knighton remotely downloaded archive footage from the camera on the street corner. The lieutenant had filed for a warrant on his complink back at the first apartment. They still had to wait several minutes on the busy streetside curb for a response. J.D spent the time watching the hectic city traffic. Emily was documenting the license plate number and reviewing the vehicle's parking violations when Eddie's complink beeped. "Go" instructed the lieutenant.

Still wearing her byglex latex gloves, Emily reached into the wheel well above the passenger rear tire to find a secret compartment. The detective then rotated her position and crawled part way under the vehicle. Switching her copcam to a portable extender rod, she then recorded the underside of the vehicle to show the secret compartment. While concentrating on recording her movements properly, Emily awkwardly opened the secret compartment and retrieved two weapons. The first weapon was a Colt 1919-38 pistol; the second weapon was a .29 caliber Roulluse Special. She had pulled the odd .29 caliber gun from car wheel well's hidden compartment of the car registered to suspect Veedan Downmore. Both weapons were placed in evidence bags and sealed as both Emily and Eddie recorded the process.

Without discussion, Lt. Knighton led the way into the apartment building to talk to Veedan Downmore. "What made you think to look there?" asked J.D. curiously.

"Three previous incidents led us to look there. One, about eight months ago, Veedan accidently shot his brother's television and refrigerator with the Roullouse. Two, Veedan's vibrant vehicle was impounded by Cathedral police for unpaid parking tickets about six months ago. Three, a Cathedral patrol officer caught Veedan in the act of hiding a small amount of drugs in that secret compartment under his vibrant vehicle almost five months ago. The Cathedral PD had records of Veedan Downmore's accident prone gun, poorly parked sports car, and secret hiding spot." Emily explained. While explaining, she had remotely downloaded the lobby camera's recent video footage over the last 24 hours to her complink.

The trio had transversed the dank and dirty lobby and were now climbing the dingy and dirtier stairs. "How did the lieutenant and you know this Downmore's background?" J.D. questioned still curiously.

"We were working a homicide two doors away from his brother's place the night of the accidental appliance shooting. Then we happened to be on a stakeout nearby the night the patrol officer caught Veedan hiding drugs. He also had the Roullouse Special on him that night. Eddie's intervention prevented Veedan from getting shot that night." Emily expounded following the explanation with a sad sigh. The trio had reached their destination floor and were entering a narrow dimly lit hallway.

"Text Huana, please." Eddie politely ordered Emily. Detective Huana Beuhalaurr would inform the victim's next of kin for the 271st precinct homicide division. Emily quickly sent Detective Beuhalaurr an insta-text on her instant texter app from her complink as they marched down the dirty hallway to Veedan's apartment.

Although shabby, the apartment hallway had been recently cleaned. It was complete contrast with the filthy lobby and stairway. The police trio did not have far to walk before reaching the apartment that was their destination. Reaching the apartment first, the lieutenant knocked sharply on the white painted door. Raised voices in an argument could be heard coming from inside the apartment. It took a couple of knocks and several minutes before Veedan answered the door.

Upon seeing Lt. Knighton standing outside the door, Veedan declared, "I did not shoot my cousin. I do not even have the .29 caliber gun anymore."

"Who said your cousin was shot?" Emily challenged.

"I was just assuming he got shot. That's why homicide is here." Veedan answered.

"Good assumption. Who said he was shot with a .29 caliber?" Emily challenged again.

"That was my guess. You came to see me because my cousin was shot this morning with a .29 caliber and I used to own a .29 caliber gun." the suspect replied.

"You seem to be a good guesser. Who said your cousin was shot this morning? Why not guess he was shot last night?" Emily continued to question.

"I saw him last night around 10pm and he was alive so it must have been this morning." Veedan poorly lied.

"Why did you see him last night?" Emily wondered.

"Asked to borrow some money but he would not lend me any money." Veedan responded. The conversation continued around the doorway as the suspect had not invited the detectives into the apartment.

"What? You told me he was done given you money." a voice called from inside the apartment.

"That's my girlfriend. Ignore her. She's not helpful." Veedan disclosed while shouting the last part over his shoulder.

"So how do you explain that the video camera in the lobby and the video camera on the street corner recorded you entering the building this morning and not last night?" Emily inquired. Eddie held up his coplink to show the suspect an incriminating picture.

"Ah, the camera must have had the wrong times." Veedan lamely countered.

"Both of them got the times wrong and both of them recorded dark sky like daytime and daylight like night time. Do you own a Scorpion Turbo XL hot rod? license plate JAM 4 LIF?" Emily queried onward.

"Yes, he owns that gasoline guzzling and paycheck stealing carjack magnet. He loves that stupid car more than he loves me." the unhelpful girlfriend called from inside the apartment.

"Yes." the suspect sighed.

"So the .29 caliber gun which you don't own anymore that I found in the wheel well hideaway of that same car must be yours as well." Emily surmised.

"Somebody must have planted it on my car." Veedan stated.

"Somebody with your fingerprints planted a .29 caliber revolver which you used to own in a custom compartment for a revolver in your car's wheel well." Emily replied with heavy skepticism.

"That's quite interesting." Eddie added.

"I am getting the feeling that you don't believe me." Veedan defensively replied.

"I am getting the feeling that you are under arrest." Emily responded.

"Funny, I feel the same." Eddie shared.

Emily read the suspect his re-revised Miranda rights as the lieutenant began to handcuff Veedan Downmore. At first he began to struggle, but then he thought better of that course of action. Reluctantly, he let Eddie applied the restraints as Emily concluded the reading of his rights.

"I did not have time to shoot my cousin three times last night." Veedan protested as he was being arrested.

"How many times?" Lt. Knighton asked him. This time Veedan did not answer.

The 271st precinct homicide detectives detained Veedan and took him back to the precinct for booking. After he was processed, the detectives interviewed him a second time, this time under caution, and they had almost the exact same conversation with the foolish criminal. He offered the same poor excuses and revealed the same undisclosed details as he had done previously. Downmore may as well have worn a guilty sign around his neck.

Chapter 3

Again with the Lycans

After a predictable interrogation of Veedan Downmore and a multitude of procedural police paperwork on that case, the morning had been exhausting and it was now exhausted. MInutes before noon, the looming promise of a lunch hour was ruined when an emergency dispatch came to the 271st precinct homicide division. With expectations of a nice lunch dashed, Eddie and Emily were assigned the urgent dispatch by their captain.

Multiple shots had been reportedly fired at the city park called St. Lawrence Gardens on the corner of South Abbott Drive and Calista Road in a busy midtown section of the 272nd precinct. The dispatch indicated that one victim was down and several bystanders had been injured. A sundry of law enforcement personnel were enroute to establish order to the currently escalating chaos in and around St. Lawrence Gardens.

Eddie and Emily, accompanied by J.D., rushed to the midtown shooting location as they joined the Cathedral law enforcement's race to gain control of the crime site before the media arrived to report on how the scene was out of control. A pair of unrelated active situations had the city's special weapons and tactics, SWAT, teams busy at the moment so the remaining available units of law enforcement would have to suffice for this dispatch.

The trio's PSUV was the fourth law enforcement vehicle to arrive on the scene; six media vans had already reached the destination. The CPD was already behind in the race. The media was jockeying for prime filming positions as the police struggled to keep them back and establish a perimeter. One pair of Cathedral patrol officers were rushing to put up barricades while another pair of police officers were scrambling to get CSPs deployed. These robotic preservers had seen a lot of service and they appeared worn with many carvings, knicks, and dents. Two more Cathedral patrol cars arrived on the scene to park on the edge of the park next to the detectives' PSUV, police service utility vehicle.

Emily had already equipped her gear, vest, and electronics. The MPAR was prepared and J.D. was set to deploy it. Once Eddie had parked the vehicle, Emily spun into action, making a beeline for a section of the normally nonviolent park where Cathedral officers were putting up a police line of weatherproof yellow tape. Ignoring questions from the gathering media, Detective Oftenmarch kept her focus on the crime scene ahead.

As more media arrived at the park, a pair of private police patrol cruisers from Elite Law Enforcers appeared at St. Lawrence Gardens to aid the Cathedral Police. If the Elite Law Enforcers, ELE, was as good at police work as it was at advertising, then they would be elite class law enforcement. The employees of the private company seemed eager to get involved as they dashed from their parked cars. A Cathedral patrol officer was standing guard over a body on the park grounds. As Emily reached the Cathedral foot patrol officer, denoted by the orange and white sash worn, several CSP droids had their perimeter warning alarms blaring. In the interior of the park, the usual crowd of park appreciators had dispersed giving the area a surreal calm. It was too calm for the inter-city park surroundings. Getting her complink ready, Emily approached the Cathedral officer who had secured the crime scene.

"Good afternoon, I'm Detective Emily Oftenmarch and my partner Lt. Eddie Knighton is coming. We have been assigned this homicide. What do we have here, officer?" Emily introduced then asked as she held out her badge for inspection.

"Sgt. LeRoyson has been interviewing witnesses and it sounds like there was an exchange of gunfire between this victim and another individual. They appeared to be targeting one another." the officer reported as they indicated the sergeant with a pointing finger.

Emily knelt down to get the victim's identification. As she did, she noted that the victim had been shot twice close in proximity to his heart. "An exchange of gunfire like a midtown duel in the middle of St. Lawrence Gardens?", she puzzled.

"You never know what's going to happen in Cathedral on any given day." the patrol officer recited a common phrase regarding the city.

Lt. Knighton and trainee Fairbankers had made their way into the interior of the park. They had made their way past the Cathedral police's battle for perimeter position against the Cathedral megamedia on the outer edges of St. Lawrence Gardens. J.D. had carried the MPAR into the park and was now struggling to get the droid set-up. More CSP droid alarms mixed with police sirens loudly filled the air as Eddie approached Emily's position.

"Witnesses are saying this was a two-man shoutout like an old fashion duel, Eddie." The identification run returned results on Emily's complink. "Victim is Barrett Alexander, age fifty-nine, and current resident of Cathedral. Mister Alexander was formerly a Cathedral police officer, now retired, and reportedly working for a private law enforcement company called Elite Law Enforcers." the detective informed her lieutenant.

"Which brings ELE here." Eddie suspiciously observed.

"You never know what's going to happen in Cathedral on any given day." the patrol officer repeated.

Her complink was getting a weak signal in the park but managed to continue uploading Barrett Alexander's profile. "His police employment record is excellent with awards for good conduct, citations for bravery in the line of duty, and no disciplinary actions received." Emily added. She ran a macropulse digiscan of the body with her maxrecorder.

The Cathedral Sky Patrol helicopters passed overhead at low speed and a high noise factor. Slowing to an appropriate pace, the Sky Patrol began dropping CSPs to aid the Cathedral Police forces in St. Lawrence Gardens. As the droids' autochutes opened dispersing the robotic forces across the park, Cathedral emergency services were busy attending to injured civilians from the altercation. None of the bystanders still in the park had been shot but several were wounded in the ensuing panic to escape the shootout. Cathedral police officers were questioning any witnesses that remained in the park as J.D. Fairbankers finally deployed the MPAR, which immediately shut down again. Eddie observed the body of retired police officer Barrett Alexander as Emily prayed for the fallen former colleague.

"Thank you for your grace, love, and mercy dear LORD. Thank You for Your peace, which transcends all understanding. May Your grace and peace be with Mr. Barrett Alexander. May his future be peaceful in Your kingdom of glory. May YOU bless him and keep him, dear LORD. May Your face shine on him and be gracious to him and give me peace. Amen."

"Amen." Eddie agreed then moved off toward Sgt. LeRoyson and some witnesses. Emily sent a quick instant texter to Detective Huana Beuhleurr requesting notification to Barrett's next of kin.

The Elite Law Enforcement patrol officers had made their way over to Emily and the crime scene victim. "We respectfully would like to be highly involved in the investigation of the murder of our colleague." the lead ELE officer stated.

"Hello, gentlemen. I am Detective Oftenmarch. That is great you want to help. Could you tell us if Mr. Alexander was working on any cases currently? Or has he received any threats lately?" Emily commenced information collecting.

"Officer Barrett Alexander was an anti-burglary specialist. He did not have cases or threats." the lead ELE officer spoke indignantly.

"Anti-burglary, is that another term for security?" Emily pondered.

"ELE does not just do security, we do more than the minimum. We do not see this as just a homicide; this is policide and policide calls for all hands on deck." the ELE employee recited company policy.

"You would be surprised what can be accomplished in the hands of Steady Eddie. He is not just an ordinary homicide detective." Emily replied as she watched her lieutenant speak with Sgt. LeRoyson.

"Steady Eddie?" the ELE workers puzzled together.

"The nickname for Lt. Eddie Knighton, the officer in charge." the Cathedral police officer explained.

"Lt. Knighton has the Cathedral police record for the most closed homicide cases in a 20 year period." trainee Fairbankers revealed as he still was struggling to get the MPAR online and into action.

"That just tells us he is old." mocked the lead ELE officer.

"So when you hear the story of a legend, your first thought is old. How interesting." Emily observed as she also observed the coroner had arrived. The coroner was attempting to navigate the media infested police line. Emily continued, "My question regarding security was not meant to be offensive, it was only for clarification."

"This is still an all available officers priority. The ELE demands an update regarding this policide." another ELE officer sputtered indignantly.

Another Cathedral patrol officer had walked into the vicinity where he could hear the last comment from the Elite Law Enforcers. "The man was shot and killed. You have been updated." that officer responded.

The lead Elite Law Enforcement officer walked up close to that Cathedral officer to get face to face with him. The two of them were having a stern stare off when Emily interjected, "Barrett has a Celtic .44 pistol next to him which appears he had drawn. Would this be his service weapon?"

Distracted from his staring, the lead ELE officer responded, "Elite Law police officers supply their own weapons. It is very likely that was his service weapon and will be registered as such."

"Do you use a Celtic?" Fairbankers tried a question while still struggling with the MPAR.

"No." both ELE officers emphatically answered. A gust of wind rigorously rustled the few trees in St. Lawrence Gardens.

"The Celtic .44 is registered as his service weapon." Emily had checked her tableau to confirm. "You have a dryer sheet coming out of your pant leg." she added to the other ELE officer as she stood up from examining the victim.

"Emily, the sergeant has news." Lt. Knighton returned with an update.

"Several witnesses have indicated that the victim exchanged fire with another middle-aged man in a trench coat. Each man shot the other man as well as a passerby. According to witnesses the shooter left the park wounded heading north and the bystander exited the park also wounded to the east." Sgt. LaShawndra LeRoyson summarized eyewitnesses' accounts.

"Officer Thurnes found some blood trails supporting the exiting directions." the officer next to Sgt. LeRoyson appended.

"You never know what's going to happen in Cathedral on any given day." the officer guarding the body repeated.

"How many times did the northbound shooter fire?" Emily asked as she reapplied sealant to her gloves and prepared an evidence bag.

"Three shots were fired by each man is my understanding." the sergeant responded promptly.

"Two of the unknown shooter's shots struck Barrett Alexander." the detective declared as she pulled a numbered marker from her coat.

"Who?" asked a Cathedral officer.

"Barrett." answered the other ELE officer as he pointed downward at the deceased.

"The third shot reportedly struck the innocent bystander." Sgt. LeRoyson reported.

Emily placed the marker and took two quick pictures of the weapon with her complink. Then she scooped up the Celtic .44 and swiftly ejected the clip. "Four bullets missing in the magazine." she announced.

"How many hit his counterpart?" Eddie asked the obvious question.

"Did he have a full mag at the start of the duel?" wondered trainee Fairbankers.

Not waiting for any answers, the lieutenant pointed at Sgt. LeRoyson and the Cathedral officer next to her. "With me, blood trail north."

"The 154th precinct should be in pursuit as we speak." LaShawndra added.

"Take J.D., blood trail east." Lt. Knighton instructed Emily.

After bagging the Celtic .44 pistol into evidence and following several procedural logging steps, Detective Oftenmarch looked at the Elite Law Enforcer officers. "Either of you care to join us?"

"No." the lead ELE office replied curtly.

"I'll go." the dryer sheet wearer volunteered.

"Leave it, J.D. We have to move; the blood is running on the innocent passerby." Emily ordered as she stored the evidence bag in the MPAR's containment compartment. She locked and sealed the MPAR's primary compartment. Trainee Fairbankers stopped struggling with the complicated robot to follow Emily already on the move. They left the MPAR where it was, silently flashing in a stationary position in the park.

Quickly hustling across the park, Emily noticed three things of interest. First, the CSPs had increased in number and had managed to move the crowd and most of the media out of St. Lawrence Gardens. Second, the coroner and crew had navigated the crowd and were in the park nearing Barrett Alexander's resting spot. Third, and most importantly, there were two sets of blood drops about fifteen yards apart. As she pointed each set out to Jeremy Dean, Emily also noted their positioning was consistent with an easterly route out of the park. Still moving quickly, Detective Oftenmarch reach the Cathedral police barricade first. CSPs had formed an impressive line full of lights and flashers separating the park from a mass of people. An officer with Cathedral, working the barricade, let them pass.

Shouts of questions from reporters came their way as they crossed the barricade. Without slowing Emily made a statement as she exited St. Lawrence Gardens. "Now is a time for Cathedral to recover. It is a time to speak of the recovery of Cathedral from an unfortunate incident and not to cry of negative news. Thank you."

Emily had to battle her way through reporters, cameramen, and onlookers with questions. Leading the way through the maze of humanity, the detective zigzagged and said excuse me about a hundred times. She had just about reached Calista Road when a man approached her holding up a universal parallel bus, UPB, digipod drive.

"I was able to record some of the shooting. A pair of TV crewmen gave me 350 dollars each for a copy of the recording. How much...", the man started his pitch to her.

Emily snatched it out of his hand with catlike reflexes. "How much the Cathedral Police would appreciate being given a copy. Thank you for your kindness. You are a good citizen doing your civic duty." the detective interrupted and then put the UPB digipod drive in her inside coat pocket. She left the man standing at the edge of the crowd dumbfounded and stammering "but, but". Emily kept moving and made her way to Calista Road.

Traffic had been rerouted to keep Calista Road clear. Detective Oftenmarch lead the way across the blocked street with trainee Jeremy Fairbankers close behind her. The ELE officer was several paces back. Once across the street, Emily spotted a couple more drops of blood leading down North Grant Street. Rows of more onlookers hovering at the barricades were blocking the sidewalk on North Grant Street. Emily had to politely struggle her way through the crowd of spectators. As the amount of people in her path thinned, Emily feared she had lost the trail of blood drops. Ignoring some suggestive comments from the crowd, the detective urgently scanned the ground for the blood trail. Her persistence paid off after a couple of minutes as she found another blood drop further along the sidewalk. This droplet had been stepped on and smeared along the walk.

North Grant Street was busy on any given workday and that was true on this day. The sidewalks were crowded mostly with people on their lunch hours. The traffic was heavy full of delivery trucks, service vehicles, public transport trolleys, and general public travelers. Detective Oftenmarch continued straight on North Grant Street in an attempt to follow the blood trail. She passed multiple music stores, a couple of clothing stores, and a popular shoe store called Trends. Cathedral was known for its glamorous glass-front stores. Like most stores in Cathedral, the ones they passed on North Grant Street had fancy all glass fronts. There was so much foot traffic on North Grant Street, following the blood trail was becoming like looking for needles in haystacks.

Two blocks into their search, just as Emily was thinking they had lost the trail, she found another smudged pair of blood drops. They were outside The Eisenhower Hotel just before its curved front driveway for valet service. Across the street was the thirty-five story Cliffton midscraper with its giant digital television screen, or jumbotron, displaying Channel 11 news coverage currently showing St. Lawrence Gardens. Several people had stopped to watch the news footage. Between the pedestrians and the news watchers, the sidewalk was packed solid on this block. Seeing the sidewalk pavement was difficult enough but finding blood on the pavement was becoming impossible. Additionally, it was hard to look down for more than two seconds without having to look up again to avoid running into anyone.

Reaching the corner of North Grant Street and West 422nd Street, Emily lucked into finding another blood spot. She was just about to pass by it when a man in a business suit dropped his pen. As he blocked foot traffic to scoop it up, the detective spotted blood. This droplet was swirled into the pavement and mixed with some dirt. Looking around, Emily did not like her chances for following the trail for much longer. Both West 422nd and North Grant Street had electronic billboards attracting spectators. The foot traffic was not subsiding and West 422nd was known as restaurant row, or the pub and grub zone, therefore attracting many lunch hour partakers. On the far corner of North Grant and West 422nd was NextGen Longtrans Cellular, which attracted a lot of customers at any hour.

"We are going to have to split up." Emily decided aloud.

"Three officers are not nearly enough to search this crowd effectively." the ELE officer spoke his opinion. He had somehow stayed close by her even through the city crowd.

Fairbankers had fallen behind a little and was scrambling to catch up to them. Now that Emily had stopped, he had a crowd dodging and go with the flow fighting chance to do so. "Seems like we would have a better chance looking for a gunshot victim than more of the blood trail. A gunshot victim should stand out even in Cathedral." Emily reasoned.

"There is a hospital about three blocks south on West 422nd Street. That seems like a likely place for the victim to go" the ELE officer informed her.

"I can try to continue our search along North Grant Street." Fairbankers offered as he had caught up with them.

"Ok, then I will go north on West 422nd Street towards Copious Curl. There is an alley behind Copious that is notorious for homicide crime scenes. Radio in on Police Channel 3 if you find something." Emily formulated a plan.

"I don't have a radio." Fairbankers indicated as if he had just realized this fact.

"Call my complink from your cell phone." Oftenmarch instructed him. The ELE officer had already left them to cross North Grant Street to head south for the nearby hospital. By his demeanor, it seemed like he was done working with them as a team. Fairbankers nodded that he understood and as he waited for the light to cross West 422nd Street, Emily started her trek north on West 422nd's busy sidewalk.

West 422nd Street was almost as crowded as North Grant Street. There was a street performer doing a dance for a sizeable group of spectators which Emily had to circumnavigate. The next challenge was getting around a hot sausage vendor. Emily was no longer spotting any blood on what she could see of the sidewalk. More importantly, the detective was not noticing anybody in distress. Across the street was a midsize digital viewscreen running an advertisement for an upcoming music concert. As Emily weaved past some slower walking pedestrians, she could see Copious Curl up ahead.

Copious Curl was a horseshoe, or half circle, shaped street with both ends connecting to the western side of West 422nd Street. The inner semicircle was home of the well-known playhouse theater called The Prestigium. The theater had an ornate architecture and was quite often decorated lavishly. The outside semicircle of Copious Curl was mostly occupied by restaurants and pubs. Popular eating establishments like Taco Teddy's, The Stout House, The Captain's Galley, and Four Beer Minimum all resided on the outer semicircle. Emily was headed for the back alley behind the buildings on the outer semicircle of Copious Curl.

Dodging a passing biker, the detective continued to scour the sidewalks for traces of blood. Emily picked up her pace towards the back alley while keeping a lookout for any traces of blood on the ground. After avoiding several more people on the sidewalks, she reached the top of the back alley to immediately begin a search. Within seconds of the search, she noticed there was a slight discoloration in the pavement in the back alley. Emily spotted what could have been a blood spot. Maybe, maybe not, thought the detective. It could be something, it could be nothing. The detective returned to looking for something more definitive in the alley, like an injured person.

Quickly, Emily hunted around piles of garbage, underneath cardboard boxes, between discarded shopping carts, and behind an abandoned broken-down washer as she moved along the alley. The detective continued the hunt at the first of several dumpsters in the alley. At the first dumpster, Emily circumnavigated it in exploration to find nobody hurt or unhurt. With no success at this dumpster, she hustled to the next dumpster. Once at that dumpster, Emily repeated her merry-go-round inspection.

Satisfied nobody was behind or alongside the second dumpster, Emily progressed her search farther down the alley. Two quick steps brought the detective to an abandoned armchair where she had a rapid three hundred and sixty degree scan. Finding nobody, Emily pressed on with her search. On her third step from the armchair, the back door to the restaurant called Sir Loin's Banquet Hall, a local lunch time favorite, opened. Out of the door came a pair of familiar fellows, Detective Hedra Shippendarrow and Detective Alexy Millacotta. They had come into the alley to indulge in their bad habit of smoking. Both immediately noticed her.

"Emily, what brings a hard-working detective like yourself to a back alleyway in this precinct?" Detective Millacotta wondered.

"It couldn't be for the lovely view." joked Detective Shippendarrow.

"I'm searching for a wounded civilian who witnessed a criminal act." Emily explained.

"An odd place for your search to lead you." Alexy commented.

"You think the injured party came into this alley?" Shippendarrow questioned as he lit his cigarette.

"We were following a blood droplet trail which seems to have stopped at the corner of North Grant Street and West 422nd Street. The continuation of the search led me to the start of this alley." Emily explained further.

"Not an ideal spot to seek medical attention." Shippendarrow shrewdly observed.

"There is a community health clinic about one block east on West 421st Street." Detective Millacotta helpfully informed.

"A group of us split up to cover more ground, I need to search this alley quickly even just to eliminate it." Emily revealed as she took several steps toward the third dumpster.

"I'll go settle-up my bill then give you a hand." Millacotta indicated then hustled to get back into the restaurant.

"Good idea, you pay our bill while I help Emily." Shippendarrow expressed as Millacotta went through the back door.

As Detective Oftenmarch checked in and around the third dumpster, a few raindrops started to fall from the afternoon sky. Emily found only trash, which she threw a couple of pieces of that trash into the dumpster before moving further along the alley.

Detective Shippendarrow called out to Emily, "A wounded victim would not have come down this alley to hide." He took a puff of his cigarette to indulge his bad habit then reluctantly snuffed it out and tossed it into the dumpster.

Emily, with her quickness, was already checking around the fourth dumpster then she called back, "If I don't check and the victim is here then they could die in this alley undiscovered."

"Think about it, Emily. Is there any evidence that an injured individual went down this alley?" Shippendarrow asked as he moved closer to her, now smokefree.

"You are correct, there is no evidence." she quietly admitted, looking farther down the alley.

"If you were a wounded victim and perhaps had poor health care insurance, then where would you go for help?" the older detective wisely posed a good question.

Emily thought for a moment then had some colossally calming clarity come to her. "The charity clinic run by the Cathedral Minority Respect Foundation back on North Grant Street." she answered aloud with her hand on her forehead.

"Now you're thinking wisely. Work smarter and not harder." Shippendarrow encouraged.

"Thanks, Hedra." Emily offered her gratitude and then accelerated into a run to exit the half-searched alley.

"I will search the rest of the alley just to make you feel better." Shippendarrow shouted in farewell.

Emily gave him a wave mid-run. Another raindrop landed on her shoulder. As she was dashing out of the alley, Emily saw a woman watching her from a second story window. The lady was giving her a strange look like she was wondering what the detective was doing. Not letting that trouble her, Emily exited the alley and was back on West 422nd Street.

The detective moved with as much haste as possible as she reversed her path on West 422nd Street. Rushing back to the corner of West 422nd Street and North Grant Street as quickly as she could manage, Emily was no longer looking for blood. As a few more raindrops fell on the city, the detective had a feeling the blood trail was soon to be washed away. Once she maneuvered through the lunchtime crowd and reached the intersection of the two roads, Emily had to wait for the crosswalk beacon light before crossing West 422nd Street. The wait was for about a minute but felt like ten minutes to the determined detective. When the opportunity to cross came, Emily took an intersection side wide line outside of the crosswalk to jog across the street.

Once across West 422nd, Detective Oftenmarch moved at a brisk pace with her focus fixed firmly on getting to the charity clinic three buildings from the intersection. The starting drizzle and the clumped crowds were not dampening Emily's determination. She was able to slide between and around pedestrians to get to the entrance of the charity clinic. The clinic was closed and nobody was outside the front entrance. Holding back her disappointment, the detective kept pursuing this possibility. While peering through the front windows for signs of activity, Emily kept moving across the front of the clinic.

Unlike most buildings on North Grant Street, the charity clinic had a driveway which accessed the main road. The Minority Respect Foundation-run clinic had a driveway to North Grant Street which ran alongside the building and into a small parking area in the rear of the building. The detective peeled away from the sidewalk crowd as soon as she reached the driveway. Emily darted down the driveway with track athlete speed.

While sprinting down the clinic driveway, Emily was thinking that Eddie would not have been thrilled with her wildly speculatory and erratic search for the shooting victim. More rain drops were falling and what little of the blood trail that was left was certainly not long for existence. Formulating what the next step in the search could be, Emily entered the tiny cramped back parking lot to the charity clinic. Both the Exoprofit and Sterling Morgan Commerce midscrapers on West 421st Street could be seen from the little lot. Filled with litter and debris, the parking lot contained more garbage than parking spaces. Then the detective spotted three men huddled by the clinic's back door. Two of them seemed to be gathered around the third man who was half sitting half laying on the ground. None of them noticed Emily until she was about five feet from them.

"Do you work here?" one of the huddled men asked her with a note of desperation in his voice.

"Detective Emily Oftenmarch, I am with the Cathedral Police Department." she identified herself.

"She's too pretty to be a cop." another huddled man commented.

"We don't need no cop; we need a doctor." the first man spoke out again.

She knelt down by the third man who seemed to be in distress. His face was contorted with pain." I have done nothing wrong." he struggled to faintly say.

"I absolutely agree, it seems like a wrong was done to you. Did you get shot in St. Lawrence Gardens not too long ago?" Emily queried as she saw the man was bleeding just above his hip.

"Yes." he said weakly.

"The man needs a doctor not a lot of questions." the first man protested.

"My colleagues and I have been looking for several blocks to find you, mister." Emily informed the painfully injured man, then she got on her police radio. Her moment of relief was over now that she had seen the wound. "Twenty Charlie Hotel Delta Twelve requesting immediate medical attention for gunshot victim at rear entrance of the Minority Respect Foundation Clinic on North Grant Street. Repeat immediate medical attention needed at the rear entrance of the Minority Respect Foundation Clinic."

"Medical assistant request has been received. Emergency medical personal have been contacted.", came the computerized autodispatcher on the radio.

"This is Officer Dawson with Cathedral dispatch, please confirm dispatch of EMTs to Minority Respect Foundation Clinic at 24739 North Grant Street for gunshot victim." the human dispatcher responded on the radio.

"Confirmed, dispatch." Emily confirmed.

"Ambulance is enroute." Officer Dawson returned.

"He can't afford the hospital bill." the second man pleaded unhappily.

"This medical bill will be courtesy of the Cathedral taxpayers. One of you please bang on that back door and shout police. What is your friend's name?" Emily attempted to redirect the focus.

"Teddy, his name is Teddy." the second man answered as the first man stood up to go to the clinic's back door.

Detective Oftenmarch pulled out a thin handkerchief from her inside coat pocket as she internally admonished herself for leaving the first aid kit in the MPAR still back at the city park. "Teddy, we are going to put this over your wound to try to slow the bleeding." Emily indicated then turned to the second man. "Please put some pressure on the handkerchief for me."

From outside the door the first man shouted, "Skinny woman say she's the police and to open up this mother....."

"Without the swearing." Emily interrupted with a yell.

"That's most of his words. If he couldn't swear then he'd have nothing to say." the second man shared as he attempted to put pressure on the bleeding wound. Teddy grimaced.

"Police, open up!" the first man tried again without profanity as he pounded on the clinic's back door.

As Emily looked around the alley for anything better than a hankie, she noticed that the huddled men both had signs near them. One sign laid on the ground and read: Beware the Lycans. The other sign was propped up by a half-torn cardboard box and read: The Lycans are Coming. Again with the lycans, thought Emily. Next, she observed an unopened delivered package by the back door.

"Police. Open up or she will shoot." the first man bellowed still banging on the door.

Emily sprang to her feet and rushed over to the box. Using her car key as an improvised knife she gouged open the box.

"Is that legal?" the second man asked doubtfully.

Emily went tearing through the box of supplies and as luck would have it found some bandages. "Thank you, GOD." she said aloud.

"I don't think she cares. Woman's not messing around." the first man replied no longer smashing his fist on the door.

"We care more about Teddy; he is more important than ownership of supplies." Emily replied as she returned to the injured man with bandages and gauze. The detective quickly got to work replacing the handkerchief with the new found bandages.

"Why did you come looking for Teddy?" the second man inquired as he watched the detective adeptly apply the fresh first aid.

"Teddy was both a victim and a witness of a criminal act. The Cathedral Police Department wants to come to his aid and hear his testimony." Emily explained while progressing in soundly securing the bandages.

"Teddy told us two fools were blasting bullets trying to smoke each other." the first man relayed as he returned from the unanswered door.

"And one of these gunmen got you by mistake, Teddy?" Emily asked the ailing witness. Teddy nodded affirmatively a couple of times. "Nobody should get shot having a nice walk in a Cathedral city park, you poor fellow Teddy." Emily sympathized as a light drizzle of rain began to fall. She carefully and cautiously concluded the bandaging.

"You're too pretty to be a cop and you speak too sweetly to be one." the second man stated his opinion.

"I noticed your signs about lycans." she indicated and pointed at the signs then continued, "Where have you seen lycans?"

"They cruise the streets at night marking their territory. Some of them walk through tent city at midnight looking for prey." the second man answered.

"They're all over the news. They don't mess about, have this city in their clutches. You can smell the fear all around." the first man expounded.

"I have heard stories of these lycans and you need not be afraid." Ofternmarch replied, cleaning up some blood.

"You don't understand. They come in the night and take people away never to be seen again." the second man fearfully forewarned.

"Some say they are demons coming for lost souls, some say they are thugs doing the bidding of their tyrant masters, but I say they are beasts looking for death and destruction." the first man relayed.

"The lycans bring death and misery. They're killers.", the second man indicated.

"You are right, I don't understand. However, the LORD understands and HE has sent me to tell you good news, the good news of JESUS CHRIST. John 3:17 says *For GOD did not send his SON into the world to* condemn the world, but to save the world through HIM." Emily paused then continued, "If the lycans come they cannot destroy those who believe in CHRIST. It is written in Hebrews 2:14 and 15 *Since the children have flesh and blood, HE too shared in their humility so that by HIS death HE might destroy him who holds the power of death-that is, the devil-and free those who all their lives were held in slavery by their fear of death.*"

"You're saying the lycans want us to fear death but CHRIST has removed their weapon." the first man deduced.

"How does GOD know who to free?" the second man wondered.

"Romans 3:23 states *for all have sinned and fall short of the glory of GOD.* Romans 6:23 *says for the wages of sin is death but the gift of GOD is eternal life in CHRIST JESUS our LORD.* John 3:16 reads *For GOD so loved the world HE gave his one and only SON, that whoever believes in him may have eternal life.* From those three passages we know GOD set everyone free." Emily spoke the truth. Ambulance sirens could be heard in the distance.

"Craziest talk I have ever heard from a cop." the first man declared.

"So everyone is free?" asked the second man.

"Will they accept their gift? Will they trust in their freedom? John 1:12 says *Yet to all who received HIM, to those who believe in HIS name, HE gave the right to become children of GOD.*" Emily answered while positioning herself to block the light rain from landing on Teddy's face.

"So believing he existed makes you free?" the second man puzzled pulling on his collar to keep out any rain.

"Not just his existence, Romans 10:9 reads *That if you confess with your mouth, "JESUS is LORD", and believe in your heart that GOD raised HIM from the dead, you will be saved.*" Emily clarified.

74

"Tell this stuff to the werewolves, not us." exclaimed the first man while feeling the air for raindrops.

"I would like to hear more. Why free us?" Teddy quietly and faintly asked as the ambulance siren grew much louder and closer.

"GOD loves you, Teddy. As it says in Romans 5:8, *GOD demonstrates HIS own love for us in this: While we were sinners, CHRIST died for us.* Then Ephesians 2:4 and 5 says *But because of HIS great love for us, GOD, who is rich in mercy, made us alive in CHRIST even when we were dead in transgressions- it is by grace you have been saved.*" the detective testified.

"Wow, that's deep." the second man expressed.

The ambulance could now be heard coming down the side driveway to the charity clinic with its siren ear-splittingly close. Emily gave Teddy a reassuring pat on his shoulder and then a smile of hope. The rain remained light and mild as the ambulance arrived.

"*Everyone who calls on the name of the LORD will be saved*, Romans 10:13."Emily confirmed as one of the EMTs jumped out of the ambulance to rush over to Emily and Teddy. The paramedic had a field medical kit and a blanket ready to use. Without wasting any time, the paramedic began to treat Teddy and prepare him for transport. Emily prayed for Teddy as the medic was working. After parking the ambulance, the second paramedic unloaded a stretcher to bring over to the wounded civilian. They worked with professionalism and competency to assist Teddy.

As the paramedics were securing Teddy for transport, J.D. Fairbankers arrived in the back parking lot to the charity clinic. He looked as if he had been running and that running had got the best of him. The trainee ran over to Emily as soon as he spotted her.

He needed a moment to catch his breath, so Emily spoke first. "J.D. meet Teddy.He is our VIP for today; poor man was shot while minding his own business. Teddy, this is J.D. Fairbankers. He is working hard to become a great detective." Emily made introductions. Teddy just nodded. J.D. just waved at the man. Emily turned to where the other two men had been to find that they had silently left. Both the lycan related signs had been left behind, discarded in the parking lot.

"Emily, there is a woman waiting up front who needs our help." the young trainee finally managed to speak.

"Ok J.D., first things are first. Let me say goodbye to Teddy. Did you see Detectives Shippendarrow or Millacotta on North Grant Street?" Emily returned calmly.

"I don't know who those people are." Fairbankers replied still short on breath.

"Teddy, this is where I must say goodbye. The paramedics will take good care of you. There will be a Cathedral officer to look in on you later this evening. Please take care." Emily said her farewell.

Teddy winked at her and softly said, "Thank you for everything."

As Teddy was being loaded into the ambulance, J.D. Fairbankers regained his breath. "Emily, this lady is really desperate for some help."

Emily nodded she understood as she watched Teddy being placed into the ambulance. "Lead the way, J.D. Let's go help this woman." the detective responded. And so she followed trainee Fairbankers back up the charity driveway, back onto the sidewalk of North Grant Street, and to a woman pacing back and forth by the front door to the closed charity clinic.

Emily's police communicator radio received a call. "This is Sgt. LaShawndra LeRoyson for Detective Oftenmarch."

"This is Detective Oftenmarch, go ahead Sgt. LeRoyson." Emily responded on her radio.

"We found the second shooter deceased in his car in a parking garage on Second Prospect Avenue. He had multiple gunshot wounds." the sergeant reported.

"We found the victim alive behind the charity clinic on North Grant Street. The poor man was shot once and not in a condition to give us a statement. EMTs are taking him to the hospital on West 422nd Street." Emily counter reported.

"The second shooter's car is on the tenth floor of the fifteen-story parking garage at 1531 2nd Prospect, which is why it took so long to find him. The lieutenant says to come join us." Sgt. LeRoyson updated.

"Copy that." Emily replied.

Finishing her radio conversation, Emily turned to J.D. Fairbankers now standing beside the troubled lady. Fairbankers introduced Emily to a very upset lady. The detective offered both the distressed lady and J.D. a mint. Then Emily attempted to calm the lady down before listening to her story about a missing niece and a mysterious van in her neighborhood. Her tale was troubling and was extremely difficult for her to tell through all her panic and emotion. When she finished in tears, Fairbankers took out an electronic device which projected a holographic image of a neatly dressed lady in an emerald green dress with a silver lace pattern. She had a pretty face, wore a green beaded necklace and silver ribbons in her hair. It was an electronic assistant J.D. used to get the poor lady's contact information.

Chapter 4

Seventh, Eighth, and Ninth

Detective Oftenmarch sat down at her desk with a mug of hot earl grey tea and a spinach arugula tortilla wrap. Her long early morning had been followed by a very long day. A warm beverage and some food were welcome prospects. Emily had stopped at the thrift mart two blocks from the 271st Cathedral police precinct to buy a couple pairs of inexpensive low-cut socks. Having removed her boots, Emily put on both pairs of the newly acquired socks. The footwear was not great quality but they were far better than no socks, which had been that morning's unintentional option. She put her police recorder and her portable tableau in the charging station on her desk. Both devices were in dire need of a recharge.

After the coroner had retrieved the second shooter and his rental car had been impounded, Lt. Knighton had gone to the forensics lab with both firearms used in the shootout at St. Lawrence Gardens in an attempt to get them processed urgently. Most detectives thought his silent watchful hovering caused the forensic scientists to give him first priority just to get rid of him. However, Emily suspected he bribed them. The lieutenant was also still trying to identify the second dueler; his fingerprints were not in the Cathedral PD database.

When Emily and J.D. had returned to the park to collect the MPAR on their way to the 2nd Prospect Avenue parking garage, they had found the robot had been damaged. One of the Cathedral patrol officers still on the scene informed them the ELE officer had attempted to open its main containment compartment by force after they had left. This was after the private law officer attempted to hack into the droid and caused a majority short in its electronics. The compartment remained sealed tight, but the robot was fried and broken. J.D. had gone to the technology department to get the MPAR repaired. While he was waiting for the robot, the trainee was going to start looking into the case of the missing niece and the mysterious work van.

Which left Emily on her own to get some deskwork completed. After waking up her cyberlinked desktop computer, Emily logged into the CaseBuilder program used by the Cathedral Homicide Department. Her files were shared with Lt. Eddie Knighton along with the additional program he had installed called Kilosource Information Multiseek Manager Internet Edition, KIMMie. An added benefit was that this particular program had voice recognition. While speaking to KIMMie, Emily could simultaneously work in the CaseBuilder program. As her programs were loading, the detective had a bite of her wrap, a swig of warm tea, and placed her police 19G complink, also in dire need of recharging, in its charging station. Feeling weary the detective looked at her desk clock. It felt much later than the time indicated; there was still about an hour left in the work day.

Emily opened up her email as KIMMie came online. Dozens of emails appeared unread in her inbox. The lab results came back in the Lobowry case from earlier in the week; the fingerprints matched, the blood type matched, and the DNA was a ninety-five percent probable. Emily noted the trifecta in CaseBuilder and attached the lab report.

"Kimmie, search for a company called Pulchra Lunae HVAC Repairs." Emily used the voice command option.

Dr. Brownling had emailed her and the lieutenant a copy of the autopsy reports for the two bottling plant victims. Cause of death for both victims was knife wounds and not wolf mauling. Stabbed to death was the good doctor's conclusion. Even though the case was no longer their case, Emily still entered this information into CaseBuilder. Earlier that morning when the detective had reviewed the plant's sad security video footage, she had also attached the link to the recordings into the CaseBuilder.

"No results found for a Pulchra Lunae HVAC Repairs.", voiced KIMMie.

A rectangular pane popped up in CaseBuilder indicating that the Incancennio Bottling Plant case was no longer assigned to Knighton and

Oftenmarch. Emily clicked on the residual button option to close the rectangular pane.

"Kimmie, search the area case files for any mention of a Pulchra Lunae HVAC Repairs." Emily requested the next search.

While the Incancennio Bottling Plant case was open, the detective went to the section that listed the two victims. She crossed referenced their names to any other files in CaseBuilder. Both names yielded results, multiple results. Clicking on the first result, Emily quickly skimmed the case section regarding the victim, then closed the file. Selecting the second result, she repeated the fast perusing and quick exiting process.

"There is one entry in the Cathedral PD files and there are four entries in the Granthum PD files." KIMMie voiced the results.

"Kimmie, read line of first Granthum result." Emily commanded.

"Suspicious work van for Pulchra Lunae HVAC Repairs reported in St. Gregory's Cemetary after hours." the computer autoreplied.

"Kimmie, read the line of the second Granthum result." Emily continued the process.

"Company listed for illegally parked van was Pulchra Lunae HVAC Repairs." the computer autoreplied.

"Kimmie, please read the line for the third Granthum result." Emily proceeded numerically.

"Company listed for illegally parked van was Pulchra Lunae HVAC Repairs." KIMMie repeated.

"Kimmie, please read the line for the final Granthum result." Emily commanded.

"No sign of the van belonging to a Pulchra Lunae HVAC Repairs reportedly blocking a fire hydrant." KIMMie voiced in response.

"Kimmie, please read the line for the Cathedral result." Emily concluded.

"Resident complained of suspicious work van for Pulchra Lunae HVAC Repairs parked in vacationing neighbor's driveway." KIMMie voiced the entry.

Emily returned to opening, speed scanning, and closing other files relating to the bottling plant victims. The detective got the gist and exited the Incancennio Bottling Plant file. The first plant murder victim had been scheduled to appear in court to refute witness testimony against a Cathedral narcotics detective charged with falsifying evidence. The second murder victim had recently recanted a pair of testimonies, both giving an alibi to the same suspect for separate burglaries. That suspect was subsequently arrested by a private police firm called Elite Law Enforcers. It was a small world after all. Detective Oftenmarch began to wonder if the lycan masquerade killers eliminated their intended targets after all. Or could it have been two out of three?

"Kimmie, how many missing women from Cathedral were reported in the 24-hour period before the first Granthum entry?" Emily asked for a new search.

While the program searched, Emily opened the Barrett Alexander case file to begin her official work. She needed to give a report on her movements and observations then start a background on Barrett Alexander.

"Twelve women were reported missing." KIMMie voiced the answer.

"How many are still missing?" Emily follow-up quiried.

"Eight women are still listed as missing." the computer digitoned.

Emily observed that Eddie had added the name of the second dueler to the file, Mitchell Moe Gertzin. Mitchell Moe Gertzin was a registered private investigator licensed for the state of Illinois. He had tax records for a Gertzin Detective Agency based in Chicago. What an inventive name for the agency. How did he ever think of it? The lieutenant had made a note in the file that Gertzin Detective Agency did contract work for a private law enforcement company based in Cathedral called Crimestoppers, Inc.

"Kimmie, how many missing women from Cathedral were reported 29 days before the first Granthum entry?" Emily requested.

Emily ran a search to see if Barrett Alexander was involved in any current cases assigned to Elite Law Enforcers by the city of Cathedral. Then starting a secondary search, she looked for any open cases regarding Barrett Alexander personally. The officers from the ELE stated Barrett only worked security or what they called security instead and did not have any ongoing cases. Emily wanted to determine if that was the truth.

"Four women were reported missing." KIMMie synthesized.

"How many are still missing?" the detective duplicated her follow-up question.

"Two women are still listed as missing." KIMMie digitoned in reply.

Results started coming back on Barrett Alexander regarding any open legal proceedings or current law enforcement work; there were only two hits. First, there was an open case for grand theft auto in the 191st precinct in which the investigating officers consulted with Mr. Alexander. Second, there was an open case in which Barrett Alexander was hired by the Cathedral Police Department's Commissioner's office to protect a key witness. He was to protect a witness to the murder of a lawyer from the Cathedral prosecutor's office. The case was still ongoing, which led Emily to question where was the witness. Their name was redacted from the file. Immediately, the detective put this information into an email and sent it to Lt. Knighton. Did the ELE officers know about Barrett's protection assignment? Were they at St. Lawrence Gardens to locate the witness? None of the witness statements Emily had heard or read thus far had mentioned anyone accompanying Barrett Alexander in the park at the time of the shooting. As far as the Cathedral PD knew, he was alone at the time.

"Kimmie, how many missing women from Cathedral were reported 59 days from the first Granthum entry?" the detective pondered.

A murdered witness at the bottling plant, a murdered false witness at the same plant, and now a potentially missing witness whose city police commissioner's office hired bodyguard had been killed were all important to current criminal cases. To Emily, this was suspiciously looking like a hunt for silence. Was Gertzin independent from the lycan masqueraders or was he working in conjunction with them?

"Four women were reported missing." the computer voiced.

"And how many are still missing?" Emily wondered again.

"Two women are still listed as missing." KIMMie's answer was digitoned.

"Kimmie, for Granthum entries two and three, who paid the fine for the illegally parked vehicle registered to Pulchra Lunae?" Emily asked the computer.

Emily switched her Barrett Alexander inquiries to focus on the Celtic .44 pistol. She discovered he bought it after he had retired from the police force. There were no records in the Cathedral area police files of him firing the weapon. The weapon was manufactured by a company that was a subsidiary of a private law enforcement company called Defenders of Law and Order. Defenders of Law and Order was a competitor of Elite Law Enforcers, who employed Barrett Alexander. That was probably why the other ELE officers were so quick to say they did not use a Celtic .44 pistol. Barrett, according to city records, owned two other registered weapons. He had an old fashion revolver and a Beretta 3 in his possession; both had stronger firepower than a Celtic .44 pistol. The Celtic .44 was more easily concealed and was registered as his ELE service weapon. Was he on duty when he was exchanging gunfire in the park, Emily asked herself. If so, was he on the job for the ELE or the commissioner's office?

"The registered vehicle to Pulchra Lunae had its parking fines paid by None of Your Business, LLC." KIMMie autoreported.

"Oh really. Kimmie, who is the executor of None of Your Business, LLC?" Emily requested, suppressing her amusement.

"Mr. Santa Claus, resident of the North Pole." the computer autoreplied.

"Kimmie, flag None of Your Business, LLC as fraudulent." Emily instructed.

"Compliant." the computer digitalized.

A fake company displayed on a work van registered to a fake company having its parking fines paid by a fake corporation was incredibly suspicious. Emily's desk phone rang, which was unusual. "Cathedral Homicide, Detective Oftenmarch speaking." she answered.

"Oh good, I was able to reach you. My name is Dr. Thomas Wiley and I am an assistant coroner with the Cathedral coroner's office. I have some peculiar information regarding the victim named Barrett Alexander and you were listed as the investigating officer." the doctor greeted over the phone.

"Good afternoon, doctor. I am investigating the murder of Mr. Alexander but was not expecting the autopsy to be this soon." Emily confessed.

"Oh no detective, the autopsy has not been done yet. The oddities were discovered when we removed the victim's shoes. He had notes or messages stored in his shoes under his feet." the doctor explained further.

"That is strange, doctor." Emily replied with curiosity.

"It gets stranger, detective. The messages themselves are cryptic and written in purple colored crayon. We took pictures of them which I will email you but in the meantime I think I should read them to you." Dr. Wiley continued.

"You definitely have my undivided attention, doctor." Emily admitted.

"The first message says: There are no pickled peppers for Peter Piper to pick. The second message says: The weasel went around the mulberry bush but no monkey gave chase. And the last message says: The lycans are coming." the kind doctor read the crayon crafted notes.

"A variation of a tongue twister, a reference to a nursery rhyme, and another werewolf warning certainly qualify as odd and cryptic messages to hide in your shoes, doctor." Emily agreed.

"Hopefully you can make more sense out of them than I have managed. Like I said before, I will email pictures of the messages. Good luck, detective." Dr. Wiley concluded.

"Thank you and have a good evening, doctor." Emily farewelled.

Detective Oftenmarch quickly updated the Barrett Alexander file with this bizarre new information. KIMMie had mistaken some of the phone conversation for commands and was in a confused frozen state, so Emily restarted the program. She paused to take a drink of her now lukewarm tea.

Taking out the UPB digipod drive obtained from an onlooker, Emily took a risk and plugged it into her desktop computer. Immediately running a virus scan on the drive, she minimized some of the risk. After the virus scan cleared the drive, Emily opened the drive and played the lone video file on the device. The video ran for about a minute and a half and did actually show the exchange of gunfire at St. Lawrence Gardens. Distant and blurring, the footage did not provide much detail but was clear enough to show the two men did indeed shoot each other. On the grainy recording, the entire duel was captured. It had started abruptly with Gertzin firing and then the rapid exchange of shots took a short period of time. The duel was over as quickly as it started. Emily copied the video file and attached a copy to the Barrett Alexander file in CaseBuilder. Next, she attached a copy to the Mitchell Moe Gertzin file in CaseBuilder. Finally, she emailed the tech lab a copy of the video file with an official request to attempt to clean-up and enlarge the duel footage.

Emily started filling out departmental forms for the case file when her personal cell phone rang. Pulling her phone from her inside coat pocket, Emily saw from the display it was her younger sister Ninth calling.

A brief history on the evolution of Emily's name. She was born the eighth child of the Day family and her birthname was Eighth Day. When she was attending high school and college, she went by the name Emily. At the age of eighteen, she legally changed her name to Emily Day. After she married her first husband, Abraham, her name became Emily Goldsmith. When Emily joined the Cathedral Police Department, she was Officer Emily Goldsmith. After Abraham passed away Emily kept the last name Goldsmith. She met and eventually married David-John Oftenmarch around the time that she became a detective. This changed her name again. This time her legal name was Emily Goldsmith-Oftenmarch and at work she was known as Detective Emily Oftenmarch.

"Hello, Ninth. How are you feeling today?" Emily greeted as she answered her phone.

"Sorry to bother you at work, Eighth. We need your help with Seventh." Ninth began worriedly.

"Our brother is a grown man, Ninth. He doesn't need a babysitter anymore." Emily interjected.

"He missed work today, Eighth, and none of us can find him. Mom looked at his apartment. Fifth and Sixth drove to his friends' places and around the neighborhood. With you being a detective, I was hoping you could find him and make sure he is alright." Ninth explained speaking rapidly.

"It is more likely his little shadow of a sister could find him than Detective Oftenmarch." Emily speculated.

"There is that too. Please find him, E. You know I would not call and ask unless Mom was worried." Ninth pleaded.

"Alright Ninth, I will slip away for awhile to find Seventh as I have an idea where he might be located. This is only because you ask so nicely, Ninth." Emily agreed.

"Thank you, E. You really are the best. Will you be at the New Carnelian Knights game tomorrow night? If so, you can meet my new boyfriend." Ninth shared excitedly.

"Wait a minute. Didn't you introduce your new boyfriend to David and I two weeks ago?" Emily asked in confusion.

"That was my old boyfriend, E." Ninth said with a giggle.

"Of course it was, how silly of me. Talk to you later, Ninth. I am off to find a wandering big brother." Emily concluded the phone call.

"Thank you again, E." Ninth said goodbye.

Emily put her phone back into her coat pocket, took off her work boots, and put on her black athletic shoes. After finishing her wrap, the detective downed the last of her cold tea. Leaving her copcam and tableau to charge, Emily grabbed her complink. Springing to her feet, Emily then grabbed her coat and headed out of the homicide department.

The detective hustled down the third floor main hallway and then took the stairs to the ground floor. Emily weaved through foot traffic in both booking and the main lobby. Once outside the 271st precinct's confines, Emily jogged four blocks to the electric monorail station on Easy Street. She hoped her jogging looked like some late afternoon exercise.

At the electric monorail station, Emily went up to the northeast inbound city platform to wait three minutes for the next available monorail train. Fortunately, the station was not too crowded and the detective would be able to get a place on the next train. She used her personal rail pass to pay the monorail fee and boarded the electric train. Standing quietly amongst the railway passengers, Emily rode the monorail for seven stops.

On the seventh stop, she exited the train and then promptly departed the monorail station on Northern Norfolk Street. First crossing Northern Norfolk Street, Emily then cut across Blackheart Square where the old Cathedral Courthouse still stood. The old courthouse bell was chiming for the bottom of the hour.

As Emily was crossing the square, she saw someone who caused her to halt her haste. Standing behind some hedges next to a small white flowering dogwood tree was the private investigator, Emerson Plumwine. Curious as to what he was up to, Emily decided to go talk to him. As the detective walked over to the private eye's position, she noted that Emerson was watching a side entrance to the Old Cathedral Courthouse. Plumwine was friends with homicide detective Darious Cole, or at least used to be. Detective Cole had introduced her to Emerson and as Plumwine's work intersected with Eddie's and her investigations, Emily came to know Emerson quite well. His current behavior was more usual than his typical unusual. Emily was not accustomed to seeing Emerson this early in the day. Usually the wayward private detective was not about until around dinner time or very late in the evening, at his typical stomping ground and watering hole, Club Arden.

"Good afternoon, Emerson." Emily greeted him from the other side of the hedge.

Emerson flinched in surprise. "You startled me, Emily. I am a little preoccupied at the moment." the private investigator stated. The private eye had a poetry book upside down in his hand, which he was clearly pretending to read.

"Busy working on a case I suspect." Emily returned.

"This is on the double hush. I am but a daydreamer in the square." Emerson indicated.

"All your cases are on the double hush - triple hush, Emerson." Emily reminded him.

"This case really is on the double hush, Emily" he seriously replied. He put his index finger to his lips to make a libraryesque quiet gesture.

"The old Cathedral Courthouse is an interesting building and has unique architecture but not much going on there these days, Emerson." Emily indicated.

"People have been stealing and altering police records and court documents that are stored and archived in this old building." Emerson Plumwine shared. "I am keeping track of who is coming in and going out of this building."

"Now that is interesting. I did not know Cathedral kept records in the Old Cathedral Courthouse." Emily admitted.

"Few people do, Emily. Now please forgive me, I must get back to my watch." the private investigator apologized. He resumed pretending to read his upside down book.

"Your book is upside down. Best of luck to you, Emerson." Emily bid the eccentric man farewell and continued across the square.

Halfway across the square Emily noticed a man who was walking in the opposite direction from her giving her a peculiar look. He was the second person today to look at her strangely. For a moment she started to feel self-conscious or insecure but then decided to once again forget about it.

Exiting Blackheart Square and then passing Ebotics robotics gaming store and training arena, the detective was on the fast-paced move again. Next, she passed the circular glass fronted Cathedral Megamedia Building with its three outdoor jumbotrons playing to the city crowd. Three blocks, two street crossings, and one clothing boutique front display crowd navigating later, Emily reached her destination. She entered the luxury suites building called The Grand Getaway. The detective showed her badge to the robotic doorman to gain building access, then showed it again to the human working the security desk to retain access.

Taking the stairs to the fourth floor, Emily moved purposefully with more interest in her final destination than her journey. Each step was padded with a tread making them faster for Emily to climb. Passing nobody on the stairs, the detective arrived on the fourth floor quickly. The fourth floor hallway was full of lavish decorations but only one other visitor, a man patiently waiting for the elevator. Emily hustled down the hallway and an oversized wooden door of a corner suite. Pressing the suite's front buzzer activated the automated door assistant.

"Name and password, please." the electronic device requested.

"Emily Oftenmarch. By the hair of my chinny chin chin." Emily responded.

The electronic system paused a moment before replying, "One moment, please." It was now Emily's turn to patiently wait in the hallway.

An attractive young lady neatly dressed in an elegant red gown and adorning several well-polished articles of rich jewelry came to the door. Emily recognized the lady as her brother Seventh's friend Sandra Silvers.

"Hello, Sandra. Sorry to bother you. I need to see my brother." Emily greeted.

"Sorry Emily, you know I can't let you come inside." Sandra apologized.

"I didn't ask to come inside, Sandra. I just asked to see my brother. Please tell your guests the dealer needs a five minute break and he can come to the door." Emily suggested.

"Wait a minute." Sandra replied and then closed the suite's wooden door again.

Once again Emily was left to patiently wait in the hallway. As Emily waited, a man dressed in a black leather jacket and wearing sunglasses inside the building stepped off the elevator. He strutted down the well decorated hallway to the corner suite where the detective was queued.

"You here to play, good looking, or is Sandra hiring some fresh eye candy." the confident arrival asked her as he checked her out.

"Neither one, I am waiting on my brother." Emily answered. She stood off to the side to allow him to push the suite buzzer and reactivate the automated door assistant.

"Name and password, please.", the electronic assistant requested.

"Johnny 'River' Ferry. Sarsaparilla." the arrogant guest revealed with air quotes and then a double finger point gesture. Emily observed that he actually had an ace up his sleeve. She did not even need to see the playing cards to know this man was in for an expensive session of losing poker.

Emily smiled politely as the door assistant welcomed him. The oversized wooden suite door opened. "Welcome, Mr. Ferry." the door assistant greeted.

"Wish me luck, beautiful." Johnny stated before waltzing exuberantly through the suite door.

Not long after happy go lucky Johnny had entered the suite, the elevator doors opened again. Another man wearing a black leather jacket exited the elevator. This man was well dressed and kept his sunglasses hanging from his vest collar. The newcomer walked more confidently yet less arrogantly than Johnny 'River' Ferry. He moved purposely down the lavishly decorated hallway to the corner suite where the detective was still queued.

"Are you next or are you waiting on your companion?" the arriving man asked.

"Waiting on my brother." Emily corrected.

"Sure, you are." the man replied skeptically looking at his shiny wristwatch.

"Please go ahead." the detective politely offered as she moved farther away from the suite buzzer to give him room to activate the auto assistant.

"Name and password, please." the electronic assistant requested again.

"Kajay Malgrave. Sarsaparilla." the confident guest replied. He was subdued and waited patiently. Emily observed he had a tired look about him with bags under his eyes. This man had the look of someone who spends a lot of sleepless nights playing poker.

Emily smiled pleasantly as the door assistant welcomed this man. The oversized wooden suite door opened. "Welcome, Mr. Malgrave." the door assistant voiced in salutation.

"You're hot. If you'd dress sexier, then you wouldn't have to wait for any man." Kajay commented, then strolled casually through the suite door.

About ten seconds later, Seventh came out of the door. He was wearing a flamboyant vest, black bow tie, and black armbands over a white dress shirt. His entire outfit was cliche.

"You can't come here while I'm working, E." Seventh sternly stated.

"Correction, I should not have to come here while you're working but my knucklehead brother does not bother to tell his own mother he will be away from work for a day." Emily sharply retorted.

"Mom called you?" Seventh asked.

"She asked Ninth to call, or Ninth beat her to the phone call. Of course I got called, Seventh. That's why I am here and not working." she answered her brother like a little sister.

"I am supposed to be working too, E." Seventh countered.

"Inform your full-time employer that you're taking the day off to work your part time job, Seventh. That is what an adult does." Emily countered back.

"Mom has a fit every time I mention missing work or doing this job." Seventh complained.

"I think she wants to make sure you're safe first and foremost. Then she will tell you not to go on your typical pub hop tonight." Emily reasonably surmised.

"It is called a pub crawl, E." Seventh corrected.

"It is called stupid. And please no fighting tonight. I am not going to bail you out again." Emily told her brother as she pulled out her phone.

"You're calling her?" Seventh asked deflated.

"I'm calling Ninth." Emily replied as she dialed.

As soon as Ninth answered, Emily asked her to talk to her brother and handed the phone over to Seventh. Seventh and Ninth talked on Emily's phone for about a minute and then Emily heard Seventh say "I don't want to talk to mom. No, please don't put her on the phone. Ninth, Ninth." Then he handed the phone back to Emily. "I really do have to get back to work, E."

"Likewise, Seventh, be safe tonight my brother." the detective said farewell. Seventh went back into the corner suite as Emily headed down the hallway with her phone to her ear.

On Emily's tenth step, her mother's voice came on the phone. "Seventh, where are you?" she inquired with some concern and some anger.

"Sorry mom, he had to go back to his other job. He's safe and at some luxury suites in Cathedral." Emily explained.

"How is it that it is always you that finds your brother Seventh?" her mom wondered.

"I am a police detective, mom." Emily reasoned.

"That worries me too. Seventh goes off on his 24-hour disappearances but you Eighth have a dangerous job all the time." her mother worried.

"I am fine, mom. Thanks for worrying." Emily relayed.

"How many times have you been shot at today?" her mother asked.

"None, but I was attacked by wolves." the detective answered.

"I never know when you're joking and when you're serious." her mom admitted.

Emily had reached the door to the stairwell and stopped just in front of it. "I have to get back to work, Mom. Take care and tell everyone I love them." Emily said her farewell.

"Thank you for checking on your brother, Eighth, and please do be careful. Goodbye." her mother said her goodbye.

As Emily put her phone away and opened the stairway entrance door, she saw three men come out of the elevator. She recognized two of them from their news conferences and press appearances. They were both police captains for the Cathedral Police. One was the captain of the 160th Cathedral Police precinct and the other was a captain for one of the downtown precincts. Emily could not remember which number exactly. Pausing for a minute at the door, Emily watched them walk the hallway to the corner suite where she had just met with her brother. All three men were so involved in their conversation that none of them noticed Emily.

Once at the door, they pressed the buzzer to activate the very busy automated door assistant. In reply to the same name and password request, they told the electronic device that they were the police and to open up. And in an instant, Sandra Silvers was at the door greeting them as guests, not as police officers. Interesting, thought Detective Oftenmarch, then silently she went into the stairwell noiselessly closing the door behind her.

As Emily began her trek back to the 271st police precinct, her thoughts were on her brother's moonlight mischief and poker player police captains. When she returned to Blackheart Square, her thoughts change to Emerson Plumwine and his statements regarding stolen records from the old courthouse. On the monorail train her thoughts switched to Teddy and how the poor man could be alone in the hospital tonight. When Emily got off the train, she was wondering to herself why a Chicago-based private investigator would travel to Cathedral to shoot a private law security officer. When Emily entered the hectic 271st precinct lobby, she was making a mental note to check Gertzin's background to see if he had any history with Barrett Alexander. By the time the detective returned to her desk, she was instantly back working on the Barrett Alexander file in CaseBuilder almost as if she had never left her desk.

Ten minutes after Emily had returned, J.D. Fairbankers was back from the tech lab with some bad news. The MPAR unit was damaged by the ELE to the extent that it was going to need extensive overnight repairs, thus putting it out of commission until Monday morning at the earliest. The poor robot had been wounded in the line of duty. The two of them spent several minutes talking about Pulchra Lunae and comparing notes regarding missing women. As they were discussing, Lt. Knighton returned from the forensics lab with some good news. Ballistics had been completed for the Celtic .44 pistol and the weapon used by Mitchell Moe Gertzin. All the lab needed now was the removed bullets from the deceased to be received from the coroner's office for comparison. Alas, the estimated time on their receipt was also Monday morning.

The who, where, when, and how were all known for the St. Lawrence Gardens' midpark showdown. It was the why of the shooting that was out of focus. Since the culprits were known and off the streets, their captain would consider the case a success. Since there would not be a need to put anyone on trial for the shootings, the prosecutor's office would also consider the case a success. Eddie would naturally have several theories on the motif or motive, which he would naturally research and document in CaseBuilder. Chances were high he would have a why by Monday morning as well. There was a light at the ending of this long work day tunnel.

The prosecutor's office was satisfied with the Lobowry case. Veedan Downmore killed his cousin Dixon Downmore. Mitchell Moe Gertzin shot and killed Barrett Alexander. Barrett Alexander shot and killed Mitchell Moe Gertzin. The Incancennio Bottling Plant homicides had been reassigned through no fault of their doing. The Pulchra Lunae van mystery was not their case and might not even be homicide related.

Officially, Emily's work day was done; she could go home and rest with a job well done. She could start on having herself a nice weekend. But Emily was compelled to continue, she could not help herself. Things were not right and she wanted to make an effort to put some things right. She texted her loving husband to let him know she would not be home for dinner.

Chapter 5

Full Moon Cemetery

As hard as J.D. Fairbankers tried to persuade Lt. Knighton to get involved with the missing girl and mysterious van situation, it was ultimately Detective Oftenmarch who convinced him. Missing women every 28 days on the full moon and a bogus company van for a non-existent Pulchra Lunae company were questionable things the lieutenant could not ignore. Also, and most likely, the lieutenant agreed because he knew it would annoy the captain. Emily knew leaving their jurisdiction was a bad idea but she could not shake the feeling that it was important to intervene. Oftenmarch was motivated by compassion for the lady with the missing niece and to encourage J.D.'s desire to help. The detective had an internal prompting that this was the right thing to do. The lieutenant also appeared to discern something was amiss and the mud tusslers should intervene. There was a life and death reason to get involved.

Eddie had asked Emily to make some phone calls to the Granthum Police to inform the local law enforcement of their intentions to stake out St. Gregory's Cemetery to watch for the suspicious work van tonight. It had taken six phone calls and reciting the story and their intended plan a dozen times before anyone with authority in the Granthum PD agreed to cooperate and allow them to stake out the cemetery in Granthum city limits.

So when most of the day shift Cathedral police personnel went home at five o'clock Cathedral time, J.D, Eddie, and Emily kept working. They split their past shift hours between updating CaseBuilder, researching to find facts and evidence, and preparing for their trip to Granthum's cemetery. Eddie bought the three of them a nice dinner from a nearby Italian restaurant and after they had eaten, they left for Granthum. Lt. Knighton drove his own car while J.D. rode with Emily, who was driving the PSUV. Making the eastward trip, the drive to Granthum took about an hour in moderate traffic.

Granthum was the home of many factories and manufacturing facilities. The production of goods and services churned and continued both
day and night in the city of Granthum. The city of Granthum was also
notorious for its road construction. The orange barrel battle often raged
prevalently against the city's infrastructure. Having numerous sports
fans, Granthum was also known for its popular baseball team called the
Granthum Grey Sox. The Grey Sox, big rivals with the Cathedral Bishops,
had a home baseball game that night. They were beginning a three-
game series at home versus New York.

To avoid road construction and any remaining baseball stadium
traffic, both Emily and Eddie took the outerbelt highway to the south
side of the city, where St. Gregory's Cemetery was located. They took
the Madison Junction exit which had an electronic message board stating the off ramp was scheduled to soon receive construction. Their
journey took them past the big Clearview Glass factory, the profitable
Bellyfood snack chip plant, the Underpar golf cart assembly plant, and
one of the three megapower plants in the city. Granthum hosted three
major energy company competitors which each had a megapower plant
located there.

The streets of Granthum were far less crowded than in Cathedral
especially at this time of the evening. The trio passed a bowling alley
and a local pub that had drawn crowds but otherwise this section of the
city was quiet with few people around after sunset.

St. Gregory's Cemetery was secluded and shared its dead-end road
with only a church and a funeral home. The main entrance was closed
with a gate blocking its front driveway into the cemetery. They had to
drive further along to a secondary entrance, which appeared to be more
for maintenance crews and groundskeepers than visitors. The unpaved
drive at this entrance was muddy and slightly bumpy but had no barricade preventing their admittance.

Once on the cemetery grounds, the detectives found a concealed
spot by a rundown maintenance shed, an old tree, and a pair of hedges

to park their vehicles. From this secluded spot, they had an excellent vantage point on both entrances and an exceptional view of the front section of the cemetery grounds. Now that they had their position, all they could do was wait to see if the mysterious work van would show up.

"We might have a long wait ahead, J.D. I brought crackers and a thermos of coffee. You're welcome to share. Seeing as there are limited restroom options, you may want to go easy on the coffee for the first hour or two." Emily offered.

"Shouldn't we ask the lieutenant to join us instead of leaving him to sit alone in his car?" J.D. inquired.

"Eddie will be happier to have peace and quiet. He works better left alone with his thoughts." Emily explained.

"I don't think he likes me much." J.D. expressed.

"He likes you just fine. People often misread Lt. Knighton. They mistake his silence for lack of knowledge, unsympathetic, arrogance, grumpiness, or disapproval. It is my opinion that he is quiet because he is listening." Emily explained to the trainee.

"Interesting. What does he hear?" Fairbankers wondered.

"The notes that lead to the symphonic solution to catching a criminal. Someday you will witness it." the detective expounded.

"Do you hear these notes, Emily?" the trainee asked her.

"Most of the time I listen to Eddie. Speaking of listening, do you mind if we listen to a baseball game on the radio?" Emily returned.

"Sure, you can listen to the game. I have my indigo tooth headphones so I can listen to my favorite megawave streamcasts on my comphone." Fairbankers shared.

"This is a tough way to spend your first night working with the Cathedral Police." Emily considered.

"I don't mind. This is interesting and I hope we can save that nice lady's niece tonight." J.D. wished.

"We all would like a happy ending tonight, J.D. There are far too few happy endings working Cathedral homicide." Oftenmarch shared. She turned on the radio and tuned in the Granthum Grey Sox baseball game. Fairbankers put on his wireless headphones and became silent. He began playing a word cipher game on a handheld device that projected a bright hologram with an orange banner and bold alphanumeric characters.

The light of the moon and the puffy clouds swirled together to form a kaleidoscope of light and shadow. The orange yellow light flowed in and through the clouds, appearing bright in places and faded behind wafting clouds in other spots. The moonlight shone bright and then became cloud faded in the night sky, continually changing between its brilliance of pale light, its misty ring of hydro light, and its cloud masked and muted light positions. The moonlight blended into the various densities of the passing clouds giving off a varied array of colors and intensities.

When Emily tuned into the baseball game, it was the bottom of the sixth inning and the game was tied 2-2. The Grey Sox managed to load the bases with only one out but then their next batter hit into an inning ending double play, keeping the score tied. As she listened, Emily reviewed her notes on her complink for the Incancennio Bottling Plant homicides.

In the top of the seventh, the Grey Sox had to go to their bullpen for relief. They were unable to keep New York off the scoreboard after a two out RBI single. As the Grey Sox were giving up a run, Emily was exchanging texts with her husband. She told him she was going to be extremely late, he replied stay safe, she replied get some sleep, he replied kettle calls pot black, and both spouses finished with an I love you.

Trailing 3-2 in the bottom of the seventh, Granthum stranded a man on second base. Back-to-back batters struck out, the second one on a controversial strike three call. That call led to the Grey Sox manager arguing with the umpire, which led to the manager being ejected from the game. Detective Oftenmarch had returned to her bottling plant notes but stopped reviewing them at the conclusion of the seventh inning.

Emily watched the cemetery intently and then the night sky as the top of the eighth inning played on the radio. Through a multilayer of clouds, a swirl of light and darkness, shone the moon. The moon would be obscured by the first layer of clouds then unobstructed by the first layer to be semiblocked by the second layer of clouds. Light would peek out around the clouds and in gaps between the clouds. Then the moon would breakout to brightly illuminate the sky only to be recovered by one layer or another of clouds. The cometary was dark and uneventful. Granthum's second reliever of the night, a lefty, pitched a one-two-three inning, making that half inning also uneventful.

Having turned his holographic game off, J.D. had fallen asleep with his headphones on during the bottom of the eighth inning. Emily let him sleep as she searched the internet on her police tableau looking for any news articles regarding criminals dressed as werewolves. The only story she had found during the bottom of the eighth inning was about teenaged Halloween pranksters. Meanwhile, the Grey Sox hit a one out solo home run to left centerfield to tie the game again. St. Gregory's Cemetery remained quiet and still; if any creature was stirring, then it was as small as a mouse. The darkness of the night seemed to get darker when Emily looked back at the cemetery.

In the top of the ninth inning, Granthum struggled with their pitching and fielding. Despite walking two batters, committing an error, and failing to turn a double play, the Grey Sox somehow managed to get out of the top of the ninth without giving up a run. The baseball game went to the bottom of the ninth inning still tied. With her eyes tired from looking at electronic screens, Emily listened to the ninth inning while watching the night sky. The full moon continued to fade in and out of view as the layers of clouds rolled by it.

As Emily moongazed, the Grey Sox managed to get runners on the corners, first and third base, with two outs. The next batter fouled off five pitches and stayed alive to get a full count. Unfortunately, the pay-off pitch was hit right at the centerfielder for an inning ending flyout to center. For the second straight day, Granthum was playing extra innings.

The detective ate a couple of crackers and poured herself some coffee as the fourth Grey Sox relief pitcher worked the tenth inning. The lanky veteran reliever managed to keep New York off balance at the plate and off the base pads in the top of the tenth. J.D. had awakened before the third out and he also had opted for some coffee and crackers.

Enjoying the warm beverage and a caffeine jump start, Emily and J.D. listened to the bottom of the tenth inning as they watched the dark and lifeless graveyard grounds. The Grey Sox leadoff hitter in the tenth smashed the second pitch of the at bat off the outfield wall for a double. New York intentionally walked the next hitter to make the double play and the force-out at third options. Granthum's next two batters both recorded outs as they were unable to come through with a game winning hit. However, the next Grey Sox player who came to bat smacked a hard ground ball back up the middle. Zipping past the outstretched glove of the pitcher and racing by a diving second baseman, the ball rapidly rolled into right centerfield. Rounding third base, the Grey Sox lead runner was dashing determinedly for home. New York's centerfielder cleanly fielded the ball and threw the ball towards home plate like a low flying rocket. The Grey Sox runner dove head first for home. The catcher for New York caught the ball and spun flawlessly to attempt to apply the tag. Colliding, the runner and catcher had converged at home plate. Safe was the umpire's call. The roar of the overjoyed home crowd could be heard on the radio. By a score of 4-3, the Grey Sox had won.

The baseball game had become so interesting, Emily had forgotten about the cemetery vigil. As the radio announcer was celebrating the win, that is when Emily spotted movement. A pair of headlights were slowly moving along the dark cemetery grounds. Immediately, Emily switched off the radio and strained her eyes to make out any details for the arriving vehicle.

"I think this is it, J.D." she spoke softly unnecessarily as if the newcomer could hear.

"Can't make out the company logo from here, but I think you are correct, Emily." J.D. agreed.

The vehicle was slowly driving along the frontmost access lane in the cemetery. About halfway along the lane, the vehicle came to a stop at the side of the lane. Its brake lights went off like the vehicle had been placed in park.

Both J.D. and Emily could hear Lt. Knighton open his car door. Fastening her shoulder light and activating her copcam, Emily prepared to confront the driver of the late-night cemetery visiting vehicle. Swiftly and quietly, Detective Oftenmarch exited the PSUV and trainee Fairbankers did likewise. Eddie was standing in front of his car activating his copcam when they joined him. He nodded to Emily, it was time to go to work. Briskly but cautiously, they marched across the mushy and sometimes sloppy graveyard grounds and onto the muddy access lane. During the hike, they could see a hulking figure get out of the work van. He appeared to be a large man; he moved around to the back of the vehicle and opened the rear door. Even in the moonlight, the van looked too shabby and too rusty to be considered a legitimate work vehicle.

Lt. Knighton was in the lead position as the trio approached the van. The vehicle was an old revamped Hardwork Series III black cargo van. The van's engine was off but the key remained in the ignition, giving the suspicious brutish man interior cab lights for visibility. He was leaning into the rear of the van working on something feverishly with the van door partially closed as the detectives approached. Saint Gregory's Cemetery was extremely poorly lit, making it difficult to discern what was happening. His movements seamed peculiar and the rear door was concealing what he was doing. The cemetery was not equipped for abnormal night time visitations. One thing was apparent: his behavior was odd. Emily adjusted her shoulder light as they marched along the muddy access lane drive. The darkened remote grounds were soggy from all the recent rain in Granthum, causing their foot falls to squish.

When they were within thirty-five feet of the black van, Emily spoke out. "Excuse us, sir. This is the Cathedral Police. The cemetery is closed at this time of night." she announced.

With a jolt of surprise, the huge hulking man quickly withdrew from the van. Stepping back from the well-used van, the burly bizarre behaving man offered an awkward excuse. "Was just getting some of my tools organized for a late-night repair. Customer's furnace broke down and they need an emergency service."

"Surely there are better places to prepare then in a closed cemetery on a dark chilly night parked in the mud." Detective Oftenmarch challenged.

"I like working in peace, this is the quietest place I know." he explained.

"You like working blind?" Eddie puzzled.

"The cemetery is clearly closed. It is much too dark to properly and functionally work and you are getting your work boots caked in mud. So let us try this again. What are you doing trespassing on dark cemetery grounds late at night?" Emily rephrased her curiosity.

"Look, I don't want any trouble. I'll just get in my work van and be on my way." the muscular man declared.

"Your license plate has expired." Lt. Knighton observed holding his flashlight beam on the plate illuminating the displayed date.

"Sticker must have fallen off the plate. I hate it when that happens." the large lying man offered.

"Doesn't make it legal, sir. I would like to see your driver's license and vehicle registration please." Detective Oftenmarch calmly requested.

The brawny balking man made no move to retrieve any documentation. Instead he looked around as if he was considering what he should do next. As he was midnight deliberating, the cargo van rocked sideways a couple of times. He looked quizzically at the detectives wondering if they had noticed the movement in the dark. Eddie had his professional poker face displayed which revealed nothing. Emily held an uncharacteristic frown on her face. Then there was the young trainee Jeremy Dean, whose mouth was agape and eyes were as wide as if he was witness to a miracle. The big man burst into a run and was almost instantly sprinting across the cemetery grounds at a surprising speed for his stature.

Lt. Knighton chased after the fleeing suspect, swiftly giving transcemetery pursuit. Emily darted toward the old van while motioning to trainee Fairbankers to follow her. Efficiently and expediently, Emily reached the van to fling the unlocked rear doors open. The sight that awaited her was upsetting. A pair of naked young women were bound and gagged on the van floor. Visibly distressed, they were desperately struggling for freedom from their cruel circumstances. Their frantic efforts were thus far in vain. A poor effort had been made to spread a blanket along the floor of the van. No attempt had been made to cover their nakedness. They were given no covering. Emily rapidly put her magician assistance skills from a past part time job to work.

"This is Detective Oftenmarch of Cathedral homicide requesting immediate assistance at St. Gregory's Cemetery in Lower Granthum. Human trafficker and attempted murder suspect on the run. Multiple victims need immediate attention." Detective Oftenmarch broadcasted over her digital lawband communicator. As she spoke, Emily nimbly worked to untied the victims' hands. Within twelve seconds, Emily had the hands of one lovely young lady untied. Then repeated the under twelve second untie on the other lovely young lady's hands.

"Request for law enforcement back and medical personnel received." the computerized dispatcher autoreplied.

"This is Granthum dispatch central. Please confirm police backup and ambulance needed at St. Gregory's Cemetery." the human dispatcher spoke over the communicator.

"Confirmed" Emily replied as she unknotted the restraining ropes.

After loosening and releasing their bindings, Emily quickly unfastened their gags. Both unclad and teary-eyed women gasped for air once the gags were removed. "J.D., it's important that you cover-up and protect both ladies. Stay with them in case the dishonest villain doubles back to the van." Emily quickly instructed as she sprang away from the rundown van. Like a graceful blur in the night Emily ran graveyard bound to assist Eddie.

J.D. stammered in uncertain protest, "I don't have any women's clothing. Do I shoot the suspect if he returns? I don't know what to tell the Granthum Police when they arrive. Who is going to help you, Emily?" His protests faded in the distance as Detective Oftenmarch put her years of track running to good use. Confident that J.D. would handle the situation, she moved gazellelike across the first cemetery lawn between the access lanes. The gravestones were low to the ground in this section and gave little if any obstructions. With blazing speed, Emily reached the bridge over Reflection Creek. The ornate wooden bridge led to the second cemetery lawn.

As she sprinted across the bridge, Emily could see the lieutenant's torchlight moving upward on Bauden's Rest Hill. She could also make out the suspect's silhouette on top of Bauden's Rest Hill now that the full moon shone brightly in a now clear sky. Moonlight bathed the entire cemetery in a lambent white light. Needing to close the distance between her and Eddie, Emily increased her stride and bounded across the aesthetic footbridge and onto the second cemetery lawn. The second cemetery lawn was much like the first in size and lack of obstacles. The detective sprinted across this ground in greater speed and urgency. The second access lane was far muddier and covered in more mud puddles than the first access lane. It was probably for this reason the suspect had not parked his van on this second lane.

The detective splashed and sloshed her way across the muddy lane. She used her momentum to propel her up the first ten yards of Bauden's Rest Hill, then switched her run to a stair climber stride. Emily had lost sight of Eddie and the suspect from the upslope position of the hill. Unlike the flatter cemetery grounds of St. Gregory's, the hill was covered with taller more artistic gravestone markers. The tombstones on the lower half of the hill were about two feet high. It was easy to respectfully circumnavigate graves at the bottom of the hill. Over half way up the hill, the tombstones were three to four feet tall. The taller tombstones obstructed vision moving uphill but improved her cover from any potential gunfire. However, the markers were askew from their neighbors and the hill appeared to have neither straight rows nor clarity of how to respectfully avoid running on dead people's graves. Emily set her pace and through shear iron will determination raced past tombstone after tenebrous tombstone to reach the top of the hill. From the crest of Bauden's Rest Hill, Emily could view the cemetery valley below and the neighboring cemetery high grounds called Count Blessing's Tomb Hill. The bright moonlight allowed her to see the stocky suspect running up the taller hill while Eddie remained in pursuit down in the grave swamp valley. The fleeing suspect was now about 30 yards from her with the lieutenant trailing in pursuit roughly 10 yards behind the brute.

As Detective Emily Oftenmarch began her quickstep downhill, she saw the strangest sight of her life on the edge of the cemetery grounds east of Bauden's Rest Hill. From a distance she saw what looked like an ominous broad shouldered lycan standing roughly eight feet tall. To her it appeared to be a surreal snarling tangle furred brute sized werewolf. The massive manbeast was lumbering in the cemetery on a full moon night. In an open view to her right, the beast seemed to be growling in her direction. Even from their distant range, it appeared to be fixated on her. Emily was staring in disbelief as she moved at downhill speed. Moving at such a fast pace, she had to look away from the lycanish image to concentrate on the gravestones impeding her downhill route.

Emily had significantly closed the gap between her and the lieutenant by the time she reached the bottom of Bauden's Rest Hill. Eddie had progressed through the cemetery valley and was beginning his uphill pursuit of the oversized outlaw. The valley grounds were soggy but contained fewer gravesites. Containing some obelisk markers and family memorial marques, there were fewer obstructions to avoid in this section of the gloomy graveyard. Emily was in a full sprint across this section, kicking up mud and mushy dirt as she thundered through the valley. As she traversed the swampy cemetery field with unslowing speed, Emily could see that Count Blessing's Tomb Hill was full of statues, monuments, memorials, and mausoleums. She could also observe that the fleeing big nefarious man was slowing down as he ran the second hill.

Detective Oftenmarch reached the second graveyard hill at great speed. She was within ten yards of Lt. Knighton when she passed the hills' first statue. Passing the first monument, she was within seven yards of Eddie. As Emily passed the hill's second statue, she was about four yards behind him. Halfway up the hill, Emily had caught up to Eddie. She passed the lieutenant and began to lead the prolonged pursuit of the slowing and trudging tankish man. Emily's blistering pace continued on the steeper uphill upper half of the incline. The fleeing brute would disappear and reappear from her sight as he weaved gravesite structures, but she was quickly catching up to him.

The clear night and the full moon in the now clear sky was allowing a bright light from the moon to improve visibility as the detectives gave chase in the grim and ghastly graveyard grounds. While the giantlike evader was in moonlight view, Eddie's Phasepulser IX stunner erupted in the night, sending a stunner stream in the suspected villain's direction. The pulsewave struck the belaboring behemoth in his shoulder but it did not stop the mammoth man for even a second.

Emily's superior speed on foot had her in range of catching the big man now. He was in her sights just yards ahead when he darted behind a large statue of the virgin Mary. When Detective Oftenmarch passed the tall statue, the brute was nowhere to be seen; he had vanished from her vision.

"He's playing hide and seek." Emily called out a warning to Lt. Knighton as she dropped her pace to a seeking jog. The sky remained completely clear and the bright moonlight shone down on the cemetery like a giant overhead flashlight aiding Emily in her search for the now hiding huge fellow. The detective weaved her way through some mid-sized memorial marquees as she scanned for the problematic and resistant suspect. The ground of Count Blessing's Tomb Hill had no puddles or standing water but was still quite muddy. This section of the graveyard hill was devoid of grass like it had seen a lot of activity lately. Using her shoulder strapped light, Emily sweepingly searched the cemetery's muddy ground for fresh footprints. As she searched, playing graveyard seeker, the detective pulled out her Phasepulser IX and adjusted its setting to a higher level.

"He stayed topside of hill." Eddie indicated loud enough for her to hear. The night had become rather chilly and steam was rising up from the cemetery ground. Mixing with the moonlight, the steam was wafting into the air to swirl around the grave markers. There was a lot of stonework on Count Blessing's Tomb Hill, providing many options for hiding spots. Emily had an urge to call out Marco. Her footsteps were finding soft squishy ground but also silence following each spongy step. In the area, there was a multitude of fresh footprints on the ground. Too many footprints for an ordinary cemetery grounds. The nighttime cemetery hunt in the macabre environment was not making the list of Emily's favorite activities. Searching onward in the graveyard, Emily strained to hear or see anything to help find their hiding hulk. A dense silence fell on the full moonlit cemetery hill, giving the situation an even eerier feeling. Quiet, gravestone, quiet, mausoleum entrance, a gargoyle statue, silence, steam coming from a newly dug grave, another gravestone, and more silence was what the detective was experiencing on her creepy exploration.

Suddenly, Emily detected movement in her peripheral vision. The large suspect sprang from behind an entrance pillar of a weathered mausoleum. He forcefully tackled Lt. Knighton to the ground and pounced on top of him. The brute threw a downward punch which Eddie blocked with his arms, causing him to drop his Phasepulser IX. Reacting swiftly, Detective Oftenmarch fired a stunning stream from her Phasepulser IX and followed it with a flying front kick which struck the big man firmly on the side of his broad chin. The stun strike-front kick combination rocked the big brute backwards, shifting his weight enough for Eddie to shove him off himself.

The barbarianish brute recovered sharply and regathered himself in a position to resume attacking. However, Emily was swifter and continued her counterattack. Landing nimbly, adeptly avoiding stomping on ground prone Eddie, and keeping her momentum Emily executed a roundhouse kick to the aggressor's abdomen. She followed with another stun stream fired at close range, which struck the tough guy squarely in his chest. These punishments just sent the man into berserk mode.

The enraged man threw a forceful punch in Emily's direction, which she gracefully dodged. Back on his feet, Eddie threw an uppercut punch that landed on the big man's cheek to no effect. The furious fellow tossed the lieutenant aside like a ragdoll to pursue Detective Oftenmarch. Emily's third stun stream missed just wide as the bruiser bull rushed her. With a pirouette spin move, Emily elegantly evaded the brunt of the bull-rush. The belligerent brute just connected with a glancing push, which was enough to throw her into a nearby marble cherub statue on top of a stone grave marker. The detective's left arm and shoulder struck the statue hard, leaving a stinging sensation in her arm. Emily prevented herself from falling by catching hold of the statue and using it to keep herself on her feet. While she was propped up by the statuary, the berserking brute spun back around to punch her. With fast reactions and a quick first step, Emily swiftly sidestepped the strongman's pugilistic punch and he hit the marble cherub instead. This was followed by Eddie bringing down his backup Phasepulser IX to crack the man over the top of his head with the butt of the stunner. Emily added a down stomp to the inside knee of the giant jerk and he crashed to the ground with a powerfully potent plop. The force of his landing splattered mud everywhere.

As mud was flung about, Detective Oftenmarch was tackled from behind on her blind side. She crashed down onto the muddy ground and immediately rolled. The cloaked tackler who had partially fell on top of her ended up underneath her after she rolled. More mud was flung about the area. Once above the new aggressor, Emily elbowed the annoying assailant in the face. The man was wearing some kind of ghoulish mask which absorbed most of the blow. The detective immediately followed her elbowing with a point blank Phasepulser IX shot. The stunner strike took the fight out of the masked attacker, and Emily scrambled to her feet now no longer grappled.

Another cloaked and masked attacker was tussling with Lt. Knighton. These new arrivals were dressed like cultists from a low budget science fiction movie. The men looked like a pair of rumbling hockey players. Emily rushed to assist Eddie. With a burst of acceleration, she dashed over to the fight and drove her knee into the private region of the lieutenant's cultlike combatant. Her knee doubled the fighter over with a howl of pain. While he was bent over in pain, Emily took out her police handcuffs and speedily handcuffed the suffering stooge to an iron gate of a fence encircling a family memorial plot. The man was in too much pain to resist the rough restraining.

Two more cloak shrouded and ghoul masked miscreants were charging at Eddie and Emily. A voice bellowed out from a distance in the chilly night air. It said, "Forget the guy, get the female." Eddie replied by immediately firing off two shots from his backup Phasepulser IX, the first stream in the direction of the voice and the second pulsewave at the oncoming attackers.

"Cathedral Police, cease your assault or be arrested." Emily loudly and clearly called out into the night. Both charging cultist kept coming, hollering "For the full moon". Emily squeezed off two quick shots in succession from her Phasepulser IX and both shots struck one of each shouting lunatic. Having no effect, the stunner was not even slowing them down in their rush. As the lead charger grabbed at Emily, the detective performed an Aikido hip throw, called koshinage, to fend off his attack and send him tumbling to the muddy ground. The second attacker grabbed Emily so she countered with a forearm turn, called kote mawashi, and torqued his arm. This allowed Eddie to intervene and fasten a handcuff on the wrist of the twisted hand. He kicked out wildly in response and Detective Oftenmarch caught his ankle. She managed to hold onto it long enough for Lt. Knighton to fasten the other cuff to the kicker's ankle. As the second attacker fell down comically handcuffed wrist to ankle with shouts of protest, the first attacker tripped Emily by bowling into the back of her legs.

She toppled onto the muddy ground again. This time Emily did an Aikido backward roll, called ukemi ushiro, to avoid injury and get to a kneeling position. Eddie pounced downward on the prone clipper. The lieutenant slugged the masked madman in the gut and began wrestling with him to get his second pair of handcuffs fastened. Quickly Emily joined the melee and the pair of law enforcement detectives were able to handcuff the man's left wrist via the double team. Their wrestling took the group over some muddy ground, making it mud wrestling. With a lot of kicking and screaming, the agitated attacker continued to wrestle in resistance. The trio tussled, tossing mud amuck. There was mud everywhere.

Eddie pummeled the resister with a pair of punishing punches as the cloaked fighter defiantly held his right wrist out of reach. Improvising, Emily twisted the masked struggler's right leg then applied enough pressure to bend the leg at the knee and pin the right ankle in an exposed position. Catching on quickly, the lieutenant secured the ankle in the other cuff. As much as the first attacker squirmed, he was securely restrained in an awkward wrist to ankle position. The good news was that three hooded assailants were cuffed; the bad news was the detectives had run out of available handcuffs.

No sooner had the detectives returned to their feet when another cloaked confronter with a ghoulish mask attempted to strike Emily with a club. Swiftly dodging the strike with a quick step and lean away, Detective Oftenmarch let the attacker's momentum carry him past her. His swing and miss had him recklessly off balance. She then repositioned her front leg in her stance to trip the club carrying cultist. The whiffer crashed to the ground with a grunt as more mud splattered. More mud speckled the detectives' clothing. Once the cloaked clubber was wallowing in the mud, Emily fired her Phasepulser IX and stunned the shrouded swinger, leaving him dazed in the dirt.

As Emily was using her stunner, Lt. Knighton was surprise attacked from the dark. The battered bruiser, who had led them to this spot in the cemetery, punched Eddie right in the face. The slug sent Eddie staggering and he dropped his secondary stunner. As the brute was winding up to hit Eddie again, Emily fired her Phasepulser IX at him. The stunner stream struck him in the chest but only momentarily slowed him. As her phasepulser was beeping to indicate a low charge, the ruffian with an iron constitution turned his attention to her. He charged at her and sent a mighty overhand punch in her direction. Emily ducked the attempted blow and side bounced to put some distance between herself and any possible backhand swing. The infuriated big man threw a jab in Emily's direction which she also nimbly dodged.

Going on the offensive, Emily executed a roundhouse kick which slammed into the gut of the brute. He took the powerful kick like a rocksteady gladiator. The maniac man threw a pair of wild roughhouse punches in Emily's direction. She continued to avoid his attacks with her quickness and fast footwork. Switching from her preferred technique, the traditional Aikido, to a new American invented technique called Audokki, Emily countered. Performing a roundhouse kick to high kick combination, called the Twin Tiger longkicks, the detective pounded the bruiser brutally. Unphased, the brawny brawler grabbed Emily's leg and pulled her up into the night air like a marionette. Hanging upside down dangling by her leg, Emily was seeing the moonlit cemetery twirl before her eyes.

Then she heard a pair of nearby gunshots ring out in the night. The gorilla grip on her leg released, sending her plummeting to the cold hard ground. Detective Oftenmarch landed slightly awkwardly but fortunately was not feeling any jolts of pain. As she laid on the muddy ground, the detective could see the large lout crumpled on the ground next to her holding his buttocks. Scrambling to her feet, Emily observed the man was bleeding from his butt. Once standing again she began to recompose herself; she was covered in mud. Lt. Knighton walked up next to her with his service pistol aimed at the huge hooligan. It was clear to her now that Eddie was done with the fighting and had progressed to putting bullets into attackers. He had a no nonsense look in his eyes, one of them starting to blacken, that was transfixed on the bleeding brute.

Emily traversed in a circle, scanning the cemetery hill for more dangerous hoodlums on the attack. Seeing no more incoming threats, Emily looked back at Eddie. "You look like I feel." she truthfully told him.

"I feel like you look." the scowling lieutenant replied.

"Where is the Granthum Police when you need them?" Emily asked as she scanned the cemetery a second time. She turned back to the large goon still grounded and bleeding. "By the way, you're under arrest you big jerk." Emily informed the prone man.

After picking up one of Eddie's dropped Phasepulser stunners, Detective Oftenmarch rapidly restunned a pair of prone creepy cultists. Next she pointed the Phasepulser IX upwards, her arm fully extended, and fired a stream into the night sky to act as a flare. The stunner stream brightly lit up the already moonlit sky; its burst of illumination was like a beacon in the late-night cemetery. Distant shouts of "over there: and "hurry this way" could be heard throughout the cemetery grounds all the way from the cemetery hilltop. If there were any more wacky masked and hooded cultists, they were nowhere to be seen in St. Gregory's cemetery anymore.

"Having that gun does not make you right." the brute snarled at Eddie. The lieutenant just kept a calm and seriously steady stare.

"Having two bound and naked young women in the back of your fake repair van definitely makes you wrong." Emily sharply retorted. "You have the right to remain silent, please do so."

The barbarianish brute just growled and grunted in disapproval. The cemetery seemed quiet and peaceful at the moment under a calm clear moonlight sky, almost too peaceful. Then Emily remembered the lycan sighting on the far edge of the cemetery. She had seen the were-wolf as she was descending Bauden's Rest Hill. Turning to Eddie she asked him, "Did you see the lycan to the east on the cemetery's border?"

"What?" Eddie puzzled still watching the grumpy galoot vigilantly with his service pistol still at the ready.

Emily abruptly ran ten yards to the east to get a better vantage point from Count Blessing's Tomb Hill. Having to avoid several tomb-stones and an obelisk plot marker, Emily found a good place to view the grounds to the eastern perimeter of the cemetery. The bright moonlight gave light to that entire area to reveal no werewolves. Looking twice, she saw nothing. Did she imagine it? It seemed so real at the time. Turning to return to where Eddie had the brute detained, Emily spotted a new unsettling sight.

About fifteen yards to the north of the cemetery hill's peak was what appeared to be some type of makeshift altar. Emily took several steps closer to get a better look. As she approached, the bizarre struc-ture looked like a psycho pagan altar with full moon globes on poles around its perimeter. The globes gave off an afterglow light suggest-ing they were made of a phosphorescent material. The altar itself was covering in strange cryptic symbols. Next to the spooky satanic looking altar were two shallow graves freshly dug. They were sloppily shoveled and had no nearby markers ready to identify the spot. Both graves were empty and probably meant for the poor young unclad women previ-ously tied-up in the back of the rusty old van. Moving closer, Emily could discern more of the creepy altar. It had restraints chained to a stone surface stained with blood. Rapidly taking out her complink, Emily shot several photos of the sadistic sight in swift succession.

Approaching nearer to the creepy construction, Emily observed a pair of stone werewolves standing about four feet tall. Very detailed and disturbing, the lycan statues flanked a stone podium at the head of the abdominal altar. The unfriendly looking statues seemed to be a focal point of the evil erection. The sides of the stone surface were blood-caked, revealing it had been used more than once. When Emily got up next to the pagan faux altar, she saw movement out of the corner of her eye. Turning quickly, the detective aimed the Phasepulser IX she was carrying in that direction, expecting an attack. Detective Oftenmarch found a man wearing an ornate robe, tall well decorated headdress, and a shiny ghoulish mask hiding behind a stone monument.

Coming out from his hiding spot, the oddly dressed man was holding a staff with a moon shaped headpiece which he rested against the stone monument. This allowed him to raise his hands palms out. "I offer you no violence; it is beneath my nobility." he proudly stated.

Emily used her complink with her non-stunner carrying hand to take a picture of the now unhidden possibly head cultist based on his attire. "Are the cloaked men who attacked us friends of yours?" Emily accusatorily asked the fancy robed man.

"They are children of the moon; they are performing their duty. You are gorgeous. It is a shame, you would have made an excellent sacrifice to the lunar lord on the full moon." the fancy robed man explained nothing but revealed much.

"So you meant to kill those two young ladies tonight." Emily posed a new accusation.

"That neanderthal led you here tonight, didn't he? It is so hard to find decent servants these disappointing days." the headdress wearer obfuscated.

"The big man in the rundown van works for you?" Emily asked.

"He is but a lowly servant for the children of the moon." the proud man stated.

"And the lycan on the eastern section of the cemetery, was he also part of your group?" Emily tried another question.

The fancy robed man's eyes grew wide under his grotesque mask. "You saw a lycan here tonight in this very cemetery." he exclaimed excitedly. "That's wonderful!"

"The lycan did not look overly happy to be here." Emily countered.

"You must be a princess of the moon, that is why you are here tonight and that is why we were unable to capture you. What a wonderous night." the looney man ridiculously rambled.

"I am with the Cathedral Police Department and we are here to stop criminal activity on this night. You, Mr. Nobility, are under arrest for conspiracy to commit murder, accessory to kidnapping, and ordering the assault of police officers." Emily clearly indicated.

"If I had known a moonlight princess, a searer of the werewolves was to be here tonight, then a child of the moon would have been sacrificed to the lunar lord. My apologies." the crazy cloaked man prattled as he ignored Detective Oftenmarch's statement.

Emily read him his re-revised Miranda rights as he continued to speak of full moon magic, the importance of lycans, and how special this night had been. "A werewolf came, if only that oaf had brought you here properly then this would have been beautiful, almost as beautiful as you." he concluded merrily.

Emily answered the man, "I am a child of GOD. Hebrews 10:12-14 states: *But CHRIST gave HIMSELF once for all sins and that is good forever. After that HE sat down at the right side of GOD. HE is waiting there for GOD to make those who have hated HIM a place to rest HIS feet. And by one gift HE has made perfect forever all those who are being set apart for GOD-like living.*"

"Amen." said a Granthum patrol officer now standing nearby. "The lieutenant asked me to come check on you." he added.

"Please secure this gentleman, he is under arrest and agreed to go peaceable." Emily replied. Then turning to the now speechless fancy dressed man she concluded, "The love and mercy of GOD is what makes tonight wonderous."

The fancy dressed fanatic goggled at her as the Granthum police officer was handcuffing him. "But you saw a lycan. How could you see a werewolf? How could you see a werewolf if you do not speak for the full moon?" he puzzled.

"The lycan was not a werewolf hunched on all fours like in the movies but was standing upright and quite tall. Not feral, but fearsome in any movements. The eyes were not dark red but pale and searching. Searching, the lycan appeared to be searching not hunting." Emily described what she thought she saw.

"But only a royal child of the moon could see." stammered the now restrained madman as the Granthum policeman removed his headdress.

"It is not about the moon and children of the moon. It is about CHRIST and faith in CHRIST. Galatians 3:26 and 27 reads, *You are all sons of GOD through faith in CHRIST JESUS, for all of you who were baptized into CHRIST have clothed yourselves with CHRIST.*" Emily explained as she was looking up into the pale moonlight in the night sky.

"I don't understand how this can be. It should be us who received the honor, we are the blessed children." screamed the extravagantly cloaked lunatic as the Granthum police officer began to lead him away.

"1 John 3:10 says, *By this it is evident who are children of GOD, and who are children of the devil: whoever does not practice righteousness is not of GOD, nor is the one who does not love his brother.*" the detective recited to the detained deranged man as he was led away.

"You should listen to the lady." the police officer suggested to the lunatic as they walked along Count Blessing's Tomb Hill.

Exhausted, Emily walked back to the spot on the cemetery hill where she had last seen Eddie. Having been awake since the early morning hours, the lack of sleep was taking its toll on her. As the detective trudged her way back towards the lieutenant, she could see that paramedics were loading the brutish kidnapper onto a gurney. She could also perceive cloaked cultists being escorted down the cemetery hill in handcuffs by the Granthum Police.

Lt. Knighton was making notes in his old fashion paper notepad as Emily approached him. "They were going to sacrifice the women to the full moon and dump their bodies into a pair of shallow pathetic graves already dug." Emily informed her partner.

"Charming." the lieutenant responded.

"How is the sore butt bruiser?" Emily asked.

"He'll live." Eddie replied flatly.

"How many suspects did we arrest?" Emily wondered looking across the moonlit cemetery toward Bauden's Rest Hill. She could see several police escorted perpetrators being marched up Bauden's Rest Hill.

" I counted seven criminals." the lieutenant answered as his complink chimed for an incoming message.

"Please not another dispatch, I am too overly tired to work another homicide at this moment." Emily admitted wearily.

Having put his notepad away, the lieutenant had taken out his complink to read its display. "This is worse." Eddie indicated and then showed Emily his complink.

The display of the lieutenant's complink had an incoming text that read: The Cathedral Police High Commissioner would like to see you in his office at One Police Plaza ASAP.

Chapter 6

The Commissioner's Chessmen

With the two young women safe, sound, and secure, the night felt like a triumph. J.D. had been the distressed damsels' knight in shining armor. Neither young lady could stop thanking him before medical personal chauffeured them to better places. The Granthum police officers congratulated him and several GPD officers gave Fairbankers encouragement by telling him what a fantastic law enforcement officer he was going to become. J.D was excited and cheerfully chatted about how great the night had been during the entire drive back to Cathedral. Emily bought the on-top-of-the-world trainee some 2 AM tacos as a job well done treat before dropping him off at the 272nd precinct. The lieutenant had decided that J.D. should get some well-earned sleep and did not have to accompany them to the high commissioner's late-night postmortem. Eddie was expecting that high-ranking members of Cathedral law enforcement were going to be less than pleased with cowboy style crime-fighting. He was expecting a tongue lashing from the high commissioner and the young trainee did not need nor warrant that experience. Emily wished J.D. a well-deserved good weekend and then drove downtown to meet Lt. Knighton outside the Cathedral Police Plaza city block.

The Cathedral Police's central downtown location was the Police Plaza, which consisted of four buildings covering an entire city block. One Police Plaza was a forty-one story ornate glass building called Cathedral Central, or the Police Tower by Cathedral law enforcement. The building was primarily black with tinted glass windows and blue lettering identifying it. The structure was sleek, striking, prominent, and fit in nicely among the skyscrapers of downtown Cathedral. One Police Plaza contained the offices of high-ranking police officers, senior members of the District Attorney's office, and the departmental heads of the coroner, the crime lab, forensics, and information technology.

Two Police Plaza was a twenty-eight story building that was wider, squatter, and less attractive than the Police Tower. This building was very much in contrast with its neighboring building. It housed police media liaison officers, police union facilities, conference rooms, and press conference halls. All the lights inside the Police Tower were off overnight but 2 Police Plaza had several lights still lit on several floors, suggesting the burning of the modern day midnight oil.

The eclectic building behind Two Police Plaza was Three Police Plaza, which was also referred to as the Old Police facility. This building with two annexes and three renovations was once the old Arden district jail. No longer recognizable as the old jailhouse, Three Police Plaza was an administration building with overflow storage and some robotic technology development in the basement. Most of the modern day paperwork or computer work for running an organization and managing a large work force was done in Three Police Plaza. All the upper management for health and regulation compliance worked in this building. The Cathedral Police Department's primary computer center was also in the basement of Three Police Plaza. A few people worked in the old remodeled jailhouse during the day, but at night the building was a ghost structure.

The final building in the plaza was the 1st Cathedral Police precinct. The first precinct was more for posterity than functionality. It was primarily a historical landmark and seldom used for practicing law enforcement. In the east wing of the building was a museum of police history. The structure had more tourists visit its jails than criminals.

This dark and clandestine meeting was scheduled to take place not in the high commissioner's office atop 1 Police Plaza but in a modest sized highly secure conference room in 2 Police Plaza. Eddie and Emily were greeted by an assistant to the commissioners' office named Edward P. Holly. They knew his name was Edward P. Holly from not only his verbal introduction but also the bright silver name tag he was wearing. Edward was very talkative, especially for such an early hour. Edward P. Holly escorted them to the third floor conference room where four unanticipated people were waiting for them.

There was not a large conference table surrounded by a multitude of swivel chairs like in a stereotypical conference room in this room. Instead, this conference room had a dozen cushioned tallback armchairs placed in a circle around an oval mahogany coffee table. There was also an elongated wooden table along the back wall which appeared to be for snacks and refreshments. Currently the table only had a coffee pot and some paper cups on it. Each armchair was on a royal blue rug and had a tableau docking station by its right hand side. The room was well lit, with a bright interior emanating outward, mostly from an extra large domed light fixture in the center of the room's ceiling.

The four waiting people were the four Cathedral Police commissioners. The city of Cathedral had four police commissioners, all of whom reported to the high commissioner of the Cathedral Police Department. One commissioner was in charge of the border precincts, precincts numbered 200 and above. Another commissioner was in charge of the midtown precincts, precincts numbered 100 to 199. The third commissioner was in charge of the downtown precincts, precincts numbered 1 to 99. The downtown precinct commissioner was traditionally the second in command and took charge while the high commissioner was away. The fourth and final police commissioner was the commissioner-at-large who served as a floater who could help out where there was need and back fill for leaves of absence or vacation.

Sitting in the armchair furthest from the door was downtown precinct Commissioner Paul Hopkick. After years of undercover detective work, he had steadily made a reputation for himself solving burglaries for over thirty years. Nearing seventy years old, Paul Hopkick preferred old fashioned police work. On this morning, he was dressed far more casually than his colleagues. Seated next to him was Angela Fartherbridge, the border precinct commissioner. She worked both fraud cases and cybercrimes for decades. Known as the queen of the scamspotters, for years Angela uncovered conspiracies before the conspirators were even done conspiring. She was neatly and well dressed, the polar opposite of Hopkick. Next to her sat Harold Chinchinocippi, the commissioner-at-large. He was a highly educated man with bachelor's degrees in criminal psychology and forensic psychology from St.

Francis University in Cathedral. Harold also had a criminal justice degree from The University of Cathedral, a bachelor's degree in business from Cathedral State University, and a master's degree in business from Gryphon University. First working for the crime lab with the Cathedral Police, Chinchinocippi had worked his way up the ranks to commissioner. Harold also served as the 3rd Cathedral Police precinct chief. His workaholic schedule had contributed to three failed marriages. He was wearing dress khaki pants, dress shoes, and a half unbuttoned cardigan sweater with a tee shirt underneath which read: I survived the 5th Annual Cathedral Police Department 10k Charity run. Sitting across the circle from the other commissioners was Zahlen Soppatellenti, the midtown precinct commissioner. Zahlen began his career as a Chatham police officer, transferred to Cathedral, and worked his way up to a precinct captain. Soppatellenti like to follow rules and regulations and was known for looking at things by the numbers. He was dressed professionally but his necktie was untied and his hair was ruffled as if he had experienced a long rough day.

None of them rose or greeted the detectives upon their arrival, perhaps because the police commissioners were half asleep. Silently, Eddie and Emily sat in a pair of armchairs closest to the door after removing their mucky jackets. Emily had no sooner gotten comfortable in an armchair when High Commissioner Benson Harden entered the room. He was accompanied by a man that Emily did not know. The second man closed the conference door behind them. Lt. Knighton and Detective Oftenmarch rose to their feet, they were the only ones to do so.

"Please have a seat. Sorry if I kept you waiting long and I do apologize for the terrible hour of this meeting." High Commissioner Harden began as he sat down next to Paul Hopkick. "Commissioners, these are detectives Knighton and Oftenmarch. Detectives, these are commissioners Hopkick, Fartherbridge, Chinchinocippi, and Soppatellenti. The good man standing by the door is chief security officer Brown" the high commissioner made brief introductions. He looked at Eddie and Emily, both seated once again. "I am aware that Commissioner Fartherbridge calls you the mud tusslers. Until now I thought she was being whimsical. You are literally covered in mud." he continued. The chief security officer remained standing guard in close proximity to the door.

"The name was metaphorical, sir. They seemed to have lived up to their nickname tonight." Commissioner Fartherbridge conveyed.

The high commissioner nodded his understanding. Still looking at Eddie and Emily, he asked, "How are you two doing?"

"Overworked and underappreciated, sir." answered Eddie.

"No complaints here, sir." Emily responded.

"I see. Before we discuss the real reason we are meeting at this frightful hour, I would like to review the St. Gregory Cemetery incident. My understanding is this began when a citizen in Cathedral approached you regarding her missing niece." High Commissioner Harden stated.

"Correct, sir. We looked into her story and found a pattern and some information that pointed us in the direction of St. Gregory Cemetery in Granthum." Emily explained.

"So you decided to travel to Granthum unbeknownst to your captain and have a midnight confrontation with killers in the middle of a desolate cemetery. I am uncertain if this was dedication or stupidity on your part." the high commissioner expressed.

"This was my fault, sir. I very much wanted to help the upset lady who approached us and recover her missing young niece." Emily confessed.

"Officially, I am telling you in the future you will report to your superiors first. Then the Cathedral Police and the Granthum Police will work together to restore law and order. Unofficially, I say outstanding job stopping these monsters." High Commissioner Harden informed the detectives.

"Granthum Police Department's preliminary report says the gang leader who confessed everything refers to you, Detective Oftenmarch, as the moon princess. He claims you told him that you saw a werewolf in the cemetery. Did you see a werewolf in the cemetery?" Commissioner Hopkick asked Emily.

"I am not sure what I saw, commissioner. It was dark and the cult was wearing costumes." Emily answered.

"We captured all known culprits." Eddie supported.

"Were any of them dressed like werewolves?" the border precinct commissioner asked curiously.

"More like cultists in a Cthulhu horror movie." Emily revealed.

"I have spoken with the Granthum Police Commissioner and we have agreed that the city of Granthum will take over the case from here. The Granthum Police will search for unmarked graves at St. Gregory and their legal team will prosecute the guilty. Let us speak no more of this topic." the high commissioner concluded.

"Agreed, sir." Commissioner Fartherbridge seconded.

"Now to discuss the problem that confronts us, the reason for this late hour meeting. Allow me to start at the beginning, commissioners, for the benefit of the detectives. On a quarterly basis, the commissioners' office reviews the arrest and conviction statistics for all Cathedral law enforcement." High Commissioner Harden opened.

"If I may, sir, I have an example to give the detectives for the 272nd precinct." Commissioner Soppatellenti requested.

"Please do." Harden granted.

"For a 90-day period earlier this year, the 271st precinct had 29 unsolved cases, 32 arrested suspects acquitted, 44 charges dismissed or dropped, twice arrested multiple people for the same crime, 28 cases contracted to private law enforcement companies, 10 cases reassigned to other precincts, 3 suspects escape custody, and 3 wrongful arrest lawsuits." Commissioner Soppatellenti read the statistics.

"Earlier this year we were seeing disappointing results similar to this example in almost every Cathedral precinct. We started investigating to determine how things had gone so far wrong and discovered that our numbers did not add up correctly. Our statistics were wrong." Harden explained further.

"It was then discovered that our computer systems had been broken into or hacked. The Cathedral Police main computer database had a security breach." Commissioner Soppatellenti revealed.

"Grand Rebellion of Viralcrackers Elite." Lt. Knighton stated.

"How do you know about GRoVE?" Commissioner Soppatellenti asked with a surprised tone.

"Dixon Downmore case." the lieutenant responded. He had read the papers at Downmore's apartment containing notes for computer equipment requests for Grove and propaganda literature for Grove.

"Mr. Downmore was a murder victim who had done business with this group." Emily extrapolated with some speculation.

"So these cybercriminals known as Grove had illegal hacked into our computer network and altered our records. Therefore, we had to hire a private network security company to secure our database and a private software technology company to fix our altered data." Harden continued the story.

"This process took longer than we had anticipated." Commissioner Fartherbridge admitted.

"The physical backup copies at the Old Cathedral Courthouse in Blackheart Square had been stolen." Emily connected.

"How do you know about the stolen records at the old courthouse?" Commissioner Fartherbridge asked, also with a surprised tone.

"A private investigator named Emerson Plumwine has been investigating the thefts." Emily responded.

"Emerson Plumwine. Emerson Plumwine. He died last year in a car explosion, detective." Commissioner Fartherbridge remembered.

"Sure he did, commissioner, and he always paid his taxes and his alimony before his untimely death." Emily replied.

"You are suggesting that he faked his death?" Commissioner Hopkick inquired.

"Whole agency is phony." Eddie theorized.

"Lt. Knighton believes the private investigating agency works under a fake name or a pseudo name. There is no Emerson Plumwine, different people play the part of the detective in order to secure work." Emily expounded.

"Getting back to the topic, the theft did delay the private IT company in fixing the police database. But once the data was corrected, we had a new problem.", Harden explained further.

"The numbers got worse." Eddie responded.

"Again, how do you know this?" the shocked midtown commissioner wondered.

"Educated guess." Lt. Knighton replied.

"Yes, lieutenant, the numbers were worse. Our police force's performance had deteriorated and the cybercriminals had covered it up. Fortunately, through the hard work of the Cathedral Cybercrimes Division, Cathedral police had caught several of the cyber rebels in Grove." Harden progressed.

"These crackers, or hackers, were given nonprosecution agreements in exchange for their testimonies against those who hired them." Commissioner Hopkick explained.

"We wanted to catch the people who hired the cybercriminals. We wanted to catch the architects of this crime and the masterminds behind this deception. All the apprehended cybercriminals agreed to cooperate and testify against those who hired them. The prosecutor's office, the district attorney himself, was filing charges against the grand perpetrators. Much to our chagrin, some of the suspects were police officers." Harden continued his narration then paused. There was a sadness showing in his eyes.

"The prosecutor's office began looking into the validity of the accusations against the accused orchestrators especially those in law enforcement." Commissioner Chinchinnocippi added.

"We thought we were making progress towards catching those responsible for corrupting our law enforcement forces." Commissioner Fartherbridge indicated.

"The villains countered with the lycan masquerade killers." Detective Oftenmarch deduced.

"Why do you say that?" inquired Harden.

"Cathedral homicide has been seeing their wicked handiwork and criminal misdeeds." Emily shared.

"We believe these so called lycans were hired to eliminate the district attorney and the hackers. They unfortunately succeeded with the DA." Harden sadly expressed.

"But there was a witness to his murder, who the commissioners' office has been protecting." Emily returned.

"And how do you know that?" the downtown precinct commissioner puzzled.

"The Barrett Alexander case. Mr. Alexander was murdered today in St. Lawrence Gardens. In the course of our investigation I looked Barrett Alexander up in our police records. Our police records show he was employed by this office to protect that witness." Emily informed.

"His eighteen year old girlfriend." Eddie added.

"Again, how do you know that?" Commissioner Hopkick asked in surprise.

"Who doesn't know?" Eddie offered.

"Worst kept secret in Cathedral." Chinchinocippi admitted.

"The young lady is actually quite mature for her age." Commissioner Soppatellenti defended.

"Please, Zahlen. The girl wants to be a sugar pop singer, a bikini model, and a fashion commentator with a smiley face hearts as a rating system." Fartherbridge disagreed.

"Regardless of her age, she was a witness and is a citizen of Cathedral who needs our protection. Now our discussion has arrived at the problem which currently confronts us. We need the lycan masquerade killers apprehended. That must be our next move in this deadly and sadistic game of chess. The lycan piece needs to come off the board." Harden expressed earnestly.

"Parnes and Barsons are struggling." Eddie stated knowingly.

"Again, how do you know?" now the high commissioner was perplexed. "How did you know they were asked to catch these villains?"

"Incancennio Bottling Plant homicides." Eddie answered.

"They were not exactly subtle about needing to be there." Emily added.

"Parnes and Barsons have had trouble trying to catch the lycans." Commissioner Fartherbridge admitted sadly.

"The bottling plant plan of Captain Thackery did not go as planned either." Commissioner Soppatellenti sadly admitted.

"Not the best plan Cathedral PD has ever had." the commissioner-at-large conceded.

"That plant is like a bad omen." Commissioner Hopkick stated his opinion.

"Detective Shippendarrow told me that bottling plant was known for moonshine running. It might be possible the lycans had shady inside help to access the plant." Emily shared.

"Deceased Detective Hedra Shippendarrow?" Commissioner Fartherbridge asked.

"Before he died." Eddie replied.

"Yes, he was a hero." Emily appended. She tried to keep her expression neutral as her mind raced in horror. She had two conversations that day with a man she knew had died in the line of duty years ago. Not that long ago she was describing a lycan in detail to a murder suspect. She had been so certain she did not imagine the beastman. Did she see a wolfman? Was Emerson dead? Was she going crazy? Emily was in horror as she questioned her own sanity. As her thoughts tumbled in turmoil, externally Emily stayed quiet as Commissioner Hopkick spoke about how Incancennio's moonshine business had nothing to do with this issue.

"We allowed one of the hackers to return to work, to earn a living. He works at the Incancennio Bottling Plant. In addition, we had a plan for this cyber rebel. He was also supposed to access a work computer which was fast enough and sophisticated enough for him to check if the criminal masterminds had recruited new hackers to monkey with our systems." the high commissioner divulged.

"Zeke Ryerson, Jr." Lt. Knighton exposed.

"The weasel went around the mulberry bush but no monkey gave chase." Emily recited.

"What is she talking about?" Commissioner Fartherbridge asked Eddie.

"The coroner's office emailed me photographs of cryptic messages which they had discovered in Barrett Alexander's shoes. That was one of the messages. Code for Ryerson did not flush out any new hackers." Emily responded as calmly as she could manage.

"Good grief. One of them is an antisocial savant and the other is a half-mad genius. Are you sure about this, sir?" Commissioner Soppatellenti expressed his doubts.

"I also have my doubts, sir. Oftenmarch is a beauty and a good detective but she's a borderline mad sleuth who converses with the presumably deceased and possibly sees werewolves. Knighton is a great detective but an arrogant know it all. He could solve the case and you would never know it because he would not have said more than ten words to you. One is a mute and the other is a maniac." Commissioner Hopkick harshly added his doubts.

"Tell us how you really feel." Security Chief Brown mused.

"I detect, not bloviate." Eddie calmly retorted. Emily sat silently saddened that her superiors thought her insane.

"Anything you like to add, Angela?" Harden asked.

"The mud tusslers would not have been my second or even third choice, sir. They are unpredictable and unconventional. However, their successes are remarkable and their results are undeniable." Commissioner Fartherbridge gave her opinion.

"How about you, Harold?" Harden requested the thoughts of the last commissioner.

"Question for you, detectives. If you were the high commissioner, would you choose the mud tusslers?" the commissioner-at-large posed.

Eddie just peered at Commissioner Chinchinocippi like the commissioner was an idiot and did not answer.

"We appreciate High Commissioner Harden's support and will do the job assign to us to the best of our ability." Emily responded diplomatically.

"Not a yes between the two of them, Benson. That says it all." Chinchinocippi gave his conclusion to the high commissioner.

"Thank you, commissioners. I apologize again for the hour of this meeting. Thank you for your time and input. Have a good weekend. I would like to speak privately with the detectives now." High Commissioner Harden thanked and dismissed the commissioners.

Quietly, the four police commissioners rose and left the conference room. They all looked tired and had worrisome expressions as they exited the room wordlessly. Chief Security Officer Brown nodded to the high commissioner in understanding then followed the commissioners out of the room, closing the door behind himself. It was just High Commissioner Benson Harden and the two detectives left in the room. The room had fallen completely silent after the long conversation. It sounded more like St. Gregory Cemetery than a conference room at that moment. Benson sighed and rubbed his temples for a moment. It appeared like he was making a difficult decision. Emily was wondering if he was waiting on them to break the silence with an objection or a question when the high commissioner finally spoke.

"Each of the commissioners had already picked a pair of detectives to catch these lycan masquerade killers, as you have called them. None of them have come close to catching the killers. It has been weeks and those criminals have eluded us. Now it is my turn. The pair of you are my pick. I knew your father well, Eddie. Your old man was the best I have ever known and I would still pick you over him for this assignment. You two are my pick because when the going gets tough you do not quit. The lights go out and giant wolves attack, you do not retreat. Your captain reassigns you to another case, you work both cases. When your work week is done, you go to a Granthum cemetery to fight villains and save lives. I also picked you two because you don't miss many things. It was clear from this morning's conversation you have been paying attention. So you have probably not missed that members of our police force are selling us out to private law enforcement for personal gain on my watch. They are purposely flubbing Cathedral PD cases and passing the solutions to private law enforcement for kickbacks. They are destroying the Cathedral Police Department from within under my very nose. This is my reputation, my life's work, my legacy, and I am asking you to help me save it. Save the Cathedral Police Department. In the game of chess, each piece moves in a prescribed manner. In life's game of chess, some pieces move in many multifaceted ways. You look at the board, you calculate the moves and then the opponent breaks the rules. The opponents broke the rules and the law. They activated the lycans to eliminate opposition and silence collaborators. The opponent has added their lycan piece; now it's my turn to add a piece. You are the commissioner's chessmen. You are the piece they will not be able to predict, to misdirect, or to break. Many may say this is a zwischenzug. They will say that I am delaying the inevitable. That this would be an intermezzo before I have to resign and turn this whole mess over to the state authorities. I can assure you that this is not the case. Now I would like the pair of you to take the weekend off and get rested. The stress of this job can be great, so I would like both of you to see a departmental psychiatrist on Monday morning to help you with that stress. I will have those scheduled for you. Finally, I want you to go and catch these lycans. Any questions?" the high commissioner made his heartfelt speech.

When neither Eddie nor Emily asked a question, Benson Harden rose from his seat. "I am done bloviating then." And with that said he departed the room. The room once again fell silent as a cemetery.

The detectives sat in silence for a moment until Eddie uncharacteristically broke the silence. "You're not crazy, Emily." he stated.

"You were correct in your hunch that private law enforcement companies are sabotaging police cases and then picking-up those cases." Emily admitted.

"Plus the poison pill" Eddie added.

"If you were a deranged lycan masquerade killer, what would you do next, Eddie?" Emily probed.

"Go after the witness." Eddie surmised.

"Agreed. Possibly go after Ryerson as well. If they can attack Ryerson or the witness, then they have a fork in this chess game. What should be our defense?" Emily pondered.

"Attack instead of defend?" Eddie suggested with uncertainty.

"Zone defense?" Emily suggested with less conviction. After mulling over her own question for a moment she asked a new question. "Should I call him?"

"He's dead, really dead." Eddie responded decisively.

"Then I just might be crazy, Eddie." Emily replied.

"Sanity is overrated anyway." Eddie decided.

"You're not underappreciated, Eddie." Emily stated.

"Good night, Emily." Eddie wearily wished as he rose from his seat.

"Good night, Eddie, and have a good weekend." Emily returned.

"You as well." Eddie replied. With that said he too departed the room. The conference room fell silent for the third and final time that morning.

Still troubled with questions of her mental state, Emily slowly rose to her feet and put on her filthy three-fourth-length black leather jacket. When she had left Granthum, the workday had felt like a success and she wanted to celebrate. Now the world seemed to have turned upside down. After this meeting, the morning felt like a disaster and the last thing she wanted to do was celebrate. Yesterday she was happily unaware that she was talking to dead people. Today she was frightfully aware of that fact. As Emily left the room and headed for the exit of 2 Police Plaza, she prayed for the sanity to get home safely to Chatham Hills. Still overwhelmingly upset over feeling crazy, Emily kept replaying things in her head. What had she seen? At this time of the morning, the southwestern drive home would take her about 45 minutes. The prospects of going home and having a couple of days off from work was one piece of good news. That was the piece Detective Oftenmarch was going to play on her chess board of life.

Chapter 7

Saturday

Chatham Hills is a wealthy suburb of Chatham, one of the daughter cities of Cathedral. Chatham has similarities to the central city; it is a cleaner scaled down version of Cathedral. Chatham Hills sits on the southeast border of Chatham. Chatham Hills has similarities to Chatham; it is a more affluent version of the daughter metropolis. Chatham Hills is the home for many people who work in Chatham and for many people, like Emily, who commute to Cathedral for work. Chatham Hills is primarily an affluent neighborhood with low crime rates. The reason David-John and Emily could afford to buy a home in Chatham Hills was largely because of the money Emily had inherited from her generous late husband Abraham Goldsmith.

Their beautiful home was a two-story, three-car-garage Jacobean style house, with a Bergamont style southeast wing, which sat on a hill, which was common in Chatham Hills. The hillside home was located in the Royal Demesne Estate development. From the north side of their home, they could see the skyline of Chatham. From the south side of their home, they could see most of Grand Maple Valley Park, the county park in the valley. They had a long backyard which, from the back doors, started out as a lovely open lawn and then became a staggered pine tree grove (no correlation to cyber criminals) as it sloped downhill. David liked to decorate the pine trees for Christmas.

Being a full-time pastor at the First Baptist Second Birth Church and a part time librarian at the Chatham Hill Public Library, David-John had an affinity for books. The house had a wonderful and extensive library, full of books David-John had collected over the years. He kept a work desk and his computer in a central location in the library where he spent many hours both reading and writing. Emily purposely did not have a home office. The detective tried as much as possible not to bring her work home with her. She was much happier in rooms like the living, dining, or family room.

David-John had heard his wife come home early that morning. He had then heard his wife showering but she never came to bed. Since she had been at work for over a day, he was relieved she had finally come home. Having to wake up to get ready for work, David-John needed to get cleaned up in the bathroom. Emily was no longer in the bathroom when he went to use it and she had still not gone to bed when he had finished in the bathroom. Puzzled, he went on a hunt for his lovely wife. His knee arthritis was bothering him that morning, so David-John grabbed his cane before he began his search.

His search did not take long. He found her sitting on the largest guest bedroom floor leaning against the wall. She was barefoot in an old pair of exercise spandex pants hugging her legs as her head was down resting on her knees. Emily was wearing her old worn flannel shirt, which her father had given her, unbuttoned and the left side of the shirt had slid down her shoulder, revealing part of an ace bandage wrapped around her left arm. Her hair was a tangled wet and disheveled mess which hid her face, but he could hear Emily sobbing softly. Emily looked wilted and dejected; her posture suggesting insecurity as she clung for composure. David-John's heart broke as he saw his wife sitting in a sad fetal position.

"Sweetheart, you look uncomfortable. Let me get you a chair and perhaps some hot earl grey tea." he greeted sympathetically.

"You married a crazy person." Emily declared softly.

"No, I married a loving and caring woman who is under a lot of continuous stress and has to endure more than her share of traumatic events." David-John replied as he steadied himself with his trusty cane.

"I am seeing werewolves and talking to dead people." moaned the tired detective.

"So things were not as they seemed. Sometimes our minds can play tricks on us. But in the end we are not fooled because we knew the truth. Isaiah 26:3-4 says *YOU keep him in perfect peace whose mind is stayed on YOU, because he trusts in YOU. Trust in the LORD forever, for the LORD GOD is an everlasting rock*. Then there is John 14:1 where JESUS is speaking, *'Do not let your hearts be troubled. Trust in GOD; trust also in ME'*." David-John comforted his wife.

"Two of the Cathedral police commissioners called me mad." Emily told her husband.

With some effort, David-John sat down on the floor next to his wife. "Well, the police commissioners do not know who you really are like I know you. They may not love and appreciate you but I do. GOD also loves you, Emily. 1 John 3:1 says, *How great is the love the FATHER has lavished on us, that we should be called children of GOD! And that is what we are! The reason the world does not know us is that it did not know HIM*. And Jeremiah 31:3 says, *The LORD appeared to us in the past saying: 'I have loved you with an everlasting love; I have drawn you with loving kindness'*. Therefore, you are loved, Emily, by those who know you." David-John lovingly told her.

Emily lifted her head to look at her husband and she looked exhausted. "I wish you were with me earlier this morning. Your encouragement would have been refreshing." she admitted.

"Sometimes it is difficult to remember the joys in life and too simple to dwell on the troubles in life." David-John observed.

"Have you ever felt too tired to sleep?" Emily wondered.

"Thankfully, I have not. Eventually you will have to sleep, sweetheart." David-John reasoned.

"Just hearing the word sleep is encouraging." she admitted.

"So here is my plan. Give your husband a hug and then help him up off the floor. While I am at work at the library information desk, you get some sleep. When I get home this afternoon, we can drive to New Carnelian where I will buy you a nice dinner and we will watch the soccer game." David-John suggested.

Giving her husband a big hug Emily said, "You have the best plans."

After Emily had helped him off the floor and to his feet, he gave her an affectionate kiss and said, "Have a good sleep, sweetheart."

"Thank you. Have a great day, dear." Emily replied, managing a smile.

David-John said a prayer over her and gave her a farewell kiss before he headed off to work. Emily had the house to herself and she used that quiet time for some much needed sleep. She headed to the master bedroom and laid down on their Cathedral king size bed. Extremely comfortable, it was the best mattress she had ever owned. Peacefully, she laid in silence trying to forget about work.

After awhile Emily drifted off to sleep. She was dressed like little red riding hood. Her cape was bright scarlet and was flowing in the wind. It was a chilly wind so she put her bright red hood over her head and pulled it tight. She looked around but did not recognize her surroundings, some type of clockmakers factory but it was an outdoor factory. This did not make sense to her. Then she saw off in the distance a big bad wolf. Or was it a werewolf, she could not tell at first but as it approached, she saw it was a big bad werewolf. The beastman had its eyes fixed on her and it growled menacingly. Quickly it began to run at her and Emily ran from the bolting beast. The werewolf chased her through the clock factory but it was a forest now. She was running through a dense forest as the big bad werewolf chased her. She looked back to see if the werewolf was gaining on her, but she saw megawolves instead. Three or four megawolves were chasing her, they seemed to be coming too fast to escape. They were here, they were there, they were coming from everywhere. Emily ran harder and passed several cattywampus cottages in the forest then some reporters were running beside her asking questions. She was running across St. Lawrence Gardens and the megawolves chased only her and nobody else. Emily ran past CSP units but none of them tried to help her. One by one they fell apart in a pile of broken electronic parts. So Emily kept running. She ran so fast and so far that she was now in a cemetery, a cemetery different in appearance from St. Gregory. This cemetery was darker and spookier. It was misty all around the grounds filled with barren trees and the gravestones were all oblique. Emily spun in a circle searching for an exit. The cemetery seemed to have no beginning and no end, with gravestones shrouded in mist every direction she looked. A cultist popped up from behind a gravestone, then faded into smoke. Then she saw the man she knew as Emerson Plumwine dressed as a cavalier taking pictures of black gravestones. He said to her while pointing to the graves, "They cannot hurt them unless you let them." Emily wanted to answer but before she spoke she next saw a band of gloomscroungers, called Malreapers, marching double file across the cemetery. Creepy and shadowy, Malreapers were fictional monsters attracted to misery and despair. They searched for humans in pain and suffering. All the ghastly gloomscroungers stopped marching and simultaneously looked at her. Their eyes glowed in deep garnet as they maniacally giggled in an earsplitting pitch. With grim expressions, the gangly gloomscroungers, cowled in evil, made their wicked intentions known. They immediately came after her and as hard as Emily tried she was quickly trapped in the cemetery between the wolves and the Malreapers. Cackling and creeping, the eerie gloomscroungers soared closer. Teeth bared and menacingly growling, the megawolves attacked. Emily had nowhere to go when she abruptly woke-up.

Emily was home safely in her comfortable bed and her phone was chiming from the nightstand next to her usual side of the bed. She looked at the bedside alarm clock; it was a couple of minutes past noon. After stretching and trying to shake off sleepy mental cobwebs, Emily looked at her phone to see that she had a text from her brother Seventh. He was asking if she would ecredit him some cash so he could get a Dial-A-Ride service. Instead, Emily purchased a ticket for an autoshuttle on her account with Zoomer and emailed him the voucher so he could get a ride on the nearest autoshuttle. With that completed, she got out of bed and took her second hot shower of the day.

The second shower helped her wake up. Emily put on a light blue tank top shirt and a pair of denim jean shorts. She grabbed a pair of Pregrotta soft sandals and headed downstairs. Stopping in the kitchen, Emily programmed a light snack from the robocook unit. The robocook quickly and efficiently prepared her meal as she looked at the weather forecast on the house's weather tracker unit. After eating some food, Emily put on her sandals and a pair of Solarwear Ultra slimeline sunglasses and headed for her car. She was not taking her gun, her phasepulser, her badge, or her police electronic equipment. Feeling one hundred pounds lighter, Emily started her car and drove to the Grand Maple Valley Park.

From her home, the drive to the county park's main entrance was about five minutes. Parking her car in the main lot, Mrs. Oftenmarch was glad to see that the park had a lot of guests on this pleasant Saturday afternoon. After locking her car, Emily casually made her way toward the main walking path in Grand Maple Valley Park. She walked past the children's playground full of happy energetic children, then past a pair of picnic pavilions full of happy, feasting, and less energetic adults, and then across the white wooden footbridge over a small creek. She entered onto the main walking path and started her Saturday afternoon stroll in the park. The section of the park she was walking was full of maple and oak trees. There were some white birches and chromodendrons living among the predominant maple and oak trees. The wood chipped walking path was dry and mostly leaf free. It was a beautiful day for a walk in the park.

Rounding a bend in the path, Emily entered a section where the park forest thinned and there was a nice open meadow full of field flowers, tall grass, and busy little birds. A slight breeze was in the air as Emily walked through the pleasant serene meadow. She said hello to some fellow path hikers as they passed by her. Once across the meadow, Emily entered another wooded area along the path. The trees were much taller in this section of the park. Mostly maple trees, with some pine trees sprinkled into the mix, occupied this forest section. The trees swayed calmly in the light breeze. As Emily continued along the path, the forest grew a little denser and she saw a rabbit scurrying along the forest ground. Her cell phone suddenly rang, breaking the wonderful silence of the park. The phone's display revealed it was her captain calling.

"Good afternoon, captain." Emily answered.

"Emily, I am sorry to bother you on your day off. I tried asking Lt. Knighton but Eddie only gives me three-word answers." Captain Bronzesmith began.

"What would you like to know, Captain?" Emily inquired.

"Why did the high commissioner want to see the both of you?" Captain Bronzesmith counter questioned.

"He wanted to discuss handling any future midnight investigations to Granthum more collaboratively. Then he assigned the Incancennio Bottling Plant case back to us." Emily summarized.

"I heard about your capture of the serial murder gang. Are you all right, Emily?" the captain wondered.

"I am fine, thank you." she reassured him.

"Did Eddie ask for the bottling plant case back?" Captain Bronzesmith suspiciously asked.

"No, the high commissioner initiated the topic." Emily divulged.

"Why does High Commissioner Harden care about the bottling plant case?" the baffled captain queried.

"The lycan masquerade killers have been thumbing their nose at the Cathedral Police Department." Emily shared.

"And he wants Lt. Knighton to take the wind out of their sails. I get it." the captain responded. "Now for the second reason I called you, Emily. I would like you to take the lieutenants exam. I have already recommended you for the promotion to lieutenant."

"Thank you, sir. Only problem is that the Cathedral PD does not put two lieutenants together as partners." Emily hesitantly thanked.

"Yes, this would mean the end of the mud tusslers. Cathedral will soon be initiating a special division of homicide that will handle high priority homicide cases citywide. Knighton's name has come up numerous times for that division. If Eddie moves on to greener pastures, then I would like you to stay with the 271th precinct, Emily." Captain Bronzesmith explained.

"How long do I have to decide?" Emily wondered.

"Take the weekend and give it some thought. Let me know on Monday please. Enjoy the rest of your weekend, detective." the captain said his farewell.

"You as well, sir. Goodbye." Emily replied then closed the phone connection.

Emily continued her picturesque walk in the Grand Maple Valley Park. The walking path went uphill onto a rise where the trees thinned out again. Maple trees were still in the majority but with a few poplar trees comingling with them. There were several wildberry bushes on either side of the walking path. There was a small clearing at the top of the rise where Emily could get a scenic overlooking view of the park. The sun intertwined with the trees and brightened the sky above them. The colors of the leaves were starting to change around the edges. She was unsure of what she had seen last night but Emily could now definitely see GOD's beautiful creation in the park.

Continuing along the path, Emily went downhill, around another bend, and over another white wooden footbridge. This footbridge went over a small pond. There were some ducks swimming lazily on the pond. The sunlight reflected off the surface of the water and Emily enjoyed seeing its brilliance through her Solarwear Ultra slimline sunglasses. The sun created a glistening lane of light on the surface of the water. After exiting the bridge, Emily entered another forest section of the park. This area had spruce, sycamore, and gibbous trees cohabitating with the maple trees. The trees continued to make peaceful companions on this sunny Saturday afternoon.

Emily thoughts briefly turned to how much should she trust Captain Bronzesmith. Highly respected, the captain came to the 271st precinct about eight months ago. The homicide squad did not yet know him all that well. Was his insistence to stay off the New Terranceville case solely for his desire for the of the 271st homicide division to prosper? Or did the man have ulterior motives? Bronzesmith could be genuinely focused on his department's success. Or the captain might have something to hide. Emily decided he would be presumed innocent until proven guilty.

A friendly warning of 'on your left' was called out before a pair of polite bicycle riders passed Emily as she walked along the picturesque path. The pleasant park was often enjoyed by people on warm and sunny weekends. Emily's thoughts returned to peacefully enjoying nature. This was the perfect day to go for a walk, ride, or run in the beautiful Grand Maple Valley Park. A squirrel scurried across the path about 50 feet up the path from Emily. The squirrel was hustling from one maple tree to the next maple tree where it began its ascent up that tall tree. Wildlife in the park always seem to be plentiful and they were peaceful creatures who shared well with human visitors to their home.

As she walked along the path through the park, Emily again became lost in her thoughts. She was thinking about the events of yesterday and the early hour conversation with the commissioners. Emily began thinking if she should call the gifted number. There was a story behind the gifted number.

Once not so long ago, there was a rich old man who lived in Cathedral. The rich old man liked very few people but he loved Emily Oftenmarch because she caught the person who murdered his dog when no other police officer in Cathedral would assist him. Not long after the death of his dog, the wealthy elderly old man moved away from Cathedral. He sold all his real estate, packed up his belongings, and left the city of Cathedral, never to return. Before he left Cathedral he gave a phone number to Emily. If she ever needed help he told her to call that number. Not long after the elderly man had moved away, the news of his death made the media. Emily had never called the gifted phone number. However, she received calls from that number last Christmas and again on her birthday. No one spoke on the other end; the caller would just hangup. Eddie and Detective Murkendale had both looked into the mysterious calls for her. Both confirmed the wealthy old man had passed away and the phone number cross referenced to a nursing home in Florida.

Emily sat down on a park bench looking at her cell phone. She decided to call for help, it could not hurt. An automated voice message answered for the nursing home. The detective decided to leave a message and go the distance with the attempt. She followed the saying in for a penny, in for a pound.

"This is Detective Emily Oftenmarch with the Cathedral Police. I need help. Please call me back, you have my number. Thank you." Emily left her message.

Emily kept her seat on the bench for a moment. Enjoying the breeze, she watched a pair of dogs chase a squirrel up a maple tree. As the dogs' owners tried to call them back, the dogs ran around the base of the tree trying to figure out how to catch the squirrel. The sunlight continued to prevail as it shone through the trees and over the forest trail.

Getting up from the park bench, Emily resumed her scenic hike through Grand Maple Valley Park. She walked past a row of bushy shrubs flanked by a scattering of Japanese maple trees. Behind the Japanese maples were taller trees. As Emily continued down the walking trail, chromodendrons increased in number to vie for majority with the maples. However, it was the maple trees that maintained the majority along the trail. There were also a couple of flowering ficuses freely frolicking in the wind. The ground was getting grassier as Emily's walk was circling back toward the main parking lot. Warmth from the sun mixed with a refreshing breeze made the woodland walk splendid.

Passing a cluster of maple trees, Emily continued her relaxing hike. The trees spread from a tightly clumped spacing to a lattice-like spacing. There was a fallen section of tree sprawled out on an angle amongst the other maples. Its decay was in contrast with the beauty of the living trees. The dead section of tree was being partially propped up by a couple of healthy maple trees. They were like teammates helping a fallen companion. The woods had a calming effect on Emily in its beauty and peacefulness. A patch of wild sweetberries ran along the path. Both attractive and enticing, the berries had layers to their attractiveness. From behind her, someone called out on your left. Emily stepped to the edge of the path as a pair of bikers passed by her. The off-duty detective took a deep breath of fresh air then continued forward.

As she walked, Emily looked at her left arm. She had some bruising where her arm had struck a graveyard statue. As Emily was considering using an ice pack once she returned home, she was greeted by another nature hiker.

"Good afternoon, Detective Oftenmarch. I'm Officer Dirk Gray from the Cathedral 275th precinct." the off-duty policeman greeted.

"Hello, Dirk. Please call me, Emily. Are you enjoying your Saturday in the park?" Emily replied.

"It's lovely. My wife and I saw you on television last evening speaking to the media outside St. Lawrence Gardens. We both liked your comments very much." Dirk complimented.

"Thank you. I did not know they had broadcasted my response to their questions." Emily admitted.

"I knew Barrett Alexander from when he used to work on the Cathedral Police force. He was a good guy. Did you catch his killer?" the officer wondered.

"Yes, we have his killer. Mr. Alexander put some bullets in his attacker and did most of the work. We just found the assailant's dead body." Emily shared.

"Barrett was the second retired police officer to be murdered in Cathedral this week. Retired officer Kenneth Brahmson was murdered on Wednesday. It's a shame." Officer Gray revealed.

"It is a shame." Emily agreed.

"Kenneth was only retired six months and was working part time security for Conglomerate Warehouses. He was shot and killed working his security job at the warehouse yard. He never even made it to fully retired." Dirk shared.

"The hope is for people to have long, enjoyable, and relaxing retirements but sadly that does not happen often enough." Emily admitted.

"All those years, police officers put their lives on the line to try to serve and protect the community. It's disheartening to see them murdered after their retirement. You would wish them a safe danger free life as a civilian." Dirk dreamed aloud.

"It would be nice for them to enjoy some peaceful life after working for many years to maintain peace for others." Emily agreed.

"Yes, it would.", the off-duty officer also agreed.

"My hope is that they may have peace in heaven. Matthew 5:9-10, *Blessed are the peacemakers, for they will be called children of GOD. Blessed are those who are persecuted because of righteousness, for theirs is the kingdom of heaven.*" Emily replied.

"I have taken up enough of your time, detective. You enjoy some peace on this wonderful afternoon in this wonderful park." Officer Gray said his farewell.

"You as well, Dirk. Enjoy some well-earned peace and quiet before retirement." Emily suggested in departure.

The detective finished her pleasant park valley Saturday hike and then drove home. Once home she started on getting some chores completed. Emily loaded her and her husband's laundry into the autosorter for the autowashers, including her muddy jacket. She then wrapped an ice pack around her left arm. While her clothes were being autocleaned, she started making snacks for church tomorrow. With the help of the robocook and the HomeChef unit, Emily was able to get the strawberry kolaches and blueberry muffins into the BakeMaster 3000 ovens before the clothes had to go into the autodryer and autopresser. While her and her husband's clothes were drying and the treats were cooking, Emily packed two new reserve bags for work. She made sure that both bags had extra socks, double checking each one.

Once those three tasks were complete, Emily refreshened then changed into a New Carnelian Knights shirt, a light fleece jacket, a lace-up assymetric plaid skirted leggings, and a pair of heeled dress boots. The skirt was a black, grey, and white color combination and the leggings were black. This matched with the New Carnelian team colors.

David-John got home from work as Emily was changing. He had to take some medication and his prescribed painkillers before getting ready. Once he felt better, David-John very quickly got dressed and prepared to go out for the evening. He loved going out with his wife on Saturday nights as much as she enjoyed going out with him on Saturday nights. They drove to a nice Italian restaurant in downtime New Carnelian. After enjoying a nice meal and each other's company, they did a little bit of sightseeing by driving around the city of New Carnelian.

New Carnelian was a city built around mining and oil drilling. When most of America had moved on to more modern machinations, New Carnelian went back to old fashioned industrial business. Not everything in New Carnelian was blue collar driven, but enough things were that way to give New Carnelian a reputation for blue collar business.

Jaycox Motors had its headquarters in New Carnelian. Emily's late husband Abraham's uncle Jared Goldsmith was Jaycox Motors' vice president and he lived in New Carnelian. Jared Goldsmith was passionate about three things: Jaycox sportscars, the city of New Carnelian, and the New Carnelian FC Knights. Jared together with his brother Jeremiah, who was Emily's former father-in-law, owned the Penultimate League football club (called soccer in the United States).

Jared Goldsmith always liked Emily and every year as a present he would give her a pair of season tickets to see his team's home games. Most of the time, Emily would have to give the tickets away because of conflicts with her work schedule, or David-John's work schedule, or both their work schedules. Then there were special nights like tonight when they could go to the game and those nights were typically enjoyable outings.

The New Carnelian FC Knights' home stadium was on the western edge of Carnelian and was called StoneBridge Castle. All the entrances to the stadium were old fashioned stone bridges and the stadium itself was built to look like an old medieval stone castle. The theme of the unique design was that the castle-formed stadium was home to the Knights of New Carnelian. On the north side of StoneBridge Castle was a pair of round stone towers with adjoining circular turrets. One tower contained the VIP lounges and the other tower contained the media boxes. On top of each tower and turret flew the team flags for the FC Knights. StoneBridge Castle had a capacity of 72,000 fans and the only group more ruckus than the stadium fans were the tailgaters outside the stadium before the match.

A massive crowd had come to cheer on the Knights this game day. Spirits were high and fans laughed and cheered as they merrily made their way into the stadium. The Knights were playing well enough to be in contention to make the playoffs. They were playing the Northern Division's second place team, the Ontario Renegades, on a pleasant Saturday night in front of a sellout crowd. Both teams were healthy and hungry for a win.

The game started at a fast pace with both teams creating scoring chances early in the match. Then the game slowed its pace as the Renegades were maintaining control of the ball in a methodical attack for most of the time. Fouls being committed by New Carnelian started piling up as the Knights were on the defensive for long stretches. Ontario had earned multiple free kicks and a half dozen corner kicks by staying aggressive. It was a free kick in the fortieth minute that led to the Renegades goal. They had made a nice pass into the box which allowed for a header past the Knights' lunging goalie and into the back of the net and the one to none go ahead score. The Knights were unable to mount a quality counterattack before the intermission. At halftime, the Renegades lead the Knights, 1-0, to the home crowds' disappointment.

At halftime David-John and Emily went to the food court in concourse C of the stadium to meet Ninth and her new new boyfriend. Any of the food courts at StoneBridge Castle were packed to capacity at halftime and the food court in concourse C was no exception. It took some time for them to find Ninth and her new new boyfriend among the throngs of hungry fans. It was Emily who first found them but it was David-John who was first greeted. Running up to him with a tackling style hug, Ninth embraced him with a shriek of glee. Ninth was always happy to see David-John and her sister. Usually a good mood person, Ninth was full of her typical cheer and joy spreading. Her most recent boyfriend, who look very similar to her last boyfriend, was much more subdued and less energetic than Ninth. In his defense, most people were. Kind as always, David-John was warm and welcoming to the young man. He engaged in a pleasant conversation with the latest boyfriend as Emily hugged her sister Ninth.

Ninth had a thousand things to exuberantly tell her sister. Emily listened to tales about their family, the family business, their mom's new puppy, Ninth's new workout routine, her new workout outfit, Friday night techno mini golf, and the recently opened coffee shop in her neighborhood. As Emily listened to Ninth's non-stop news, David-John had a conversation with Ninth's date. The conversations continued as they waiting in line for some beverages, purchased some beverages, and then drank those same beverages. At the conclusion of the conversations, David-John said a prayer of blessing over the current boyfriend. After exchanging hugs and handshakes, the group said their farewells and headed back to their respective seats to watch the second half.

Starting the second half well, the Knights passed the ball in quick progressive combinations to work the ball deep into Ontario's defensive zone. The Knights had an early shot on goal which required a diving save from the Renegades' goalkeeper. After that shot, the Renegades returned to their ball controlling slow pace and were keeping possession away from New Carnelian. This time the Knights were able to intercept a pass and go on a quick counterattack. The counterattack caused Ontario to commit a foul on defense and this gave New Carnelian a free kick. The Knights used the free kick to cross the ball into the box for an opportunistic shot on goal. This shot was partially blocked by an Ontario defender, deflecting the ball just wide of the goal. Handball was called as the defender had outstretched his arm to get the deflection off his upper arm area. New Carnelian was awarded a penalty kick and a sensational opportunity to tie the game. The Knights' captain took the penalty kick and blasted his shot past the goalkeeper, which erupted the home crowd into jubilation.

With the game once again tied, the Renegades began a more up-tempo offensive style of play. Ontario maintained possession of the ball with efficient passing to keep pressure on the New Carnelian defense. Staying on the offensive, the Renegades kept probing the Knights' defense for openings. New Carnelian worked relentlessly to hold strong. For the next ten minutes, Ontario pressed forward and took multiple shots towards goal. New Carnelian weathered the attack and kept the game tied, one to one. Then New Carnelian's superstar striker with a sizeable salary and a premium transfer fee made his presence in the game known. On the counterattack, a deep crossing pass was corralled and controlled by super striker Hugh Zammellamiore. The Ontario defenders were unable to close down any open space preventing a shooting alley. Taking advantage of the opportunity, Zammellamiore sent a sensational superpowered strike soaring past the outstretched goalkeeper into the upper lefthand corner of the goal. The home crowd exploded in an exuberant roar celebrating the go-ahead goal. The stadium stands became a giant gregarious party zone.

Still hosting a party in the stands, the game continued. A unison chant echoed throughout the stadium as New Carnelian tried to keep momentum by staying aggressive. Motivated from gaining the lead and having the support of an energized home crowd behind them, the Knights gained inspiration in their play. Under pressure by the Knights' defense, Ontario lost possession on an errant pass. New Carnelian charged forward on a counterattack forcing Ontario to concede a cornerkick when blocking an on-target shot out of bounds.

With well timed accuracy, the cornerkick was skillfully placed were a New Carnelian midfielder leaped over a defender and was able to head the ball toward goal. The hard struck header slid passed the goalie to ricochet off the crossbar and bounce dangerously back into the field of play. Ontario's zonal marking was in complete disarray after the rebound and their breakdown led to a Knights' opportunity. Taking great advantage of that breakdown, Zammellamoire seized the moment and brilliantly boot blasted the ball into the back of the net. Once again the crowd erupted into a mighty cheer. In a state of euphoria, the home crowd was rocking in jubilation as the Knights took a 3-1 lead. Fans were literally jumping for joy. Shouts of Zammellamoire for MVP were cascading through the stadium.

A rhythmic chant emanated from the energetic fans as the game continued. The Knights had both a multiple goal lead and momentum, giving the happy fans joyous reason to party in the stands. Grand in magnitude, the crowd celebration crescendoed to uncontained jubilee with expectations of victory. Enjoying the moment, Emily forgot about her worrisome work woes and questions of self-sanity. She simply enjoyed the atmosphere as the Knights went on to joyous victory, 3 to 1.

New Carnelian FC Knights

Chapter 8

Psalm Swim

With its tall slender bell tower standing among a colorful cluster of trees, the First Baptist Second Birth Church was located at the end of a cozy cul-de sac. A structure of simple architecture, the church blended in very nicely with the surrounding residential area. The church was a well maintained medium sized building with a tidy well landscaped property. On the backside of the church, not visible from the road, was a newish ordinary looking addition which consisted of a spacious fellowship hall and several classrooms. On the front of the church was a pair of wide stained glass doors which led into a quaint welcome area. The church used to have a robotic greeter at those front doors. However, David-John had the robot removed because he preferred people welcoming people to church.

In front of the First Baptist Second Birth Church was its prize winning rose garden. Originally, the garden was where the church's first pastor practiced his hobby of cultivating roses. Years later, the rose garden became a prayer garden tended by the church's garden club. The church's rose garden was now well known in the neighborhood and often received visitors. Around the outer edges of the garden grew smooth roses, mostly in pink. In a layer laid a variety of vibrant old garden roses. Populating the main section of the garden were grandiflora roses. In a mixture of pinks, reds, and whites, the grandiflora roses were the jewels of the rose garden. In the back section of the garden grew the brilliant Arden roses. In bright reds and yellows, the Arden roses flourished in the church's rose garden. It had taken decades of diligent plant breeding to grow these roses, but their beauty definitely made it worth that time.

The First Baptist Second Birth Church had three Sunday morning services, the early riser 7am, the family oriented 9am, and the casual 11am. In preparation, David-John almost always left the house at 4am on Sunday mornings to head to the church to pray for the congregation, the sermon, the church, and anything else that came to heart. More often than not, Emily was a much later Sunday morning riser. When not interrupted by work, Emily typically woke up around 6:45 in the morning and went to the 9am Sunday morning service. She sat with her husband in the front row until he went up to the pulpit to preach, at which time she would sit attentively alone. For the 11am service, Emily would usually serve as a barista at the church's coffee bar.

On this Sunday, David-John left at his normal time but Emily slept in fifteen minutes longer. This caused her to hustle faster than normal to get ready for church. She wore a cowl neck button embellished cadet blue shirt, a layered ruffle hem silver skirt, white nylons, a simple silver necklace, and a pair of high heels. Emily packed a jug of ice tea, a carton of apple cider, a package of oatmeal raisin cookies, the container full of kolaches, and the container full of muffins into a large tote bag. After a light traffic drive to church, which was vastly different from travelling in Cathedral, Emily arrived at church with two minutes to spare. Like every Sunday, the church was full of friendly faces and crowded with cheery conversations. Despite being behind schedule, Emily found time to exchange warm pleasantries with several people and still was sitting next to her husband when the opening worship song began the 9am service.

Most attendees of the church knew Emily was a police officer. The majority of them assumed she was a traffic cop or a desk clerk. Very few of them knew she was a homicide detective in Cathedral, and she was fine with that being the case. One of the few attendees who knew her occupation was Common Pleas Court Judge Betty Strong. Mrs. Strong would usually greet Emily on her way to her seat. Today, the judge was atypically not at church. Emily made a mental note to give the judge a call later to see how she was doing.

Full of bright light, the sanctuary had tall slender windows along its side walls and several modestly ornate chandeliers dangling from its twenty-four foot high ceiling. Completely carpeted with a nice plush carpeting, the sanctuary had four sections of neatly arranged rows of modular seats. The center aisle had a second elongated red rug on top of the carpet that travelled the length of the room to the altar. This was an attractive feature which was a draw for weddings. After a three-step rise, the altar itself was a simple design with a lectern, a wooden cross, and equipment for a worship team.

Like most Sundays, the church service was excellent and her husband's sermon message was instructive. David-John seldom practiced his sermons with her, so the messages were often new to her, like today's message. Her husband always gave a heartfelt passionate message with the hope of helping people love GOD more and loving other people better. No matter how much was going on at work, Emily always did her best to focus on her husband's sermon on Sunday mornings. Some Sundays it was easier to focus than others.

Like most Sundays, the church service helped renew her mood. Emily was able to leave her detective work worries at the door and just worship. Again, some Sundays it was easier to do that than others. But she always had friendly people to talk to, takeaways from the sermon, and a rewarding church family to enjoy. Here she was the pastor's wife Emily and not Detective Oftenmarch. Sunday morning church service was often a highlight of her week and this week was no exception. Hallelujah to the KING of KINGS.

After the service, Emily went to the coffee bar and began serving the Sunday school students, church parishioners, and church visitors. As was often the arrangement, Mrs. Edith Springsparrow, a kind septuagenarian, was serving at the coffee bar with Emily. They were giving out treats and beverages, all with warm greetings, to people and having polite conversations with partakers same as a usual Sunday morning. Edith and Emily would see both post-9am worshippers and pre-11am worshippers come visit them at the coffee bar. Nothing was out of the ordinary for about fifteen minutes of serving at the coffee bar that morning. Again, it was like any other Sunday. Emily had just served a decaf coffee and a cookie to a kind man when she saw Hedra Shippendarrow standing at the coffee bar.

"Eddie won't go for help, that will have to be your move." Detective Shippendarrow said. Emily closed her eyes and took a deep breath.

When she opened her eyes, Mr. Patrick was standing where the detective had previously appeared.

"Edith won't give me a helping, it will have to be your doing. Something about me getting too fat." Mr. Patrick said, patting his sizeable pot belly.

"Too many treats has he been eating." Mrs. Springsparrow stated from further down the coffee bar.

"Edith is the wiser of us. I am the softie, what would you like Mr. Patrick?" Emily asked calmly as she was internally uncalm. It happened again; it had seemed so real. Emily served Mr. Patrick the snacks he had requested and he thanked her profusely.

A version of a poem came to Emily's thoughts, a version of a poem that she could related to recently.

The other day from nowhere, I met a man who wasn't there

He wasn't there again today. Oh how, I wish he'd go away.

From behind my office chair, talked to a cop without a care

He didn't speak that fateful day. Oh how, I wish he'd stay away.

After Mr. Patrick had departed, Mrs. Springsparrow came up to her. "Are you alright, my dear? You seem slightly discomposed." she asked with concern.

"I am afraid I have been letting my work get to me, Edith." Emily admitted.

"Don't let life get you down, Emily. When I am feeling sad or overwhelmed, I pick a Psalm from the Bible and just keep reading and reading it until I forget my troubles or at least forget to remember them." Edith kindly shared.

162

"That sounds like a great idea." Emily confessed.

"Old folks like me have a trick or two to use because we have experienced a trick or two or three in our lifetime." Edith continued sharing.

The pair of them returned to serving snacks and beverages until the crowd dissipated and the food had been depleted. The 11am service was in full worship as they started to clear and clean the area. In the process of tidying the counter, Emily's cell phone rang. The area code of the number on the phone's display was for Florida. It was the number she had called yesterday. She answered the phone after the third ring. After hearing two beeps, the dial tone was all Emily could now hear as the phone call had ended. Emily hoped that odd call meant her message was received and help was on the way.

After finishing serving at the church, Emily returned home on her own as David-John would be busy well into the afternoon. She spent some time completing some much needed housework. Work occupied so much of her weekdays, Emily often found herself catching up on housework on the weekends. With the aid, of some music, the work went relatively well as she was not hindered by her injuries. Since she was unhampered by those injuries, Emily also completed her choirs in a reasonable amount of time.

There had been some swelling in her left hand early Saturday morning. The swelling had now gone down. Emily flexed her hand a couple of times and felt no discomfort. Then she looked at her left arm, which displayed only a slight discoloration. Since her injuries were healing nicely, she decided to get some exercise. Emily jogged to the Royal Desmesne Estate clubhouse two streets from her home. The clubhouse had a pool which was available to neighborhood residents of the homeowners coalition. It was a quick jog to the clubhouse and the weather was delightful for a run. Once there, Emily used her electronic passkey for the building and the locker room. After changing, she began to swim laps in the pool. The clubhouse pool was only four lanes wide but was twenty-five meters long. The pool was often empty on Sunday afternoon and provided Emily both a nice place to swim and a quiet place to think. Even the robotic pool cleaner was deactivated on Sundays. Neither a creature nor a thing would be stirring, not even a droid.

Initially her thoughts troubled her as Emily began her recreational swim. She could not go crazy. She could not let people down. The captain and Eddie needed her. The commissioner had personally asked her and Eddie for help. She could not lose her mental stability. She could not disappoint her husband. The citizens of Cathedral trusted her to serve and protect the community. The police department of Cathedral entrusted her to catch murderous law breakers. She could not go insane. Insanity was not an option. How could she help her family if she went crazy? How could she continue to be a detective as a lunatic? Who would believe her testimony for CHRIST if she were viewed as a crazy nut? She just could not go crazy.

These thoughts swam through her mind as she swam through the lukewarm pool water. The rhythm of her swimming strokes increased as her thoughts quickened through her mind. Emily moved smoothly through the water, propelled by her desire to not be crazy. With her thoughts on her sanity, Emily's swimming was efficiently on autotechnique, relying on muscle memory. Her plan was simple: she sought some peace in the tranquility of swimming.

As Emily continued to swim, she pushed thoughts of work aside. Furthermore, she pushed thoughts of anything work related aside. Beginning with a freestyle stroke, Emily set a steady pace for her first few laps. She swam at her even pace and let the quiet immerse her. Emily soon found a steady rhythm to her swimming strokes. Continuing to calm herself, she traversed through the lovely lukewarm water. While she swam, Emily began reciting Psalm 100 to herself.

Shout for joy to the LORD, all the earth.

Worship the LORD with gladness; come before Him with joyful songs.

Know that the LORD is GOD. It is He who made us, and we are His; we are His people, the sheep of His pasture.

Enter His gates with thanksgiving and His courts with praise; give thanks to Him and praise His name.

For the LORD is good and His love endures forever; His faithfulness continues through all generations.

Then Emily switched to the breaststroke. She cleared her mind of seeing and hearing deceased detectives. No more thoughts of lycan masquerade killers or moon cultists. Emily focused on her swimming technique and the silent aquatic surroundings. As she swam, Emily developed a steady rhythm to her breaststroke. Finding comfort in the exercise, Emily moved through the blissful blue water. As she did the breaststroke, Emily then continued reciting Psalm 100 to herself.

Shout for joy to the LORD, all the earth.

Worship the LORD with gladness; come before Him with joyful songs.

Know that the LORD is GOD. It is He who made us, and we are His; we are His people, the sheep of His pasture.

Enter His gates with thanksgiving and His courts with praise; give thanks to Him and praise His name.

For the LORD is good and His love endures forever; His faithfulness continues through all generations.

Next Emily changed her stroke to the butterfly. Forgotten were the doubts of the police commissioners regarding her. She pushed away thoughts of people looking at her oddly. Continuing to swim, Emily endeavored to enjoy the water and the surrounding pool serenity.

Moving across the pool, Emily found a rhythm to her butterfly strokes. Continuing to calm herself, she navigated the tranquil tepid water. Putting her focus on breathing as she swam butterflies, Emily returned to reciting Psalm 100 to herself.

Shout for joy to the LORD, all the earth.

Worship the LORD with gladness; come before Him with joyful songs.

Know that the LORD is GOD. It is He who made us, and we are His; we are His people, the sheep of His pasture.

Enter His gates with thanksgiving and His courts with praise; give thanks to Him and praise His name.

For the LORD is good and His love endures forever; His faithfulness continues through all generations.

Switching to the backstroke, Emily changed her perspective. Listening to the peaceful underwater rush of current from her strokes, she was looking up at the ceiling. Light fixtures would pass by her view as she swam. Away melted thoughts of coroner's reports and forensic results. As she swam, Emily transitioned into a steady pace with her backstrokes. Swimming peacefully, she negotiated the wonderful warm water. Emily sailed through the carefree waters of harmony. She continued to repeat Psalm 100 to herself as she swam backwards.

Shout for joy to the LORD, all the earth.

Worship the LORD with gladness; come before Him with joyful songs.

Know that the LORD is GOD. It is He who made us, and we are His; we are His people, the sheep of His pasture.

Enter His gates with thanksgiving and His courts with praise; give thanks to Him and praise His name.

For the LORD is good and His love endures forever; His faithfulness continues through all generations.

Returning to the free stroke, Emily began to swim harder and faster. Reaching longer and kicking quicker, she pushed to go faster. As if driving herself to overcome her troubles by outswimming them, Emily pushed herself to swim even faster. Must go faster, must go faster, she thought. Now moving quicker, Emily increased the rhythm to her swimming strokes. As she speedily slashed through the warmer water, she challenged herself further. Fueled by the desire to defeat bad thoughts, Emily forced herself to keep swimming at a rapid pace. Sprinting across the pool, Emily returned to reciting Psalm 100 to herself.

Shout for joy to the LORD, all the earth.

Worship the LORD with gladness; come before Him with joyful songs.

Know that the LORD is GOD. It is He who made us, and we are His; we are His people, the sheep of His pasture.

Enter His gates with thanksgiving and His courts with praise; give thanks to Him and praise His name.

For the LORD is good and His love endures forever; His faithfulness continues through all generations.

Emily slowed her pace and her racing mind began to calm again. Emily deaccelerated to find a slower steady pace to her swimming strokes. As she calmed her pace, Emily calmly traversed the water of refreshing ripples. Her thoughts turned to reminiscing about childhood swimming lessons. She was not Detective Oftenmarch solving a case at that moment; she was Emily having a swim. The water was pleasant; the pool was peaceful. GOD was great; He was King throughout everything. As she swam, Emily recited repeatedly Psalm 100 to herself.

Shout for joy to the LORD, all the earth.

Worship the LORD with gladness; come before Him with joyful songs.

Know that the LORD is GOD. It is He who made us, and we are His; we are His people, the sheep of His pasture.

Enter His gates with thanksgiving and His courts with praise; give thanks to Him and praise His name.

For the LORD is good and His love endures forever; His faithfulness continues through all generations.

She kept swimming. Emily did not want to stop. She felt compelled to keep swimming and reciting Psalm 100 to herself. Emily regained a modestly paced steady rhythm to her swimming strokes. As she continued to seek calmness, Emily pushed through the crystal clear water. Emily felt at peace as she kept swimming and remained focused on Psalm 100. The more she swam while going over the Psalm, the better she felt. Her worries drifted away as lap after lap she recited Psalm 100 to herself.

Shout for joy to the LORD, all the earth.

Worship the LORD with gladness; come before Him with joyful songs.

Know that the LORD is GOD. It is He who made us, and we are His; we are His people, the sheep of His pasture.

Enter His gates with thanksgiving and His courts with praise; give thanks to Him and praise His name.

For the LORD is good and His love endures forever; His faithfulness continues through all generations.

Easily keeping a steady rhythm to her swimming strokes, Emily persisted in her swimming. Continuing to push herself, Emily battled through the deep delightful water. Continuing to push herself, she fought to conquer the tides of her inner storm. Finally, Emily stopped worrying about lycan masquerade killers, cemetery werewolf sightings, and all the pressures from police work. No longing focusing on herself, she remembered the loving people the LORD had put in her life. She had a loving husband, a caring family, a wonderful Wednesday night study group, a kind church family, helpful members of her late husband's family, and some dedicated co-workers. Emily was not alone in this tumultuous world. Most of all, she would always have the love of the LORD. She silently repeated Psalm 100 to herself again.

Shout for joy to the LORD, all the earth.

Worship the LORD with gladness; come before Him with joyful songs.

Know that the LORD is GOD. It is He who made us, and we are His; we are His people, the sheep of His pasture.

Enter His gates with thanksgiving and His courts with praise; give thanks to Him and praise His name.

For the LORD is good and His love endures forever; His faithfulness continues through all generations.

Exhausted and fatigued, Emily left the pool completely drained of energy. Weak and lethargic, Emily made her way to the locker room to change. Tired to the bone, she left the clubhouse and trudged home. The walk home seemed much longer than the run to the clubhouse had been. Even though she was spent physically, her mind was now calm and she no longer felt troubled. Her Psalm swim had refreshed her and renewed her spirit. As she plodded home, the air she was breathing seemed fresher. It was like a gift of replenishment.

As Emily walked back home, she listened to a podcast on her slim-line microheadphones. The podcast was a daily dose of good news and today they were discussing Psalm 28:6-9. *Praise be to the Lord, for he has heard my cry for mercy. The Lord is my strength and my shield; my heart trusts in him, and he helps me. My heart leaps for joy, and with my song I praise him. The Lord is the strength of his people, a fortress of salvation for his anointed one. Save your people and bless your inheritance; be their shepherd and carry them forever.* The topic matched well with her psalm swim, it seemed very apropos. Emily listened intently as she peacefully and wearily hiked back to her house.

When Emily finally returned home, she ate some food and then had a long hot shower. After the wonderful shower, Emily took two hair dryer stands and a third handheld hairdryer into an upstairs sitting room. She put on a New Carnelian Knights t-shirt which had been a giveaway. Emily had caught the shirt, which had been thrown into the crowd as a team promotional during a match. This shirt was far too big for her, size 3XL, so she wore it as a night shirt. She let the soothing warm dryers run as she rested in a lounge seat. As her hair dried, Emily drifted off to sleep, a warm tranquil sleep. She woke up when David-John returned home from his Sunday afternoon pastors' prayer meeting and luncheon. By his own admission, the pastors ate more than they prayed on their Sunday after-noon gatherings. David-John often took a nap after the luncheons. So Emily got up, turned off all the dryers, and went to go nap with her husband.

Searching for her husband, it took Emily some time to find him. David-John was not located in the typical rooms for his normal Sunday routine. Usually he would go to the living room to read where he would fall asleep in his comfortable reading chair or he would go to the family room to watch intervision, where he would drift into slumber in his relax-ing recliner. Not finding him in the living room or family room, Emily finally found David-John in the library. The library had four tall bay windows, two located in the front of the house and two located in the back of the house. Each bay window projected outward at pronounced angular sections to create an alcove in the library. David-John was standing silently in one of the library's cozy front alcoves staring out the picture window.

The library was one of the nicest rooms in their home. David-John used the room as a home office and he had a nice oak writing desk here on top of which he accomplished a lot of his work. In the room were a dictionary stand, a pair of black armchairs, and a half a dozen floor lamps. There was an oversized globe located between the armchairs. Also in the majority of the library were over thirty 6-foot-tall classic bookcases. Most of them were in a pair of rows consisting of bookcases standing back-to-back. As most of the bookcases were over half empty, the library was still more of a vision of what it could become as David-John assembled it over time. Every year Emily bought David-John a couple of books for his birthday, their anniversary, and Christmas.

Emily strode over to her husband and cuddled up beside him. David-John put his arm around her and tenderly held his wife closely. He had leaned his cane against the wall, which meant he was going well and had both arms free to give her a proper hug. The married couple quietly embraced as they gazed out the picture window together. Quietly they shared a moment of peace and tranquility together. It was a lovely moment filled with a love that could not be expressed with words.

"There is so much heartache in this world, there is no such compassion in this world." David-John lamented breaking the silence.

"A wise man once told me to be compassionate and then there will be compassion in this world." Emily responded.

"Not sure about the wise part but the rest of that statement sounds correct. Thanks for the reminder, Emily." David-John thanked.

"I was looking for a snuggle buddy for a long Sunday's nap." Emily shared her desire.

"As wonderful as that sounds, sadly I cannot nap with you. Have to review my speech for tomorrow night at Chatham Community

College, write some prayers for Tuesday's spaghetti night at church, then prepare for Wednesday night adult Bible studies, and finally work on the lesson for Friday night study group. I have a lot of work to get done." David-John sadly informed his wife.

"Well, that is disappointing but understandable. I, on the other hand, have to get some rest now because there may not be much opportunity to sleep in my near future." Emily informed her husband.

"Rest well, Emily. And let us pray for the wisdom to act when we don't know and the faith to move when we don't see. May we always remember to find rest in the FATHER." David-John bid her farewell followed by a passionate kiss.

After getting the maximum amount of pleasure out of the kiss, Emily left her husband in peace to work. Returning upstairs, she went to the master bedroom to have a long Sunday slumber. The exhausted detective quickly fell asleep on their comfortable Cathedral king size bed. And when Emily fell asleep, she fell into a deep sleep for the remainder of the day.

Chapter 9

Intruder in the Datacenter

Interrupted during a deep peaceful slumber, Emily had been awakened by Lt. Knighton's phone call around 2:30am. There had been a lycan mask sighting; Eddie told her the weekend was over and it was back to work. Emily told Eddie he was not her favorite person at that moment, then dragged herself out of bed. Dressing quickly and putting on her police necessities, Emily wasted little time getting on the road. She had opted for the black Superflex X3 Trim athletic shoes again but chose her three-quarter longline black duracloth jacket with scarlet trim this time.

Detective Oftenmarch used her portable police dashlight and sped along the highways to get to Cathedral. Doing so was not completely in compliance with the Lincoln-Lofton rule, but nobody was really going to mind at this time of day. A few minutes after three o'clock, she was inside city limits. Emily was cruising along the Transcathedral Highway, which was completely clear at this time of the morning. In less than three hours time this stretch of road would be absolutely bumper to bumper gridlock. From the highway, Spiral Towers could be seen in the distance, nicely illuminated even at this early hour. Listening to sports talk radio as she drove, she heard the Granthum Grey Sox lost to New York, the Cathedral Bishops won, and the Cathedral Crusaders won their exhibition preseason football game 20-17. The Crusaders' first round draft pick and rookie wide receiver had five receptions for 83 yards and a touchdown. Passing quickly by Victory Tower, known for its v-shaped peak, and the fourteen big bank skyscrapers off the second downtown exit of the Transcathedral Highway, Emily knew she was getting close to her destination. The sports news continued with the bad news for Chatham Lynx hockey fans. Construction on their new arena was delayed and the facility would not be ready in time for their home opener. The team would either have to start their season playing home games at Chatham State University or the BigCo Arena, home of the Cathedral Caribou.

Driving in the early morning streetlamp superlights, Emily drove past the BioHeart Center, Cathedral General Hospital, and both Getmore Insurance skyscrapers. There was an excellent view of Solomons Entertainment Casino from the highway. Taking the third midtown exit, Lincoln Boulevard, Emily departed the Transcathedral Highway and was at her destination three minutes later. It was one of the rare times that Cathedral was docile. This morning's crime scene was at Superior Private Eyes Surveillance. Known for its first rate camera coverage and high detection success rate, the home and office security company was becoming well renown. They offered 24 hour, 7 days a week surveillance coverage and cybercloud video footage retention for up to five years depending on the level of service the customer desired. They were the apex of security surveillance and security video capture. Superior Private Eyes Surveillance had a sleek gray five-story midtown building in the jurisdiction of the 113th Cathedral Police precinct.

Detective Oftenmarch parked her car next to a row of three Cathedral police cruisers. Their lights were somewhat muted in the partially foggy morning air. Light wisps of fog danced throughout the streets and buildings of Cathedral. The neighboring buildings had very few internal lights shining, giving the area a somber atmosphere. Emily noticed that there were no CSP droids working the scene, which was generally a good sign. With her car parked in the parade of police cars, Emily made sure she had her complink, copcam, police communicator, tableau, Phasepulser IX, and Maxwell Trialloy XL-2 handgun on her person. Since the MPAR was still in the tech department for repairs, Emily had to bring a detective field kit with all the items usually kept in the servicebot.

Once ready for work, the detective made her way to the entrance of Superior Private Eyes Surveillance. Lt. Knighton was waiting for her by the door. The building had a unique long front entrance which Eddie had been sketching a picture of it. After showing their badges to the Cathedral police officer at the front entrance, the duo did the same for the security guard at the front desk. Two other Cathedral police officers were quasi-patrolling the small front lobby. One of them was eating a breakfast burrito and the other one was leisurely drinking a cup of coffee.

"Nothing was stolen, security checked twice and is making one last check but it looks like a failed burglary." the coffee drinking cop stated.

"Some fool broke into the building and was seen by a night operator wearing a wolf mask. The idiot then tripped an alarm and had to make a run for it." the burrito eating cop updated.

"Are you new to the 113th precinct commercial crimes division? I have never seen you before." the coffee lover asked.

"We are with the 272nd precinct homicide division." Emily verbally released an unexpected curveball.

"This is a burglary. Why is homicide here?" sputtered the breakfast muncher.

"Someone cried wolf, which then calls us. When you catch the wannabe thieves, let them know they are also under arrest for murder." Emily revealed.

"One or two intruders?" Eddie asked the security guard. The security guard shrugged and pointed at the lobby cops. Both preoccupied lobby cops looked at each other and then also shrugged.

"Well, it is after 3am. We have no idea if anything was taken or how many intruders entered the building. This seems fitting for a CPD Monday morning." Emily complained.

"Where is the 113th CCD?" Lt. Knighton questioned the police officers lollygagging in the lobby. They both shrugged again.

"Nothing was taken, suppose they stayed in bed." one of them speculated.

"Paul is in the bathroom, maybe he knows." the other offered.

Emily turned to the security guard at the desk. "Please call your super-visor and let them know the Cathedral detectives are here. We would like to have an investigation and make another check." she requested.

"The real police have arrived." Eddie added.

With a chuckle, the security guard picked up his portable two-way radio transceiver. "Desk to central, come in.", he transmitted.

"Central" came the radio reply.

"Two Cathedral police detectives are here asking for you." the guard reported.

"Will be there in thirty seconds." the staticky response came over the radio.

As they waited at the security desk, Emily could hear the lobby snacking policemen snickering and muttering something about homi-cide working break-ins. The desk guard had techno beatrap music play-ing moderately quiet. One of the lobby ceiling lights was making a hum-ming sound.

"How many alternate exits does this facility have?" Emily queried.

"Three, two side emergency exits and the loading dock in the back." the guard disclosed.

"Did you see any intruders?" Emily asked him another question.

"No. I have only seen employees all night." the security guard answered.

A set of double doors opened from behind the security desk and a pair of Superior Private Eyes Surveillance employees entered the lobby.

One was dressed in a security uniform and the other in a business shirt and skirt.

"I am Miranda Philcox, security shift supervisor. Thank you for coming. This will be a waste of your time because whatever the thief came to get they failed to get anything." the lady greeted then expressed.

"The thief wore a wolf mask, is that correct?" Emily questioned.

"Our datacenter night operator said they saw the infiltrator wearing a mask." Miranda confirmed.

"Which makes the intruder potentially dangerous and brings us to your front lobby. I am Detective Emily Oftenmarch and this is Lt. Eddie Knighton. We are going to need some of your time to investigate what this potentially dangerous individual was doing while illegally on your premises." Detective Oftenmarch explained.

"Nobody was hurt and nothing was taken but we can accommodate you." Miranda reluctantly agreed.

"Thank you. May we speak with the datacenter operator who saw the intruder? Then may we see the locations where the intruder was seen and where the alarm was tripped?" Emily requested.

"Take them to the back datacenter hallway and I will send the operator to meet you there." Miranda told the security guard accompanying her. Her tone suggested this was an imposition.

Miranda left the lobby and the non-desk stationed security guard led the detectives through to the datacenter office's main hallway. Upon entering the hallway, the ambient lighting changed drastically. This area of the building had all its lights very dim, providing low visibility. It took some ocular adjustment time to see after having come from the well lit lobby. Both detectives simultaneously turned on their copcams.

"What happened to the lights?" Emily wondered.

"It's a security measure for when the security alarms are triggered." the security guard explained.

"Wouldn't lights improve security?" Eddie asked.

"Employees are trained to get to light zones or safe zones, like the lobby, in the event of a security alarm. An intruder would be left in the dark, unsure where to go." the security guard expounded.

"Interesting." Emily replied. "How long do the lights stay in this state?"

"I don't know. We have never had a security alarm go off before today." the man unveiled.

They had walked down the main hallway past a half dozen doors and two large glass windows. Inside the windows appeared to be darkened datacenters full of computer equipment with their LEDs, indicator lights, and illuminated displays glowing in the dark. At the end of the main hallway was a t-intersection where the security guard turned left. Halfway down this hallway, the security guard stopped.

"This is where the infiltrator in the mask was seen." the guard disclosed as he halted.

"And where was the security alarm triggered?" Emily inquired.

"At the next set of datacenter doors on the right." the security guard returned with a pointing gesture. The indicated doors did not have an emergency exit sign above them.

"Did they access that door?" Eddie asked as he took a picture with his complink.

"The datacenter operator says they did. The security logs show no entry for those doors since around 10pm yesterday." the guard responded.

"The eyewitness account and the security logs contradict each other." Emily observed.

"Affirmative, detective." the security guard agreed.

"And you saw nobody when you checked the room behind the doors?" Emily looked for clarification.

"Security has no authorization to enter datacenter floors. Only certified IT staff and system administrators are allowed on the datacenter floors." the guard revealed policy.

"Who checked that room?" Lt. Knighton questioned.

"The night ops supervisor searched the datacenter." the security guard divulged.

Miranda Philcox entered the hallway followed by a young man in a Cathedral Rocks tee shirt, blue jeans with holes in them, and bright neon yellow sneakers. His sneakers could be clearly seen in the dimly lit hallway. The young man looked uncomfortable as he followed Miranda. Miranda had a purposeful march that was unmistakable even in the dark.

Once close to the detectives she ordered, "Tell them what you saw, Jimmy." Then to the security guard she added, "I will be in my office."

As Miranda walked away, Jimmy started talking, "Yo, I was coming back from having some munchies and an energy boost heading for my workstation when I saw a dude in a creepy wolfman mask standing about here in the hallway. I was like no way. "

"How far from you?" Eddied asked.

"I was coming out of the lobby hallway so not far." Jimmy replied.

"Good morning, Jimmy. I'm Emily and he is Lt. Knighton. We are Cathedral police detectives. We have some questions for you that will help us. Did it look like the man was walking away from you and then stopped to look at you?" Emily wondered after greeting Jimmy.

"Maybe, not sure. I was surprised and distracted by the weirdo mask." Jimmy admitted.

"A wolf mask?" Eddie looked for confirmation.

"Definitely, gave me the heebee geebees." Jimmy replied.

"Did the man run or walk away from you?" Emily asked.

"Kinda ran away, seemed like a run I think." Jimmy recalled uncertainly. He furrowed his brow as he thought.

"Was he carrying anything?" Eddie questioned.

"I don't know. Don't remember." Jimmy blanked.

"And he went through those doors? You're sure he went through the doors, Jimmy? He didn't just try to open them?" Detective Oftenmarch looked for a definitive statement.

"He for sure opened that door. Acted like he knew the door would open. Ran straight over there and cruised through the door, no card scan. I was like whoa, how did he do that?" Jimmy testified.

"How was he dressed?" Lt. Knighton inquired

"Think he wore a shirt and jeans. Wolf mask for sure." Jimmy supplied.

"Can you please give me access to that room, Jimmy?" Emily asked politely.

"No problem. That floor is mostly in-house tech, no customer secure level stuff." Jimmy replied then walked casually towards the doors being discussed.

"While I am checking this datacenter floor, Lt. Knighton has a few more questions for you, Jimmy." Emily explained.

"Cool." Jimmy was agreeable as he scanned and then opened the door.

"Thank you, Jimmy." Emily thanked him as she entered the datacenter.

If the hallways were low visibility, then the datacenter was no visibility. Detective Oftenmarch turned on her shoulder light. Between the darkness, the rows of computer equipment, and the size of the room, an intruder could hide for hours in there and not be found. The detective set her field kit down next to the doors. Emily suspected the night operations supervisor did not search very thoroughly since there was a box of cables tipped over about six feet into the room. Emily scooped up some cables, righted the box, and placed the cables into the box.

Collecting herself, Emily calmly began to inspect her dark surroundings. In the torchlight, clear vision was limited to the first couple of rows of equipment. Darkness swallowed up and obscured anything after that point. Judging by the sound of a plethora of running cooling fans, the datacenter seemed to be a sizeable room full of equipment. The detective began to make a long scrupulous scan of the datacenter as she cautiously walked forward in the darkened room. Looking to-and-fro, Emily started down what seemed to be the main aisleway. As she peered into the darkness, the datacenter did not seem to be out of the ordinary. But suddenly, what was that?

Emily could have sworn she saw something moving in the datacenter. The facility had only its emergency exit lights running due to their loss of power. Their backup generators supplied power to their computer and storage array equipment, which was the backbone of their business, but neglected to restore lighting to their facility. Therefore, Emily relied on her shoulder light as she stealthfully walked the datacenter. As the detective walked, she was on the watch for more movement.

A shadowy figure passed by the center power regulator unit and darted into the last aisle between the computer rack cabinets. Emily, spotting the figure, swiftly moved to intercept the unknown intruder. Opting for speed over stealth, Emily made a little more noise than she would have liked. In seconds, the detective had travelled across an aisle. Moving further into the datacenter and closer to the trespasser, Emily moved down the right side aisleway. As she passed the second to last aisle, Emily thought she spotted the shadowy figure again back in the center aisle. When the detective reached the last aisle, it was empty.

Realizing the intruder must have doubled back on her, Detective Oftenmarch sprinted up the right side aisle. Passing fifteen or sixteen aisles, Emily finally picked an aisle to transition back to the center aisleway. Again in seconds, the detective had travelled across the aisle. Back in the center aisleway, Emily started swiftly surveying the datacenter with steadfast scrutiny. Most people would begin to think they had imagined the fleeting faint image or think their mind was playing tricks on them, but Emily's certainty held and her determination tripled.

After about thirty seconds into her sweeping scan, Emily saw the shadowy figure again. It was moving rapidly. This time it moved from behind a datacenterwide power generator and into the second to last aisle between the cabinets heading left. The detective hustled down the center aisleway. This time she did not take any of the aisles to the left but went straight to the second to last aisle. As she reached the penultimate aisle to peer across the aisle, Emily just caught a glimpse of the elusive figure.

Rapidly, Emily rushed back one aisle to look down the row. Yes, she spotted the figure again. Keeping her speed high, the detective moved to the next aisle to look for the figure passing the other side. Emily saw nothing, bounced back an aisle, and still saw nothing. Emily was puzzled by what she could be seeing. Hastily, Detective Oftenmarch hustled forward three aisles and still saw nothing. Back to hide and seek, thought Emily.

She removed a pen from her jacket pocket and threw it back in the direction she had just left. Hitting the floor, the pen made some clattering noises as it unevenly landed. As the pen made noise, Emily crept slowly along the current aisle heading left and attempting to be silent.

The shadowy figure passed by the far end of the aisle, and she was off running like she was discharged from a cannon. At full speed Emily rounded the end cabinet of the aisle and ran onto the left side aisleway. The shadowy figure switched directions and bobbed before scurrying into another aisle. Emily had momentum on her side and carried that momentum to follow into that aisle.

The intruder was quick as they moved down the aisle, but Emily was faster. She could clearly see the trespasser and had them in her sights as she ran them down. This individual was clearly not imaginary. They had on jeans and a hooded sweatshirt with the hood pulled over their head. As Emily closed within about a couple of yards of the elusive intruder, they jumped. They jumped unbelievably up and over the row of computer rack cabinets to the right. Detective Oftenmarch reached with an outstretched arm to narrowly miss grabbing the leaper. Amazed and annoyed, Emily rushed to the center aisleway and one aisle to the right.

When Emily reached the adjacent aisle, the intruder had vanished. "I am with the Cathedral Police. I know you're in here now. Come out with your hands up. This is your chance to be leniently arrested for break-ing and entering." Emily called out as she unholstered her Phasepulser IX. Her declaration was met with silence or as silent as all the running datacenter fans would allow. The detective crept softly first up and then started back down the center aisleway. She kept her eyes scanning for movement and her head on a swivel.

As Emily moved down the center aisleway, detecting nothing, her notion for the need of assistance was growing. This datacenter sneak was probably going to require teamwork to trap and arrest. The detec-tive had just about made it back to her hurled pen when she spotted movement again. Leaping from a row of cabinets to a center power converter, the elusive intruder had taken to a higher elevation for their evasion. The evader was about mid-datacenter and had the option to move in all directions, an emphasis on in all directions.

Emily paused her creeping and held her spot. Trying not to look in the intruder's direction, the detective was keeping a sly watch on them. Momentarily waiting atop the power unit, the shadowy figure remained cautious. They remained motionless for awhile. Satisfied they were undetected, the evader leapt from their current position.

Emily rapidly rotated and suddenly shot two successive stunner streams from her Phasepulser. Both shots struck the intruder in mid-air. Twice stunned, the leaper was still able to nimbly land on a computer rack cabinet. Once on the cabinet, the shadowy figure began their retreat. They attempted to clamber forward onto the roof of a storage array. After firing, Emily sprinted towards the intruder. As the evader began to maneuver, Emily fired a third stunner steam in their direction.

In order to dodge the new incoming stream, the intruder dropped from the cabinet roof and disappeared behind a row of cabinets. An electronic computer room was not an ideal place for a rogue stunning stream. The stream struck high up on the far computer center wall. The datacenter doors opened at the far end of the room, where Eddie and a security guard stood in the entranceway.

"What in the world are you doing?" screamed the security guard.

"Shut the door. We have an intruder trapped." Emily loudly ordered as she raced for the aisle where the evader had descended.

"The sensors have only shown you in this room, detective." the security guard hollered as Lt. Knighton closed the datacenter doors.

"Someone has defeated your sensors. And they are crafty." Emily called back over the fan noise while looking at an empty aisle where the intruder would have dropped.

"What you are suggesting, detective, is not possible. Our sensors cannot be outwitted no matter how clever a gatecrasher may be." the security guard disagreed as he walked towards Emily.

Emily did not reply as she began renewing her silent search for the intruder. Adjusting the power level on her Phasepulser IX, Emily moved to the next aisle. Between the ambient noise and the shouting guard, the datacenter creeper was able to reposition without producing any audio clues. There was nothing for Emily to find in the next aisle. Coming to stand next to the detective, the security guard spread his arms in a what are you looking for gesture. Ignoring him, Detective Oftenmarch reversed course and slowly started back down the center aisleway with her Phasepulser IX at the ready. Row after row of running equipment Emily passed by without a sign or sighting of the elusive trespasser. By keeping her movements slow and steady, the detective also kept her movements stealthy. Before reaching the last aisle in the datacenter, Emily spotted the shadowy figure again. It appeared momentarily in the fringes of her shoulder torchlight in the opposite direction from where she had expected. Somehow the intruder had been able to slip behind her and move to the opposite side of the datacenter.

Turning off her shoulder light, Emily radically changed her position and speed. She jogged up the center aisleway and positioned herself in the left center area of the center aisleway. Quietly taking out her hand-held flashlight, the detective turned it on facing the ground. Pointing it to the right, Emily rolled the flashlight down the center aisleway like a bowling ball. As the light twirled down the center aisleway illuminating the aisles to the right, Emily kept her gaze leftward searching for movement. Shrouded movement caught her attention at the far left end of the aisle where she was positioned currently.

"Far left side heading for the doors." Emily bellowed as she bolted up the center aisleway in the same direction, doorward. Passing her first aisle, she saw the figure again. On her way by the second aisle, it could be seen again. At the third aisle, it was gone again. Emily came to a sudden stop and turned back on her shoulder light. Aiming the light at the top of the row of cabinets she had just passed, the detective scanned systematically along the roofline of the row. She was on the lookout for the higher altitude line of escape. About eight cabinets into her sweeping search, Emily put her light directly on the intruder.

"I see them, Emily." Eddie called from his door guarding spot.

The evasive sneaker tried to reverse course to get out of Emily's torchlight but the detective anticipated this move. She kept her light focused on the tricky trespasser. Soon, Lt. Knighton had his torchlight on the uninvited datacenter guest. The intruder was lit up like a stage performer dancing on top of computer equipment cabinets.

Emily fired her Phasepulser and before the runner could get to the end of the row they were forced to dodge the stream. Their dodge caused them to vacate the rooftops of the row. Expecting the intruder to come to ground level, Emily had already moved back one aisle and was in a full sprint across the aisle as the sneaker dropped to the floor. Emily fired her Phasepulser again, this time straight down the aisle to greet the fallen floor lander. This stunner stream struck the intruder squarely in the back.

Unfazed by another stun, the evader instantly fled. They moved for the end of the aisle. Fortunately, Emily was at top speed as she surged across the aisle. The detective was yards from the dodger when they reached the end of the aisle. The determined intruder turned right to head down the left side aisleway but Emily performed the turn sharper and quicker. With the detective closing in, the elusive evader attempted to jump again. Only this time, Emily was ready for this move. Instead of reaching out, the detective lunged upward and caught the leaping leaver by the foot.

Their footwear felt like metal and looked like a roller skate as Emily grabbed it. Pulling downward with all her strength, she prevented a successful jump. The fleeing trespasser came far short of the cabinet rooftops to instead come crashing to the floor with more of a clunk than a thud. The twice fallen intruder immediately tried to get to their feet.

186

Acting faster, Emily tackled the intruder back to the datacenter raised floor. They felt like a rock as Emily applied the takedown.

Once on the ground, the intruder attempted to pull free from the detective. Emily held tight, preventing the escape. The security guard had arrived as she clung to the resistant trespasser. Jumping on top of the intruder, the security guard tried to pin them to the ground. The two of them started to grapple. As they struggled, Emily reached for her handcuffs. She heard what sounded like the whirring of gear noises coming from the uninvited guest.

The more the wrestling continued the more the security guard was losing the match. The intruder had tussled to the top position and the security guard was losing hold. Reacting quickly, Emily cuffed the trespasser's right wrist with difficulty in the darkness. Once cuffed, the intruder stopped wrestling and tried to run again. Still holding the other end of the handcuffs, the detective yanked downward, pulling the stumbling intruder back on top of the security guard. Letting out a grunt of pain, the security guard ceased grappling with the perp.

Still half cuffed, the intruder tried to regain their feet again. Unable to move the intruder's arm for an armlock or to get it near to their other arm, Emily had to improvise. She moved the guard's arm instead and fastened the other cuff onto his wrist. With the intruder left struggling and cuffed to the guard, Emily stood up. Once on her feet, Emily put her boot to the side of the intruder's hooded face and pressed them force- fully to the floor. Their head smacked against the ground. With their head pinned under her foot and their one hand cuffed to the security guard, the intruder started making an odd electronic beeping noise. Suddenly, they became motionless.

Eddie was now standing next to Emily with his Phasepulser IX drawn. He looked down at the trespasser and asked, "Had enough yet?" The intruder did not answer, they just stayed motionless.

"I don't think our mysterious guest is human, Eddie." Emily specu- lated keeping her foot pressure applied.

The security guard began to struggle to a kneeling position. Eddie gave the laboring man some help. With her phasepulser aimed point blank at the intruder, Emily removed her foot. With both Eddie and Emily having their shoulder lights spotlighting the prone evader, they remained still.

The security guard reached over with his free hand and pulled down the trespasser's hood. It was a robot and its main facial display had lights spinning like a slot machine in mid-play. It had a barcode scanner for eyes and the scanner was flashing red at a fast rate. The phrase fatal error was scrolling in red on a smaller subfacial display.

"It's the maintenance droid for the datacenter." exclaimed the security guard.

"You dress your maintenance droid up like a college frat boy?" Emily inquired quizzically.

"No, it is dressed in a baggy maintenance coveralls with the company logo." the guard answered.

"Can't have naked droids now." Eddie jested.

"The real intruder must have switched clothes with the maintenance droid." Emily speculated again.

"Left looking like an employee." Eddie agreed.

"Does your maintenance droid usually play hide and seek or leap-frog?" Emily wondered still aiming her stunner.

"No, it's typically extremely docile. Goes about its work and stays in plain sight. Someone must have tampered with it." the security guard disclosed.

"Was maintenance scheduled for today?" Lt. Knighton asked seriously.

"Yes, Sunday night to Monday morning is always a weekly maintenance window. The droid keeps a timely schedule." the security guard responded, still kneeling over the robot.

"So somebody tripped an alarm, activating your security protocols and then swapped outfits with your now crosswired service droid." Emily recapped.

"That appears to be the case, detective." the guard admitted.

"There is not any property theft, but would you be able to determine if any data was stolen?" Emily reasonably wondered.

"If the intruder attempted to access any equipment, then there would be a time-stamped log of their activity on that equipment." the security guard explained.

"And what data was accessed?" Eddie questioned.

"That is above my pay grade. I don't know that." the guard replied.

"Being a company that records and stores security footage, you should have security footage which recorded and saved all the intruder's movements here today. We should have video showing what they did and what they touched." Emily optimistically reasoned.

"We don't have any datacenter security cameras. We only have perimeter security cameras." the security guard revealed.

"You are kidding." Lt. Knighton stated in disbelief.

"Ok. Please notify the personnel who can determine what equipment was accessed, what data was accessed, and if any security data was copied, taken, and/or erased. The sooner we know this information, the better it would be for all of us. In the meantime, we are detaining your trick or treat droid and especially taking his new wardrobe into evidence. Any questions or concerns, sir?" Detective Oftenmarch instructed.

"I thought you were a crazy hot chic, but now I see you're not crazy at all." the security guard gave his opinion.

"Please get to work." Lt. Knighton expressed as he unlocked the handcuff on the guard, then helped the man to his feet.

"I am on it, detectives." the security guard assured as he scurried away.

"Who gets the honor of stripping off the maintenance droid?" Emily inquired.

"That's your buddy." Eddie indicated as he pointed to the prone droid, then handed her the uncuffed end of her handcuffs.

"Did you notice the droid did not get to wear a wolf mask?" Emily rhetorically asked as she began disrobing the robot.

"It's not a killer." Eddie stated as he started his trek out of the datacenter.

Emily was left by herself with the task of undressing the malfunctioning droid. Emily removed her complink and took several pictures of the maintenance droid. Setting her Phasepulser IX to its robotic restraining mode, the detective engaged the stunner's restraining port and magnetically attached the phasepulser to the prone droid. Having secured the robot, Emily walked back to the datacenter entrance to retrieve her field kit. With the field kit in hand, she returned to the restrained droid, then sanitized and sealed her hands so she could begin disrobing the droid. Removing clothing from a droid in the dark was a creepy and odd job. After removing the Chatham State University sweatshirt, Emily left her handcuff attached. She removed the faded bootleg cut jeans and fastened the other end of the cuffs to a metallic section of the robot's mechanical thigh just in case. With the droid undressed and partially double restrained, Emily folded the clothes neatly. The detective bagged and labeled both articles of clothing into separate evidence bags. Next, Emily struggled to get the heavy droid to its robotic feet. Once in a semi-standing position, Emily spun it toward the exit. Then with the removed bagged clothes in hand, the detective half led half dragged the lumpish dysfunctional droid out of the datacenter.

When she had managed with much effort to pull the maintenance droid to the datacenter door, Emily remembered her flashlight and pen were still laying on the computer room floor. Normally, the detective would send the MPAR to retrieve those items. Since the MPAR was unavailable, Emily was going to have to do it herself. Half dropping half setting the robot down, Emily sat the unit next to the door. After setting down her field kit and bagged articles of clothing, the detective went to retrieve her discharged items. She would have to hunt some for the pen but her flashlight should still be lit, leaving a beam of light to find.

Within a minute, Emily had found and recovered her pen with minimal trouble. She turned her attention toward looking for a torchlight beam. In another minute or so, Emily located the flashlight from its torchlight beacon in the dark. It had rolled all the way to the far datacenter wall. As she went to scoop up the flashlight, Emily noticed something shining or glistening in the torchlight. Putting her shoulder secured light in the direction of the object, the detective now saw two tiny objects reflecting in the light. With her hands still sealed, Emily picked up both small shining objects. They appeared to be some type of miniature metal cased electronic devices. Emily held the devices in her shoulder light beam to examine them closer. Not entirely sure what they could be, the detective held on to them so she could place them into an evidence bag. Picking up her flashlight, Emily made the dark datacenter walk back across the room.

Having traveled the center aisleway several times that morning, Emily could have navigated it in dark, but did not have to do so. The emergency protocols for the building disengaged and the datacenter lights came on after detecting her movement. Now that she was almost done in the datacenter, the building lights returned to normal. Back at the datacenter door, Emily proficiently placed the tiny electronic devices into an evidence bag. Once bagging and labeling was complete, she picked up her field kit and fought to pull the droid back up onto its robotic feet. With the cumbersome computerized robot literally in tow, Emily left the now well lit datacenter.

As Detective Oftenmarch hauled the droid through the doorway and entered the hallway, she saw Lt. Knighton speaking with an employee of Superior Private Eyes Surveillance she had not met yet. The man was watching her drag the maintenance droid into the hallway with much interest.

"It looks as though the robot's positronics were crossed with its negatronics. The unit may have to be entirely reprogrammed." the interested Superior Private Eyes Surveillance employee assessed.

"I would be happy if it would just walk on its own again." Emily admitted.

"Thaddeus Marketseller, night operations center manager here at Superior P.I.s." the employee introduced himself.

"Detective Emily Oftenmarch, nice to meet you." the detective returned in greeting.

"When will you know?" Lt. Knighton asked Thaddeus as he continued their discussion.

"It will take some time to figure out if any information was accessed and if so, what information was accessed. We will have to recover our systems, then access our security firewalls and user access timestamps, and then we will have to search for unauthorized entries. My best guess is that we should have answers by the end of the day." Thaddeus postulated.

"Please inform us upon discovery." Lt. Knighton requested.

"Absolutely, we pride ourselves in having an excellent reputation with the police and would be happy to share any information which helps the police and protects our clients." the manager gave the pro-corporation response.

"Any objection if we take your redressed robot to our police facilities as evidence?" Emily added her own request.

"Absolutely none, anything to help the police. I will let the front security desk know you will be taking the unit." Thaddeus pleasantly complied.

"Can I use your restroom?" the lieutenant asked.

"Sure, it's the third door on the left down this hall. Now if you would please excuse me, I have to get back to work. We have a lot of recovery work to get done." Thaddeus pleasantly directed then departed.

Eddie rubbed the back of his neck in annoyance; he did this when something was bothering him. The lieutenant turned to look at Emily with the damaged droid. "That's still your friend." he told Emily.

Without another word, the lieutenant walked away and down the hall toward the previously indicated restroom. This left Detective Oftenmarch alone with the uncooperative carcass of a robot to haul on her own. After letting out a sigh, the detective resumed her tussle with towing the damaged robot along with her. Who needed Pilates exercise when you could get your workout by hauling a dead droid around.

Emily lugged the lumpish lifeless robot to the exit. Next she dragged it into the lobby after struggling with the door. The security guard working the front desk briefly looked at her as she entered the lobby, then went back to looking at something at his desk, showing no interest in helping the detective.

"Who's your date, detective?" a Cathedral patrolman at the front door asked.

"Not the best dance partner I have ever had." Emily admitted. "Could you help me with this heavy heap of a droid?"

"Is the robot under arrest?" the officer sarcastically asked as he approached to assist the robot toting detective.

"This robot was violated and is being taken in as evidence." Emily explained.

With the help of the patrolman, Emily got the droid out the front door and into the calm Cathedral city street. The early morning air was still chilly as there was a lack of temperature in the pre-sunlight hours. Swirling winds amidst the city buildings added to the morning bitterness. Detective Oftenmarch took in several breaths of cool air as she carried the bulky droid to the police vehicles with the help of one of the junior Cathedral police officers who was ordered to take over droid carrying duties. On the bright side, the arduous task of manual droid transporting at least would not be in hot weather.

Since Eddie had brought the city police SUV, Emily decided that would be the preferrable vehicle to transport the malfunctioned droid rather than her car. Opting for the PSUV's backseat, she further decided that Lt. Knighton could chauffer the cumbersome droid through the city of Cathedral. The offline robot's lack of verbal communication would make it a good riding companion for the lieutenant and Eddie could enjoy his customary silence.

As Emily loaded the droid into the PSUV, she had the feeling that this was going to be a very long day. After thanking the officer for his assistance, Detective Oftenmarch loaded her detective field kit into her trunk. As soon as Eddie exited Superior Private Eyes Surveillance, he was eager to get going and asked Emily to follow him to their next stop.

Chapter 10

The Warehouse Surprise

Eddie had updated Emily that he had been working with the Cathedral police traffic division over the weekend. With the help of members of that division, Eddie had the traffic camera archive footage reviewed from Friday morning. Having the bottling plant security footage of the truck in the loading dock gave them a vague starting point. The light traffic leaving Cathedral and entering New Terranceville on the recordings for Friday morning allowed them to find two possible trucks.

In exchange for tickets to a jazz festival, Lt. Knighton persuaded a traffic monitor watch warden on the graveyard shift to review footage from other area cameras to attempt to retrace the trucks' routes. The first truck was quickly and successfully traced back to a gas station on the border of Cathedral. That truck was recorded from an intersection video camera as it sat for hours in a gas station parking lot. First, it was broken down waiting for repairs for almost an hour. Then a mobile mechanic arrived to work on the truck for over an hour. Thinking for megawolves to sit in a truck unnoticed or unheard for hours to be unlikely, Eddie eliminated this truck.

The second truck took longer to find on video and was significantly harder to trace. After hours of difficult work and inspecting dozens of cameras' video footage, the video reviewer in the traffic division was able to track the second truck back to a warehouse facility on the western border of Cathedral. According to Eddie, the facility was sizeable and moderately secluded. Both aspects made the warehouse facility advantageous for concealing megawolves. Therefore, the lieutenant had this facility scheduled as their next stop. Lt. Knighton had already issued an all-points bulletin for that truck earlier in the morning.

Detective Oftenmarch followed Lt. Knighton, who was driving the PSUV, in the opposite direction of the growing inbound city traffic along the Transcathedral Highway. The apprehended slash confiscated maintenance droid rode in the back of the PSUV. After passing the Silversteeples skyline, Eddie led the way onto the Grand Cathedral Junction. Overnight construction on the well-used junction had finished for the pending rush hour, so they had minimal delays on this section of their journey. They passed through the south campus region of Baroque Cathedral University. Then they passed what once was the old Arden shopping plaza which previously had become St. Silas Mercy Hospital and had now become the Albatross Global Shipping and Distribution Center. One exit before Commerce Falls Shopping Village, they took the right option at the fork in the Grand Cathedral Junction to enter the Cathedral Outerbelt Highway. More congested than the Grand Cathedral Junction, the outerbelt took them longer to travel. Fortunately, they only needed to drive approximately four miles on the Cathedral Outerbelt Highway. Lights from the Bettermans super silicon manufacturing plant could be seen from the highway. Taking the Lincolnshire exit, Eddie turned onto Truckers Run Road and headed for the warehouse district. Several lengthy traffic lights later, they had reached their destination, Conglomerate Warehouses.

Eddie and Emily both pulled into the small visitors' parking lot and entered the economical makeshift security trailer stationed next to the front gates. The trailer was in need of repairs and could have used a coat of paint. Looking exhausted and overtired, the night security guard was struggling to assist them. Probably in the final hour of his shift, the guard was more prepared for going home to bed than aiding the police. He sluggishly labored to contact someone who could help them. Both his supervisor and shift manager were not onsite and unreachable by phone. The assistant supervisor was on vacation and the dayshift manager would not arrive for over two hours. Eventually the assistant shift manager and acting assistant supervisor came to the security trailer to assist them.

Thick spectacled, sweater over her uniform, pen behind her ear, and with two electronic tablets in hand, the assistant shift manager looked more like a clerk than a security guard. The kind lady was fully cooperative and eager to help Eddie and Emily. She informed them that their security procedures only logged incoming vehicles and not outgoing vehicles. As part of their security measures, they did have security cameras at the gates and throughout the grounds. Those cameras focused more on entry points and main access roads than individual warehouses. It was up to the warehouse renters to install any additional security cameras for the purpose of monitoring individual warehouses. With that said, the assistant shift manager escorted them to the security command center, where the security monitors and logs where located, to review the video archives for last Thursday night to Friday morning.

Outside the buildings, the warehouse grounds were unimpressive and ordinary. Gravel driveways, modular maintenance buildings, and basic unornate warehouses were present. The warehouse facility seemed low tech and rudimentary around the property and on the outside of the central building. Inside the central building however, the facility was impressive and high tech. Full of computer stations, maintenance droids, brand new vending mechchef machines, and digital checkpoint stations. When the assistant manager escorted them into the central security command center, their surroundings increased in technology and sophistication. With two walls of television monitors, a half dozen control stations, a holographic status and traffic display, and a digital security sentry, the central security command center was extremely impressive and extraordinary.

The security watch crew was less impressive than their command center surroundings. Two of the three security officers looked half asleep while the third member actually was asleep, snoring at his station. Having visitors arrive in the security command center did not perk up the patrol personnel to peak performance. Instead their sluggishness was coupled with frustration and annoyance by getting an arduous complex task at the end of a long night shift.

The assistant shift manager worked with Lt. Knighton while one of the still cognizant security officers worked with Detective Oftenmarch. After the acting shift manager had loaded up security footage from the Thursday night to Friday morning time frame, they each worked in pairs at a single control station. Each control station brought video images onto ten monitors for each team to watch. Emily focused on the displays showing video recordings closest to the main front gate.

Attempting to watch all ten screens at once was insurmountable and unproductive. Running the backlogged video footage at fifteen times speed, each team was reviewing an hour's worth of recording in four minutes. Approximately twelve tedious minutes into the process, Eddie and the assistant manager found footage of the truck they were searching to find.

While Eddie played the video backwards to trace the suspicious truck from the front exit back through the warehouse grounds, the assistant manager looked in the security records to find which company and warehouse the vehicle had been registered. With Emily's help as she had switched control stations, Lt. Knighton traced the truck back to section D-5 in the facility. There they lost any video footprint of the vehicle. Reviewing the logs, the assistant manager discovered the truck had been cleared to enter the facility on Wednesday and was headed to a warehouse being rented by the company Lawtech.

Unfortunately, Lawtech rented twelve warehouses from Conglomerate and eight of those warehouses were in section D-5. They had narrowed their search down to eight possible warehouses, none of which they had a warrant to search. Just as it seemed like the detectives had hit a dead end, a thought occurred to Emily. A recollection from her conversation with Cathedral police officer Dirk Gray at the Grand Maple Valley Park on Saturday. He had told her about a murdered retired police officer working security at this warehouse facility.

"There was a homicide at this facility last Wednesday. Someone murdered a security guard within the grounds of this company. Is that correct?" Emily looked for confirmation.

"Security Officer Kenneth Brahmson was slain on his patrol rounds during the day shift on Wednesday." the security officer who had teamed with Emily confirmed.

The assistant shift manager seemed visibly upset. She answered in a shaky voice "Kenneth was one of our best security officers."

"Was he murdered in section D-5?" Emily continued questioning.

"Yes, I believe so." answered the other awake security guard.

"In or around which warehouse?" Eddie asked.

"Warehouse D505. It has been closed since Wednesday." Emily's former video review partner answered.

"He was killed just inside warehouse D505." the assistant manager replied on the verge of tears.

"Who are the detectives from the Cathedral PD working his homicide?" Emily wondered.

"Just one, Detective Jebson something." the assistant manager spoke in a highly quaky voice, then began to weep.

"Jebson Bunkle." Lt. Knighton interjected.

Both Eddie and Emily pulled out their police tableaus and began searching for the Brahmson case file in the Cathedral Police database. While she was searching, Emily asked another question. "Did Detective Bunkle search warehouse D505?" she inquired.

Now awake, the third guard answered groggily, "Day shift said the detective was kinda lazy. Just wanted the video."

"Conglomerate doesn't place security surveillance in that sector. Lawtech has their own cameras in and around their warehouses." the second guard answered.

"He said it was a Lawtech problem, not his problem." the assistant manager choked back tears to respond.

"Any objections to us searching?" Lt. Knighton posed.

"No, sir. Cathedral homicide has the full cooperation of Conglomerate Warehouses and its renters." Emily's previous video review partner responded.

Emily turned to the sad assistant manager and stated, "We don't see this as a problem. We see it as a search for justice. Please lead the way to warehouse D505."

"Lawtech has a security tech who works night patrol for the company. He oversees and monitors their night security droids. We will give him a call to let him know you are heading to warehouse D505." the non-napping and non-assisting guard explained.

"I can take them to warehouse D505, Cathy." the now fully awake security officer offered.

"No, that's alright. I can take them. I want to take them." the assistant manager replied with a sniffle.

"You are an unusual pair of Cathedral police officers. You are going to search a crime scene in a spooky Lawtech warehouse where none of your co-workers could be bothered to visit." the guard who had partnered with Emily commented.

"Unusual is one description." Eddie responded.

"Please call Lawtech's tech. I am taking them out there now." Cathy informed her crew. With that said she led the way out of the security command center. Lt. Knighton silently followed her.

"Thank you for your help." Emily thanked the guards then followed Eddie's exit.

Reversing their route into the central building, they were back outside in minutes. Emily was glad she remembered to bring her field kit as they strolled onto the main access drive. Their walk along the gravel drive towards section D-5 was a quiet trek. Eddie was his usually silent self and even though Emily tried to converse and console assistant shift manager Cathy, she was uncommunicative as well. The woman was clearly upset over the loss of a co-worker. As they walked, the early morning fog was fading away. Light was sneaking into the sky like a prelude to morning daylight. There was still little activity in the warehouse complex at this hour on a Monday morning. Detective Oftenmarch only observed one warehouse building with an open door and glowing indoor lights. To Emily, the wordless walk seemed to last longer than it actually took. Lt. Knighton was diligently reading his police tableau display as they hiked. Before arriving in section D-5, they had to pass by a patrolling sentry robot. The machine beeped and flashed as it scanned assistant manager Cathy's employee badge. The droid displayed a green light, then continued on its programmed patrol path.

Section D-5 was slightly downhill from the main path they had been walking. Assistant manager Cathy had taken them left onto a side gravel drive, which consisted of more gravel than the main drive. About thirty yards of walking the side path revealed a shadowy figure of a man standing next to two flashing droids about five hundred feet ahead. With each step closer to the droid flanked figure, the man became more clearly visible and less shadowy.

When they were in range of hearing him, the short robot companioned man called out to the assistant shift manager. "This is a terrible time to come inspect a warehouse, Cathy. Not only is it ridiculously early in the morning and the last hour of the night shift, the incident in question happened five days ago." he bellowed.

"There is never a good time for murder." Emily called back.

"Lawtech Police investigated the homicide and believe the security guard encountered warehouse trespassers. They are pursuing accordingly without Cathedral police assistance." the little man declared.

"Bad news. Those trespassers took a vehicle from this warehouse section and traveled to New Terranceville to murder two more people." Detective Oftenmarch counter-declared.

"Same deep stab wound MO." Lt. Knighton stated as he pointed at his police tableau. They were now close enough to the man and his droids to speak at a normal volume.

"Did you call them, Cathy? I know Kenneth and you were good friends but involving the Cathedral homicide again was not necessary." the small man indicated.

"I did not call them, Hermannie. They came here on their own accord." assistant manager Cathy responded quietly.

"Has Lawtech solved the homicide and do they have the perpetrators in custody?" Emily questioned the Lawtech employee.

"Well, no, but I'm pretty sure they soon will." he replied.

"Appears we are necessary." Eddie sternly stated as he held up his police badge for one of the droids to scan.

"We did not come as an insult to Lawtech. We came because there is a group of wolf masked killers which are seriously out of control." Emily appeased as she held up her police badge for the other droid to scan.

"I am not going to stop you, Cathy. They are your responsibility when you take them into that warehouse. Be aware, that when Lawtech warehouse security director Quincy and Lawtech Detective Varper find out about this visit, they will both be absolutely furious." the Lawtech employee indicated.

"We will be sure to pass their concerns on to the Brahmson family." Emily replied as the droid cleared her credentials with a chime and a green light.

"What she said." Eddie supported as the other droid cleared his credentials with a chime and a green light.

The droid accompanied Lawtech employee who Cathy had called Hermannie wordlessly turned away from them and departed their company. As he went, he stomped with his every footstep to let his displeased disapproval be known to them. While, the short man marched away in a huff with his security droids in tow, Cathy spoke softly again.

"Thank you for doing this. Warehouse D505 is on this upcoming lane to the right. It will be the second warehouse on the right side of the lane." Cathy quietly expressed.

"No need to thank us, Cathy. You are helping us. All of us, except for maybe Mister Lawtech loyalist, want to catch the wolf masquerade killers who murdered Kenneth Brahmson." Emily reasoned calmly.

"Is that Lawtech's security camera?" Eddie inquired pointing to a camera on the side of a warehouse at the corner of the upcoming intersection.

Cathy nodded in the affirmative before Lt. Knighton took out his complink. After aiming his complink in the direction of the wall-mounted security camera, Eddie began feverishly working on his complink as they walked. Another Lawtech sentry droid rolled past them heading in the opposite direction. This one went about its electronically run patrol without stopping to scan them.

As Emily watched the patrolling robot move along, she had another thought occur to her. "It is curious that trespassers could get past so many Lawtech robotic sentries without being detected." she commented aloud.

Making the turn at the intersection, Eddie was still working on his complink and Emily observed another robot sentry two warehouses away from them. The new driveway they entered was composed of more dirt or mud than gravel. Sections of it were well worn with tire treed tracks. Emily could see their destination now; the identifying D505 could be seen on the warehouse and a marquee at the far warehouse entrance also had a visible D505 printed on it.

"Eddie, there is another Lawtech security camera on warehouse D505." Emily observed.

"Roger that." Eddie returned, then turned his complink and attention onto that camera.

Some of the warehouses had more external lighting than others. Conglomerate warehouses seemed to provide a single uniform bright light over every warehouse garage door. Security and path lighting appeared to be renter provided and varied from warehouse to warehouse. Lawtech warehouses had more security light than any of the other warehouses they had encountered on this walk. Emily observed yet another robotic sentry in the surrounding area. This section of the facility would not be the choice of a random trespasser. Any intruder who came to Lawtech's area of this facility would have done so deliberately with an intended task. Next, Emily spotted motion sensors around each Lawtech lit warehouse in the area. As she walked, Detective Oftenmarch took out her complink and took several pictures of the surrounding area and warehouses.

"Are you forming the same suspicions that I am, Eddie?" Emily wondered.

"Formed and cured." Eddie replied, still busy on his complink which was still aimed at the warehouse security camera.

Observing yet another robotic sentry in the nearby area, Emily took a picture of it. "I seriously doubt anyone snuck into this warehouse without Lawtech knowing about it." Emily stated confidently.

Uneventfully, they reached the first entrance of warehouse D505. As Eddie continued to work with his complink on the cameras and Emily took a few more photos of the perimeter, the assistant shift manager unlocked the warehouse door. Once the door was unlocked, assistant manager Cathy led the way into the warehouse. Detective Oftenmarch followed her into the building as Lt. Knighton held back, still working on his complink.

Cathy turned on the warehouse's overhead lights to illuminate the vast building. The warehouse was a massive open space internally. There was a dividing partition being used that split the space in half. The side of the warehouse space Emily could see appeared cavernous and mostly empty. One modest sized delivery truck, a pair of crates, a rusty pallet jack, a stack of cardboard boxes, a stack of old splintered pallets, and some scattered rubbish on the floor was all that was in this half of the large warehouse. Cathy pointed to an open area near the door they had entered. This section of the warehouse looked cleaner and was less dusty than the rest of the warehouse. It was also litter free, which was in contrast to the rest of the space.

"This is where security officer Brahmson was killed. They took the crime scene tape away and cleaned his blood off the floor." Cathy meekly divulged, appearing to become emotional again.

Emily took a picture of the open pristine space and then took a couple of pictures of its surrounding warehouse grungy space. The difference was so stark it was ridiculous. Looking up, the detective spotted an inside security camera mounted along the wall facing away from the door. It was the only one but its current position had it aimed fortuitously in the direction of the cleansed area. Switching from the camera application to the uplink application on her complink, Emily used her complink to attempt to connect to the security camera. Access denied, encryption key required was the message that quickly came up on her display. Emily entered the Cathedral PD's default override encryption key passcode and that came back invalid, access still denied. Now Emily knew what Eddie was dealing with on his complink. Trying the police default override code again, in case she misspelled or mistyped something in it, Emily still had no luck.

Pausing for a moment to think, Emily searched her memory to recall another work around solution. She had a flashback to when she was a rookie police officer and a pair of security tech consultants were trying to impress her to get a date. Every security camera company programmed a master code for their products in the last ten years, they had told her. Then they rattled off a list of those codes, which were mostly science fiction based. Remembering the code they showed her as an example, Emily entered a nerdy word followed by the number 69 and then the pound sign, #, into her complink. Access granted! The detective immediately started wirelessly downloading video footage feeling triumphant. However, the victory was short lived as she discovered the archived footage only went back approximately thirty hours to around midnight Sunday morning.

"Cleaned the crime scene and wiped the security footage. Obstruction of justice charges are in Lawtech's near future." Emily surmised aloud.

Lt. Knighton walked into the warehouse through the now unlocked door. As he surveyed the warehouse space for the first time, anger appeared on his face, which was extremely rare.

"Absurd nonsense." Lt. Knighton interjected loudly. His two word statement echoed in the wide-open warehouse.

"Security video only goes back to early Sunday morning which is consistent with their nonsense." Emily informed Eddie. She turned to assistant manager Cathy to speak. "Cathy, we are thinking this whole warehouse is a crime scene. We think we had better search it all." Emily declared as she pulled out byglex latex gloves from her field kit and began to seal up her hands. Lt. Knighton likewise had taken a sealed package of byglex latex gloves from his pocket and was beginning the same process.

Determination forged in Emily and the detective began to studiously search the warehouse floor. Starting along the wall nearest them, Emily swept down the entire length of the warehouse, then began a return trip about six feet from the wall. As Emily carefully surveyed the warehouse floor, Eddie went over to the pallet jack and prepared to violently ram it into both crates in an attempt to make puncture holes in each of them. Then he thought better and abandoned that plan, pushed the pallet jack aside, and went over to the crates to discover they both were unfastened and opened easily. As Eddie impolitely opened the crates, Emily spotted some interesting things in the rubbish on the warehouse floor.

After taking a picture with her complink, the detective picked up two large sized syringes. As she studied them, both syringes appeared to have a liquid residue still inside them. The residue was colorless and had ample viscosity. Detective Oftenmarch bagged both syringes into evidence. As she finished bagging the syringes, Emily spotted another find. It looked like tufts of hair or fur. Brushing the strands into a pile with her hand, Emily assessed the find further. Deciding that this could be part of a megawolf's fur coat, Emily began to bag the hairlike strands into evidence.

As Emily was bagging furlike follicles, Eddie was pulling bubble wrap out of crates and then empty cardboard boxes with Chinese writing on them. He was placing the bubble wrap on one pile and the boxes in another pile. All the boxes appeared to be identical. As he stacked his piles of shipping materials, Emily continued her search of the floor. Just to the right of the first step of syringes, the detective found a third sizeable syringe. Again, Emily took a picture of the syringe as it lay on the floor before picking it up and bagging it.

"Canine growth hormones." Eddie translated as he pointed to the stack of empty boxes with Chinese writing. He had used his translation app on his police complink.

"Make sense, Eddie. I found three syringes on the floor over here and what could be wolf fur. These villains could have been injecting canine growth hormones into those megawolves right here in the warehouse." Emily reasonably speculated.

"What are megawolves?" Cathy curiously posed.

"Oversized wolves that were apparently given growth hormones. They were aggressively attacking people at a facility in New Terranceville and were delivered by the truck we traced back to this very warehouse." Emily narrated the megawolf tale.

Eddie had broken down about a half dozen empty cardboard boxes with the Chinese labels and had carried them over to Emily. "Bag these boxes please." he requested. His demeanor was more serene now that they had something to show for their early morning efforts.

As Emily bagged the cardboard boxes into evidence, Lt. Knighton walked over to the delivery truck to inspect it. He was circumnavigating the vehicle as Detective Oftenmarch returned to profoundly perusing the warehouse floor. In less than a minute, she found more animal hair and another substantial syringe. After taking another photo, Emily proceeded to the bagging process. The detective was starting to get accustomed to not having the MPAR's assistance. She had now gathered enough hair and syringes to start a collection.

As Emily added to her collection, Lt. Knighton began searching inside the cargo bed of the unlocked truck. Unlike the section of the floor Emily was searching, the floor of the cargo bed was clear and clean. The lieutenant searched and researched the space for any clues. He retraced his steps twice but still could not find anything. Eddie was not only unable to find any useful evidence, he was not able to find anything.

As Eddie was having no success within the truck, Detective Oftenmarch had discovered another two syringes to add to her growing collection. Emily progressed in her systematic search of the warehouse floor. The next areas of floor she searched had scraps of wood, metal shavings, packing peanuts, bent nails, a well used paint stirrer, scraps of cable insulation, dust bunnies, popped bubble wrap shreds, swirls of sawdust, more dust bunnies, more pesky packing peanuts, broken staples, and discarded lock washers, but nothing germane to a murder or megawolf related.

As Emily surveyed the warehouse floor, Lt. Knighton moved to the truck's unlocked cab to search. The cab was much less tidy than the cargo bed had been. Mud covered the floormats and the floor of the cab. Eddie removed seven crushed beer cans from the passenger's seat and placed them in a plastic bag he had found crumpled on the dashboard. He found a half-torn receipt for coffee and two bags of fast food rubbish and remnants. Like Emily, the lieutenant was finding nothing worthy of being considered evidence. Dropping the bag of old beer cans onto the driver's seat, Eddie decided to proceed by opening the glove compartment.

While Eddie moved his attention to the glove box, Emily had decided to halt her floor rubbish scavenger hunt and switch to something with more promise of results. What was on the other side of the dividing partition, she wondered, and quickly decided to go find that answer. Instantly switching from a slow-paced searching walk to a fast-paced purpose driven stride, Detective Oftenmarch strode over to the mandoor in the dividing partition. Without hesitation she pushed open the hinged dooresque section of the partition and walked through to the other side of the warehouse.

The bright overhead lights were illuminating the entire warehouse on both sides of the dividing partition, which meant Emily could see fine on the other side of the divider - and what a sight she saw. Row after row of neatly lined-up droids stood like soldiers at attention, filling up this entire half of the warehouse. They looked like a brigade ready to be given the forward march command. These droids were not like the robotic sentries they encountered on their walk to warehouse D505, nor were they like Cathedral PD's crime scene preservers. These droids were also not like the Superior Private Eyes Surveillance's maintenance droid. They were elegant and impressive. These droids had the look of sophisticated premium machines. Having human-formed bodies and human-like faces, these droids were made to look like robohuman police officers. A long ways from being considered cyborgs, the droids were clearly designed to be shiny alloy robotic police officers. Their face plates and chest plates were highly detailed and none of their joints, wires, or circuitry was exposed. All the droids were well shielded as well as well polished.

A banner hanging on the back wall of the warehouse read, in large artistic block letters, **Lawtech Lawbotic Patrollers**. Underneath that bold line of text was a smaller less fancy line which read MasterForce 10000 series. From the droids' pristine well finished appearance, Emily had the impression this was to be Lawtech's latest innovation in their fight against crime. This was their high technological solution to modern day lawbreaking. Emily could hear the propaganda in her head, a masterforce of tireless justice to bring peace to the law abiding citizens in this modern world.

Admiring their tall sleek forms, Emily walked along the ranks of the robots. Emily picked a row at random and began walking across the row. She inspected each patrol droid as she strolled by it. Each droid looked exactly the same as the last one to her. One by one, the detective admired each Lawbotic Patroller in the row. Every last one of them was spotless, like showroom model sports cars. When Emily reached the end of the row, she moved to the next row and started walking back across that row. Again, she took in each droid as she paced along the row of robots.

When the detective got to the fourteenth or fifteenth droid in this row, she found something she did not expect to find. Emily found something that should not have been there. This particular droid did not look like all the other droids, this particular droid had something none of the other robots neatly displayed in rows had. It was wearing a wolf mask. Not just any wolf mask, but a wolf mask identical to the style worn by the wolf masquerade killers. Emily had to rub her eyes before taking a second look to ensure she was not imagining things. Upon a second look, the wolf mask was still there.

"Eddie, can you come see? Can you come see? Can you come see, Eddie? Eddie can you come see? Won't believe this, when you come see. There's a mask on this robot. That will give you a crescendo, Eddie. They came into this big warehouse. They left the wolf mask on the robot. They gave into their boredom. They'll be struck down. It is their doom. Eddie can you come see? Can you come see? Can you come see, Eddie? Eddie, can you come see? Can you come see? Can you come see, Eddie?" Emily sang loudly as she took several pictures of the masked droid.

As Emily took her last photo of the masked robotic patroller, she saw Eddie standing next to her. He was giving her an are you through look, which he was known to give. "You found the Wehrmacht, Emily." the lieutenant jested.

"I found you a buddy, Eddie. This is your buddy." Emily replied pointing to the wolf mask adorned droid.

A rare expression of incredulity appeared on the lieutenant's face followed by an even rarer occurrence, he smiled. "No buddy. Mask only, please." Eddie decided.

"Oh no, Lawtech is not getting off that easy." Emily decided as she turned on her copcam manually. "On. Activate. Where is your on button or switch? Hello." Emily verbally worked on trying to activate the robot as she knocked on its chest armor plate. Then she looked around the back of the droid. Still not finding an activate button, Emily tried a different tactic. "Help." she told the droid.

"Officer online. Obstruction detected." the droid vocalized.

"Exactly. You have an obstruction. Who put that obstruction there?" Emily returned as she pulled the wolf mask off the robot and then held up her badge for the droid to scan.

"Obstruction removed. Is this officer to go on duty?" the robot roborequested. Its eye lights were now visible to view glowing brightly.

"Yes. Yes, you are. First task is to tell me who put the obstruction on you." Emily instructed the droid.

"Unknown. Officer online for twenty-eight seconds." synthesized the droid.

"You have been pranked by a smooth criminal and you are stating you do not know who did it. Is that correct?" Emily asked the droid.

The robot was unresponsive for a moment presumably processing her question. Then it responded with a synthesized, "Correct."

Emily looked at Eddie, who shook his head in the negative indicated he knew what his partner was thinking.

Reluctantly, Detective Oftenmarch told the droid, "Officer is now off duty."

"Should this officer go offline?" the droid roboqueried.

"Yes. Yes, you should." Emily answered, then turned off her copcam.

The bright lights representing the droid's eyes went dark and the robot returned to a statue figure. Now appearing like every other droid in the ranks, it returned to being just another Lawtech Lawbotic Patroller. Another robotic private in their mechanical army of law enforcement and self-proclaimed superiority. The detective like the droid better with the wolf mask on its robotic head.

Emily turned to Eddie and began to reconstruct the villains' tragic misbehavior, "They came to this warehouse to do work for Lawtech or on the pretense of doing work for Lawtech. They make themselves at home injecting growth hormones into wolves and putting wolf masks on droids. Then security officer Brahmson discovers something is amiss or hears something suspicious and enters the warehouse to investigate. He catches them in the act of misbehaving or they possibly were trespassing. An altercation ensues and one of them murders security officer Brahmson during the day shift on Wednesday. They could not stay here at the scene of their crime, but they did not take the truck to New Terranceville until late Thursday night. It appears they left this warehouse hastily, leaving behind syringes, boxes, and masks. Furthermore, we have established the truck containing the megawolves left from this warehouse section late Thursday night. So the question becomes: Where were they located or keeping the megawolves after the homicide until their departure time?"

"Another warehouse in section D-5." Lt. Knighton proposed.

"The warehouse next door to this one is currently vacant. It has been undergoing maintenance during its period of unoccupancy." Cathy informed them as she spoke from down the far end of an orderly aisle of pristine dormant droids. She had quietly followed them over to the Lawbotic Patroller side of the warehouse.

"Any objections to us having a look at the adjacent warehouse?" Emily inquired.

"After seeing this warehouse, I am actually personally interested, not just professionally interested, in seeing next door myself." Cathy admitted.

"Let's have a look then. Please lead the way." the lady detective requested.

After quickly bagging and tagging the remaining evidence, the pair of detectives followed Cathy to the next warehouse. The sky was much brighter as daylight had emerged, as dawn had arrived. As they walked to the adjacent warehouse, it appeared nearly identical to the one they had just exited. One notable exception both detectives noticed was that this warehouse had no external security cameras.

Another difference was the destination warehouse had a notice-ably fresh coat of exterior paint. The group of three made a quick march to the neighboring warehouse. With no cameras to attempt downloads to complinks nor Lawtech employees to interrupt them, they made great time. They swiftly arrived at the main warehouse door and Cathy efficiently worked the lock.

As soon as the door opened, a foul smell powerfully and potently struck them. A wave of stench cruelly greeted them. The nasty odor wafted towards them forewarning the unpleasantness which laid inside the warehouse. This odor permeated the area as Cathy stepped aside to allow the detectives to enter the stinky warehouse. Detective Oftenmarch steeled herself and forced herself to enter the building first. Lt. Knighton begrudgingly followed closely behind her. As Emily found the light switch, Eddie unholstered and readied his Phasepulser IX in case there were any unwanted squatters. Upon Emily flipping the light switches, the illumination from the oncoming lights revealed several things including the source of the stench. There were actually multiple sources.

The first thing they saw was a large jumble of metal that was robotesque. A cabled mess of wires and twisted metal, a robot that looked like something out of a mad scientist's lab. With exposed gears, missing parts, and wires tangled to and fro about the mechanical creature, the robot was an abomination. The best description for the machine was either a robomess or a droid monster. This monstrosity was cabled, via a snarled spaghetti-like tangle of cables, to a pair of oversized globed electrodes. Each globed electrode stood about five feet tall and had a two foot in diameter shiny metal sphere mounted on top. These bizarre mad science structures were connected to a portable power generator which looked severely charred and burnt. If the robot ever worked, which was doubtful by its appearance, then the mishap which scorched the generator certainly also disabled the droid.

Also easily noticeable and a source of the stench was a dead megawolf lying in the middle of the bare concrete floor. A pool of dried blood had formed around the deceased animal. The slain creature was surrounded by sizeable piles of feces scattered about the vast warehouse. The array of messy waste randomly placed across the warehouse floor was clearly created by confined oversized megawolves. Between the forest of fecal matter and the deceased and decaying megawolf, the source of the resulting stench was evident and strong in origins. The warehouse looked like it smelled and it was as awful as it actually smelled.

In the corner of the warehouse could now be seen a standup vacuum cleaner which was still plugged in to an outlet. Someone must have been vacuuming pre-megawolf defecations because clearly nothing was swept post megawolf droppings. Finally, the light revealed pieces of paper sprinkled about the floor. Some of the pieces of paper were crumpled while other pieces remained uncrumpled. All of the paper was scattered about the floor like some lazy careless litterer was working overtime.

214

As Lt. Knighton holstered his stunner and began taking pictures of the disgusting warehouse, Emily circumnavigated the landmine field of poop. The foul facility aroma gave her motivation to move quickly. As she approached the slain megawolf, Emily noticed more used syringes, more empty packages of growth hormones, and a less rumpled slip of paper. She picked up the somewhat unmangled piece of paper. It was a receipt for the Breakfast and Brew Cafe in West Cathedral. Timestamped for Tuesday night, the order was for a substantial amount of food.

"Think I know where our mess makers got dinner on Tuesday night. They left a receipt behind for Breakfast and Brew in West Cathedral." Emily revealed.

"This is beyond a mess." the lieutenant commented with a frown. He was carefully moving through the organic mine field towards the robomess, or droid monster.

After placing the receipt into an evidence bag, Detective Oftenmarch turned her attention to the dead creature. Still remaining cautious in the fecal minefield, Emily travelled over to the slain megawolf. Doing her best to avoid standing in the pool of dried blood, she studied the wounds on the deceased animal and to her they looked quite similar to the wounds on the victims at the bottling plant. There seemed to be stab wounds inside of claw-made gashes. As Emily examined the slain megawolf, Lt. Knighton took photos of the robomess and its tangled and disorganized mass of cables running to the science fiction looking electospheres. The lieutenant made a complete circle around the droid monster as he photographed it. Eddie hesitated between pictures as he attempted to decipher what he was seeing and deciding how to best get photographs of the oddity.

"Paging Dr. Frankenstein." Eddie commented.

"Can you make any sense out of that experiment?" Detective Oftenmarch wondered.

"No." the lieutenant answered flatly and honestly.

"These intruders could not have left a more disgusting mess if they tried." Emily commented as she surveyed the waste filled warehouse.

"Call an EVAC team, please." Eddie requested as he had clearly had enough of the stinky warehouse.

Evidence validation and collection teams were used by the Cathedral Police Department for extensive or important crime scenes. They were referenced by the EVAC acronym by half of the Cathedral police. The other half referred to them as vacuumers or sweeper squads.

"Should we request a standard team or a maximum supersized crew for this feces filled fiasco?" Emily wondered.

"Take the lot." Lt. Knighton decided.

"Requesting a full deluxe EVAC squad to come as soon as possible." Emily confirmed.

"Not the poop." Eddie added.

"Collect the trash, take the robotic whatever, get the dead megawolf, and leave the poop." Emily summarized the pending request.

"This is awful, completely awful." Cathy cried as she held her hands on the sides of her face. The woman looked as if she was overwhelmed with disbelief.

"I agree. There is no acceptable excuse for creating a mess of this extent. This is ridiculous, completely ridiculous." Detective Oftenmarch agreed.

"This whole world has become cruel and nasty. Nice people like Kenneth are killed by monsters who leave behind monsters, death, and poop. The awfulness of this wicked world makes me sad and depressed. It is so horrible it makes me wonder what's the point." Cathy sadly stated with tears in her eyes.

"Kenneth was someone special to you, was he not?" asked Emily, suspecting she knew the answer.

"Yes. We were engaged to be married this coming October. I am still wearing the engagement ring." Cathy replied as the tear were now a steady flow.

"I can empathize with you, Cathy. When I lost my first husband, Abraham, I felt the same pain. I know the deep sadness that consumes, the empty lonely feeling, and the lingering depression. Then when happiness finally returns, you then begin feeling guilty for being happy." Emily shared.

"How can I live without him?" Cathy cried.

"You don't. You live in remembrance of him." Emily responded.

"All I can feel is misery. Life is so sad it still makes me wonder what's the point." Cathy restated still in tears.

"Then let us start with hope. With GOD, there is a hope. Isaiah 40:30-31 reads: *Even youths grow tired and weary, and young men stumble and fall; but those who hope in the LORD will renew their strength. They will soar on wings like eagles; they will run and not grow weary, they will walk and not be faint.* Then in 1 Peter 3-4, it reads: *Praise be to the GOD and FATHER of our LORD JESUS CHRIST! In his great mercy HE has given us new birth into a living hope through the resurrection of JESUS CHRIST from the dead and into an inheritance that can never perish, spoil or fade - kept in heaven for you.*" Emily encouraged Cathy.

"How can we hope in such a heartless world? The horrible things in this world just keep crushing down on us." Cathy commiserated.

"1 John 5:5 says: *Who is it that overcomes the world? Only he who believes that JESUS is the SON of GOD.*" Emily replied, then continued, "And then we find hope again in John 3:16-17, *For GOD so loved the world that HE gave HIS one and only SON, that whoever believes in HIM* shall not perish but have eternal life. For GOD did not send HIS SON into the world to condemn the world, but to save the world through HIM."

"He can save this world?" Cathy doubted.

"In HIS passionate love HE sacrificed to save us from ourselves. By HIS grace, the people in this world have a chance at redemption." Emily reassured.

"How can GOD love this world? How can he save this world?" Cathy sorrowfully continued to wonder.

"That is the beautiful thing about GOD's love. Romans 5:8 reads: But GOD demonstrates HIS own love for us in this: While we were still sinners, CHRIST died for us." Emily expressed. "Then there is GOD's wonderful grace and compassion upon this world. In Romans 6:23 it says: For the wages of sin is death, but the gift of GOD is eternal life in CHRIST JESUS our LORD."

"There will be eternal life?" Cathy questioned.

"There will be eternal life unlike life here on earth. Revelations 21:4 says: HE will wipe every tear from their eyes. There will be no more death or mourning or crying or pain, for the old order of things has passed away." Emily exclaimed.

"Sounds like nonsense." Cathy protested.

"Not nonsense. In 1 Corinthians 1:18: For the message of the cross is foolishness to those who are perishing, but to us who are being saved it is the power of GOD. Then 1 Corinthians 1:25: For the foolishness of GOD is wiser than man's wisdom, and the weakness of GOD is stronger than man's strength." Emily explained.

"You seem so sure, so confident. I cannot tell if you're correct or if you're crazy." Cathy puzzled.

"I may be crazy but this is not craziness, GOD's love and CHRIST's sacrifice have brought hope to this world. GOD's living hope is not only a great thing, it is the very best of great things. GOD's love is the apex of greatness." Emily proclaimed.

"So we just hold on and hope for the best?" the downtrodden Cathy wondered.

"More than just hold on, GOD's loving gift is to be shared and we are meant for more than just to endure. In Ephesians 2:8-10 it reads: *For it is by grace you have been saved, through faith-and this is not from yourselves, it is the gift of GOD-not by works, so that no one can boast. For we are GOD's workmanship, created in CHRIST JESUS to do good works, which GOD prepared in advance for us to do.*" Emily replied.

"Can there be good done in this wicked world? It seems like there is so much bad that any good that may be done is drowned out in a sea of misery. It seems like it cannot be outdone, that it is overwhelming" Cathy responded.

"In 1 John 5:4-5 it reads: *for everyone born of GOD overcomes the world. This is the victory that has overcome the world, even our faith. Who is it that overcomes the world? Only he who believes that JESUS is the SON of GOD.*" Emily shared, then continued, "JESUS has overcome this cruel world, he told us this truth himself in John 16:33. He said: *I have told you these things, so that in ME you may have peace. In this world you will have trouble. But take heart! I have overcome the world.*"

"The way you speak does give me hope." Cathy admitted as she wept.

As Cathy wiped away a tear from her cheek, Emily went over to her and gave her a hug. She gave her a long heartfelt hug. Then the detective continued to comfort the poor woman until the EVAC team arrived.

Chapter 11

The Improv Breakfast Meeting

The Breakfast and Brew Cafe was in West Cathedral, a neighboring suburb of Cathedral. West Cathedral was known for its crazy political landscape full of turmoil, corruption, and partisan dissension. The inbound city traffic was becoming increasingly congested. However, the outbound city traffic was unclogged open roads, which was good for Eddie and Emily. As they drove, the taller Cathedral buildings were replaced by the more modest West Cathedral buildings. The architecture of the buildings also shifted from the more modern designs of Cathedral to the more retro nostalgic designs of West Cathedral.

The surface roads in West Cathedral were in need of some repairs. Long periods of neglect were one reason for the shabby shape of the streets. The large amount of traffic, especially truck traffic, which travelled on West Cathedral roads every day also undoubtedly took its toll on the city's roads. Street after street which the detectives travelled were in sad shape. There was so much deterioration on Old Patterson Street that most of the street had no edge lines. Camden Street was bumpy enough to qualify as a roller coaster. North Main Street had two steel plates covering larger holes in the road and five construction barrels with warning signs covering smaller holes in the road. Polymer Parkway had about a three-mile construction zone with absolutely no construction being done. The cafe was located off of Van Buren Drive, which had dozens of poorly patched potholes just in the five hundred feet the detectives drove.

The Breakfast and Brew Cafe was located in an expansive shopping center. The restaurant's property was tidy and the building was well maintained. It looked out of place with its cleanliness being in contrast with the surrounding area.

The post-sunrise morning was warmer and more pleasant. There was no longer a chill in the air. Emily switched from her three-quarter trenchcoat to her Cathedral PD windbreaker upon exiting her car. She put some gloves and evidence bags into the windbreaker's pockets and kept her detective kit in her car.

As they headed for the entrance, the pair of detectives scanned the building and property searching for security cameras. This seemed like the sort of neighborhood that could do with more cameras.

"Eddie, we need to talk. The captain wants me to take the lieutenant's exam." Emily opened the discussion of future partnership.

"Bronzesmith's boosting you two grades." Eddie wondered.

In the Cathedral Police Department, the detective class had third grade, second grade, first grade, and then senior first grade. The next promotion for a detective was lieutenant. Most lieutenants worked years as a senior first grade detective. Emily was currently a first grade detective and a promotion to lieutenant would be a double elevation.

"The captain is trying to replace you for when you are selected for the special detective division." Emily replied.

"He's getting rid of me." Eddie countered.

"Why would the captain want to do that, Eddie?" Emily challenged.

"Optics and politics over accomplishments." the lieutenant responded.

"The captain is lucky to have you in his precinct." Oftenmarch complimented.

"Murk is getting passed over." the lieutenant remarked.

"Kenny is planning on retiring soon. His pending retirement is probably why the captain asked me." Emily reasoned.

"Murk says wrong is wrong." Eddie returned.

"I have disagreed with Bronzesmith in the past." Emily protested.

"You politely correct him." Lt. Knighton explained the difference.

"I would like for us to continue to be partners. If I go for lieutenant, then that most likely separates us. Would you like to continue to be partners?" Emily probed for Eddie's thoughts.

"GOD's will, Emily." the lieutenant quietly answered.

"But what would you like, Eddie?" Emily probed again.

"To catch these killers." the lieutenant responded.

"That's all you would like in our future partnership?" Emily examined further.

"Ecclesiastes 4:19." Eddie answered.

Detective Oftenmarch had to take out her personal complink phone to look up the Bible verse. "*Two are better than one, because they have a good return for their work.*" she read aloud. "I was hoping for a more sentimental response, Eddie." Emily admitted.

Eddie did not answer. A determined expression had returned to his face, a calculating stare kept his eyes forward. As his partner, Emily knew that the lieutenant's focus had returned to the current case and Eddie liked to address one problem at a time. So she dropped the subject for now. Wordlessly, Lt. Knighton led the way through the cafe's front door. As the detectives entered, a small old fashioned bell jingled from over the door to announce their arrival.

The cafe was a small privately owned establishment with a community based decor. There was a lot of local historical artwork and local high school sports memorabilia on the walls. The small coffee and sandwich shop had a basic breakfast menu, not as basic as take it or leave it, but still rather simplistic.

In a booth in the corner of the cafe, a group of four men were seated having a collectively somber conversation. Detective Oftenmarch recognized state internal affairs agent Bradley Stiggers, who investigated Detective Darius Cole last year, and former security agent to the previous state governor, Danny Dotson. Stiggers was almost seven feet tall and proudly spoke of his Viking ancestry. Dotson was 6 feet 5 inches tall and over 300 pounds of mostly muscle. Neither man was hard to miss. Lt. Knighton had also recognized them because he headed directly to their table.

"Two detectives and two bodyguards." Eddie opened the conversation.

"How do you know I am a detective?" asked a slovenly dressed private detective with bloodshot eyes.

"A detective recognizes a detective." Eddie enlightened.

"What do you recognize, sweet cheeks?" the private detective asked Emily.

"Conversely, chauvinism can be recognized by most people." Emily replied.

"Gamble, meet the mud tusslers. The somber one is Lt. Eddie Knighton and the smiley one is Detective Emily Oftenmarch from the 272nd Cathedral Homicide division. Both of them work too hard." agent Stiggers introduced them.

"Nice to meet you, Emily." the private detective greeted her ignoring Eddie.

"Good morning, Gamble." Emily counter greeted.

The man sitting next to Dotson asked him, "Do you know them, Donny Boy?"

"They have saved my life, twice." Dotson answered.

"I do not understand how you can still have the nickname Donny Boy. You left boyhood long ago, Don." Emily expressed.

"What can we do for you, Eddie?" agent Stiggers soberly asked.

"Pre-hack Cathedral PD statistics." Eddied quickly returned.

"Shit, I always liked you, Eddie. You get right to it." Stiggers now chuckled.

"The Cathedral Police Department is infested with corruption. It perpetrates more crime than it prevents." private eye Gamble stated without sugarcoating.

"IA was working with the DA?" Eddie speculated.

"I can't answer that, lieutenant. You know I cannot comment regarding internal affairs business." Stiggers sternly stated.

"You're sitting here with two members of Cathedral's Special Police Security officers before 8am on a Monday morning. One of which we know has been assigned to protect a witness to the district attorney's murder. Eddie already knows the answer, he was just being polite." Emily retorted.

"Did they follow you here, Donny Boy?" Stiggers suspiciously asked.

"The lycan masquerade killers had dinner here, we are thinking Tuesday night. We came to find out for sure and surprise, surprise, we find this fascinating foursome fraternizing." Emily responded strongly.

"I really like her." Gamble revealed to the group.

"Her husband's a priest. She's a Bible thumper." Stiggers replied.

"No Bible thumping. My husband's a pastor. I am a follower of CHRIST, that is a good thing." Emily calmly corrected.

"Are you investigating the DA's murder?" Dotson wondered.

"We are working the murders at Incanncennio Bottling Plant first. The thought process is that the solution to those murders will lead to the DA's killers." Detective Oftenmarch explained.

"Brass wants the ring leaders." the lieutenant expanded.

"These two are the detectives that caught the Skyscraper killer and she was on television on Friday after Barrett was killed in the park." the other security officer realized.

"Oh, great. That's just what the mud tusslers need, more fame and encouragement." Agent Stiggers complained.

"This is my partner, Security Agent Reggie Brownsides. You'll have to forgive him, he's a rookie." Dotson introduced his inexperienced partner.

"Hello, Reggie. Have the two of you been assigned to protect a free-lance hacker by the name of Zeke Ryerson, Jr. recently?" Emily inquired.

"Yes, he is one of three hackers the Cathedral PD has had us pro-tecting. We have been working around the clock protecting people from the DA's killers." Dotson replied, clearly annoyed.

"How is Zeke?" Emily asked genuinely interested.

"Alive." the massive security officer answered.

"Dude is scared all the time. Cathedral PD security is having to guard these hackers all the time. The new program director has been getting doctors to prescribe drugs to security forces to keep us awake for all the overtime we have been getting lately." Brownsides shared.

"That should make High Commissioner Harden proud." Stiggers jested.

"Cathedral PD's division of witness protection director Odgenpiper Petrov has been approving the use of a specific prescription drug to counteract drowsiness and sleepiness. They are supposed to be safer than working exhausted." Dotson informed them.

"Some of the security officers, or bodyguards, have become so addicted to this drug that they have been given a nickname. They are being called peppers, both the drug and the addicts." Gamble expounded.

"Most of the peppers take peppers to recover from heavy off duty drinking." Brownsides shared with a chuckle.

"These affected officers are starting to miss work instead of working more." Dotson added with amusement.

"Hence, this meeting." Lt. Knighton deduced.

"I can't answer that, lieutenant. You know I cannot comment regarding internal affairs business. Stop me if you have heard me say this before." Stiggers repeated internal affairs policy.

"Stop." Eddie returned.

Drug enhancement administrator Odgenpiper Petrov had no drunk pepper takers available to select for protection duty. He had to resort to an alternative plan which was hiring former police officers like Barrett Alexander. Detective Oftenmarch began better understanding what led to the St. James Park murder.

"There were no pickled peppers for Peter Piper to pick." Emily recited from memory.

"What are you talking about?" Stiggers asked in puzzlement.

"Barrett Alexander had cryptic messages hidden in his shoes. One of them was: There were no pickled peppers for Peter Piper to pick. These messages were found during his autopsy." Emily explained.

"What did the other messages say?" wondered Brownsides.

"The Lycans are coming." Emily relayed rapidly.

"Did you catch Barrett's killer?" Gamble questioned.

"Yes." Eddie responded.

"A private detective licensed in Illinois named Mitchell Moe Gertzin is being posthumously charged for Mr. Alexander's murder. He had a history of run-ins with the law and a history of working for dubious people." Detective Oftenmarch informed.

"I can look up this independent detective to see if he was registered with the National Grand Union of Private Investigators." Gamble announced.

"His history also contained federal work." Eddie offered evenly.

Stiggers was clearly agitated. "The Federal government is free to hire any vermin that they desire."

"Like Lawtech?" Lt. Knighton asked.

"How can you know, Knighton? How could you possibly know? Furthermore, how do you always seem to know things that nobody is supposed to know? Why is that?" Stiggers rattled off a series of questions in astonishment.

"There are a lot of shiny Lawtech Lawbotic Masterforce 1000 Patrollers in the city of Cathedral." Emily expressed, hoping this would be bait to learn more information.

"You have seen the new Lawtech Patrollers? Those were not supposed to be deployed into action yet." private detective Gamble took the bait.

"Lawtech is not the problem. It is a result produced because of the problem." Stiggers clarified.

"Is the FBI investigating?" Eddie asked flatly.

"His question is not about internal affairs business." Emily added.

"Yes, they are investigating. The alleged corruption in the Cathedral police department has drawn a lot of attention." Stiggers admitted.

"Some might say too much attention." Gamble appended.

"Are Cathedral PD officers committing murders?" Lt. Knighton asked with trepidation.

"I don't know, Eddie. I honestly do not know." Stiggers admitted again grimly.

"Throwing cases to help private companies, sending solutions to private companies for money, trading information and informants for cash, auctioning off cushy cases to private detectives, hiring hackers to alter official Cathedral Police records, and hiding evidence and witness statements then later selling them to private law enforcement companies are all being done from inside the Cathedral Police. The probability that the Cathedral Police are involved in the murders preventing the prosecution of these crimes is extremely high." Gamble expressed his logical opinion bluntly.

"I really hope these killers are not cops." Dotson shared.

"No way there are any cops involved in killing the D.A." Brownsides confidently gave his opinion.

"A private detective named Mercury Bryphos tells some pretty compelling stories which suggest the Cathedral Police are involved. He has been investigating police corruption in Cathedral and has made some rather disappointing discoveries. It may be worth talking to him, lieutenant." Gamble disclosed.

A waitress for The Breakfast and Brew Cafe approached Eddie and Emily. She appeared hurried and flustered as she greeted them. By the looks of her, it had been a difficult morning of work thus far. With an egg stain on the side of her uniform, she introduced herself as Lucy Anne and apologized for their wait.

"Good morning, Lucy Anne. We are with the Cathedral Police Department and would like to speak with your manager regarding last Tuesday evening and your security footage. On a side note, I would like to place a to-go order for two dozen spinach, bacon, and egg snack wrappers and the largest to-go container of black coffee you sell, please." Emily greeted then ordered.

Lucy Anne briefly studied Eddie's displayed badge, jotted down the detective's order, and then hustled off to find her manager. With newfound motivation and unfazed professionalism, she moved quickly and efficiently like a well-seasoned veteran of the job.

Once the waitress departed, Stiggers spoke again. "I wish you good luck on this case, Eddie. I really do but I have nothing to tell you which can help. We have no leads on these masked murderers." he confessed.

"Any more thoughts about Lawtech?" Eddie renewed his line of inquiry.

"Lawtech tries to use overpriced droids to do a man's job." Stiggers answered. "Or a woman's job." he then added.

"Cathedral PD has been trying to use those tin canners for protection detail and they are terrible guards. They could not guard toilet paper in a restroom properly." Brownsides offered.

"They're meant to be back-up to the real protection." Dotson contributed.

"Stupid droids...More obstacles then guards...", Brownsides continued to bad mouth Lawtech robots with a mouth full of food.

"With people, you can determine who they work for and from whom they take orders. But with droids, it is difficult to tell who controls them and commands them. Most of the time the security droids stand there like old fashion statues because nobody is taking responsibility for them or operation of them." Dotson explained.

"It is sad times when people cannot count on other people to help them. We are dependent on machines, but there is no love or compassion from them." Gamble interjected.

"Lucas Dockett from the 102nd precinct is retiring this week. His co-workers are throwing him a retirement party tonight." Dotson changed the subject.

"We are going to miss it because we have to work the Ring and Wing tower tonight." Brownsides lamented.

"Lucky you." Gamble jokingly replied.

"Eddie and I will have to send Lucas a gift. He is both a gentleman and a good detective. Eddie and I have to get back to work, this was a nice meeting. Thank you for the chat and enjoy your breakfast." Emily bid them farewell as she detected a middle-aged man in a Breakfast and Brew company shirt and tie approaching them.

"Later, Eddie." Stiggers said goodbye.

"Later indeed, Stiggers." Knighton countered in farewell.

The Breakfast and Brew attired man was medium height, heavyset, and slightly balding. He was sweating profusely, suggesting that he had been working hard in a hot kitchen before coming into the dining area to speak with the detectives. He looked calmer and less stressed than the waitress had appeared. With a friendly smile he warmly greeted them.

"I am Lou Gallop, shift manager. Lucy Anne said you needed some information. Please come to our back office." Lou introduced himself and then led them away from the dining area. They followed him behind the register counter into a hallway that led to a small office off to the side of the busy kitchen.

"Good morning, Mr. Gallop. I am Detective Emily Oftenmarch and this is Lieutenant Eddie Knighton with the Cathedral Police Department." Emily returned introductions as they walked toward the office. The tiny office had just enough room for the three of them but not enough room for anyone of them to sit.

"How can I help you, detectives?" manager Lou Gallop asked.

"We would appreciate if you could help us identify some of your customers from last Tuesday evening. We have their discarded receipt from Breakfast and Brew. It has found at the scene of a crime." Emily revealed as she showed the slightly crumpled receipt in an evidence bag to Lou Gallop.

Lou squinted a little as he analyzed the receipt. "Ten to six, paid in cash." he said aloud reading the slip. Lou shook his head a couple of times then continued, "This would have been a takeout order as we close our dining room at 3pm and our dining counter at 4pm. This take-out would have been just before closing time at 6pm."

"Who was working here last Tuesday evening before close? We are hoping they may recall anyone pulling into the parking lot with a box truck or who had picked-up such a large order of food." Emily inquired.

"I was here for the Tuesday closing shift. We had Jack and Benny working in the kitchen and Beth was working the cash register. The guys in the kitchen would not have seen the customers, only Beth and myself. I don't recall any box trucks and don't remember any specific customers from that night." Lou responded unhelpfully.

"Were there any rowdy customers or anything unusual on Tuesday evening?" Emily queried onward.

"Not that I recall, just another work day." the manager answered unhelpfully again.

"Could we get your security footage from that evening?" Emily asked.

"Sorry, detective. We do not keep our video recordings past 24 hours. We record over the footage from the prior day unless there is an incident. We've had no trouble in the last couple of weeks." the manager disclosed quietly.

"What about the parking lot cameras?" Emily followed with her next question.

"Those are mostly for show. The camera focused on the door is the only one that records. Its recording is also only kept for 24 hours unless there is a problem." Lou continued the trend of less than helpful answers.

"Would an order of this much food be unusual?" Emily wondered.

"It would be uncommon but not remarkable. We do get large orders from time to time even at that hour." Lou replied.

"Do you recall how many customers you had last Tuesday evening just before closing time?" Emily interrogated further.

"We don't get a lot of customers at the end of the day. I would guess three or four last Tuesday, but I would have to check our register records to be sure." he responded.

"Would you be willing to give us a copy of Tuesday evening's register records please?" Emily requested politely.

"Sure, that would not be a problem." Lou consented.

"Is Beth here right now?" Emily hoped.

"No, Beth works second shifts. She has morning classes at the local community college." Lou informed them.

"Could we get a contact number for Beth so we can call her to ask her about Tuesday evening?" Emily requested.

"Sure, I can get you that info." Lou answered then began moving paperwork off the small office desk's computer keyboard.

As Lou began typing, Detective Oftenmarch looked toward Lt. Knighton. Eddie was surveying the small office and sparse security video equipment. When he made eye contact with Emily, he shook his head no indicating that he did not have any questions. Briefly looking at the small security monitor in the tiny office, Emily could see that any video that might have been obtained would have been limited.

"Do you use a security company, Lou?" Emily posed to the manager.

"We used to have Dayco and Nightwatch, Inc. The senior management decided the service was not worth the expense and cancelled it." Lou informed them. He seemed to be struggling with whatever he was doing on the computer.

"This shopping center must be a fairly safe location for them to feel that way." the detective was making conversation at this point.

Lou looked puzzled and flustered. "I don't know how this could have happened. The register records for Tuesday evening are not in the system. There is nothing listed after 5pm on that day." he disclosed with confusion.

Emily remained calm for the both of them. "We would settle for a copy of any records you do have for Tuesday and a contact number for Beth." the detective amended.

"Of course, of course. I will gladly get you that information. I am sorry I could not be more helpful." the manager apologized. He typed frantically on the office computer and a pair of printouts were produced in about thirty seconds. Lou was rummaging through some paper files as the printouts were coming out.

"How long has Beth worked for the cafe?" Emily queried mostly making conversation.

"About a year." Lou answered as he grabbed the printouts and wrote on the top sheet. "Here is the information you asked for. Beth's number is written at the top of the page. Sorry, I could not be more helpful." He handed the pages to Emily.

"Thank you, Lou. We appreciated the help you have given us." Emily thanked.

"Have a nice day." was all that Eddie said. And with that said, the pair of detectives took their leave from The Breakfast and Brew Cafe.

The detectives left the cafe disappointed and dejected. Having followed the trail of the van of megawolves to a road block, they were feeling less than triumphant with their current results. They walk in silence as Emily took the fresh coffee and breakfast food she ordered to her car. Lt. Knighton looked around scanning the shopping center and the businesses that occupied it. With a pensive expression on his face, the lieutenant was mulling over one of his infamous wonderments. "Why stop here?" Eddie finally asked aloud.

"Maybe they like this restaurant." Emily speculated.

"Breakfast for dinner desire, doubtful." Eddie doubted.

235

Emily joined the search and seek for an answer to Eddie's puzzlement. The shopping center seemed rather ordinary. Looking at the neighboring businesses in the shopping center, Detective Oftenmarch offered some more explanations.

"Perhaps they wanted some fireworks from the Grand Finale Factory. It could also be possible one of the killers likes to vape and wanted to purchase some product at the Beat the Smoke Vapor Emporium. Or they wanted some do it yourself technology or gear from Independent Circuits." Emily speculated.

"All possible but none strong." Eddie retorted.

"It is interesting that they did not choose to eat at the dine-in restaurant but went with the carry out option." Emily stated.

"An unattended truckload of megawolves." Eddie postulated a reason.

"Excellent point, Eddie. None of these other businesses appear to be unique enough to be the reason for picking this shopping center as a pit stop. Maybe the stop was just random. One other observation is that dumpster three doors down is big and completely unrestricted. It is very convenient for unimpeded public use." Emily thought aloud.

"Yes, it is." agreed Eddie. Without further discussion, the lieutenant began a motivated stride towards the unsecured dumpster.

The pub three doors down from the Breakfast and Brew had a temporary closed sign posted and appeared to be in the process of remodeling. Large quantities of scrap materials and demolition byproducts filled the well-used waste container. Nobody was working on the project at the moment and the container was completely unimpeded from use or inspection. The dumpster was sitting out in the open in the middle of the large plaza shared parking lot, taking up several parking spaces. On the side of the dumpster was a do not fill above this line message, so of course over half the dumpster had trash piled so far over the line that it visibly spilled over the top of the container.

As the pair of detectives strode for the unrestricted dumpster, Emily noticed something from the corner of her eye, on the edge of her peripheral vision in the distance. Slowing her pace, she turned back to look with more scrutiny. Off in the distance away from the parking lot was a super cellular tower and next to the tower's security fence was what appeared to Emily to be a person watching them. Peering from around the fence, the distant figure was staring in their direction.

"We are being watched, Eddie." Detective Oftenmarch shared while still walking.

"From where?" Lt. Knighton asked.

"Far corner of the fence to the super cellular tower." Emily returned.

Eddie turned his head in that direction but after a few steps he replied, "Don't see them." The lieutenant then resumed facing forward and kept walking.

Slowing down more, Emily spun around to walk sidestep. She too could no longer see anything. Did they move back behind the fence, she wondered. Continuing to watch for several more lateral strides, Emily observed intently but still saw nothing. Had she seen somebody? She had thought she saw somebody out there watching them. Now she was uncertain. Three more watchful sidesteps later, the detective still spotted nobody. Abandoning the watch, Emily turned around and increased her pace to catch-up to Lt. Knighton.

The dumpster had some height, higher than an average dumpster, as it was roughly ten feet tall. The lieutenant had made his way to a built-in ladder on the side of the dumpster. Without hesitation, Eddie scaled the dumpster and stood on the top rung. He mumbled something under his breath that sounded like curse words to Emily before proceeding to climb into the dumpster. The inspection had rapidly become a dumpster bound expedition. Detective Oftenmarch quickly climbed the ladder to join the lieutenant. If Eddie was heading into the dumpster, then she knew it was for good reason. When Emily reached the top of the ladder, she could see those reasons. In the midst of the garbage about one layer deep was another slain megawolf and on the near side wall of the dumpster, also one layer deep, was an empty box labelled as growth hormones identical to the ones in the warehouse. There was little to no doubt that the lycan masquerade killers had been here. Even if they had a functional MPAR with them, Emily doubted the robot would have been much help in this situation.

As Eddie half treaded, half swam through deconstruction trash, Emily took out her complink to take some pictures. She primarily shot the pictures for evidence but truth be told she also wanted pictures of Lt. Knighton wallowing in a garbage dumpster.

Reluctantly, Emily switched on her copcam. As the lieutenant was struggling his way through the garbage, Emily climbed over the container wall to join the rummage through the rubbish. Just a few feet into her garbage travels, Emily got chalk on her sleeve and ketchup from discarded fries on the back of her hand. Eddie had made it to the discarded megawolf but was starting to sink in the garbage as he tried to unbury the dead animal. The more the lieutenant unburied the megawolf, the more buried he was becoming. He was disappearing into the debris. Detective Oftenmarch fought her way through the waste to help Eddie. More graceful in her trash trek than the lieutenant, she made it to his location with minimal sinkage. Emily discovered a half intact wooden pallet that was secure enough to use as an anchor point. Once she was in an unsinking position, Emily fished her partner from his precarious position.

When Eddie was repositioned, the pair of detectives untrashed not one but two deceased megawolves from their garbage graves. The second oversized wolf was hidden partially beneath the first oversized wolf. Both animals smelled foul and were attracting flies. Surrounded by ghastly garbage and decaying dead animals, Emily scanned the vicinity for anything else that could possibly be evidence. This was like searching for an unknown needle in a trash heap. As she was about to abandon the search as folly, something shiny caught her attention on the hind quarters of one of the wolves.

After swiftly putting on a bilatex glove and pulling an evidence bag from her pocket, Emily very carefully retrieved the object so as not to lose it in the multiple layers of the garbage pile. The object had stuck to the megawolf in a clump of dry blood. Once in the bag, she examined it closely to discover it was another small microchip. Not as small as the chips she had found at Private Eyes, but still quite tiny.

As Emily was making her discovery, Lt. Knighton had struggled over to the side of the garbage container where the growth hormone labelled box rested. He pried the box free from its neighboring waste materials and then set it on top of the garbage container wall. He flung some trash aside and then placed a smaller box next to the first one.

"Call the collection team." Eddie requested.

"First a poop filled warehouse and now a stinky dumpster- both with dead megawolves. The evidence collection squad is going to love us." Emily expressed.

"Like we chose the dumpster." Eddie replied with disgust then hauled himself out of the trash and rolled over the container wall disappearing from Emily's view.

Emily navigated her way through the refuse towards the side container wall. Sliding past copious amounts of sawdust and drywall dust, she felt like the inside of a vacuum cleaner. Emily plucked debris from her path as she went and circumnavigated some severely jagged metal beams. She half climbed half crawled her way to the dumpster's sidewall. With agility she pulled herself up to sit on top of the container wall. The top of the dumpster wall was covered in filth and grime. From her perch, Emily pulled out her complink and took several more photos of the inside of the dirty dumpster. Emily noticed on the second empty box the lieutenant had placed on top of the dumpster wall was a shipping label still securely taped to the garbage stained box. It was addressed to the Cathedral Guardian Company for a location in Cathedral. After photographing the box, Emily pulled her right foot out of the garbage. Her boot was covered in some well used oil.

"I deserve a raise after this morning." Emily commented as she took pictures.

"Add me to that list." Eddie returned from the ground.

"I would settle for a nice hot shower and a warm cup of herbal tea. Do you think the Cathedral PD would re-imburse us for replacing garbage soiled clothing?" Emily continued lightheartedly.

"There and there." Lt. Knight spoke seriously as he pointed out into the distance.

At first, Emily thought he had spotted people watching them, but after further inspection of the places he had indicated she realized he was talking about traffic cameras. The lieutenant had located a pair of nearby traffic cameras. One was located next to the traffic light at the top of the driveway into the shopping plaza. The second camera was positioned at the entrance ramp to state route 144 about one hundred feet up the road. Both devices would have captured video of the truck last Tuesday evening.

Lt. Knighton was already on the phone calling the West Cathedral traffic department. Emily had a feeling he was going to owe them a favor this time around. She gracefully glided down from the container wall and promptly called for an evidence collection squad. The detective now had no doubt that this was going to be a very long day.

Back in the parking lot, Emily could see private detective Gamble watching them from inside his parked car. They had to be a funny site to behold.

Chapter 12

Sane or insane, that is the question

Leaving the evidence collection squad to complete the task of gathering items from the dumpster in the West Cathedral shopping plaza, the detectives made the difficult drive from West Cathedral to the 271st Cathedral police precinct. Emily followed Eddie as they headed for their home base. Instead of going east from West Cathedral directly into Cathedral and congested workbound traffic, the lieutenant travelled south into the suburbs in an attempt to circumvent the rush hour traffic. Travelling through the towns of Grantburg, Whitechapel, South Royalton, Hillock Pines, and finally New Terranceville, the detectives made very little improved progress in the Cathedral bound traffic on their alternative route. Silly enough to follow the lieutenant, Emily fell behind Eddie as the city traffic had intensified. Eddie made it back to the 271st precinct several minutes before Emily. While working on his coplink, or police issued complink, the lieutenant waited for Emily to arrive in the restricted parking garage for the precinct.

It was well after eight o'clock in the morning by the time the mud tusslers made it back to the 271st homicide division and they had missed the captain's daily morning announcements. When they had arrived, their fellow homicide department co-workers were happy to see them. Of course, that was mainly because Emily had brought food and coffee from The Breakfast and Brew Company for the squad. J.D. had found an unused chair somewhere and had pulled it up next to Detective Oftenmarch's desk where he was eagerly awaiting her. The young man was excited to get started on another day of Cathedral police work. He was ready to go with his electronic device at the ready, the device with the holographic personal assistant neatly dressed in her emerald green dress with a silver lace pattern.

Emily apologized to the ambitious young trainee, "I am sorry, J.D., but you won't be with the lieutenant and I today."

"Did I do something wrong?" J.D. asked as he showed his disappointment.

"Not at all, J.D.", Emily answered. Then she turned to Detective Kenneth Murkendale and asked, "Murk, can J.D. please work with Cole and yourself today? The lieutenant and I have been put in the penalty box."

"Emily Oftenmarch in trouble, is that even possible." Murkendale mused.

"She got two minutes for congeniality." Vallens-Scantling joked.

"Eddie got two minutes for a moment of silence." his partner Mark Maxson mused.

"Emily got two minutes for vivaciousness." Detective Joppers jested.

"She clearly got a five-minute major for elegance unbecoming an officer." Detective Cole continued the joking while eating a breakfast snack wrapper.

"I love you guys as well." Emily responded.

"Need you today, Murk." Eddie broke his silence to somberly state.

"We got you, lieutenant. We have your back, sir." Detective Murkendale said seriously. "Should we bring Huana in from field interviews to help?" he asked. Eddie just nodded in agreement.

Detective Oftenmarch looked at her desk to discover a pile of items that was not there on Friday. "What is all this stuff that has appeared on my desk?" Emily asked.

"You've had visitors looking for you this morning." J.D. started to helpfully answer.

"You were visited by the ghosts of Christmas this morning and they all brought you generous gifts. The ghost of the past, named Kenneth Barsons, brought you a thick case file with a note and the message of tag, you're it. The ghost of the present, named David-John Oftenmarch, brought you a delicious breakfast and the message he loves you. We ate the food for you; you are welcome. And finally the ghost of the future, one techie head named Prithard Jergens, brought you new departmental gear and the message this is only for Emily." Theo Vallens-Scantling had his fun.

"He did not bring anyone else new gear. I think he likes Detective Oftenmarch." Detective Darius Cole noted while still eating.

"The food was delicious." Detective Joppers commented.

"More people visit you when you're not here then when you are here, Emily. If you want more visitors then you should leave more often. " Detective Maxson jested.

"Still love you guys, too. Not sure why but I do." Emily retorted.

As Murkendale began a discussion with Fairbankers, Emily began opening the packages the technology development department had dropped off at her desk. She had requested these items weeks ago. The first package was a new stunner, called the Phasepulser XII. It had an improved recharging time, a rapid double stream setting, and a higher stun pulse than the older models. The second package was a lightweight Kelvar3 quad-weave TovolMax aramid alloy vest. Her old vest had served its purpose and protected her from a particular nasty villain recently. Emily hoped this vest would serve her equally effectively. The third and final package was an auto-tracker. It was designed to scan and detect life signs and electronic pulses.

"Wonder how it autotracks?" Emily quietly asked to herself.

Trainee John Paul Tuttle had come over to her desk to get some food. He had left his fellow trainee Monkhouse sitting by himself playing a word cipher game on a handheld device that projected a bright holo-gram with an orange banner and bold alphanumeric characters. John Paul was playing with the Breakfast and Brew Company to-go bag and happen to hear her question. "You push the green button on the top right to start tracking." he kindly informed her.

"So you manually press a button to start autotracking. Manual intervention is required for the device to be autofunctioning, of course it does. Thank you for the heads up." Emily replied.

"J.D. says you're a really good cop." Tuttle told her.

"I'm an effort cop, John Paul. There are going to be good days and bad days in law enforcement. Whichever comes, just keep putting forth your best effort and nobody can ask for more." Emily offered some advice.

"Is the lieutenant an effort cop?" John Paul asked still looking over the breakfast food and then helped himself to some coffee.

Vallens-Scantling interrupted before Emily could answer. "Yo JP, leave Emily alone. She is a very busy woman with a note on a very large case file. Come help me with my computer." he shouted from his desk.

Picking up on Theo's hint, Emily set the gear to one side to look at the note on the recently delivered casefile overfull with a thick stack of pages. It read: *Sweetcakes, here is all we have on the first five werewolf kills. At least one of these killers is a seriously bad dude. When you go to arrest them call for some male backup. - Barsons*

"Knighton, where have you been this morning?" bellowed Bronzesmith as he entered the open office area.

"Busy working." Eddie calmly responded from his desk.

"We have cases to work in our jurisdiction. Leave the bottling plant case for the 272nd precinct or Sycamore Hills." ordered the captain.

"Speak with the high commissioner." Eddie retorted.

"Why would I do something like that?" Bronzesmith objected.

"Because he says different." the lieutenant answered.

"We will hire a private detective contractor to appease the commissioners. In the meantime, we have murder cases to close. This squad has a lot of work to get done." Bronzesmith declared.

"Harden gave us orders." Eddie disagreed with the captain's plan.

"This is not a debate, lieutenant." Bronzesmith shouted angrily.

"No argument there." Lt. Knighton evenly replied.

"High Commissioner Harden was very specific that the bottling plant case and the lycan masquerade killers are of the utmost priority and we are to focus our attention accordingly to solve it." Emily interjected, attempting to keep peace.

"This precinct cannot afford to have detectives away from solving precinct homicide cases to work high profile cases." the captain argued.

"With all due respect, captain, the city of Cathedral cannot afford to ignore this important case." Emily contradicted.

"My partner speaks the truth." Eddie indicated.

"There are cases pending that still have to be assigned to you. If you choose to devote your time to the bottling plant case, this will not excuse any lack of progress on those cases, Lt. Knighton. And Detective

Oftenmarch, I would like to speak with you in my office in ten min-utes." Bronzesmith yelled and then the captain stomped out of the bullpen area.

"Well, the captain appears to be in a cheery mood. This might be a good time to ask him for a raise." joked Vallens-Scantling after the captain had left.

"Mondays are getting less jolly every week here at the old 271st. You can find more happiness at a homicide scene." Joppers commented.

Nobody else spoke and the department fell into silence. Everybody got to work on whatever open cases they had going. All amusement had been sucked out of the room. Emily did her best to get some productive work done in a limited amount of time. Struggling to get some notes into CaseBuilder, the detective was preoccupied with her thoughts on impending meetings with both the captain and the psychologist. She was giving off a scent of dumpster which was also distracting and dis-turbing. Furthermore, her early start this morning was starting to catch up with her.

Fighting off sleepiness, the detective proceeded with determina-tion to get some kind of work completed. She simply cracked on with the job. At least she had not acquired any new injuries today and was feeling well. Emily's previously hurt hand was no longer bothering her. It felt like it was back to normal. The bruise on her left arm had signifi-cantly faded; it was barely noticeable now. The detective had healed up just in time to go back to work. This was a glass half full, half empty type of situation.

After fruitlessly endeavoring to get something productive accom-plished, Emily finally decided to postpone her work to prepare to meet with the captain. Getting up to get some water, Emily collected her thoughts as she formulated in her mind what she was going to say to the captain. Every time she thought she had worked out what to say, she changed her mind. Each revision seemed good at first but then faded into a poor idea. Finally deciding she was overthinking it, Emily went to the captain's office with no plan. As she knocked on Captain Bronzesmith's door, Emily figured she would keep her statements simple.

"Enter." called the captain in answer to the knock.

"You wanted to see me, Captain." Emily opened as she entered the office.

"Yes, please have a seat Emily. We have important topics to discuss." Captain Bronzesmith indicated.

"Captain, I have given the offer of taking the lieutenant's exam a lot of thought." Emily informed her superior.

"Forget about that for now. We need to talk about your psych eval scheduled for today. This department cannot afford for you to fail that evaluation. You cannot go bats in the belfry crazy on me, detective." Bronzesmith expressed.

"I have no plans to go crazy, Captain. Have you changed your mind regarding giving me the lieutenant's opportunity." Emily replied.

"Let's not worry about that now. Yes, we will have to put that on hold." Bronzesmith repeated sounding distracted.

"Sure." Emily politely capitulated albeit confused.

"The QuadPs start today, the new departmental stratagem called Proper Police Precision Prioritizing. This will affect our precinct's RAP, or results achieved performance. Our division must improve our metrics; precinct homicide cases must trump all other priorities. Our goal must be solving cases and high QuadP ratings." Bronzesmith explained.

"The lieutenant and I always try our very best to solve murders, Captain." Emily reassured him.

"The precinct's cybercrimes captain unexpectedly resigned last Friday and the chief has appointed me as the interim cybercrimes captain. This division must be running efficiently and effectively so I can divide my attention between both departments. I cannot afford for my homicide detectives, especially the lieutenant, to be territory roaming, renegade wandering, or improperly prioritizing. We must be on task and align with the Cathedral Police Department's agenda. The QuadPs will be heavily linked to our performance reviews and future funding." Bronzesmith continued his pro-departmental explanation.

"We do our best to represent the homicide division well." Emily replied.

"How important can a case outside of our precinct possibly be? On a scale from one to ten, what priority would the Cathedral PD evaluation committee give the Incanncennio case originating from New Terranceville?" the captain pondered.

"Since the assignment came from the committee's boss, High Commissioner Harden, they should give the case a ten plus rating." Emily answered confidently.

"I am not confident the committee would agree with that logic. We have to go by their defined precalculated grading scale. This has to be scrutinized from the perspective of an outside assessment group and how they would score things." Bronzesmith reasoned.

"I have no idea how lycan masquerade killers, megawolves, or mad scientist made robots would rate on the committee's grading scale." Emily retorted.

"Do you hear how absurd those things sound, Emily? You cannot go bat dung crazy; we cannot afford another Jimmy "Jumblehead" Danks. This division needs you and needs you at your best, detective. I depend on you and need you at your best, Emily." Bronzesmith pleaded with the detective.

"Detective Danks preferred not to be called Jumblehead and he was reassigned to traffic records because of stress, not insanity. As I said earlier, I have no plans to go crazy but thank you for your heartfelt concern, sir." Detective Oftenmarch responded.

"Whatever the circumstances, whatever the situation, you must pass your evaluation, Emily. This department cannot afford to lose you or even have you temporarily sidelined. You must clear your psych eval and you must get back on point with new departmental policies. This is paramount, this is my primary assignment for you." Captain Bronzesmith expressed with urgency.

"Yes, sir." Emily replied, not wanting to be contrary anymore.

"Good, get that done. You're dismissed, thank you." the captain concluded.

Emily exited the captain's office unsure if their meeting was a good one or a step backwards. The detective was also still conflicted by how much could she trust her captain. With increased pressure she felt toward the meeting with the psychologist, Emily was now dreading the evaluation even more. Slowly heading back to her desk, Emily switched to strategizing for this meeting. The closer she got to her desk, the less she felt there existed a good plan. By the time Emily reached her desk, she was certain there was no good plan to be had. Once at her desk she discovered a handwritten note on her computer plasmonitor. Lt. Knighton had left Emily a note informing her that he had gone to the evidence specialization facility to clarify some details and expedite the process.

Every six Cathedral police precincts shared one evidence specialization facility which contains the coroner's lab, the forensics lab, the technology lab, the electronics lab, the advanced research lab, and the crime reconstruction team. The 271st precinct shared the evidence specialization facility at the intersection of West Washington Circle and Anglenarrow Boulevard with precincts 267 through 270 and precinct 272. As Emily was meeting with the psychologist, Lt. Knighton would be at this facility to put a rush on the processing of all the evidence they had collected that morning.

Earlier that day, Detective Oftenmarch had received the notice for the scheduled appointment with the psychologist. Receiving the notice on both her complink and her personal phone, Emily had been given the time, location, and name of the psychologist. Both the time and the location had changed as the day had progressed. The new time was disadvantageous because it was an earlier time; the new location was advantageous because it was moved to the 271th precinct. The only piece of information that remained consistent was the name of the psychologist.

Dr. Lynnanne Quinnmacher had multiple university degrees in psychology, psychological behavior, sociology, and philosophy. The doctor had been published numerous times and had testified hundreds of times in courtrooms across the United States as an expert. Having been awarded for her excellent service to the Cathedral Police Department, Dr. Quinnmacher was held in high regard and distinction by both the High Commissioner's office and the Cathedral police union. She was a premier psychologist assigned to only the most important cases by only the highest ranking individuals such as High Commissioner Harden. This was the lady that was requested to travel to the 271st precinct to analyze Detective Emily Oftenmarch.

The doctor had arrived earlier that morning and had been given 271st precinct Chief Thigby's office to borrow to meet with the detective. At the appropriate time, Emily reluctantly made her way to the police chief's office. Heading to the chief's office required her to go up to the third floor. Electing for the stairs over the elevator, Emily slowly and unenthusiastically hiked up to her appointment. Light in foot traffic, the third floor was a quietly peaceful level. Adding to the silence, Emily noiselessly travelled to her appointment.

As Emily approached the office of the 271st precinct chief, she saw somebody she did not recognize. Outside of the Chief Thigby's office stood a man who appeared to be waiting. He was dressed in long sleeve blue polo shirt with the shield of the Cathedral Police Department emblem, a pair of nice slacks, and swayback loafers. He was dressed too professionally to be a policeman but not sophisticated enough to be in management. Emily was uncertain if the man was waiting to see the psychologist or waiting for something else. When the man saw Emily approaching, it became clear to the detective that he was waiting for her. Having seen her, the man immediately advanced towards Emily.

"Good morning. I am Diego Lowendowski, your Cathedral PD union representative and I am here to provide you with any assistance you may need." the man introduced himself.

"Is there a reason that I should be worried?" Emily inquired.

"No reason to fret, but there is a reason to be upset. You deserve more respect and consideration from the police commissioner's office." Diego expressed.

"You think this appointment with the psychologist is meant to be disrespectful?" Emily looked for clarification.

"This is unfair that someone of your exemplary service record should be asked to make an abnormal appointment with a psychologist on short notice. The union will be objecting on your behalf." Lowendowski informed her.

"This is not a bother. If the High Commissioner's office wants me to take this appointment, I will oblige them, and then carry on with my duties same as I have been." Emily gave a reply which was calmer than she felt.

"Spoken like a professional police officer who deserves better treatment. There were certainly far better ways for management to handle this circumstance. I am here to help you overcome this cruel request." Lowendowski conveyed.

"I could use any advice that you may have." Emily admitted.

"Here are some guidelines to help you. Answer truthfully but do not add any information. Stay on topic, answer the questions, and nothing more. Keep your answers short. Go with the minimum and just answer the question." Lowendowski offered.

"That sounds like what my lieutenant would also do. The truth, the whole truth, and nothing more. Anything else I should know?" Oftenmarch replied.

"Never admit if you think you're unfit for duty. Just answer truthfully and let the psychologist decide your mental state. That is what they are paid to do and it is what they are good at doing." Lowendowski continued.

"Are there many Cathedral police officers who get asked to visit psychologists?" Emily wondered.

"Yes, multiple officers are often asked to speak with psychologists. The majority of those appointments are because the officers have experienced a traumatic event. Some run into weird or twisted circumstances which are disturbing. But they are always scheduled appropriately and not last minute." Lowendowski explained.

"Well, the lieutenant and I have certainly seen some strange things recently. One of our current cases is full of bizarre." Emily admitted.

"I have been told that you were assigned the homicides committed by the lycan murderers. That's important work, you feeling up to the challenge?" Diego probed.

"The lieutenant and I will do our best." Emily indicated.

"These are tough and crazy times for the city of Cathedral. Seems like there are no end to the difficult cases produced by the people of this city." Lowendowski lamented.

"It is not all bad. There are still people worth helping in this city." Oftenmarch countered. An administrative assistant for the chief had exited the chief's office and was coming towards Emily.

"Let's hope you catch the killers before they find the right Ryerson or stab the proper buxom companion of the former district attorney." Diego wished.

"The lieutenant and I will do our best." Emily repeated distracted by the assistant.

"Dr. Quinnmacher is ready to see you now, detective." the administrative assistant for Chief Thigby interrupted them to let Emily know the psychologist was ready.

"Thank you." Emily politely replied.

"Good luck with the appointment and the investigation, detective." Lowendowski offered.

"Thank you." Emily again thanked.

As the union representative departed, Emily took a deep breath. It was time to get this over with and behind her. With as much confident as she could gather, Emily strode over to Chief Thigby's office door. After knocking politely, Emily took another deep breath and entered the chief's office.

Chief Thigby's office was a nice office with no frills and few decorations. The chief's office was a modest sized room which was kept meticulously tidy. The chief was an old school policeman who preferred to keep things simple. His office reflected that preference. Free of any wall hangings, the barren walls were a pristine white in color, which gave the room a vacant appearance. With two exceptions, the chief's desktop was likewise free of any clutter or decorations. Those two exceptions were a framed picture of his family, which included his wife, six children, and himself, and an encased service merit badge for the old Arden national guard armory which belonged to his great-great-great grandfather. With the carpet removed, the chief's office floor was bare wood which had been varnished and polished quite nicely. The only items on the pristine wooden floor, apart from the chief's desk, were the chief's armchair, an old filing cabinet, a tiny garbage can, a well-used metal coat tree, and two wooden visitor chairs, neither of which were particularly comfortable.

Seated in Chief Tigby's armchair was Doctor Lynnanne Quinnmacher. She rose to greet Emily as the detective entered the office. Quinnmacher carried herself with great poise and excellent posture. Standing next to the psychologist was a droid assistant, called a roborecorder. Positioned next to the roborecorder was a shiny servicebot. As the psychologist walked over to greet Emily, both droids emitted several soft quiet beeps. The doctor's attire and appearance was as neat as a pin. Lynnanne was wearing an A-line pleated skirt, an amaranth pink ruffle-trimmed blouse, a twirled Japanese obi with a decorative pattern, a silver locket necklace, petite silver earrings, and open toe high heel shoes. Dr. Quinnmacher had a pleasant smile which gave her a warm and friendly appearance.

"Good morning, detective. My name is Lynnanne. Please have a seat." the psychologist pleasantly offered Emly one of the visitor's wooden chairs.

"Thank you, doctor." Emily replied, taking the offered chair.

Dr. Quinnmacher sat next to her in the other visitor chair. "Please call me Lynnanne. Can my servicebot get you something warm to drink?" the doctor politely requested.

"No, thank you. I've had my fill of warm beverages this morning." Emily replied.

"Could I interest you in a jelly roll or some crackers?" Lynnanne offered.

"No, thank you." Emily again declined.

"Before we get started, I would like to inform you that this session will be recorded by my droid assistant. If this bothers you then please let me know now and I will use less intimidating and more discreet means of recording this meeting." Dr. Quinnmacher informed Emily. This revelation made sense since the doctor carried neither pen and paper nor any electronic devices.

"The roborecorder is fine with me." Emily answered as she adjusted her position in the uncomfortable wooden chair.

"The second thing I would like to mention is that there is a negative stigma on seeing a psychologist. However, therapy is not a negative thing but meant to be helpful. This session is meant to be beneficial for you." Dr. Quinnmacher expressed.

"I understand, thank you." Emily nodded in understanding.

"Begin recording. Discussion with Detective Emily Oftenmarch." Dr. Lynnanne Quinnmacher ordered her robotic assistant.

"**Recording has commenced**." voiced the droid assistant.

"Please tell me a little about yourself, Emily. Are you married? How long have you been in the Cathedral Police Department? Did you attend college? That type of information." the doctor requested.

"Yes, I am married. Have been in the Cathedral PD for over six years and went to the University of Cathedral." Emily dutifully answered.

"Let's try this again, detective. You don't have to answer all my example questions. Please just tell me a little bit about yourself." Dr. Quinnmacher clarified.

"Ok, I am a pastor's wife and married to a wonderful man named David-John. My hobbies are swimming, megafit exercising, reading, bow fishing, Arden style triathlons, and collecting candleworks. I am the youngest detective in the 271st precinct and I spend a lot of hours at work." Emily answered again.

"Interesting. I also like to swim, read, and collect candleworks." Dr. Quinnmacher admitted.

"It is nice to be in good company." Emily confessed.

"According to police department records, you have been working many long hours recently, detective. Have you been able to get enough sleep lately?" inquired the doctor.

"Some days are better than others. The work hours for this job can be unpredictable and the time to sleep can be erratic. A detective needs to take advantage of downtime to sleep when it is available." Emily replied in a way as to not admit the answer was no.

"How many hours of sleep per day do you think you averaged last work week?" Dr. Quinnmacher wondered.

"Maybe five hours on average." guessed Detective Oftenmarch.

"Are you familiar with the effects of sleep deprivation?" the doctor continued her line of questioning.

"Not really. If I ever feel weary at work, then I typically go for the caffeine solution." Emily admitted.

"When did you have your werewolf sighting?" Dr. Quinnmacher continued.

"Early Saturday morning at St. Gregory's Cemetery in Granthum. This was off in the distance in the dark." the detective explained.

"I understand. We will get back to St. Gregory's Cemetery. How many hours of sleep did you get on Friday night?" the doctor asked, returning to the quizzical topic.

"None." Emily answered Knighton style.

"Did you sleep during the day on Friday?" the follow-up question came from the doctor.

"For maybe five minutes at my desk." Emily answered.

"How many hours of sleep did you get on Thursday night?" the doctor chronologically continued in her questions.

"That was when the murders in New Terranceville at the bottling plant occurred. Got about four hours of sleep before the dispatch." Emily tried to estimate.

"How many hours of sleep did you get on Wednesday night, detective?" Quinnmacher continued in questioning.

"The lieutenant and I worked late into the night on Wednesday. By the time I got home and went to bed, I think it was again about four hours of sleep." the detective recalled.

"Did you get any sleep during the day on Thursday?" the doctor queried in hope.

"No." Emily gave her second Eddie-like answer.

"So, it would be fair to say that you did not have a lot of rest the days leading up to the werewolf sighting?" the doctor reasoned.

"That sounds like a reasonable statement." Emily agreed.

"Do you work a second job, Emily?" Dr. Quinnmacher asked.

"No, I just have my job as a Cathedral police detective." Emily confirmed.

"Have you worked any cases in the past which involved wolf attacks or late night work in a cemetery?" Dr. Quinnmacher questioned.

"I don't recall any cases involving late nights in a cemetery and I definitely have never experienced a wolf attack on any past case." Oftenmarch revealed.

"Do you have a history of seeing werewolves? Have you ever seen a werewolf in the past?" Lynnanne wondered.

"No, I have never seen a werewolf. This was the first time I thought I saw a werewolf." Emily responded.

"Have you ever had any nightmares about werewolves?" the doctor questioned.

"No. As far as I can recall, I have never had any dreams involving werewolves." the detective answered.

"Have you ever had a fear of encountering werewolves? Any symptoms of Lupophobia?" Dr. Quinnmacher continued to question.

"I never expect to see a werewolf. Since they are something you usually see in a horror movie, I never give them much if any thought." Detective Oftenmarch replied.

"What was your initial reaction when you first saw the strange wolflike image in the cemetery?" Quinnmacher inquired.

"Confused. My first thought was what could that be?" Emily replied.

"Was this figure threatening to you?" Dr. Quinnmacher wondered.

"No, it was in the distance but it seemed to just be standing there. It didn't react towards me at all." Emily disclosed.

"Have you seen strange things on the job in the past?" Dr. Quinnmacher asked.

"I once saw a man try to escape a crime scene in a gondola being pulled by a pair of goats, one of which was being ridden by his monkey sidekick." Emily disclosed.

"I meant to ask if you have seen any strange creatures or sightings like werewolves in the past?" Lynnanne clarified the question.

"No. I have not seen anything remotely as odd as a werewolf in the past." the detective responded.

"Perhaps, you were subconsciously afraid of something else. Have you encountered anything that frightened you recently?" the doctor asked.

"Startled me maybe, concerned me sure, but nothing that scared me." Emily reasoned.

"What is your biggest fear?" Quinnmacher queried.

"That people think I am crazy. If people think I have gone crazy then they wouldn't believe my testimony as a detective in a courtroom. If people think I have gone crazy then they wouldn't believe me when I tell them about JESUS." Emily admitted.

"Does this fear make you doubt your beliefs?" the doctor posed.

"Fear can do funny things to a person, but my feeling is the stronger your faith in GOD the better off you will be. I may be weak, my flesh may fail, but the LORD never will fail." Emily replied.

"If you fail, then does this cause you to doubt?" Dr. Quinnmacher asked.

"I have made mistakes and this world is full of trouble, but that does not change who GOD is and what HE has done for us." Emily answered.

"Are you not frustrated when your prayers go unanswered?" Dr. Quinnmacher queried.

"Just because things don't go my way or I don't get want I want does not mean I give up on GOD or lose faith. When you truly trust and love someone, then you do not lose that love and trust when life is difficult. Romans 8:28 reads, *And we know that in all things GOD works for the good of those who love HIM, who have been called according to HIS purpose.* Even when we don't see it, GOD is working all things for our good. Even when we don't understand it, GOD is working. And we know GOD will continue to be faithful. In Philippians 1:6 the verse reads, *being confident of this, that HE who began a good work in you will carry it on to completion until the day of CHRIST JESUS.*" Emily replied in length.

"Would it be considered insane to be confident or self-assured?" Dr. Quinnmacher proposed.

"Confident in myself would be insane. Confident in GOD would not be insasne. Having a feeling of certainty in GOD, having a feeling of trust and believe in GOD would be wise." Oftenmarch imparted.

"Is it crazy to believe in GOD?" the psychologist questioned.

"Is it crazy to have faith? People trust in currency. Is that lunacy? Every day people put their faith in planes, helicopters, and air shuttles. Are they crazy? Every time a person undergoes surgery, takes medication, or drinks a beverage without testing it for poison, it takes faith. Everyone who crosses a bridge puts their trust in it. Are those all actions of craziness?" Emily assessed.

"Maybe their trust comes from what they can see." Quinnmacher suggested.

"People cannot see oxygen yet they trust they don't need oxygen tanks every day. Is that crazy?" Emily countered.

"Do you think people find you crazy to trust in GOD?" Dr. Quinnmacher inquired.

"No. There exists nothing better to trust in than GOD. GOD is the most trustworthy presence of all in my opinion. Why should people think me crazy for trusting in the most trustworthy thing there is?" Emily replied.

"Do you think people find you crazy to love GOD?" Quinnmacher continued her questioning.

"GOD is the most loving presence in the universe, why should returning his love be considered crazy? That's crazy. If a powerful king offers you an all expenses paid trip to eternal paradise, allows you to inherit unfathomable riches, and loves you unconditionally despite any of your ugliness or foolishness, then would you feel love and gratitude? It would be crazy not to love that king and what he offered you. To me, it would be insanity to not love the most loving." Emily conveyed.

"But do you think other people see if that way?" the doctor countered.

"I don't know, but I hope they would. I am sorry if this is not relevant but it helps to say these things out loud." Emily expressed.

"No, need to apologize. That is completely understandable." Lynnanne responded. The psychologist paused for a moment then gave a command to her roborecorder, "Pause recording."

"**Recording has been paused.**" voiced the droid assistant in acknowledgement.

"Excuse me a moment while I get a drink of water. Would you like a drink of water, Emily?" the doctor indicated to the detective. The service droid began travelling toward Dr. Quinnmacher as soon as she requested a pause.

"I am still good. Thank you for the offer." Emily politely declined. She shifted her position in the uncomfortable chair again, searching for a more favorable posture.

"It helps to pause a moment, have a stop and smell the roses type of a moment. I always enjoy a little water with a respite." Dr. Quinnmacher replied as she got a bottle of water from her service droid.

"It's old school but I like listening to the radio. Sometimes it is background noise when I am thinking. Other times it gives me something new to think about." Emily made conversation. She reshifted, still searching for comfort.

"Reading has always been my preferred distraction." Dr. Quinnmacher commented then took a dainty drink of water.

"It's nice to have peaceful distractions." Emily agreed.

"Let us now conclude this conversation. Continue recording" the doctor commanded.

"**Recording has commenced.**" voiced the droid assistant.

"Changing the subject, please clarify what you meant when you referred to speaking to a former Cathedral detective." Lynnanne politely wondered.

"I was remembering the things the former detective used to teach me, their sleuthing knowledge. I was recalling their whimsical wisdom, recalling past conversations with them and reminding myself of their words in my thoughts." Emily explained.

"So you were remembering past conversations." Lynnanne proposed.

"More like replaying those conversations in my head, if that makes sense." Emily clarified.

"Do you often replay these conversations in your head?" Quinnmacher wondered.

"No, only when I encounter a situation which takes me back to a similar situation in the past. Instances where former detectives gave advice or shared knowledge." Emily supplied.

"Are these internal conversations helpful?" the doctor asked.

"Often extremely helpful, I find them to be beneficial reminders more than moments of madness. But they're hard to explain without people thinking that I am odd." Emily expressed.

"You learn from others' experiences; this would be a good thing. But this has you concerned about your image again?" Quinnmacher posed.

"It would be nice to be perceived as credible. Where the means may be unconventional, the method is not necessarily insane." Emily explained.

"Do you find being unconventional causes people to question you?" the doctor inquired further.

"I don't mind being questioned. The concern I have is being dismissed as a lunatic. The things which I have to say are not lunacy. The facts collected in an investigation, the observations I have made, the comparisons to previous cases, events I have witnessed, and especially the truth about GOD are not to be dismissed." Emily explained.

"Does it hurt your feelings to be disbelieved?" Quinnmacher questioned.

"It feels sad and frustrating to not be believed. I often feel like saying to people, do you see what I see? There's beauty to behold. Do you hear what I hear? But nobody seems to hear anything. There is a Bible verse, Matthew 11:15, which reads: *Whoever has ears, let them hear.* It is also written in Mark 4:9 *Then Jesus said, 'Whoever has ears to hear, let them hear.'* But it seems like these days people only hear what they want to hear." Emily responded.

"I hear you, Emily." Dr. Quinnmacher reassured.

"Thank you, Lynnanne. It's good to be in good company." Emily commented.

"My advice to you, detective, is that vacations can be extremely helpful. More rest would go a long way towards helping you cope with a stressful job. I see a significant rise in rates of post-traumatic stress and work related stress in Cathedral law enforcement. Allow me to share some statistics with you: 72 percent of active police officers have encountered a work related traumatic event at least once and roughly 88 percent of Cathedral law enforcement have reported having experienced stress at work. There is also a surge in sleep deprivation and long work hours in Cathedral law enforcement. Again allow me to share some statistics with you: 87 percent of all surveyed Cathedral Police force personnel do not get enough rest. Also, 81 percent of the police workforce work for over 40 hours a week. Approximately one out of four members of the Cathedral Police Department work for a private law enforcement company as well. Both are rising trends which put a strain on the members of the police. There are countermeasures which can easier be taken to alleviate this strain, beginning with more sleep and more time off. Conclude recording." the psychologist ended the official session.

"**Recording concluded. Session file saved, Oftenmarch alpha one one echo**" voiced the roborecorder obediently.

"It was nice to meet you, Emily. I enjoyed our conversation and hope you found it helpful. Sometimes it's good to talk about your troubles, help clarify your feelings. Any time you would like to speak with someone or tell someone your concerns, please give me a call. I would love to talk with you again, Emily." Quinnmacher closed as she produced a business slimchip from nowhere like a magic trick and handed it over to the detective.

"Thank you for your time, doctor." Emily returned in equal kindness.

Chapter 13

Down the Rabbit Hole

Private detective Mercury Bryphos had a small office in the basement of the Wallace-Franklin Building on the far northeast side of Cathedral. Lt. Knighton drove himself and Emily in the PSUV across the hectic city in brake-repeating city traffic. They listened to an audio recording of Lt. Jack McSummer's case logs from CaseBuilder recordings for the lycan masquerade killers' murder of the district attorney while they slugged through abysmal traffic. Most of the logs were in regards to mishandled evidence and poor video surveillance, which made them of little help.

Driving past Tivioli Tower, Johnman's Arcade, Pixel Palace Theater, the Catholic Museum, Brown and Brown headquarters, and the Cathedral Clock Towers, the detectives crawled through significant road congestion. Slowdowns increased while trying to bypass the almost always busy Grand Commerce Square. A broken down delivery truck blocking the center lane of East Chapel Blvd. only made the traffic situation worse.

By the time they reached their destination, Emily was overjoyed to be out of the PSUV and traffic. In the not-too-distant skyline, the triple towers of St. Francis University in Cathedral could be seen. The gleaming campus towers were one of the three iconic trademarks of St. Francis University. They were well known amongst Cathedral's locals and the university's alumni. Unable to park in the street because a row of cars was already parked along the roadside, the lieutenant had to find alternate parking. Many of the cars parked on the road were in front of a restricted parking lot, which was completely empty and devoid of cars. Therefore, the detectives parked in a building maintenance and security zone before entering the twelve story tower via the side revolving door entrance. Across the street, a pair of buildings were undergoing reconstruction, which made the area around the side entrance both noisy and dusty. Once inside the building, the noise dissipated, but the dust did not diminish.

Eddie and Emily took the creaky building stairs down one flight to the basement level. This subterranean level was musty and murky but considerably cleaner than the building's lobby level. The main hallway in the basement was wide but had a low ceiling, making the corridor short and squat. Each office on this sublevel had a nice cherry stained wooden door. The third broad door on the left was the office of Mercury Bryphos, private investigator.

Lt. Knighton knocked on the solid wooden door. After waiting thirty seconds, he knocked again, this time louder. Another thirty seconds passed without a response, prompting Eddie to open the door on his own. On the other side of the unlocked door was a small but quaint reception area. In one corner was a short wooden desk with absolutely nothing on it. It gave the appearance of a receptionist desk for an office which no longer had a receptionist.

On the far wall of the room was an empty coat tree in disrepair, a folding chair with its rummage sale price tag still attached, a dead and withered potted plant, and a wall mounted clock which had stopped running at three minutes to twelve next to an inner office door marked private. Having a half abandoned appearance, the room was also depressing.

On the near wall were two old fashioned Arden style highbacked and wingbacked chairs with a small round wooden coffee table positioned between them. Two magazines, one restaurant menu, and a cocktail napkin rested on the table. In the further away old Arden wingbacked chair sat an interestingly clad man.

He wore a black suit coat with tails and long garnet trousers. He also had on a dark purple vest, a pink and white polka dot tie, a black and blue striped shirt, long white socks, fuzzy blue bedroom slippers, a white leather belt, and an extremely tall dark green stove pipe hat.

"I have been waiting for Emerson Plumlee, you see, and you are not he." the oddly dressed man greeted them. "Or was it Plumwine in clandestine. Forgive me, I forget these things sometimes." he added.

"Emerson was who I was waiting to see and you two are most definitely not he."

"Sorry to disappoint." Eddie answered without emotion.

As Emily viewed the sad room she asked, "Are you Mercury Bryphos?".

"The mundane detective? Oh no, my talents are much greater. I do not partake in sleuthing misery, I am a man of mystery." he jovially replied.

"Are you waiting to see the detective, sir?" Detective Oftenmarch wondered reasonably.

"We do not seek, young lass. It is unbecoming. It is far more digni-fied to be sought." the seated man said.

Emily looked at Eddie and cautiously asked, "Do you see what I see?".

"Unfortunately, yes." Eddie flatly replied, then walked over to the inner door and knocked on it sharply.

"We see only what we wish to see." interjected the fancy dressed man.

"Our apologies, we are with the Cathedral Police Department and are going to have to intrude to speak with Mercury Bryphos." Emily explained to the peculiar man.

"It is clear to me, you are Cathedral PD. But it is not clear to you as to your who through and through." the man declared as he took a red lensed monocle from his vest breast pocket. Putting the red spectacle to his left eye he continued, "You're a villain hunter and a guardian of the doomed. You see evil doers differently than normal people in this world, you see their true inner form. You're a twilight blight combatant, a luminescent equalizer for good."

Eddie knocked on the inner door again with more force and fre-quency. He was clearly uninterested in the current conversation. Of course, the lieutenant was normally not a big conversationalist but he was particularly adverse to this conversation.

"Good afternoon, sir. I should introduce myself. My name is Detective Emily Oftenmarch. I am a Cathedral Police homicide detective and a follower of JESUS CHRIST." Emily introduce herself with resolve.

"The good king sends aid to this troubled city. The peace keepers cannot see what lies ahead when their ethics lie in shambles dead. The hours grow late for times once great, so bent men of power look for means less sour." the abnormal man riddled as he put away his unique monocle.

"Let's talk about lawlessness and broken jails where justice seldom prevails." Emily returned, attempting her own riddle.

"You wish to defeat it?" he asked amused.

"We wish to prevent it." the detective answered with continued resolve.

"And who is we?" the strange man queried for clarity.

"Anyone who wants to join." Emily countered. Eddie started knocking again.

"There are no good guys. There are no bad guys. There is just you and me and we can no longer afford to disagree." the silly man mused.

Eddie stopped knocking to say, "Agreed."

At that moment the main door from the hallway opened and in stepped a man with a loosened tie, partially unbuttoned dress shirt, coffee-stained trousers, a deep frown, and a paper bag of fast food. He glanced around the room before saying, "Thank you for watching the office, Uncle Javal."

"It was quite a delight." the seated uncle welcomed with a tip of his tall hat.

"How may I help the pair of you?" the newcomer inquired.

"Cathedral Police, homicide division. This is Lt. Eddie Knighton. I am Detective Emily Oftenmarch. We are investigating murders committed by a group of lycan masquerade killers and the possibility of Cathedral law enforcement being involved. We have been told that a private detective named Mercury Bryphos would be an excellent person to discuss this topic with us." Emily introduced as she displayed her badge.

"Masked as descendants of William Corvinus or disguised as common werewolves?" Uncle Javal asked skeptically.

"Thank you again, uncle. I am detective Bryphos, please join me in my office." the private detective responded, then strode toward the inner door.

"If you see Emerson, please tell him that Emily kept it on the double hush." Detective Oftenmarch requested to Uncle Javal in parting.

"There is no rush when on the double hush." Uncle Javal responded.

Both detectives followed the private detective into his office. The private detective's office was quite cluttered and cramped. An oversized wooden desk with an elongated credenza sat almost in the center of the room. In one corner of the room was one filing cabinet and around the desk and along the far wall were multiple stacks of paper piled on the floor. These stacks of papers ranged from knee high to waist high in height. On the top of the desk was an assortment of objects in a sea of scattered papers. Behind the desk sat a large leather luxury lounge chair and a four-foot floor lamp. In front of the desk there was an antique loveseat and a lowback cushioned chair. In the far corner was a small bar with a modest selection of alcoholic beverages and a pair of bar stools. In the opposite corner was an unpowered old jukebox. Next to the jukebox sat a pair of empty Melchizedek champagne bottles. The walls of the office were full of classical mystery movie posters.

"Please have a seat, detectives." the private detective offered.

Lt. Knighton grabbed one of the barstools, pulled it closer to the central desk, and took a seat. Emily went to take a seat on the loveseat where she discovered a dog curled up and resting on about half of the antique seat. The sleeping Schnauzer showed no intention of making any movement either towards greeting her or towards making room for her on the loveseat. Oftenmarch hesitated upon seeing the dog.

"Don't mind Apollo. He mostly sleeps these days and will not bother you." Bryphos reassured Emily. With some caution and delicacy, Detective Oftenmarch sat in the unoccupied half of the loveseat.

"How may I help you, detectives?" Bryphos asked as he sat in his desk chair.

"Are you familiar with the prosecution the former district attorney was working?" Emily asked him.

"Yes, multiple ranking Cathedral Police personnel were scheduled to be tried for tampering with evidence, taking bribes, misappropriating cases, falsifying records, lying under oath, fraud, and other similar crimes. This disease of corruption was allegedly widespread throughout Cathedral law enforcement." Bryphos gave his answer.

"Had the D.A. hired you?" Lt. Knighton questioned.

"No, the State Department of Justice hired me. They hired me to investigate if Cathedral law enforcement was abusing and misusing private law enforcement companies for personal profit. Ironically, for an investigation regarding the use of private law enforcement, they hired a private investigator." Mercury explained.

"Were you hired to investigate specific people's involvement?" Emily posed.

"The state DOJ asked me to ascertain two things. First, could a private detective acquire case solutions from Cathedral Police for cash? Second, could a private detective obtain work from Cathedral police via a bribe? Both of which were possible for me to do. The state prosecutors are currently proposing new work for me. They would like to discover if these two things are possible to accomplish in the daughter cities of Cathedral. They are concerned that Cathedral's corruption is spreading to other cities." Bryphos disclosed.

"Were you able to determine if Cathedral Police work was available to be purchased?" Detective Oftenmarch wondered.

"There were a lot of cases being offered by the Cathedral PD. It was harder for a small private investigator like myself to acquire those cases. Most of the work was being obtained by the larger companies like Lawtech, SuperSafe, and Superior Police Plus." Mercury explained.

"You were able to purchase solutions to active cases?" Emily asked for clarification.

"Which precinct do you work?" the private detective counter-queried.

"Precinct 271." Oftenmarch answered.

Spinning around in his leather lounge chair, the private detective began rummaging through his stacks of papers. Eddie and Emily shared a look as the private detective searched. After about a couple of minutes, Bryphos spun back around with two folders full of papers in his hand.

"I do not have anything for the 271st precinct, but I do have one for a 269th precinct burglary case and another for a 275th precinct homicide case that has been open for over a year." Bryphos revealed as he held out the files. Lt. Knighton stood up from the bar stool and accepted the offered files. "You may keep those if you like." the private eye continued.

Eddie began to review the files as he sat back down on the bar stool. He had a deep concentrating look on his face.

"Thank you, Mr. Bryphos. Our concern is that law enforcement could be involved in the murder of the district attorney. During your investigations, did you encounter any law enforcement which concealed murder, conspired to murder, or partake in any activity with disregard to the crime of murder?" Emily interrogated.

"Most, if not all, of the corruption I encountered involved greed, deception, deceit, or laziness but not homicide. And please call me, Mercury." the private detective replied.

"Were there any members of the Cathedral law enforcement who you felt had a lot to lose from the DA's prosecution?" Emily probed further. As she spoke, Apollo shifted to put his head on her lap. She gave the dog multiple affectionate pets behind the ears.

"I mostly dealt with intermediaries, like a college student working as a courier, a real estate agent, and a part time bartender. It was never made known to me who specifically from the police department was supplying the cases or collecting the payoff. Rumor had it that there was a downtown precinct captain who owns a private law enforcement company which is making millions upon millions of dollars off of thrown cases and reassigned work. This is a rumor that has been often told." Mercury Bryphos told the detectives.

"Does this rumored captain have a name?" Detective Oftenmarch wondered as she stroked the sleepy schnauzer. Lt. Knighton pulled out his complink as he continued to scrutinize the case files Bryphos had given them.

"Oppenheimer Gifts, he is the 16th precinct captain of the illegal substances division. He supposedly owns the Gifted Special Police Company. Rumor has it that he is making a fortune in the current climate of cop corruption." Bryphos offered.

Emily took out her complink and ran a couple of quick searches, temporarily suspending the petting of Apollo. "The captain of the 16th precinct illegal substance division is Randall Lewis; he has held that position for fourteen years. The only Gifts organization in Cathedral I can find is Specialty Gifts Private Club which is a nightclub." Oftenmarch shared.

"Must be a bad rumor." Bryphos admitted.

"There was another popular rumor that a group of Cathedral precinct chiefs owned a technology company that was selling tons of robots to the Cathedral Police." Mercury shared, attempting to be helpful.

"Let's not discuss rumors please." Emily replied as she returned to petting Apollo.

"I understand, detective." Mercury agreed.

"It has been suggested to us by other private detectives that you would be the person to whom we should speak with in regards to the Cathedral Police possibly being involved with the murder of the district attorney. Please do not take offense, Mercury, but nothing you have told us thus far would warrant such recommendations from your colleagues. What are you not telling us?" Emily challenged Bryphos as she stroked Apollo under his chin. Glancing down at the dog, Emily noticed the canine's dog tags.

"You got me, detectives. I embellish the truth and exaggerate what I know when speaking with other private eyes. Just trying to show-off and appear impressive. I never meant for those tales to cause you to come visit me and waste your time." Bryphos conceded.

"What tale did you tell Gordon Granite?" Emily shrewdly asked. Lt. Knighton abruptly stopped reading the files and quickly put his complink away.

"The fictional movie detective?" Bryphos wondered in confusion as he pointed to one of the movie posters on the wall.

"Very good response, Mercury. Now could you please explain why Apollo's name tag says Zeus." Emily replied. The dog sat up swiftly at the sound of his name.

"Oh, no. My uncle picked up the dogs from the groomers. He must have switched my sister's lazy dog with my dog. This is what I get for asking him for help. I feel foolish because I did not notice." Mercury lamented with a sad sigh.

"Well, we just met your uncle so that does make a lot of sense." Emily understood.

"My uncle is unique and leaves quite an impression, that is for sure." Bryphos replied with another sad sigh.

"Do you have any reason to believe the Cathedral police are directly involved in the murder of the district attorney?" Emily queried.

"With all the corruption in the Cathedral Police Department I have a hard time believing they are not involved. The D.A.'s killers had to have connections to the police because they knew exactly where and when to strike when the man had substantial police protection." Mercury reasoned.

"The Cathedral Police Department has a bad reputation?" Emily asked as she petted the now more energetic Zeus.

"Without betraying confidence, all I can is say is that it is not difficult for a private eye to find Cathedral law enforcement members who are willing to bend a few rules or turn a blind eye for the right price." Mercury answered.

"But the State Department of Justice was more concerned with Cathedral Police's poor ethical relationship with private law enforcement?" Emily looked for clarification.

"Most of the rule bending by the Cathedral Police involves and benefits private law enforcement in Cathedral." Mercury shared.

"If I were a client with information about the district attorney's killers and needed protection, then how would you help me and what would you advise me to do?" Detective Oftenmarch posed, still petting the now happy dog next to her.

"I would tell you to run to the hills, run for your life." private detective Bryphos replied with seriousness.

"May we keep these files?" Eddie requested confirmation, holding up the two case files Bryphos had given him.

"That's fine with me." Mercury capitulated.

"Thank you for your time and assistance, Mercury." Emily thanked as she rose from her seat and ceased petting the dog. Zeus laid back down and closed its eyes.

"You are welcome, detectives. Stop by anytime, I am always happy to help the Cathedral Police." Bryphos said his farewell.

When they left Mercury's office to return to the waiting area, Uncle Javal was no longer there. For some reason, he had sprinkled orange, aureolin, yellow, and white flower petals around the chair where he had been sitting and had left them in the wake of his departure. Other than that, the room was as sad and depressing as it had been when the detectives first entered it.

Back in the dank, musty, wide, and squat hallway, the detectives walked in silence. Lt. Knighton was still engrossed in the files they had acquired from the private detective. He was still perusing them as he walked. Emily was reminiscing about her sister Sixth's amateur mystery detectives club from their teenage years when her cell phone chimed, thus breaking the silence. She was surprised to get such good reception in the basement.

The incoming call was from a Florida area code phone number. Detective Oftenmarch answered the phone but received no reply other than three quick beeps followed by a dial tone. Eddie was looking at her expectantly. "Call me crazy, but I believe the calvary has come to the city of Cathedral." Emily told him as she put her phone away.

The lieutenant stared at her for a moment then shook his head prior to resuming his reading material. The pair of detectives resumed their subterranean walk once again in silence. After travelling down the hallway and up the dusty steps, they returned to the lobby of the Wallace-Franklin building. As Emily began walking toward the exit, it was Eddie who broke their silence this time.

"We're going to floor eight." he revealed and then pointed at the building's directory. He moved closer to the marquee and tapped it by a name under floor eight's listings. "Suite 840." Eddie concluded.

Emily traversed her latest steps and then walked up to read the directory. Suite 840 in the Wallace-Franklin building was occupied by the Cathedral Guardian Company.

"Small world after all." Emily commented.

The detectives boarded the elevator and began their ride to the eighth floor in renewed silence. Making stops on the fourth and fifth floors to pick-up additional passengers, the silence was broken with chit chat. The next stop was at floor eight where Emily and Eddie parted the other lift riders and departed the elevator. As they exited the elevator, they were greeted by a waiting elevator passenger.

"Steady Eddie and the woman formerly known as Eighth on the eighth floor, how coincidental. You two are almost as far from your precinct as I am from mine." greeted the waiter. He was Detective Braxton Dean with the 303rd Cathedral PD precinct's narcotics division.

"Happy Monday, Braxton. We're on the trail of some homicidal maniacs. What brings you to this section of the city?" Emily responded cordially.

"CGC caught a court date skipper on their bounty list with a large bag of wacky tabacci. Captain sent me to collect their reports so we can process this dumb dude." Detective Dean shared.

"How are your wife, Tami, and your son, Jimmy, doing?" Emily inquired.

"They're good. How's your brother, Second, been? I don't see him at the gym anymore." Braxton counterinquired.

"He's been busy at work. Second has been working out at his new girlfriend's gym lately." Emily informed him. Detective Dean served in the United States military with Emily's older brother, Second.

"I bet he has been." Braxton cracked.

"Wrong interpretation." Emily replied.

"Tell your brother I said hello." Braxton Dean requested.

"Please tell Tami the same for me." Emily reciprocated.

The elevator returned to the eighth floor this time with the down arrow indicator light.

"This is my ride, detectives." Braxton said as he headed for the elevator. Then he added as he entered the elevator, "Oh yeah and E, Go Bishops."

"Go Grey Sox." Emily countered without missing a beat. Eddie just waved goodbye and gave no verbal support to any baseball team.

Resuming their silent walk to their destination, the detectives used their deduction skills to ascertain the direction of the ascending suite pattern in the hallway. Suite 840 was at the far end of the main hallway towards the back of the building. The Cathedral Guardian Company suite had an all-glass front covered in posters and marketing flyers. The posters were bold and glossy; the marketing materials were extremely anti-Cathedral Police Department. The third poster the detectives passed showed droids almost identical to the Lawtech Patrollers they had discovered at the D505 warehouse earlier that day. Under the poster's image was the text, The city of Cathedral's New Defenders.

"Look familiar." Eddie said to Emily as they passed the poster.

The marketing brochure displayed next to the Lawtechlike droid poster contained graphs and statistics presenting how much more efficient and effective the CGC was over the Cathedral Police Department. Its central graph and stat showed the CGC had a 35 percent higher conviction rate than the CPD. The substat was that the Cathedral Guardian Company also spent 45 percent less money per conviction than the CPD.

"Figures don't lie." Emily started.

"But liars can figure." Eddie concluded.

Once the pair of detectives were past the plethora of procompany propaganda, they reached the fancy glass entrance to the Cathedral Guardian Company. Passing through the tall glass door, they walked into a plush well-furnished reception area. An elongated reception desk ran the length of the highly decorated room and it had three designated sections, each with a receptionist. Those three sections were labelled guests, case file pick-up, and new cases. Lt. Knighton headed straight for the young female receptionist working the guest section.

"Oftenmarch, Knighton for Dr. Halibut." Eddie told the receptionist.

"Do you have an appointment with Dr. Halibut?" the young recep-tionist asked.

"Yes." Eddie flatly responded.

"What were your names again, please?" the young lady sought clarification.

"Detective Emily Oftenmarch and Lieutenant Eddie Knighton with the Cathedral Police Department." Emily restated for the receptionist in a less cryptic fashion.

"Thank you. I will let Dr. Halibut know you are here. Please have a seat while I contact him." the youthful receptionist indicated.

As the detectives patiently waited, Emily seated and Eddie stand-ing, in the swank reception room they observed several uniformed police officers enter the Cathedral Guardian Company. In the span of about three minutes, three Cathedral police officers, each from differ-ent precincts, went up to the receptionist at the case pick-up counter. They each collected some hardcopy files, Emily never noticed any elec-tronic devices being used or given, and promptly exited without looking at their obtained documents. Eddie began to pace as they waited. Emily was noting the stark contrast between the CGC's vibrant reception area and private detective Bryphos's bleak waiting area when a young male assistant approached them.

"Dr. Halibut will see you now. Please follow me." the assistant cheerily told them. After his happy greeting, the young assistant led the detectives back into the private office area to the office of Dr. Bennathan Halibut. The back of the house area of the suite was far less decorative than the lobby but still quite well furnished.

The assistant moved briskly to the doctor's office and reached his tall sleek door in little time. An animatronic miniature robot was installed over a digital 3-D lock on the doctor's door. The display brightly illuminated a colorful keypad of numbers, letters, and symbols. As the assistant approached the door, the tiny droid came online and digitally said, "Welcome to Dr. Bennathan Halibut's office. Please enter your valid passcode to visit the doctor."

The assistant expediently and quickly entered a code, involving numerous entries on the brilliant keypad. Not accepting the code he entered, the device let out an unpleasantly loud buzzer noise and flashed red. The tiny droid made an annoying halt gesture and digivoiced, "Sorry, your passcode is invalid. Please enter your valid passcode to visit the doctor."

Muttering to himself, the assistant again thunderously fast pressed a series of illuminated keys in quick succession. Again rejecting the code entered, the device let out another loudly unpleasant buzzer noise and flashed bright red. Repeating its annoying halt gesture, the tiny droid whirled about and repeated its unwelcoming phrase. "Sorry, your passcode is invalid. Please enter your valid passcode to visit the doctor."

"This happens sometimes. This unit can be temperamental." the assistant explained to the detectives. Emily smiled. Eddie nodded in understanding. Then turning back to the temperamental electronic keypad and mini-robot, the assistant said "Geshuntit."

"Welcome to Dr. Bennathan Halibut's office. The doctor will see you now. Have a great day." the device synthesized as the little robot vigorously waved hello.

Dr. Halibut's office was completely full with bookshelves, desks, credenzas, high back leather chairs, model robots, more bookshelves, awards, filing cabinets, computer equipment, and three dry erase white boards. His multiple diplomas for engineering and robotics hung orderly on the office wall.

"Lt. Knighton, I received your emails. Please have a seat and let's discuss that fascinating robot you photographed." Bennathan eagerly welcomed them. "Where did you find this unique design?" he curiously wondered.

Eddie remained silent as he sat. Emily took his silence as a cue to answer the doctor. "In an abandoned warehouse on the far western border of Cathedral." Then she switched to questioning, "Can you tell what this robot was design to do?"

"From the photos, it is hard to determine its intended use and impossible to know its programming. What I can say is that it was constructed with high energy capacity. The robot was made to produce massive output or to operate for a long period of time." Dr. Halibut educated with his focus still on Eddie.

"So it would be fair to say that the robot was built to be productive and not necessarily nefarious." Emily speculated.

"Nothing about its design suggests destructive applications. There were no features or accessories which could be misused as a weapon. The robot was designed to be high powered and that power could potentially be used for productivity." Bennathan replied shifting his focus to Emily.

"What about data storage capacity?" Lt. Knighton wondered.

"There appears to be some internal storage capability but the robot does not seem to have any wireless network connectivity features. If that is correct, any data capture would be limited to the robot's inner hardware. Perhaps this was a prototype and the networking features were pending." the doctor of engineering and robotics indicated, looking back at the lieutenant.

"Could the robot be built as an elaborate bomb?" Emily queried.

"There is nothing explosive in nature from looking at the pictures of the robot. Any eruption from the unit would be due to malfunction and limited in scope, not bomblike. Also this robot appears to be very intricate in design, despite its disheveled appearance, and it would be peculiar to work in such depth of design and precision to construct a bomb." Dr. Halibut informed them, turning his attention back to Emily.

"Could you suggest a reason why the robot had so many wires?" Emily puzzled.

"This unit did have an excess of wires for a single robot. One possibility is that this robot was given multiple wiring paths for redundancy purely for precautionary backup. If this robot was meant for multitasking, then it is possible the abundance of wiring could be used for running multiple computations at the same time. Load balancing could be another option. If its processing is distributed over many paths, then the robot could be more efficient and faster. Another option is this was a radical design maybe made more out of creativity than practicality. Another possibility is this robot was designed to interface with other robots. The extra wiring could be used to connect and communicate directly to other robotics. There are a number of possibilities, it is difficult to pinpoint a specific one from just the pictures." Dr. Halibut speculated.

"Did you see anything to suggest why the robot had such a complicated design?" Emily asked a follow-up question.

"When inventing a robot, there is usually a tug of war between simplicity of design verses additional features. The design starts basic then grows and grows until it no longer resembles anything like the original concept. This could have been a case of an evolving bot build that went on a wild ride of additional inspirations." the doctor conjectured.

"Could it be robotically parasitic?" Lt. Knighton postulated.

"What an intriguing thought. The biggest limitation with any type of service robot is battery life. Designing a robot that could recharge itself by siphoning power from other robots would have tremendous benefits. Then the most important and valuable resource robots contain is data. Extracting information from other robots could also be advantageous. Stripping another robot of both its power and data could render it useless and increase the productivity and efficiency of the robot which absorbed them. This unit in question certainly has the probes and receptacles for such a function, but it is difficult to ascertain if the robot would have the capability to accomplish absorbing tasks from just the photographs. Of course, there could also be the possibility of piggybacking off of another robot instead of absorbing from it. But again, the pictures I have are inconclusive as to the feasibility of that function by this robot." Dr. Halibut considered the prospect.

"A definitive maybe." Eddie summarized.

"Could this be a radical design just for the purpose of being unique?" Emily wondered.

"My area of expertise is in robotical design and the practical methodology of robotic engineering but not in the motivation or philosophical desires of the designer. I can intelligently discuss the robot which was constructed but the thoughts of the designer are as mysterious to me as they are to you, detective. Much like a food critic can analyze and discuss the dish they are presented but would have no idea what the chef was thinking while cooking the dish." Bennathan explained.

"So any thoughts you would have on technical designs for galvanism or intraware designs for nefarious artificial intelligence would be purely speculation." Emily responded.

"Artificial intelligence itself, or the lack thereof, is never nefarious, detective. It is the programmer that brings the wicked intentions, whether intentionally or unintentionally, but never the programmed. But you are correct that any thoughts I may have on those designs would be speculative since I am working with limited data. Although I will speculate that I seriously doubt this robot has anything to do with reanimation." the doctor specified.

"If you were to use this robot for criminal activity, then how would you use it?" Emily hypothetically inquired.

"I wouldn't use the robot to break the law. And if you can judge a man's intent by the design of his robot, then lady you're a better man than I." Dr. Halibut stated.

285

"Thank you." Eddie concluded the conversation.

"Thank you for taking the time to speak with us." Emily warmly thanked the doctor.

"You are welcome, detectives. Please return any time you have interesting robots to discuss." the doctor said farewell.

The pair of detectives left Dr. Halibut's office and headed for the company's exit in silence. Still full of activity, the lobby of the CGC was as busy as when they came. As the detectives left the Cathedral Guardian Company, Emily spotted a company logo at the end of the hall which grabbed her attention. She turned to ask Eddie if they could make a brief detour but to her surprise, she should not have been surprised, the lieutenant had also noticed it and was already walking in that direction. They were both on the same page.

Just as Emily thought she had seen, the company logo for the corporate suite at the end of the hall was for Moonlight Security. Moonlight Security was the security company used by the Incanncennio bottling plant. All the entrance security guards and the loading dock security at the bottling plant were employees of Moonlight Security.

Unlike the CGC's office, this office did not have an all-glass front wall. Instead, Moonlight Security's unit had double glass doors. Free of displayed literature and posters, the security office had a plain and simple exterior. Only its logo and company name were on display for the office of Moonlight Security.

"We can ask them if they have any cloud based video footage for the bottling plant." Emily suggested. The onsite security video for the bottling plant was poor quality and limited coverage.

"We can ask." Lt. Knighton replied shaking his head doubtfully.

Upon reaching the office doors of the security company, Lt. Knighton's coplink sounded. He briefly looked at it as Emily tried the doors. They were open and the pair of detectives entered Moonlight Security. Passing through the front entrance, the detectives had entered a tiny lobby with absolutely no furniture or decoration. The only item present in the little lobby was a piece of paper taped to the lone wooden door across the room.

Both detectives walked over to the lonely door to read the simple white plain typed sheet of paper. It read: Moonlight Security permanently closed. We are now Evereyes, Inc., a division of Middleton, AJC, and Hoyt Enterprises. Below that message in smaller print was the nearest Evereyes, Inc address. Emily made a mental note that the security company for the bottling plant in New Terranceville had been purchased. As they read, Emily's coplink sounded. With an urgent request to return to the 271st precinct, Captain Bronzesmith wanted them to come help work the precinct's current caseload on this busy day.

As Detective Oftenmarch read the captain's call for aid on her coplink, Lt. Knighton tried the lobby's lone wooden door. Surprisingly unlocked, the door opened without obstruction or setting off any audible alarms. Following the lieutenant, Emily walked through the doorway into the defunct company's closed office. They had entered a wide open area which was absolutely empty. This cavernous void did not even display vestiges of Moonlight Security. Left as a blank space, the office was now a depressing no longer viable business and a display of sad emptiness. The space was so clean and immaculate, it was like it had been erased.

"Guess we will not be asking anyone about better video footage for the bottling plant." Emily stated the obvious. Both of their coplinks chimed simultaneously.

"This villainy has layers." Eddie stated, then exited the former office of Moonlight Security.

Chapter 14

Distraction

Captain Bronzesmith had sent a dozen texts to each of the mud tusslers while they were in the Wallace-Franklin building. Like most Mondays for the 271st Precinct homicide division, the caseload was becoming overwhelming. Unlike most Mondays, Eddie and Emily were not working homicide cases assigned to the precinct. This deviation had Captain Bronzesmith, who was still unhappy with them working the lycan masquerade killer case, pleading with them to return to their home precinct to investigate some cases. The pair of detectives capitulated and made their next destination a crime scene in the 271st precinct's assigned territory.

For the second time that day, instead of driving across the city of Cathedral back to the 271st precinct, Eddie opted to drive into the suburbs and circumvent the city and its heavy traffic. He drove east out of Cathedral into the suburb of Manchester Heights, then southeast into Manchester Hills. The lieutenant then travelled through the neighboring suburban cities of Ascension, Grand Walnut, Breckenwright, North Washington, Aldersburgh, Copley Downs, Deacon Falls, Sycamore Hills, and New Terranceville. The added travelling distance was made up for in subtracted time travelled, and Eddie was getting quite proficient at this method.

From the urgent dispatch sent by Captain Bronzesmith, the detectives had received the location of the latest homicide requiring investigation. It was in a warehouse office building in the Modern Workers Industrial Park. This location was not far from Gallium Valley, named for all the companies in the area that made semiconductor, multimetal super circuitry, and microchip products. Grimy and smoky, the area was full of blue collar and hard working companies. Between two midscrapers, the detectives found the concealed city street they sought. Behind a glass factory, a furniture warehouse, and another office building, their destination was a couple hundred feet off the main road on a muddy and unpaved dirt lane in a secluded section of the industrial park. Behind their destination was an old abandoned water treatment plant used during the days of old Arden city. Beside the unused and unoccupied plant was an old antiquated water tower. In faded black block letters, the word Arden appeared on the old fashion water tower. Above that faded word, were the words City of Cathedral written in vibrant white cursive script.

Three Cathedral police squad cars, a third-party medical examiner van, and a Cathedral PSUV were already parked around the three-story warehouse and office building. Basic in its design, the building was very similar to several other building in the area and blended in well. A dozen or more Crime Scene Preservers, robots called CSPs, had been deployed around the building. There was little vehicle traffic and even less foot traffic in this area so Emily knew something more than a standard isolate and secure the crime scene was happening with so many CSPs being used. A pair of Cathedral patrol officers were in the process of deploying more CSPs as Eddie and Emily arrived on the scene. One of the officers was frantically working on a CSP that was malfunctioning. The robot was listing to the left, flashing amber and red lights, and letting out a sad gear-grinding whine.

Hopping out of the PSUV, Emily walked toward the closest police officer on the scene to get an update of what was going on here. There seemed to be a lot of chaos and confusion. As she approached the officer who was busy deploying a CSP, Emily realized she recognized him.

"Sundance Lance, what's going on here?" Emily addressed the patrol officer.

"Too cute to cop Emily, welcome to the fun." Lance returned.

"Does not look like you're having much fun." Emily countered.

"What gave me away?" the officer asked with a smile.

"One, you're not dancing. Two, you appear to be working which is unusual for you but suits you well." Detective Oftenmarch kidded.

"Hey, I now work a second job I will have you know. Started working evenings at the cop company, Catch 'Em." the officer proudly shared.

"Well congratulations to you, Lance, and my condolences to Catch 'Em." Emily replied.

"It's good news that you're here. We're sure we have the killer trapped in the building but nobody can find them." Lance explained the situation.

"Let's start with how we are sure the killer is in this building. Could you catch me up on that part?" Emily requested.

"Officers Roberts and Worcasminitz were first on the scene. My partner and I arrived just after them. The original dispatch was for a victim of a shooting on the ground floor. That victim is in a back store room, the ME is working there now. While the four of us were securing the original crime scene, we all distinctly heard gunshots coming from the basement. No doubt about it. We have locked down this building, we followed all the procedures, nobody got passed us, but the shooter is nowhere to be found in the building." Lance told Emily. Lt. Knighton had joined them to hear this tale.

"Then there is one victim on the ground floor and one victim in the basement." Emily sought confirmation from the officer.

"Correct, confirmed by homicide already inside the building. And one shooter tucked away somewhere on the premises." Lance added.

"So we have someone playing hide and go seek. Let us see how this new technology works, just received this autotracker this morning." Emily disclosed as she pulled out the brand new autotracker. Pointing it at the warehouse, she manually pressed the autoactivate button and watched the display. The device's digital display read signal jammed repeatedly.

"Most impressive." Lt. Knighton commented then started walking towards the warehouse.

"The other police detective already tried to scan the building. It didn't work then either." Lance informed her.

Emily switched the tracking adjustment lever to life signs and tried a second time but the display still read signal jammed repeatedly. "Guess it is back to the old fashioned way. Thanks for bringing us up to speed, Lance. We are off to find a bad man." Emily told Lance.

"We will watch your butt, detective." the police officer told her.

"I'd rather you watch my back." Emily responded as she hustled to catch up with Eddie.

Emily could hear the nearest CSP whirling and humming away as strode next to Lt. Knighton. The unit was motionless on its robotic watch. The temperature had levelled off and the cloudy sky made it appear as the day would not get any warmer. After getting her first CPD windbreaker of the day dirty searching in the dumpster that morning, Emily was now wearing her second CPD windbreaker. Emily zipped her jacket up and drew it in close as the wind gusted. As Eddie and Emily approached the building, they passed a private security drone which had been turned upside down and placed in an outdoor garbage bin. The drone could be heard humming and beeping away as it remained helplessly upside down in the trash. Moving quickly, the pair of detectives reached the warehouse and office building's doors with motivation on many fronts. The officer guarding the doors greeted them as he opened the door for them.

"Detectives, the medical examiner is three rooms back on the right and your colleagues are downstairs with the second victim searching for the shooter." the officer informed them.

"Did you hear the gunshots earlier, officer?" Emily asked the helpful officer.

'Sorry, that happened before I arrived on scene. Not sorry I missed the gunfire, get enough of that tosh already. I can say that nobody's left this building through these doors since I have arrived." the officer answered.

"Roger that" Eddie responded.

"Thank you, Jones." Emily thanked him, reading the officer's name off his uniform.

Lt. Knighton opted for the subterranean route and heading for the basement victim and their co-workers. As they descended the stairs, the pair of detectives entered what looked like a mishmash of low budget horror movie props. Boxes of tentacles, a stack of fake tombstones, a container of rubber bats, a box of oversized spider webs, a pair of sarcophaguses, a pair of empty cages, a cage full of prop skeletons, boxes of zombie limbs, a half dozen old robotesque sci-fi droids, a pile of black cauldrons, a box of mangled looking imps, a row of green slimy creatures, a box of ghoulish outfits, boxes of Cthulhu style creature parts, a tall, spindly, and shiny robot, and a massive crocodile costume in three detached sections were being stored in the basement of the warehouse section of the building along with hundreds of dusty stacked cardboard boxes.

Trainee Monkhouse had pulled several boxes away from the far wall and seemed to be busily studying a section of the wall for something. Detective Weibei was crouched down by the victim, carefully looking over their body. She had a disapproving look on her face as she made observations over the fatal abuse. The poor victim was lying face up with their arms and legs sprawled awkwardly outward. Emily and Eddie passed a pair of boxes with goggling eyed monster heads at the bottom of the stairs. As the pair of detectives approached the victim, they could discern the victim had four or five gunshot wounds in their torso.

"I would ask for the bad news before the good news but I am afraid you would only have bad news, Varrity." Emily greeted her crouching co-worker.

"Well, it is good news you and the lieutenant are here. After that, things are as strange and somber as they appear." Detective Weibei replied, looking up from studying the corpse.

"From the beginning please, V." Eddie requested.

"Murkendale and Coles have two active cases going. Mark and Theo are busy with an ugly case, so that left Joppers and myself as the best option to take this when it was dispatched. It was dispatched as a single homicide, one shooting victim. So my partner and I decided he would keep working our current case with Huana and I would bring the trainee Monkhouse with me to work this homicide. We had not even arrived on the scene when reports of a second shooting for this same location were broadcast on the comms. Officers on the scene before us indicated those shots came from down here. Patrick and I immediately came down here first, discovered this body and searched this level for an active shooter. Finding nobody, we went back upstairs to search for a shooter. Still finding no one, we then identified the victim upstairs as Erin Gonzaulles, a 24-year-old inventory manager, and spoke with the third-party medical examiner who had arrived onsite. We then returned here to identify this victim as Chen Lau Bei, a local independent internet film director." Weibei ran down the sequence of events.

"What's Erin's cause of death?" queried the lieutenant.

"Third party ME indicated one of three bullets fired struck her heart and killed her instantly. As far as I know he is still examining her. He is a squirrelly fellow afraid to be here if a shooter could still be around and flatly refuses to come downstairs until we catch someone." Weibei disclosed.

"What is Patrick doing?" Emily asked.

"He believes the killer must have escaped through a tunnel since the uniformed officers are positive the shooter did not leave through the building's doors. Patrick is searching for an entrance to a possible hidden tunnel." Varrity explained.

"The autotracker registers a jammed signal. That suggests to me that instead of escaping, an individual is masking their hidden presence." Emily deduced as she pulled out her autotracker to try again.

"We've searched this area thoroughly but I don't mind trying a second subterranean search." Varrity volunteered.

"Is your autotracker jammed?" Lt. Knighton asked Detective Weibei.

After pulling out her autotracker to check it again, Varrity answered, "Yes, still out of commission."

Putting away her still jammed autotracker, Emily commented, "Likewise. Looks like we are going to have to search the old fashioned way."

"Let the search begin." Lt. Knighton decided with a scowl.

Now pulling out her maxrecorder, Emily began a micropulse digiscan of Chen Lau Bei. "If you search towards the stairs, Varrity, then I will search towards the back wall." she suggested.

"Sure, I'll search through the horror shop storage this way and you search through all the little shop of horror storage that way." Varrity jested.

"Sounds like a plan." Emily agreed as the digiscan completed. She knelt down beside the victim for a moment of silent prayer.

"Where would you like me to search?" Monkhouse wondered.

"For boxes with human weight." Eddie answered, pointing to a stack of boxes in the far corner of the gloomy basement.

"Box lifting and basement hunting for homicidal lunatics were not listed in the training description." Monkhouse grumbled.

"Every day is a new adventure in the Cathedral PD. We would not begin to know what to put in the job description. It can be both a refreshing and depressing aspect of this job." Detective Weibei responded.

Finishing her prayer, Detective Oftenmarch rose to her feet and began to scrutinize a section of the basement towards the far wall. After passing a severely damaged casket with no lid, Emily began inspecting a grouping of boxes. Nobody was hiding behind them or between them. These boxes were the extra wide and oversized type used for moving purposes. She opened one of the boxes to find creatures from the dark blackened lagoon costumes. There was an empty crumpled potato chip bag comingled with the costumes but no people. The second box Emily opened contained hundreds of worn white wax candles. Some were broken, all of them were dusty, and none of the candles were concealing a person. Progressing to the next box revealed empty cookie tins, a pair of well played dart boards, and unused rolls of macabre wallpaper. The last two boxes in the group were extremely light and were leaking packing peanuts.

The detective moved forward with her manhunt. Sidestepping an unhinged stock and a knocked over birdcage, Emily moved to the next grouping of boxes, also oversized. These boxes also hid nobody behind them or between them. Causing her to flinch, the first box Emily opened contained rubber dungeon rats which appeared quite realistic. She was glad to continue onto the next box which contained raggedy and filthy clothing probably used as zombie costumes. Box number three likewise contained shabby clothing in the zombie line of fashion. In the group's last box was stored jars of fake eyeballs, warped candlesticks, and broken brass book-ends.

Keeping her search quick and professional, Emily swiftly moved to the next potential hiding area. Moving around a sea monster head and a partially torn wyvern puppet, Detective Oftenmarch began to search around the next set of boxes. Emily could hear Monkhouse kicking boxes over as she swiftly sifted through more boxes of useless junk and second-rate movie props. Satisfied nobody was hidden among these boxes, she moved her hunt forward to the next set of boxes.

Emily partially on autopilot efficiently carried on with the search. After checking in and around this new set of boxes, Emily began rapidly riffling through more boxes of nonsense and clutter finding no cowering culprit. The detective was churning up more dust than clues in this dreary basement. Effectively searching and clearly this set of cardboard boxes, Detective Oftenmarch progressed to the next set of boxes.

After a quick visual check that no squatters resided behind or between this next group of cardboard boxes, Emily plunged into checking the contents of these boxes. The first box contained a sizeable stuffed moose head for mounting on a wall as a trophy. The second box contained a new surprise, bags of marijuana leaves mixed with paranoid hemp. Each bag was as tightly packed as possible. This box held enough pot to open a cannabinoid den.

"There is a lot of restricted substances in this box. This stash of weed would be worth quite a lot if sold on the street." Detective Oftenmarch revealed to the foursome.

"Enough to be a possible motive for murder?" Varrity inquired pausing her manhunt momentarily.

"That is a possibility." Emily reasoned as she slid the box of hemp to the side.

"Anyone hiding in the hemp?" Weibei asked hopefully.

"No pot hidden potheads." Emily answered drolly as she moved onward to inspect the next storage box.

Opening the next box, Detective Oftenmarch discovered plastic bags full of pills. The bags of brightly colored pills were labelled Party Starters, Wild Animal, and Whoa Dude. There were roughly a couple of hundred pills in each bag. Bag after bag the detective tested with the probe port on her digiscanner. Test after test came back positive for illegal substances.

"Now we have progressed to illegal substances. Possession of this box would lead to jail time." Emily called out. Having surveyed the contents of the box, she slid this box aside to join the box of hemp.

Moving on to inspect the contents of the third, fourth, and fifth boxes, Emily found bubblegum cigars, party favors, witch hats, warlock masks, rubber bats, more tattered zombie clothing, and expired cans of spaghetti but no more drugs and no hideaways. She paused for a moment before scurrying on to the next set of boxes to rethink her strategy. Even though there was an abundance of boxes in this basement, how likely would a killer choose to hide in a cardboard box, Emily riddled to herself.

As Detective Oftenmarch was contemplating this hide and seek question, a pair of Cathedral police officers came down the basement stairs. The looks on their faces displayed their bewildered reaction to the peculiar basement decor. Emily hustled over to greet them as they reached the bottom of the stairs. Still looking confused, both officers stood motionless at the foot of the stairs as they tried to make sense of all the odd items. Emily noticed they were Cathedral patrol officers from the 270th precinct. She had not realized they were that close to the neighboring precinct.

"Good afternoon, officers. I am Detective Emily Oftenmarch with Cathedral homicide. That's Lt. Knighton over by the skeletons in cages." Emily made introductions. Eddie waved distractedly as he concentrated on the search.

"Officer Linnears, reporting to help." the first patrol officer stated.

"I am Officer Spears. You having a party down here, detective?" the second officer opened lightheartedly.

"Very close, Spears. This is a search party. We are looking for a possible shooter still hiding in the basement and our autotrackers are being jammed." Emily explained.

"You're thinking the perp is hiding about this creepy freak show?" Officer Linnears checked.

"We are thinking that's a distinct possibility." Emily confirmed.

"Where would you like us to search?" Officer Spears inquired.

"One of you help trainee Monkhouse search the boxes along the back wall, please. Then the other please help Detective Weibei with her search of the nearby clutter." Detective Oftenmarch requested.

Both officers nodded in affirmation then quickly moved out to join the underground exploration for any hiding killers. As Emily began walking back to resume her cardboard box inspections, she noticed another person coming down the stairs. This time it was 270th precinct homicide detective Bret Cromby.

The heavily experienced detective strolled down the stairs like he had all the time in the world. Cromby was a hard working old school detective known for his love of fat cigars, double cheeseburgers, and thinly crowded strip clubs with plenty of whiskey in stock. He always wore a slovenly tied dark blue necktie and an untucked white dress shirt. The pouncy detective often worked alone because he preferred to work odd hours.

"Such a happy cheery place." the old detective said sarcastically.

"We often get the happy cheery locations for crime scenes." Emily replied as she looked around the basement.

"You could not be more right, Emily. This is the third dank and creepy basement in which I have had to work this month." Detective Weibei remarked.

"This is also the third dungeonlike basement this month for the lieutenant and me. But only the second time we had to play scavenger hunt in an assortment of basement junk." Emily shared.

"Instead of happy bright places, we get to search in dark dank places." Weibei lamented.

"There's enough clutter here for a week's worth of hunting in the dark." Cromby commented.

"There is a lot of stuff to go through in the dark corners of this place." Emily admitted.

"Do people actually buy this garbage?" Weibei asked.

"This is nonsense, we don't need to go through every nook and cranny to find a person. To speed up our search, we could start breaking stuff and make it even more worthless." Cromby suggested.

"I wouldn't discount anything." Emily replied.

"Feels like the more we search the more stuff we find and the less progress we make." Weibei complained.

"Is it necessary to search through all this useless rubbish? I prefer working smarter not harder." Cromby expressed.

"If we don't search thoroughly, we may miss something important." Emily reasoned as she shifted another box of stuff.

"There's more boxes of stuff over here." one of the patrol officers called out.

"This looks like it is going to be a tedious case." Detective Weibei lamented.

"This looks familiar, almost identical to the MacGinty case." Detective Cromby observed.

"It does look like it, almost too much like it." Emily admitted.

"There's even more boxes of stuff over here." called the other patrol officer.

"A long and tedious case indeed." Webei emphasized.

"Eddie, does this remind you of the MacGinty case?" Emily asked the lieutenant.

The lieutenant paused a moment from his searching. "Yes, definitively yes." Eddie agreed after thinking it over briefly.

"The lieutenant sees it now." Cromby told Oftenmarch

"Who worked on the MacGinty case?" Varrity wondered.

"Detective Bret Cromby." Eddie recalled correctly.

"We should talk to him." Detective Weibei suggested.

"He retired from the Cathedral Police Department two years ago and passed away six months ago in a retirement home down in Florida." Oftenmarch revealed. Emily looked over her shoulder and Detective Cromby was gone.

"That's too bad. We could have used his help." Detective Weibei again lamented.

"We already received his help, Varrity. Cromby showed Eddie and I how this was done and how to find the killer." Emily replied. She was both concerned and relieved about her mental health at the same time.

"When?" puzzled Weibei.

"The MacGinty case." Eddie answered. He had moved over to the row of husky robotesque sci-fi droids and seemed to be lost in thought.

Studying the robots for a moment, Eddie seemed to be pondering them. They were either archaic robots or cheap sci-fi props for a low budget film. After some consideration, Lt. Knighton came to a decision. The lieutenant pulled out his Phasepulser IX and streamed it at the first bulky droid in the line. The droid hit the ground with a loud clunk in a heap as it emanated an array of sparks. Eddie moved to the next robot and once again fired his Phasepulser IX into the machine. This unit also crashed loudly to the ground in a display of zaps and arcs. This fallen robot let out some popping and bzzting sounds. His bizarre tactic was to execute the old broken-down robots. It was so unusual, everyone in the basement was shocked and speechless as they stopped what they were doing to watch in amazement.

"That is definitively different from how Detective Cromby did it." Emily shared breaking the silence.

Continuing with his process, the lieutenant recharged his stunner and moved to the third hefty droid in the line. With his Phasepulser IX repowered, he took aim at this old robot. As Eddie fired a stream into this robot, the fourth robot suddenly moved and began to run, or as close to running as it could manage. Emily was ready for this as if she had expected it.

She shoved some partially full boxes in the path of the fleeing non-robot. Unrobotic in its flight, the runner had gotten off to a good start but the cumbersome and vision restricted outfit handicapped the fleeing non-robot from avoiding the boxes. The runner tripped over the incoming boxes, fell head over heels, and went sprawling to the floor. The robot clad basement hider slammed hard onto the concrete floor and let out a painful shout.

"You are under arrest for suspicion of murders." Emily informed the fallen faux droid as she began to hold it to the ground.

The non-robot began to squirm and struggle as Detective Oftenmarch fought to keep him pinned to the floor. Monkhouse had raced over to the tussle and started helping Emily restrain the suspect. As they were subduing the droid dressed deceiver, a beeping noise came from the tall lanky and shiny robot nearby.

Its lights and displays came on as the robot began activating. As it was powering up, Detective Weibei and one of the Cathedral police officers rushed towards the tall robot. If their plan was to prevent the shiny robot from coming online, then they were too late. Surging into action, the lanky robot maneuvered forward toward the fallen non-robot. The gleaming robot bowled over both the patrol officer and Detective Weibei. Varrity was knocked down to the ground and the officer went crashing into some nearby boxes. The spindly mechanical bot shot out a stunner stream in Emily's direction, which she nimbly ducked underneath while still restraining the fallen disguised non-robot.

Lt. Knighton returned fire, shooting a pair of stunner streams from his Phasepulser IX at the gangly bot. Both streams struck the shiny servant, but the robot absorbed the stuns. Unfazed, the mechanical bot marched forward toward the suspect being arrested. It appeared to have been summoned to come to the aid of the prone suspect. The second 270th precinct officer rushed forward and attempted to tackle the metallic menace. Smashing hard into the droid, the officer tried to haul the rangy robot off its artificial feet. Plowing through the would be tackler, the robot kept both its balance and its forward momentum. Unable to topple it, the police officer ended up clinging to the mechanical machine and being dragged along by it. The lean lanky robot discharged another stunner stream. Its aim was off target and the stream struck an undamaged bulky bot, causing it some damage.

With the police officer grappling with the robot, Eddie could no longer shoot it with stunning streams. Therefore, the lieutenant charged up close to the robust robot and began to wrestle with it. In a struggle, Eddie began to grab and try to pull out exposed wires in an attempt to remove power or disable the unit. Prying and yanking, Lt. Knighton fought vigorously to relieve the robot of some of its cabling. Sparks flew and the lieutenant released the cables he had been tugging, as he had been shocked.

Abruptly swiveling violently, the gangly bot bucked off the clutching police officer. The officer was thrown five feet and crashed into some black cauldrons before landing forcefully on the ground. The lieutenant had managed to maintain his grip on the bothersome bot and continued to grapple with its electronics.

During the bot fight, Emily and trainee Patrick had gained control of the non-robot. Despite their squirming and resisting and costume obstructions, he was now handcuffed. As Oftenmarch and Monkhouse were able to subdue and restrain the downed disguised deviant, Varrity had stood back up and regained her footing. She attempted to help the lieutenant stop the advancing robot, only to be knocked back down to the floor. For a second time, Detective Weibei found herself collapsed on the hard concrete floor. Still persistent, the troublesome techbot shot a third and fourth stunner streams. These stunner shots narrowly missed Emily and struck the concrete floor close by her. She heard hissing from the streams as they passed inches away from her.

Leaving the cuffed faux robot for Monkhouse to handle, Emily swiftly sprang over to the oncoming shiny sleek robot. Unholstering her TriAlloy Max XLT, she got right up close to the robomenace. The detective placed her TriAlloy Max XLT pistol underneath the robot's metal mechanically constructed chin and fired point blank. The gunshot sent a shower of bits, wires, circuits, chips, and capacitors spraying into the air. Quickly re-positioning her firearm, Emily fired a second shot point blank into the robot's metal-framed cranium. This shot removed a sizeable chunk of the robotic head. Oil erupted from the robot like a geyser and spewed outward onto Emily's jacket, shirt, and pants. The machine crumpled to the ground, not having the processing power to continue. Releasing his hold, Eddie let the robocarcass hit the floor.

"No domo arigato super robotto" Eddie told Emily while surveying the fallen robotic remains. He then made his way towards the area with the bulky robots.

"I've got a secret. Secret, secret." Emily answered Eddie as she helped Varrity off the basement floor. The twice knocked down detective started to regain her composure once she was back on her feet.

As Officer Linnears helped Monkhouse haul the reluctant apprehended non-robot suspect to his feet, Officer Spears examined the blasted to bits robot to make sure it was down for good.

"Now I know never to make you angry, detective." Officer Spears commented.

"Emily does not mess about when the villains get violent. She gets tough when they get rough." Varrity agreed now recomposed.

Detective Oftenmarch noticed a stunner laying on the ground by trainee Monkhouse. Picking up the stunner, Emily noted it was an antiquated short range bolt stunner. The bolt stunner was an old rarely seen predecessor to the stream stunner.

"That's mine. Must have fallen out of my pocket in the struggle." Monkhouse indicated, pointing to the stunner.

"Good job, Patrick. Thank you for your help with the arrest. We will be adding resisting arrest to this suspect's list of charges." Emily told the trainee as she returned his bolt stunner to him.

Lt. Knighton had walked over to the last standing undamaged bulky bot. With his Phasepulser IX redrawn and recharged, the lieutenant fired a stream stunner in the last sad sci-fi robot. Sparks emitted from the unit as it plummeted to the basement floor. It landed with a thud and a crackle to leave no more unscathed robots in the eerie basement. Officer Spears let out a loud gaffe at the lieutenant's disguised droid double check.

Officer Linnears was able to remove enough of the robotic costume to reveal the suspect's face. Monkhouse found a handgun concealed in a section of the non-robot's costume. Emily took out an evidence bag from her windbreaker pocket. Detective Weibei took a picture of the captured criminal's face with her police coplink.

"Where's your MPAR, Varrity?" Emily asked.

"With Joppers. Where's your MPAR?" Varrity counterqueried.

"Being repaired in the police tech shop. The ELE were unkind to it." Emily shared as she collected the discovered weapon from Monkhouse and placed it into an evidence bag.

"How kind of them. Don't know about anyone else but I am more than ready to leave this basement." Varrity shared.

"I have an ID for this idiot, detective." Monkhouse indicated as he had ungloved and fingerprinted the suspect with a digiscanner.

"It would probably be a good idea to take our friend with the robot fetish back to the 271st precinct before the lieutenant decides to stun him with a Phasepulser." Emily reasoned as she searched her pockets for her maxrecorder.

"I like your reasoning, Emily." Weibei agreed.

As Varrity and Monkhouse started perp marching the apprehended crime scene hider, Emily asked the 270th precinct officers to collect both boxes of drugs and take them into evidence. She also had found her maxrecorder and began scanning sections of the basement. Recording as she went, Emily walked over to Lt. Knighton. He was in the process of putting away his Phasepulser IX and taking out his coplink.

"I am going to go ask the third party ME to come down now and get Mr. Chen Lau Bei." Emily updated Eddie. He merely nodded in agreement.

Chapter 15

Back to the Desk

After capturing the robot disguised miscreant, Lt. Knighton drove their PSUV back to their home base, Cathedral PD precinct 271. With a brake and accelerate pattern, the lieutenant drove through troubling traffic. The traffic crawl came with a cacophony of horns, loud truck engines, and construction machinery. There were construction zones aplenty on their travel. Orange barrels littered the landscape. Unless continuous construction chaos was in progress, the Cathedral Department of Transportation did not feel like they were productive. To further complicate matters, a robodelivery drone broke down on Wilchester Road, backing up traffic for blocks and blocks. Eventually, Eddie made it back to their precinct despite all the obstacles. Once there, he dropped Detective Oftenmarch off before heading back out to aid Detectives Murkendale and Coles.

Tired and hungry, Emily walked four doors east to the local deli called Belly Joy to purchase a simple salad, a turkey sandwich with extra tomato, a bag of kettle chips, and a bottle of overpriced water to have for her late lunch. The food was not fancy but the ingredient of hunger made it taste great. The water was warm but the ingredient of thirst made it very quenching. Her late lunch break was not long but it was enough to recharge her energy.

When Detective Oftenmarch entered the 271st precinct, the main lobby was a grand circus. Packed with citizens with complaints, patrol officers with arrested people, some protesters with signs, and other people at the precinct for various reasons, Emily noticed that the robotic assistant at the front desk had malfunctioned. Because of the broken bot, Sgt. Kipperfish was working the desk and the poor man looked overwhelmed. He looked to be at his wit's end. After weaving her way up to the desk, Emily gave the frazzled sergeant her unopened bag of potato chips in an attempt to cheer up the man. With the snack delivered, Emily headed for the homicide division.

When Detective Oftenmarch returned to her desk, she discovered three things. First, the thermostat to the heating and cooling for her department was malfunctioning. It continuously recorded 85 degrees and was perpetually running the air conditioning. Second, the Cathedral PD's main computer server was offline due to unannounced updates. This limited the amount of police records accessible and database searches which could be executed. Third, the captain had put a hit and run casefile on her desk with a handwritten note of instructions which indicated what he wanted her to do.

Emily changed from her dusty shirt to a deep claret thermal mock-neck shirt with thumbholes in the sleeves and a cozy pewter sweater fleece left partially unzipped. The detective had already changed her oil-soaked pants for some fresh slacks before arriving at her desk. She rubbed some Silversilk hand cream onto her hands before making some warm herbal tea in the department's break area. Once she had taken measures to endure the office chilliness, Emily moved onto combatting computer obstacles. With the Cathedral PD's core cloudframe down due to security improvements to comply with ISO, International Organization for Standardization, requirements and FRPIP, Federal Regulations of Public Information Protection, regulations, the detective utilized a secondary option. Emily switched to a departmental server that Eddie had an overzealous intern install last year. This would at least give her enough processing technology and data access to be productive.

Once connected to the secondary server, Emily had to run software updates which required a reboot and then she had to change her password as the old entry had expired. When she completed those tasks, she had cleared the second hurdle. Or so she had thought; KIMMIE was being temperamental and took several reloads before loading correctly. Once the finicky program came online, Emily had then cleared the second hurdle.

As Emily began to work, she then saw the state of disorganization for the contents of CaseBuilder. Notes for cases were put accidently in wrong files in CaseBuilder. Case notes for #HC4014849A~2 were placed in the folder for case #HC4018329B~3. Form 442s were switched between cases #HC4014849A~2 and #HC4015659A~1. The 442 was missing from case #HC4018330A~1. Case #HC4018335C~2 was a duplicate of #HC4018012D~2 but with the victim's name misspelled. Notes for case #HC4018329B~3 were placed in case #HC4017674A~2 and for some reason translated into German. GOD only knows where the notes of case #HC4017674A~2 ended up. As Emily tried to bring up the hit and run case, she got an input error. Giving up after the third try, she had to recreate the case from backup files.

With the casefiles back into some semblance of order, Detective Oftenmarch began performing the tasks her captain had instructed for the hit and run case, HC4019105D~8. With seven people being injured and two people being killed by the speeding driver, this case was both tragic and disturbing. There were 145 witness statements recorded which Emily had to organize first by relevance, then each germane subcategory was sorted alphabetically. A couple of people were interviewed twice. Emily kept those repeat interviews with the originals. Once the witness statements were in order in CaseBuilder, Emily began downloading the traffic camera footage sent by the Cathedral Traffic Control Department. While the downloads were running, she began gathering the facial recognition reports forwarded to her by the captain in twelve intradepartmental emails. Unlike the non-robot basement hider, the hit and run driver had not bothered to disguise themselves. Their face was recorded on multiple cameras. Among the traffic department, the technology lab, the forensics lab, and two private law enforcement companies, facial recognition was run twelve times. All twelve times, the results returned with the driver unidentified. At the captain's request, Detective Oftenmarch logged all twelve negative results into CaseBuilder.

Connecting to the state department of motor vehicles, Detective Oftenmarch collected the registration information for the pick-up truck used in the crime. As Emily recorded that information into CaseBuilder, an alert appeared on her screen. It was an alert indicating the vehicle was reported stolen. The truck had been reported stolen two days ago early in the morning. Emily switched her connection to the Cathedral Police Department's division of stolen vehicles. She copied the case number, any pertinent notes, and records of the robbery incident into

CaseBuilder. Immediately after finishing the updates to CaseBuilder, Emily ran searches in the law enforcement records for the nearby surrounding area for any reports of recovered stolen vehicles. None matching the truck used in the crime could be found.

With a moment of inspiration, Emily cross referenced the family members of the hit and run victims with the family members of the stolen vehicle victim. Less than a minute into the search yielded success. Emily paused making her current updates in CaseBuilder to look at the search result. The spouse of one of the victims killed in the vehicular homicide was also the grandson of the man whose vehicle was stolen. Detective Oftenmarch pulled up the photo of this dual related individual from his driver's license on record. She then began to run facial recognition, a thirteenth attempt, on the driver in the video footage using the license photo as a comparative. The comparison quickly came back as a 98.9 percent probability as a match.

Although this dual related individual had been interviewed by a detective from a third-party law enforcement company, the interview notes on record were sad and insufficient. Emily added the weak and unuseful interview notes to CaseBuilder along with a request to have this suspect brought in for a second round of questioning. Upgrading the man from a possible suspect to the prime suspect, Emily put a high priority bulletin in CaseBuilder on his requestioning.

Saving all her work twice, once in CaseBuilder and once in a backup file, Emily returned to focusing her efforts on the lycan masquerade killers. Lt. Knighton had received an answer from the West Cathedral Department of traffic control which he had forwarded to her. Eddie's contact had come through for him with quick and helpful results. West Cathedral law enforcement had identified the killers' megawolf hauling truck a handful of times on traffic cameras' recordings for the night in question.

Emily began retracing the truck's route that evening via the West Cathedral traffic footage. Each camera had a long ridiculous identification code, street name, and time stamp on its recordings. The first video recording Emily started to review was from the camera on the ramp to state route 144. The recording showed the truck entering state route 144 at 4:54pm. Nothing particularly useful was on that footage, with the truck being so far from the camera. The next pair of video recordings Detective Oftenmarch observed were both from the camera on Van Buren Drive at the top of the driveway to the shopping plaza. As expected, the camera caught the megawolf shipping truck both coming and going. Unfortunately, this camera had a damaged lens and its recordings were of poor quality. Emily thought she could vaguely glimpse three fuzzy people in the cab of the truck. The truck arrived at the shopping center at 4:27pm, the megawolf couriers would then spend the next 23 minutes ordering food and misusing the nearby dumpster. The recording did not capture any of that activity. The truck left the shopping center at 4:53pm, three minutes after its occupants had paid for their food.

The next recording Emily watched was from a third traffic camera from 4:03pm to 4:06pm, this one was located on Chauncey Avenue just before a roundabout. This recording captured a rear view of the vehicle. The rotary was congested with traffic continuously entering and exiting. The truck full of wolves had to wait several minutes before taking its turn circling the roundabout 180 degrees to continue on Chauncey Avenue. This long distance footage did not show the truck doing anything out of the ordinary or anything to identify its passengers. The final recording also captured the back of the delivery truck. This recording was from a camera on Derbyshire Road and showed the truck going along Derbyshire Road and travelling under the old Tiedemann Pass. It maintained the speed limit as it drove uneventfully past the traffic camera, giving the police no reason to take notice. The footage was too dark and distant to discern any details. Unhelpfully, there was a faint time stamp on this video which looked like 3:54pm. Helpfully, from the route the truck was travelling on the video, Emily knew it was coming from either Harrison Heights or Hayes Hills. So they now knew that the truck full of wolves had come from somewhere farther northwest, and the megawolf pick-up took place before 4pm on Tuesday.

Having learned as much as she was going to glean from the traffic footage, Emily turned her attention to constructing an overview of the bottling plant homicides. The detective needed to review things and look at this case from a fresh perspective. This method sometimes helped Emily get a better understanding of what was involved in a case. This method also often gave Emily new ideas of where to investigate.

Detective Oftenmarch summarized what they knew about the Incanncennio Bottling Plant homicides. They knew, from the West Cathedral traffic cameras, that the masked madmen drove east into West Cathedral from Horsburgham Heights on North Lafayette Avenue. Once they were in West Cathedral, they stopped at the Breakfast and Brew Cafe where they picked-up a hearty meal and discarded unwanted items, including two megawolves, into a nearby dumpster. The detectives had discovered their dinner receipt and found their dumpster contributions.

The lycan masquerade killers then proceeded to Conglomerate's warehouse D505. They began to make themselves comfortable while injecting megawolves with growth hormones and putting masks on Lawbotic Patrollers when security guard Kenneth Brahmson discovered them on Wednesday. In a tragic confrontation the security guard was slain and the evildoing squatters were forced to relocate to an adjacent empty warehouse. The inhouse warehouse company detectives working with the local law enforcement were either incompetent or negligent as security footage was lost while masked madmen took refuge one warehouse away. The villains again made themselves comfortable while building robots and letting megawolves freely roam. In this unoccupied warehouse, the evildoing squatters left another slain megawolf, a robotic mess out of a mad scientist's dream, and an unspeakable amount of megawolf feces. They also left behind more hormone dispensing syringes for the detectives to find in the untenanted warehouse.

Leaving from the presumed unoccupied warehouse, the masked villains drove to the bottling plant in New Terranceville. From the plant's low quality security footage, the detectives could determine that a pair of accomplices entered through the plant's front entrance and made their way to the plant's loading dock. Once they were in position, they gave access of the loading dock to the evildoing squatters to make a menacing megawolf delivery.

These criminals had left a trail of lost and discarded oversized wolves that was not difficult to follow, like breadcrumbs in a fairy tale. This bizarre method did not suggest professionalism to Emily. It seemed amateur or bush league. Yet, earlier homicides were more organized, less clumsy, and left no blatant trails. Without a doubt, there was a disconnect here, or more likely, duplicity.

Detective Oftenmarch verified that KIMMIE was online and operating before using the program. "KIMMIE, how many lycan mask sightings have been reported in the last three weeks?" she began her inquiries.

Emily brought up a list of employees working the Incanncennio Bottling plant last Thursday night into early Friday morning. Running on a skeleton staff for the graveyard shift, the plant had a short list of employees working that period of time. The list consisted of the plant's night supervisor, two maintenance workers, a night janitor, a loading dock receiver, three security guards from recently acquired Moonlight Security, and a dozen plant floor workers, half of whom were temporary workers.

"There have been four hundred and seventeen reports of people being seen wearing werewolf masks." synthesized KIMMIE.

"How many sightings have been confirmed by the Cathedral Police Department?" Emily followed up her question with another question.

The murdered men at the bottling plant were one of the maintenance workers and the loading dock worker. Both had been chased by the megawolves smuggled into the plant prior to their demise. Ryerson, who appears to have been the intended victim, was not at his typical work station in the plant that night but out of position down in the basement level.

"There have been twelve sightings of werewolf masks confirmed by the Cathedral Police Department." KIMMIE's robotic answer was given.

"How many of the confirmed sightings were between sunset and sunrise?" Emily continued her questions. She paused to take a drink of tea.

"All twelve confirmed sightings were after sunset." KIMMIE digiresponded.

"When is the earliest time of day for any of the confirmed sightings?" Emily inquired.

"The earliest time recorded is 03:03 EST." digireplied KIMMIE.

"When is the latest time of day for any of the confirmed sightings?" Emily asked.

"The latest time recorded is 22:12 EST." roboresponded KIMMIE.

"Are all the confirmed sighting between sunset and sunrise?" Emily looked for clarification.

"Affirmative." KIMMIE answered.

"How many werewolf sightings have there been reported in the last three weeks?" Emily wondered.

So the lycan masked killers were striking in the dark. All the confirmed werewolf mask sightings were in the hours of darkness. Both the district attorney's homicide and the bottling plant murders were during the night time. Their crimes were always in the night, their misdeeds always in the dark.

Ryerson not being at his usual control terminal on the plant floor but down in the subterranean computer room that night appears to have been expected by the lycan masquerade killers. The high commissioner had indicated that Ryerson was performing a covert task for Cathedral law enforcement, yet the villainous intruders' approach of attack indicated they had advance knowledge of the atypical task and Ryerson's altered location. Did they have inside information, or had they just experienced good fortune? And if he was the intended victim, why were the murderers unsuccessful? Either he was not the intended target, something interfered with their evil execution, or Ryerson just experienced good fortune.

"There were two reports of werewolf sightings. Both were last Friday night." the search program voiced.

Detective Oftenmarch pulled up the list of lycan sightings. One was her alleged sighting at St. Gregory's Cemetery in Grantham on Friday night. The other sighting was by a man identified as Mad Mikey by the dispatcher who logged the received call. This was troubling knowledge; the only people seeing werewolves were a man known as Mad Mikey and herself. That was not good.

Getting back to the bottling plant, Emily found it interesting that the masked intruders knew when to depart the plant. Referring to some notes from the New Terranceville Police, Emily verified that the lycan masquerade killers had exited the plant before the first police officers arrived at the scene. Before New Terranceville police had reached the plant, the masked villains had departed and vanished into the night. The clever criminals left their megawolves behind as expendable marionettes and bolted with the job incomplete like they knew it was time to make their getaway. Were they on a time limit, or did they know law enforcement was coming soon? Impossible to say with the facts available. Detective Oftenmarch added notes and information into CaseBuilder.

The 271st precinct's detectives for the division of missing people shared the small break area with the homicide detectives. Several of them had gathered around in the break area for some coffee and conversation. They were in high spirits with much laughter and apparently not a lot of work at the moment.

One of the detectives, named Clayton Coventry, noticed Emily working at her desk and called out to her. "Hey, there's the beauty. But where is the beast? Where is the beast to your beauty, Emily?"

"Is your cruel reference to my husband or my partner?" Emily asked.

"Are you kidding? David-John is a charming gentleman. I was clearly referring to Lt. Knighton." Coventry replied with a chuckle.

Both detectives Grey and Warrington were big electronic pipe vapers. They used the break area to vape more than to eat or drink even though vaping was prohibited inside any Cathedral Police Department building. Between the two of them, they had a billow of vapor steam filling the area. A cloud of vapor steam hung over the snack and beverage counter so thick that it was obscuring the notice board on the wall behind the counter.

It was Warrington who first removed his elongated e-pipe from his mouth to speak. "It is ridiculously cold in here. Why don't the idiots in maintenance just turn the air conditioning off? We would be far better off with no temperature control." he sourly commented.

Grey removed his elongated e-pipe to join the conversation. "Rumor has it that you and Eddie are working a case for the high commissioner. Is that true, Emily?" he wondered,

With her co-workers' questions distracting her, Emily realized her work would be impeded for the near future. Besides, her tea could use refilling and reheating.

"We have been asked to investigate the murders at the Incanncennio bottling plant in New Terranceville because the lycan masquerade killers appear to be involved." Emily told the relaxing detectives as she walked over to the tiny break area.

"So the high commissioner has the lycan masquerade killers in his crosshairs." Coventry speculated then took a swig from his beverage.

"The Cathedral Police want the murders of these masqueraders to stop and the masked murderers brought to justice." Emily replied, neither confirming nor denying the speculation.

318

"Some of the detectives over in the 234th precinct think the were-wolf killers murdered the district attorney to steal one of his girlfriends. They have a bet going with the blokes in the 235th." Warrington shared mid-vape.

"Rumor has it that the district attorney would hire models to act as his girlfriends. He would switch models every four to six weeks to avoid the appearance of any long term commitments." Detective Dressler gossiped as he joined the group.

"The rumor I heard was a little different. It seems that the former DA paid multiple young women to date him simultaneously. He had a gaggle of trophy girlfriends." Coventry counter gossiped.

"These young ladies were all knockouts, absolutely gorgeous females. They were all far too attractive to be dating some middle aged overweight plain looking man." Warrington added mid-vape.

"One of those alleged models has gone missing. The 110th, 111th, and 112th precincts are all apparently busy looking for her as we speak." Grey revealed, then resumed vaping.

"I hope none of the wolfmen got ahold of the poor woman. It is bad enough having to pretend to date the former DA, the woman has been punished enough." Dressler expressed.

"Detective Smithers with the 267th told me that Lawtech Corp is now involved. They're supposedly spending big bucks on a manhunt for the missing girlfriend." Coventry shared.

"Yeah, I heard that as well. Rumor over in midtown is that one of the rich Lawtech corporate VPs is also pretending to date this beautiful babe." Warrington gossiped between vapes.

"Rumor also has it that you had seen a werewolf, Emily. Is Eddie working you too hard?" Dressler interjected, switching subjects.

"I don't know what I saw late Friday night. The whole scene and situation was bizarre." Emily explained.

"How are the QuadPs treating you?" Grey changed the subject.

"Positively poor police policy, same as usual." Warrington answered.

"Police procedure preventing progress, that is also business as usual." Dressler added.

"Proliferate paperwork per policeman" Coventry interjected with a chuckle.

"Please pass premium pints, that's my QuadPs." Warrington commented.

"It's not beer o'clock yet." Grey retorted.

"The last set of updated police policies work so brilliantly, the geniuses thought they'd give it another go." Warrington sarcastically stated, then returned to vaping.

"I am still waiting for the department to fix the Quad Fs: frustration, fatigue, folly, and futility." Coventry mused.

"Pick-up pretty perky partners, that's my QuadPs." Dressler joked.

"It's not beer o'clock yet." Grey repeated

"I think I will get a head start." Dressler returned. The missing persons detective poured himself a hearty cup of coffee heavily comingled with whiskey, then proceeded to spill the entire contents onto himself and Emily.

"We don't spill good booze on beautiful women. That's standard police practice that I actually agree with." Grey unhelpfully commented, then resumed vaping.

"I am so sorry, Emily." Dressler apologized profusely.

"Pull yourself together, man. Look at what you have done to poor Emily." Coventry expressed as he tried to help clean up the mess.

"I am so sorry, Emily." Dressler repeated as he tried to clean up his mess.

"It's ok, Donavan. It's not the first time alcohol has been spilled on me. I will be fine." Emily reassured the apologetic detective as she mopped liquid off herself and the floor.

"Well, I can tell by the mess Dressler's made that it's time to get back to work. It was nice talking to you, Emily." Grey farewelled, then concluded his vaping.

"By the way, Emily, Theo, Max, and I are all going to Crazy Skeeters for big burger night. You are welcome to join us." Detective Coventry invited her.

"Sorry, I would but I already have plans with my husband. He is giving a lecture at Chatham Community College and we have dinner plans afterwards." Emily politely declined as she attempted to remove coffee from her attire.

"C'mon Dress, let's leave Emily be so she can get back to work." Coventry told his co-worker then drained his drink and left the breakroom. Dressler followed him with one last apology as he departed.

Emily took a few more minutes to clean and compose herself before getting back to work. Now that the gossip hour and baptism of booze was over, Emily could resume work in peace. As Emily returned to her desk, she reminded herself of Lt. Knighton's ABCDs of investigating. A was for assume nothing. B was for believe nobody. C was for check everything and D was to double-check everything. Sometimes, Eddie changed D to don't forget ABC. Once she had mentally reviewed Eddie's rules, Detective Oftenmarch got back to work on the lycan masquerade murders.

There was no evidence that Emily could see which told them what the lycan maquerade killers knew or how they might know those things. Therefore, she changed tactics and decided to look at the Moonlight Security aspect. Moonlight Security gave the killers little or no resistance when they intruded the bottling plant. This was the same company which was recently purchased.

"KIMMIE, how long ago was Moonlight Security acquired by EverEyes, Inc?" Emily asked the idle search program after returning to her desk.

Conveniently, the security company given the job of protecting the Incanncennio bottling plant is sold. Most likely after the acquisition of Moonlight Security, the bottling plant is breached and two of its employees are murdered with minimal confrontation, if any, from the security guards. This seemed a little too convenient to Emily.

"There is no record of Moonlight Security being acquired." KIMMIE digivoiced in response.

So the acquisition of the company was too recent for there to be an online record of the sale, but not so recent as to allow time for the office in the Wallace-Franklin Building to be vacated. Emily was upset with herself as she realized she did not get a photo of the under new ownership sign in the lobby of what had been Moonlight Security.

"KIMMIE, does the Incanncennio bottling plant have a security company registered with the New Terranceville Police Department?" Emily inquired.

If there was no record of Moonlight Security being purchased, then it would be difficult to pursue a conspiracy theory of diluting or manipulating the bottling plant's security.

"The private security company called Moonlight Security is the company registered as the Incanncennio Bottling Plant's security." KIMMIE digivoiced its answer.

"KIMMIE, how many break-ins occurred at the Incanncennio bottling plant before last Thursday night?" Emily asked.

Detective Oftenmarch switched her focus to the bottling plant's electronic security. Like their surveillance cameras, the plant's electronic locks and keypads were outdated and sparse. There were no robotic surveillance or sentries listed for the facility. This coincided with what Emily remembered from her visit that terrible early morning. According to the Moonlight Security guards' statements, the intruders bypassed the security door and the security mantrap by cracking them. As the guards testified, the villains never approached or threatened them but moved directly to the electronics and defeated the electronic security measures. By outwitting the old technology, the villains swiftly gained access to the plant. Was this due to easy to bypass, antiquated equipment or did they have foreknowledge of equipment and possibly codes? Again not provable with the evidence available. Once they were past security, there were very few electronic locks restricting the intruders access throughout the plant.

"The Incanncennio Bottling Plant has no reports of break-ins prior to last Thursday night. The number of break-ins recorded is zero." KIMMIE supplied the answer to Emily's last question.

Had the plant's security been a sufficient deterrent in the past, had it previously been an effective pest preventer, or had it simply never been previously tested? Emily could only speculate. One thing was for certain: the outdated electronic locks put up as much resistance as old police caution tape last Thursday night. Emily added more notes and information into CaseBuilder. In contrast, the district attorney's apartment building had the latest in high tech security.

Lt. Knighton had sent Emily an email regarding the security measures for the slain district attorney's living quarters. His high-rise luxury suite had a Selitron High Sense security system. Selitron was an award winning product. This expensive system had extensive video monitoring and complexly coded redundant locks. The facility's landlord corporation had premium surveillance equipment installed, a fully staffed security desk, and state of the art robotic security with upgraded supplemental technology. The landlord was an award winning safe home company which prided itself on having premium security. Additionally, the district attorney had recently purchased a half dozen security plus robosentries which patrolled both his suite and the hallway outside his door. Each robosentry had an autodial feature for police assistance if danger was detected. Any calls from the residence of the district attorney would be given the highest priority from the Cathedral Police Department.

Yet for all the security, locks, robots, and surveillance present, the lycan masquerade killers perpetrated their crimes without detection. Never being seen by security, video, or robotic sentry, the lycan masquerade killers maneuvered past locked doors, coded passageways, restricted elevators, and a security checkpoint without restriction and seemingly minimal resistance. The Selitron High Sense front door lock was so fortified that the door could have been used on a vault, according to its national lock and safeguard rating. But the door was left wide open after the district attorney had been murdered like a post-crime boast.

Had the lycan masquerade killers been that exceptional at their villainous craft that evening, or had they received a lot of misplaced help? The next puzzlement was how could a group of killers so proficient on this job have been so sloppy and disorganized on the bottling plant invasion. Had they benefitted from luck and then their luck had run out at Incanncennio's plant? In the high rise building, the lycan masquerade killers avoided every surveillance video camera and face recognition recorder. They were like vampire reflections in mirrors, unseen. Yet in the bottling plant, the killers had more video exposure than a crooked politician on the evening news. Again, there was a disconnect here or the possibility of duplicity.

Emily pulled out the paper files Barsons had left on her desk. The portions of the file worked on by Lt. Parnes had CaseBuilder links which meant he had entered his work into CaseBuilder. The portions of the file worked on by Detective Barsons had no links. In typical lazy Barsons' fashion, he had not entered a single thing into CaseBuilder.

They had nice notes on the district attorney's building security which matched with what Lt. Knighton had found. Their notes on the district attorney's girlfriend were less helpful. Barsons had rated her a hotness score of 98 with the subcomment of babeliscous. Well that was nice, thought Emily as she crossed out the score and comment.

Their interview with her was short but interesting. She was hiding in the district attorney's bedroom when the lycan masquerade killers had invaded the apartment. She did not witness the murder. However, while hidden, she saw two of the intruders enter the bedroom, one of them without their mask being worn. Parnes later made an annotation that she had witnessed the murder, so her story may have changed. Her descriptions of the maskless man and the masked man were vague and nondescript. The witness had sat down with a police artist and the resulting sketches were in the file. Both pictures looked like generic characters out of the television show Big City Supercop. Might be a case of watching too many television shows.

Moving along in the file from Parnes and Barsons, Emily found the 272nd precinct detectives looked at a radically wide range of possible suspects with no discernible pattern of having connections or linked evidence to the crime. It was exactly like they were randomly making speculations. The pair of 272nd precinct detectives investigated inter-city gangs, third party law enforcement companies, private detective associations, military contractors, regional federal bureau agents, the New Carnelian police, the Grantham police chief, the Chatham police commissioner, the Cathedral Foundation of a Safer Tomorrow, multiple activist groups, a pair of casino ownerships, a group of collegiate scoff-laws, dozens of retired police officers, two private law offices, a pair of retired mobsters, and a partridge in a pear tree. If their investigation had been a leaf raking job, then instead of starting at one end and systematically raking in one direction, they started anywhere and raked here, there, this way, that way, and helter skelter everywhere.

Lt. Parnes and Detective Barnes had briefly looked at the Cathedral Guardian Company in conjunction with three other private law enforcement companies for any connections to the lycan masquerade killers.

More interested in the district attorney's murder, the 272nd precinct detectives did not make any reference to the CGC selling Cathedral Police case solutions or the company's plans to use Lawtech Patrollers in their CGC related case notes.

"KIMMIE, how many private law enforcement companies are using Lawtech Patrollers in the city of Cathedral?" the detective wondered.

The more Emily read the file from Parnes and Barsons, the more her head hurt. The more unnecessary commentary Emily read from Barsons, the more she became annoyed. Her head was beginning to spin with the disorganization of their file. It was so disjointed and jumbled, Detective Oftenmarch was starting to feel she understood less about this case then before she started reading their file.

"Lawtech Patrollers are currently only being used by Federal law enforcement." KIMMIE digianswered.

Struggling to find anything useful in Parnes and Barsons' tangled mess of erratic investigation lines, Detective Oftenmarch moved on to another source. All the materials collected by the lieutenant and herself and sent to the crime labs this morning would need at least another day to process. So Emily went back to the lieutenant's copcam video and her own copcam video from early Friday morning in New Terranceville. However, watching their megawolf misadventures post murders was also not benefitting the investigation. Therefore, Emily switched to watching the poor surveillance video from the dimly lit bottling plant during the invasion.

Emily watched intently to see if the masquerade intruders touched anything at the plant or if they had dropped anything which might have been missed by the police vacuuming. Viewing closely, she looked for any identifying features on the masked miscreants which might help unmask them. Twice she had to get up from her seat to get some more warm tea. Early in the video review, Emily pulled out a small throw blanket she kept at her desk for the cold winter months. Tossing the blanket over her shoulders, Emily pulled it tight to herself to combat the over-chilled office.

Not only was the plant security footage bad quality but most of it was also incredible boring. Even when a megawolf or an intruder came into the recording, it was nondescript and always uneventful. More plant security cameras would have been helpful. Neither murder was captured on video. This was bad for the investigation but this was also merciful to not have to watch a gruesome event on video replay. Emily trudged through the monotonous videos making notes in CaseBuilder occasionally until the squad room clock and micro breakroom clocks struck quarter to five. Fellow detectives had programmed the clocks to give a fifteen minute warning until end of shift.

Emily's husband, David-John, was speaking at Chatham Community College this evening and she wanted to be there to support him. Emily knew he was excited about this opportunity and had worked extremely hard on his presentation. Ending the security video's replay, she made some final notes in CaseBuilder. After sending a text to the lieutenant, Detective Oftenmarch locked up her service weapon then stored her gear which including her Phasepulser XII, autotracker, coplink, microscanner, and copcam into her duty bag. With her gear secured, Emily logged off her computer and got up to go to the ladies' room to change for this evening's affair. As Emily was changing into an evening dress with high heeled shoes and fixing her hair and makeup, Eddie replied via text that he was returning to the 271st precinct.

Returning to the still empty squad room around five o'clock, Detective Oftenmarch was now ready to be Mrs. Emily Oftenmarch. It seemed as if the rest of the homicide detectives at the 271st precinct and the Federal trainees were done for the day. She just needed to check in with the lieutenant once he arrived and then she would be off to tussle through traffic on her way to Chatham Community College. While she waited, Emily put on her double breasted cashmere wool blend coat. In the over air conditioned squad room, the dress coat worked well in keeping her warm.

Unfortunately, things did not transpire as planned when the lieutenant entered the department about two minutes later. He looked at Emily and her attire, frowned, and then said somberly, "Sorry, Emily. We're not done."

"Eddie, I am exhausted, cold, and my head aches. Not to mention, I have a husband eagerly expecting me this evening." Emily retorted.

"Noted. Labwork's ready for us." Lt. Knighton replied businesslike.

"The high commissioner's office must have put a rush on all items associated with this case." Emily deduced then asked, "Do you need me for this, Eddie?"

"One more hour, please." Eddie pleaded.

Emily looked at him skeptically. "Is that a promise, lieutenant?" she requested.

"Sure." Eddie promised unconvincingly.

Emily unhappily took out her personal phone and began dialing her husband to give him the bad news that she was going to be late.

Chapter 16

The House of Higher Thinking

As an operating practice, Cathedral Police assigned one evidence specialization facility for every six police precincts. The facility sharing method cuts down on expenses and keeps valuable experts busy. Each evidence specialization facility contains a coroner's lab, a forensics lab, a technology lab, an electronics lab, an advanced research lab, and a crime reconstruction division. All evidence requiring analysis went to the designated evidence specialization facility. The Cathedral police detectives in the 271st precinct call the building the House of Higher Thinking. Cathedral Police precincts 1 and 2 serve as historical sites and were used for ceremonial purposes. Cathedral precinct 3 is the oldest precinct still used as a functional police station operating on a daily basis. Catheral's third precinct was often believed to be the gold standard for law enforcement by the Cathedral Police Department. Always compliant with CPD policy, the precinct achieved excellent arrest records and superior efficiency statistics. Cathedral Police precincts 3 through 8 shared the longest active evidence specialization facility. The 271st Cathedral precinct shared an evidence specialization facility with precincts 267, 268, 269, 270, and 272. This shared facility was located on the intersection of West Washington Circle and Anglenarrow Boulevard, about two and a quarter miles from the 271st precinct offices.

Hoping their trip to the House of Higher Thinking would be quick, albeit still insightful, Emily drove separately from Eddie. She followed the lieutenant, who was driving the department PSUV, in her second-hand Panther Turbo 3 Hypercharger sports coupe. Halfway through their trip, a work trunk got between them after a four way stop. The work truck intermittently spewed so much black exhaust vapor or smoke, like truck flatulence, that Emily found it hard to see the PSUV just two vehicles ahead. Its emissions were so poor that the truck was leaving a trail of smog behind it. Trapped in the smog behind the slow moving truck for the second half of the trip, Emily was stopped at the traffic light at Old Station Street after Lt. Knighton had cleared the intersection on the yellow light. Cathedral's rush hour traffic was in full effect and the short trip was tedious. Emily's arrival at the facility was several minutes after Eddie had arrived.

In front of the professional specialist building was a small grassy hill in the middle of a rotary which was located at the bottom of the entrance driveway. On top of the hill was a circle of spruces and a cluster of flagpoles. Each flagpole flew a patriotic flag above a Cathedral Police Department flag. With high winds now gusting in Cathedral, the flags were whipping in the wind. Stormy weather seemed to be rushing the city of Cathedral's way. Above the flags could be seen the building's supervisor tower. The stone facade building had a wide squat cylindrical supervisor tower with a steep clay tiled roof. The city sky had become so dreary, lights were being used inside the tower and illumination was pouring out its tall slender windows.

Pulling into the compact parking lot of the facility, the detective took the last available space located next to the building's barricaded dumpster. As Emily exited her vehicle, she pulled her coat in close to herself, attempting to shield herself from the gusting winds. Between the blustery winds and the sun hidden behind thick clouds in the bleak sky, the temperature was beginning to fall in Cathedral. Leaving her gear locked and stored in her car, Emily looked westward to see dark stormy skies. Stormy weather was definitely heading the city's way.

Debris was being blown across the little parking lot. Hustling, Emily quickstepped across the front walk, which circumvented an oversized old oak tree, to the main entrance. Jogging around the old oak tree, it's a shady front pathway. Everyone's walking wearily, in the not so sunny day.

As Emily entered the lobby slightly windswept, the lieutenant was quietly waiting for her by the vending microwave and vending machines. He appeared to be deciding on what to purchase but the look on his face displayed it was a difficult and disappointing decision. Upon seeing Emily, he opted to purchase nothing. Eddie did not seem all that heartbroken over bypassing the vending cuisine.

Without saying a word, the lieutenant headed for the side hallway and began a quiet trek toward autopsy. He had decided to visit the coroner first. The hallway to autopsy was silent and vacant of any foot traffic. A soft buzz from the overhead lights could be heard in the pristine hallway. It was often a somber walk to autopsy.

Cold, quiet, and impeccably clean, autopsy was located in the rear of the ground floor. Few detective squads visited autopsy because they did not deal with the deceased as regularly as homicide. Therefore autopsy was less crowded than most other evidence specialization departments. The sterile area was devoid of any decorations or knick-knacks; it was strictly businesslike and professional in the space. An electronic sign-in board was next to the autopsy's entrance. It showed that Dr. Hogglestein, Dr. Jones, and Dr. Krinkellsome were off shift, while Dr. Brownling was displayed as on shift. The open autopsy area was filled with soft baroque music, which confirmed that Dr. Brownling was working in autopsy.

Calm and courteous, Dr. Brownling always took the time to patiently explain important details as helpfully as he could manage. The neatly attired doctor refrained from getting agitated or exasperated with any questions from the detectives. It was always positive news to find that Dr. Brownling was on shift even though he worked, and preferred, the late shift. The mud tusslers were always greeted warmly by Dr. Brownling and this evening was no exception.

"Good evening, detectives. How may I help you this evening?" the doctor greeted them then observing Detective Oftenmarch's outfit he added, "Oh Emily, you look lovely this evening my dear."

"Thank you, Doctor Brownling. Have plans to hear my husband give a lecture at Chatham Community College as a guest speaker this evening. Afterwards we have been invited to Nathaniel Hall for a post presentation gathering." Emily explained cheerfully.

"That sounds wonderful. I have always enjoyed attending collegiate seminars with my peers. They are both an instructive and an enlightening change of scenery from the mundane autopsy area." Dr. Brownling shared happily.

"The bottling plant homicides, please." Lt. Knighton redirected the conversation back to police work.

"Terrible crimes, those murders. The autopsies of those poor victims were completed last Friday." the mild mannered doctor disclosed. He began to struggle with electronic remotes for the department's computer, projector, and screen. The doctor thought using digidepth photos was more respectful than displaying the deceased.

Seeing the difficulties the doctor was experiencing, Emily intervened. "Let me help you, doctor." Emily offered and she began pressing the correct buttons to lower the screen, start the projector, and queue up digital files from last Friday.

"Thank you, Emily. Always so kind and polite. Give me a moment to find the correct set of files. Ah, there we go. Thank you." Dr. Brownling expressed his gratitude as Emily helped him project the correct photographs.

"Cause of death, doctor?" Eddie requested.

"Both victims were stabbed to death, both victims bled out. The cause was exsanguination. It was the knife wounds and not the wounds inflicted by the large wolves that were the fatal injuries. Observing the width of the incised wounds, it was most likely a military knife used as the murder weapon." the doctor answered as images and note appeared on the projection screen.

"So the attack by the megawolves did not kill these men?" Emily asked for clarification.

"As painful as the wolf wounds would have been, those wounds could have been recoverable. More than superficial, the wounds inflicted by the wolves were erratic, savage, but not significant in depth.

In contrast, the stab wounds were deep and deadly. The murderer was proficient and knowledgeably precise in where to strike. Arteries were struck. Both victims sustained damage to a common carotid artery and a subclavian artery" the doctor explained, showing more images and diagrams on the screen.

"Which wounds were first?" the lieutenant asked.

"The fatal wounds would have been second as they would have quickly caused death and none of the wounds were post mortem. There was also blood splatter on the basement walls and floor. The blood trail along the hallways suggests the murders occurred after the initial attacks." Dr. Brownling indicated.

"Would it be fair to speculate that the victims were chased down by the megawolves, weakened by the wolf inflicted wounds, and then murdered by an experienced killer?" Emily postulated.

"That method is similar to wolves in the wild. First, they injure their prey and then once it is in a weakened state, then they go in for the kill. Your hypothesis could be supported by the victims' injuries but it could not be proven by the autopsy alone." the kind doctor replied, his attention still focused on the projection screen.

"Dr. Brownling, we received a report which indicated three deceased megawolves which had been discovered were brought here to be examined. Is that correct?" Emily inquired, changing the topic.

"Yes, that is correct. An assistant in training examined the beasts this afternoon. They left some hand-written notes but no information has been entered into the computer yet so there is nothing to display on the screen." Dr. Brownling explained.

"Could you summarize, doctor?" Eddie asked.

Looking through some hand-written pages he had picked up, Dr. Brownling answered, "I will do my best, lieutenant. According to the preliminary report the abnormally large wolves had been stunned by an older close range stunner before being stabbed. The close range stunning left burn marks and the stab wounds are similar in description to the stab wounds on this case's human victims." the doctor disclosed.

"So it could be possible that the same seasoned murderer that killed the poor bottling plant employees could also have executed the megawolves. Wound first, then strike effectively." Emily suggested as she picked up a page the doctor had accidentally dropped.

The doctor accepted back the lost page. "Thank you, Emily. Your deduction could be possible but it is not provable with the evidence from our examinations. One item of interest here is that human blood was found on one of the wolves. A sample of the blood was sent to the lab for further examinations." Dr. Brownling revealed.

"Skilled but sloppy." the lieutenant commented.

"Or efficient but still fallible." the doctor suggested.

"Thank you, doctor." Eddie concluded his visit.

"Thank you for your hard work and help, Dr. Brownling." Emily thanked the doctor.

"Please be safe, young lady. This is a very nasty business. I do not wish to see any harm come to you." the concerned doctor declared.

"You are extremely kind, doctor. Pray for us and we will be fine. Thank you again, Dr.Brownling." Detective Oftenmarch said her farewell.

"You are most welcome." the kind doctor replied with a small bow.

Both Eddie and Emily exited autopsy without conversation. They both seemed to be deep in thought. They seemed to be getting answers yet the overarching questions still remained. The detectives traversed their steps down the side hallway towards the lobby, then they made a sharp left turn and travelled down a separate hallway. They wordlessly walked toward the rear of the building where the detectives entered the back stairway.

Quietly and preoccupied in thought, the pair of 271st precinct homicide detectives took the back stairs to the second floor of the evidence specialization facility. Once on the second floor, they walked down the center hallway. Silently, the mud tusslers passed a pair of offices and one of the forensics labs. Even though it was well past 5:30pm, the second floor was bustling with activity. Lab technicians were hustling in and out of offices and labs. A pair of Cathedral detectives passed them so engaged in a conversation they missed Emily's friendly greeting. A man was standing in the middle of the hallway attempting to eat a sandwich and speak on his macrocellular phone at the same time but failing to do either task very well.

Halfway down the hallway, the pair of detectives stopped outside a closed office door which bore the name Olivia Osweiller and the title senior forensic scientist. After knocking on the door firmly, Eddie held the door handle expectantly. About ten seconds passed before the entire door illuminated green and they heard a voice from behind the door give them permission to enter. Lt. Knighton wasted no time in opening the door, but then waited to allow Detective Oftenmarch to enter first.

The detectives entered an all too familiar room, the senior forensic scientist's office. They had been there hundreds of times on hundreds of cases. Olivia Osweiller was concluding a compuconference communication as they entered the room. Her desk and credenza were cluttered with papers, tablets, electronics, and an assortment of pens but the rest of the office, which included bookshelves, guest chairs, a refreshment table, a wall monitor, an award display, and a pair of tall dragon trees, was impeccably tidy. On the far wall was a full length glass window which displayed the neighboring lab and a door which led to the same.

"Good evening, detectives. Please have a seat." Olivia greeted the pair of detectives as they entered.

"Good evening, Olivia. Sorry for the late hour of our visit." Emily greeted in return. Eddie just nodded and single waved.

"What a lovely dress, Emily. I am guessing you had better plans for this evening than visiting forensics." Olivia Osweiller observed.

"My husband is speaking at Chatham Community College tonight and I still have hopes of hearing some of it. How are you this evening, Olivia?" Emily returned as she sat.

"Rather frustrated. Why is it that evidence involved in one of your cases always comes with complications, detectives?" Osweiller puzzled.

"An interesting question, Olivia. If only there was a simplistic answer I could give you." Emily replied sully.

"How complicated?" Eddie counter puzzled.

"Another interesting question, lieutenant. Now for the frustrating answer, let us begin with the discarded syringes. Hundreds of fingerprints were collected off the syringes. Fingerprints belonging to four, possibly five, individuals. Each and every time we run any of these prints in the law enforcement database, both national and international, the matching result returns federally restricted blocks. Each and every time we attempt to bypass the restrictions we are deemed unauthorized. I have been in communication with several federal law enforcement agencies all afternoon and rode on the federal merry-go-round of bureaucracy three times. Despite best efforts, the fingerprints are still restricted." Osweiller divulged the complicated news.

"An apologetic refusal or a hardline blunt denial?" Emily wondered.

"More of the latter." Olivia admitted.

"And the packaging?" Lt. Knighton prompted, moving forward.

"Both the plastic bags and the cardboard boxes which contained the syringes had far more fingerprints than the syringes. These items were like fingerprint collages. We had three lab technicians from our department and two borrowed lab technicians from neighboring facilities separating and eliminating fingerprints and handprints for hours. We performed this difficult process rapidly because this case has the high commissioner's high priority on it. At the conclusion of this arduous task, what we discovered was the same set of four, possibly five, sets of federally restricted prints had handled the packaging. Prints we are not authorized to identify. There seems to be a pattern here." Osweiller disclosed, then let out a heavy exasperated sigh.

"Second verse, same as the first." replied Emily.

"Emily the eighth, you are you are." Olivia smiled.

"Is there anyone we could appeal toward in order to get the prints unrestricted for a murder investigation?" Oftenmarch reasonably questioned.

"I have done all I can, Emily. It would be up to the high commissioner's office or the regional attorney's office to apply pressure now." Osweiller responded.

"The syringes' contents?" Eddie requested.

"Your partner's a pain, Emily the eighth." Osweiller commented, no longer smiling, before continuing. "The residue recovered from the insides of the syringes is a combination of two federally controlled substances. The first illegal substance is an advanced growth hormone developed by a foreign military contractor and that AGH is capable of producing megawolves. Well named in your report, Emily. The second forbidden substance is an adrenaline accelerant manufactured by an ambitious pharmaceutical company with far more wealth than intelligence. Known side effects of this second substance are hallucinations, faux perceptions of invincibility, and episodes of psychotic behavior. This substance would make nasty megawolves extremely aggressive. Neither substance may be legally purchased nor prescribed by a licensed doctor by federal law."

"So the combination of these two substances would be ridiculously dangerous?" Oftenmarch asked the obvious.

"The result would be a massive brute acting with little or no rational thought, like a werewolf for example." Osweiller answered.

"So if one illegal and dangerous substance was not enough, the lycan masquerade killers decided to give the megawolves a combination of two dangerous drugs." Emily summarized.

"We sent samples of the despicable compound drug to the advanced research lab for further scrutiny. Their findings confirmed forensics' conclusions. The report they sent back concluded with the message and I'll quote it: 'A good way to turn Dr. Jekyll into Mr. Hyde.' " Osweiller further explained.

"May we ask about the wolf mask we found, Olivia?" Emily inquired.

"Unfortunately, Emily, the wolf mask is more of the same revelations, full of fingerprints protected from identification by some federal institution. One piece of information the lab was able to determine is that the mask was custom made. Much of the mask was hand stitched, not machine stitched, and the materials on the mask are a mixture of yak hair, khullu, Dutch Landrace goat hair, and Northwestern wolf fur and teeth which is not used in retail." Osweiller informed them. Then she sat back in her chair, rubbing her forehead with her left hand.

"Would it be fair to say that the wolf mask is not cheaply made?" Emily posed her query.

"The wolf mask was very well constructed. It was also reinforced with a sturdy breathable cotton underlayer." Olivia returned.

"The blood on the megawolf." Eddie interjected.

"Dr. Brownling informed us that human blood found on one of the megawolves was sent to forensics for analysis. Do you have any information on that?" Emily questioned from Eddie's prompt.

Osweiller flipped through some papers on her desk, separated one page from the stack, and then answered. "The lab was able to get a blood type and partial DNA profile from that sample, but nothing more. If we got a blood sample from a suspect, then that suspect could be eliminated or remain under suspicion from a match to this sample."

"So if we catch the wolf slayer then the blood sample could be used as evidence against them but not as a smoking gun." Emily concluded.

"That would be correct." Olivia answered, setting down the paper.

"You are beautiful, Oliva." Eddie stated as he rose from his seat.

Osweiller looked perturbed. "Get out of my office, Eddie, before I use my personal stunner on you." she replied with a note of anger.

"Thank you for all your hard work, Oliva. Please pass on our appreciation to your team." Oftenmarch gratefully thanked as she got-up from her seat. The lieutenant was already over halfway to the door. His work phone was ringing, playing its familiar tune.

"Catch these idiots, E, and then please kick them once for me." Olivia Osweiller replied.

Motivated to make a quick exit, Eddie was the first one out of the office. By the time Emily had departed the office and closed the office door, Lt. Knighton was several yards down the hallway. The lieutenant increased his pace as he strode down the hallway. It was like the desire to solve this case was propelling him to move faster. He had a sizable lead on Emily by the time he reached the far end of the hallway where he began to pace back and forth in wait. His work phone started making its all too familiar chime as it rang again. The lieutenant answered his chiming work phone as he paced the far end of the hallway. Emily maintained a steady stride along the hall.

A young junior detective from the 269th precinct named Oatwhey Minmograhme sat on the floor in the hallway. The newbie detective had his head down and his shoulders slumped in sadness. Emily had met the kind youthful man over the last month during trips to the house of higher learning.

"Why so glum, Oatwhey?" Emily asked the young detective

He looked up at her with a depressed expression on his face. "I made a mistake, Detective Oftenmarch. I mixed up some of the evidence between cases and it looks like a criminal will get away with a crime because of me." young Detective Minmograhme admitted sadly.

"We all make mistakes, Oatwhey. We do the best job we can, learn from our mistakes, and try to improve. Being a Cathedral Police detective is challenging work but don't let it get you down." Emily encouraged the young detective.

"Because of me, a career burglar is going to get away with major thefts. My rookie mistake erased weeks of hard work by several members of the Cathedral Police Department. This makes it hard for me to be cheery." Oatwhey continued to shamefully admit.

"Honest mistakes happen to the best of us. Even in the worst of times, our teammates and co-workers in the Cathedral Police Department will have our backs. Together we can overcome adversity. And if we keep trying and improving then in time our successes will outweigh our mistakes. You can find solace in that." Detective Oftenmarch offered.

"This is why I could never be a Christian like you, Emily. Any good things I achieve are far outweighed by the bad things I do." Oatwhey shared with melancholy.

"Being a follower of Christ has nothing to do with doing good or bad things. There is a difference between following a religion and having a relationship with GOD. When following a religion, it's about you and what you do. If you do good things or behave admirably you think somehow you are worthy. If you do bad things or behave poorly you think somehow you are forever unworthy. The Bible tells us in Romans 3:23 *for all have sinned and fall short of the glory of God* and in 1 John 1:9 *If we confess our sins, HE is faithful and just and will forgive us our sins and purify us from all unrighteousness.* So neither religious belief is correct. In a relationship with GOD, it's about GOD and what GOD has done for you. As a gift, GOD's love and sacrifice have made us worthy. Anything you do is done for the love of GOD because HE is worthy. We learn from Ephesians 2: 4-5 *But because of HIS great love for us, GOD, who is rich in mercy, made us alive with CHRIST even when we were dead in transgressions—it is by grace you have been saved.* In a relationship with GOD, we know we have been forgiven no matter what good or bad we have done as long as we are repentant and follow GOD. The Bible reads in Galatians 2:20 *I have been crucified with Christ and I no longer live, but Christ lives in me. The life I now live in the body, I live by faith in the Son of God, who loved me and gave himself for me.*" Emily told the truth to Oatwhey.

"Is there a way for mistake driven people to be loved by GOD?" Oatwhey questioned.

"There are lies that the devil tells people. First lie, you are not worthy and never will be good enough. Second lie, you are good enough and can be worthy on your own. The truth is you are not worthy but you are loved by GOD. Because you are loved by GOD, you are not worthless. As a gift, GOD's love and sacrifice gave us worth. We know we are loved from Romans 5:8 *But God demonstrates his own love for us in this: While we were still sinners, Christ died for us.* Again we know we are loved from 1 John 4: 9-10 *This is how GOD showed his love among us: HE sent his one and only SON into the world that we might live through HIM. This is love: not that we loved GOD, but that HE loved us and sent HIS SON as an atoning sacrifice for our sins.*" Emily expounded.

"I have never heard it explained that way. It always seemed like Christianity was a religion and you had rules to follow." Oathwhey expressed in confusion.

"There is again a difference between religion and a relationship with GOD in that regard. In a religion, following rules somehow makes a person worthy. Following rules supposedly leads to earning a path to heaven in religion. If you misbehave or don't follow rules in religion, then somehow you are unworthy. In religion, a rule breaker, or sinner, could never go to heaven. However, when in a relationship with GOD we know all people have sinned and GOD, in HIS great love, forgives us despite any rules we may or may not have followed. Romans 6:23 reads: *For the wages of sin is death, but the gift of GOD is eternal life in CHRIST JESUS our LORD*. Salvation is a loving gift from GOD for all rule breakers. It's not about rules, it's about love. John 14:15 states *If you love ME. keep my commands*. This is why disciples of CHRIST obey commandments. Finally, like a parent who gives rules to a child to keep them safe or keep them from danger, GOD gives HIS followers commandments. Hebrews 12: 9-10 reads: *Moreover, we have all had human fathers who disciplined us and we respected them for it. How much more should we submit to the Father of spirits and live! They disciplined us for a little while as they thought best; but GOD disciplines us for our good, in order that we may share in HIS holiness*. So GOD gives us commandments out of love for our own benefit." Emily lovingly explained.

"So it's a gift and there is nothing more to do." Oatwhey responded.

"Salvation is a gift and we respond in love. GOD's grace gives us hope and in response we trust in GOD. As we follow GOD with faith, HE will give us opportunities to do good things. It is written in Ephesians 2:8-10 *For it is by grace you have been saved, through faith—and this is not from yourselves, it is the gift of GOD— not by works, so that no one can boast. For we are GOD's handiwork, created in CHRIST JESUS to do good works, which GOD prepared in advance for us to do*." Emily shared.

"Is it important for a believer to do good things?" Oatwhey wondered curiously.

"I think it is. Let me give you an example. You and I are going on a picnic and I told you I believed it was going to rain. If I was not wearing a raincoat, carried no umbrella, wore dress shoes without boots, and left all my car windows down, then would you believe that I thought it was going to rain? Would my actions reflect my stated belief? Conversely, if I was wearing a zipped up raincoat, held an open umbrella, wore galoshes, and had all my car windows up, then would you believe that I thougt it was going to rain? Would my actions reflect my stated belief? We should live our lives behaving in a manner which confirms we trust and believe that GOD has made us worthy. In a relationship with GOD, the actions of a believer should reflect their love and trust in GOD. As JESUS says in John 13:34-35, *"A new command I give you; Love one another. As I have loved you, so you must love one another. By this everyone will know that you are MY disciples, if you love one another."* Emily further explained.

Having finished his phone conversation, Lt. Knighton was at the end of the hall motioning to Emily it was time to move to their next appointment. The lieutenant was also no longer pacing and seemed eager to go to their next destination.

Seeing Eddie beckon, Oatwhey said, "Thank you, Emily. You have given me a lot to think about."

"One last thing, Oatwhey. Career burglars often steal again, it's what makes them career burglars. There's a good chance you will have another chance to catch this thief. Seems to me there's also a good chance they won't get away with it next time you're on the case." Emily encouraged the young detective before walking toward Eddie.

"One last thing, Emily. You look amazing in that outfit. You look like a fairy tale princess ready to go to a ball." Detective Minmograhme complimented in farewell.

"Thank you, Oatwhey. Have a better evening." Oftenmarch returned in farewell.

Hustling to the end of the hallway, Emily caught up with the lieutenant. Eddie was holding the stairway door open for her as he was typing something into his coplink. As soon as the detective passed through the doorway and into the stairway, Lt. Knighton pocketed his coplink and followed closely behind her.

The pair of 271st precinct detectives were silently climbing the back staircase of the evidence specialization facility again. This time they were quietly ascending from the second floor to the third floor. Thus far this visit had given them much to consider but nothing case breaking to progress them toward making an arrest. Actually, the visit had provided the detectives with more questions than answers. It was terrible to know Cathedral Police Department had corrupt cops in its ranks; it was worse to discover a federal agency likely had murderers in its midst.

The mud tusslers exited the quiet stairwell to enter the noisy main corridor of the third floor. A transport droid carrying refreshments had broken down in the middle of the corridor with a wailing alarm and a red flashing alert light. Two men were shouting at each other in a heated argument as they shoved flat computer laptops, flattops, in each other's faces. The second door on the corridor's right side had a wide open door from which ear throbbingly loud technopunk music was blasting into the corridor. A mechanical monkey clashing cymbals repeatedly had been left unattended against a wall. For the pair of detectives, it was like stepping into a tidal wave of thunderous noise.

The lieutenant double time strode across the corridor causing Emily to have to hustle in heels to keep pace. Lt. Knighton made a beeline for their destination in an endeavor to escape the chaotic cavalcade of noise. Upon reaching a door marked Tech Lab #2, Eddie quickly opened it without bothering to knock. Both detectives dashed into the lab without delay. They moved like they were exiting a thunder storm of noise. Stepping out of the loud noise, they entered the cluttered and chromatic tech lab.

A pair of technology lab technicians were working in the computerized workspace. There were rows of electronic equipment of all shapes and sizes throughout the room. The first technology expert present was Sam Mamye, a veteran technician with more than twenty-five years of experience. Sam worked on a lot of the mud tusslers' cases because he liked Lt. Knighton and often addressed him as the only patient detective in the city of Cathedral. Sam and Eddie were also the only two people Emily knew who collected classic vinyl records. The second tech lab worker present was Almond Gelsenkirchen. Almond was Sam's assistant, an excellent programmer, an outstanding circuit manipulator, an adept network engineer, and an accomplished GigaCraft game player. Both men simultaneously looked up from their work to peer at the arriving detectives.

"Good evening, detectives." Mamye greeted the detective duo.

"Good evening, gentlemen. Thank you for staying late to meet with us." Emily returned in greeting to the technical twosome.

"Fantastic outfit, Emily. You look far too nice to be visiting this dull place. You're dressed to be walking a red carpet somewhere." Gelsenkirchen complimented.

"Thank you, Almond. My husband is speaking at Chatham Community College tonight and I was hoping to see some of his presentation." Emily explained for the third time this visit to the House of Higher Thinking.

"Sounds interesting. If he ever comes to speak at Cathedral State University, maybe I will be able to listen to him." Almond expressed, getting up from his workstation.

"We can tell you have been working hard, Almond. You have some mustard on your labcoat from eating while you work." Oftenmarch indicated. The young assistant scrabbled to clean himself of spilled condiment.

"I am guessing the two of you came to discuss the most unusual robot we here in the tech lab have ever seen." Mayme speculated.

"We cannot decide if the robot is half finished or if the creator is half crazy." Almond interjected while cleaning his lab coat.

"What can you tell us?" Lt. Knighton inquired.

"Well first, Frankenbot, that's what I call it, is made from a variety of parts. Some parts are retail, some parts are military grade, some parts are black market, and a majority of parts are custom made. There are a ton of rare metals in Frankenbot. This robotic menagerie was put together with everything but the kitchen sink." Mamye disclosed.

"So the parts did not come from a single source?" Oftenmarch looked to confirm.

"We would be lucky if we could narrow it down to two dozen sources." Almond answered now having a cleaner labcoat.

"The second item is of extreme interest and that is regarding Frankenbot's software. It took five members of the electronics department and computer lab to gain access to the software. Once they finally did, they found extensive encrypted coding. Once they finally deciphered it, they found federally licensed programming code, a massive amount of federally licensed programming code. Next, they detected subroutines with federally protected passcodes. Then when they moved onto the lower machine levels, they discovered federal copyright firmware. Whoever created Frankenbot either worked for the federal government or they stole from the federal government. Its software is full of Federal footprints." Mamye explained.

"Federal robots, federal restrictions, and federal software. This is becoming a disturbing pattern." Emily expressed aloud.

"Were there fingerprints on Frankenbot?" Eddie wondered.

"Yes, there were multiple sets of prints. When we tried to identify the prints in the system, they were federally protection but I think you may have already known that fact." Gelsenkirchen answered with curiosity.

"Not a surprise." Eddie stated.

"Third point of interest with Frankenbot: it had remote network and telecommunication access to Cathedral Police Department systems. To be more specific, direct access with no restrictions." Sam Mayme reported with some concern in his voice.

"Not a surprise." Eddie repeated.

"What about the maintenance droid from Superior Private Eyes Surveillance? Could anything helpful be found with it?" Oftenmarch posed, hoping for something relevant.

"It was just an ordinary maintenance droid which was damaged. Nothing interesting." Mamye disappointingly replied.

"Somebody had messed with its circuitry. They sabotaged the droid in a way that left no hints nor clues to be found." Almond elaborated.

"And the clothes it wore?" Lt. Knighton quizzed.

"With the forensic lab so busy, we sent the droid's acquired outfit to a private company for analysis. The single set of fingerprints discovered on the clothing matched a set of federally restricted prints also found on Frankenbot." Mamye indicated.

"Not a surprise." Eddie repeated.

"The villains stole its clothes and scrambled its circuit boards. They showed nothing but cruelty to the poor thing." Gelsenkirchen added.

"Almost forgot, we also looked at those two small mircochips you found, Emily." Sam Mayme remembered. "It took us a few tries but we were able to connect them to a testing station and get them to execute their code." he continued as he moved to a nearby workstation.

"They seem like ordinary chips that just broke off somebody's handheld electronics." Almond surmised.

"Just need a moment to bring up the first program for you." Mayme told them as he clicked on some keys at the nearby workstation.

"I would like to get a device with these built-in programs. They were both rather good." Almond expressed.

"Here we go, Codebreakers is the first program." Mayme said as the workstation projected a holographic image. The image said Codebreakers on an orange banner and below the banner had black alphanumeric text scrolling across the image.

"It is a game where the players have to quickly decode cryptic messages into the actual messages. Guessing a character on the first try gives the player gold wording, guessing on the second attempt gives them silver, and a success on a third attempt gives them a bronze letter. The faster you decode the phrase, the more points you score." Almond explained the game.

"Oh no, Eddie." Emily moaned. "This is bad."

Sam Mayme, Almond, and Lt. Knighton all looked at Emily with puzzled expressions. When she did not elaborate and nobody responded to her comment, Sam shrugged then continued.

"Here is the second program, a personal assistant." Mayme expressed and with more clicking of keys he projected a new image. This one was a holographic image of a neatly dressed lady in an emerald green dress with a silver lace pattern. She had a pretty face, wore a green beaded necklace and silver ribbons in her hair.

Emily moved to an unoccupied chair and sat down disheartened. "Oh no, Eddie. This is both good news and terrible news. The good news is I know who has done these horrid crimes but the terrible news is I know who has done these horrid crimes." she told the lieutenant.

"Not seeing it, Emily." Eddie admitted.

"Sam, we found another microchip earlier today, slightly bigger, which was also turned in to be examined. Any chance you got that chip to project a portly well dressed detective?" Emily asked Mamye.

"That's amazing, Emily. We were able to get the larger microchip to also work. It took us a little longer to bring up that program. This one was my favorite of the three." Mamye revealed as he moved to a larger workstation and began typing feverishly. In a few moments a new holographic projection was displayed.

Emily's heart sank as she was shown the hologram. The image was a well dressed portly man with good posture in a tailored suit. He wore a neat flat black waistcoat, a tidy black bowtie, and a black derby hat.

"How may I be of service?" voiced the holographic image.

"Now I'm caught up, Emily." Lt. Knighton softly declared. Emily could see the anger on her partner's normally neutral face.

"Those projections solved the case?" Gelsenkirchen asked in disbelief.

"Turn it off, please." Eddie requested.

"I won't be attending my husband's lecture tonight. Instead, we will be apprehending some federal trainees for suspicion of murder." Emily sadly admitted more to herself than the lab technicians or the lieutenant.

"They hide in plain sight." Eddie spoke in a low grumble.

"Cathedral PD should have the trainees' fingerprints on file for elimination purposes, right lieutenant?" Emily asked Eddie with a moment of realization.

"Who knows anymore." Eddie returned as his macrophone rang. He exited the lab to take the call.

When Eddie was out of the room, Sam spoke. "It is difficult to tell with Lt. Knighton. Is he angry, Emily?" he wondered.

"Yes, he is upset, Sam. This case has had layers of stink and I believe Eddie is ready to fumigate." Emily shared as she texted, from her work phone, the names of the federal trainees to Osweiller.

"What did those programs tell you, Emily? I don't understand." Almond admitted.

"They are the programs used by FDILE trainees. There were three FDILE trainees assigned to train with our division around the time these devices were left at crime scenes. It looks like a disappointingly bad coincidence." Emily explained.

"So there is an element of betrayal in which these trainees conducted their misconducts. I can understand why the lieutenant would be perturbed." Sam realized.

"Even FDILE trainees are committing crimes in Cathedral. The CPD can't trust anyone these days." Almond expressed.

"Excellent work gentlemen, thank you both for all you have done. If you will excuse me, I have to call and disappoint my husband." Emily told the lab technicians and took her leave.

With the third floor corridor still loud and unsuitable to make a phone call, Emily made her way back to the rear staircase of the evidence specialization facility. Crossing the corridor as quickly as she could, Emily began dialing her own cell phone. As Oftenmarch crossed the corridor a young male techie hurried after her. The young man had called to Emily but he could not be heard amidst the loud racket in the corridor. With persistence, the young techie followed after Emily. Once the detective entered the refreshing quiet of the stairway, Emily found Lt. Knighton had likewise entered the stairway to take the phone call he had received. The trailing techie had followed Oftenmarch into the stairway where he patiently waited as Emily spoke on the phone. After Emily finished leaving David-John a voice message, Eddie had more news for her.

"Private Eyes called with answers." Lt. Knighton updated Oftenmarch.

"Did they find stolen or accessed video?" Emily inquired.

"Yes." Eddie replied.

"Did they determine from which location the video was being surveillance?" Emily asked.

"Yes." Eddie repeated.

"From where?" Oftenmarch requested.

"The Flockman and Bellweather Building." Lt. Knighton revealed.

"The Wing and RIng Tower that Brownsides mentioned at the breakfast café. That's probably the location the Cathedral police protection division is working tonight." Emily recalled and figured.

"Makes sense." Eddie agreed.

"Excuse me, Detective Oftenmarch. I was able to repair your MPAR for you." the robotics tech named Jackery proudly told Emily. Jackery did a lot of the repairs for the 271st homicide division.

"Thank you, Jackery. That is some much needed good news." Emily thanked.

"I am always happy to help you, Emily. If you need anything else fixed or upgraded then please let me know and I will get right on it." Jackery offered.

"We're good. Thank you again, Jackery." Emily assured him.

"We must move quickly." Eddie indicated urgently.

"Eddie, not to complain, but this long day has used up all my available work clothes. The first set of clothes smells like dirty dumpster. The second set of clothes are soiled and oiled. The last set of clothes are coffee stained and reek like a brewery. It's either this dress or my gym clothes." Emily protested.

"The outfit that private investigator from RoboWorlds gave to you as a Christmas gift last year is still down in storage. After you declined to keep it, we left it in storage for any police personnel to borrow. You could use that" Jackery suggested helpfully.

"Crisis averted." Lt. Knighton declared. Emily just gave him a disapproving look.

Chapter 17

Clash at Flockman and Bellweather

Things began moving fast. Lt. Knighton had broadcast for assistance from the Cathedral crisis response team. Requesting for immediate help at the Flockman and Bellweather Building, the lieutenant made it clear to the crisis response team how important this matter was. The mud tusslers had gotten prepared quickly, maybe too quickly. They nearly forgot their newly repaired MPAR, Emily almost forgot her new Phasepulser XII, and Eddie almost left his coplink recharging in the vending area.

Emily had to get changed very quickly, almost too quickly. Out of necessity, she wore the outfit that Jackery had suggested. The detective sported an extra long and double layered white coat, white blouse with navy blue trim, a navy blue scarf with white trim, light gray pants, her newly issued police vest, and a pair of her own black boots. She was not sure how fashionable or functional the outfit was but it was much better than her alternatives.

Leaving Emily's car behind, the mud tusslers loaded into the PSUV and left the House of Higher Learning. Police lights flashing, the lieutenant raced out of the parking lot like he was exiting pit row on a raceway track. Considering this urgent enough to satisfy the Lincoln-Lofton rule, Eddie also turned on the PSUV's sirens. He had plugged the address for the Flockman and Bellweather building into the PSUV's navigation system and zoomed down the road. They were quickly enroute towards Grand Cathedral Square moving as fast as possible.

In downtown Cathedral resided Grand Cathedral Square, a popular place for locals and a big tourist site. The square was actually a triangle, it was in the shape of a triangle. Three roads, Cathedral Main Street, Cathedral Grand Avenue, and Perennial Parkway, served as the boundaries for the Grand Cathedral Square. The triangular square resided inside the intersection of those three roads. Statues, water fountains, artwork, decorated pines, flower beds, and holographic images adorned the square. The city would decorate the square for the major holidays to make it more festive. The square was a parklike atmosphere in the middle of a hectic cosmopolitan city.

Cathedral Grand Avenue had a row of tall sleek buildings that occupied the length of the square on the opposite side of the road. Each building was well illuminated and had ornate glass centric fronts. These buildings were staggered in height but uniform in width. They were unique in style but similar in structure. These structures built an urban line-up that suggested activity and commerce. Company names and logos were prominent and highlighted on each and every building in the row. Each tall building had enough architectural bling and bright luminescence for ten buildings. Each tall building was designed and built to draw people's attention from all the other attention seeking structures on the street.

Across the Cathedral Main Street from Grand Central Square were more modest sized consumer driven buildings. Along Cathedral Main Street across from the square on the opposite side of the road stood a three-story SuperShoppers Market & Pharmacy, a four-story media and bookstore, a two-story coffee house, a three-story sporting goods store, a pair of four-story clothing and fashion stores, a trio of two-story restaurants, an indoor amusement center, a three-story night club, a two-story APEX supermax movie theater, a twelve-story hotel, a two-story pizzeria, a four-story retro urban mall, and a pair of well constructed stone churches with tall steeples and a taller belltower.

Located on the corner of Perennial Parkway and Cathedral Grand Avenue and on the corner of Perennial Parkway and Cathedral Main Street were clock towers. This pair of towers were known as the Golden Clocktowers of Cathedral. These twin clock towers were iconic Cathedral landmarks and among the most visited attractions by tourists to Cathedral. The Golden Clocktowers of Cathedral were programmed to be synchronized with each other and to chime and bong at the exact same time. This was part of their magic for most tourists.

Across the street opposite the square along Perennial Parkway was a mix of office buildings, apartment buildings, and buildings with a combination of both offices and apartments. These buildings all looked like copies of each other and were quite close together in proximity. It was among this row of clonelike buildings that stood the Bellweather and Flockman Building. The Ring and Wing tower, as Brownsides had called it, was located at 19408 Perennial Parkway in a bustling and busy section of Cathedral. A fifty-two story skyscraper, the Bellweather and Flockman Building tapered in width and length as it rose upward giving it the appearance of a pyramid style tower. This was the mud tusslers' destination.

Speeding through the city streets with their lights and sirens running, Lt. Knighton navigated the crowded Cathedral roads of crawling traffic as best he could. Full of thick storm clouds, the city sky had become very dark and ominous. High winds throughout Cathedral had increased in intensity, causing havoc with several traffic lights and the parade of advertisement drones overhead competing for air space. To avoid traffic jams, the lieutenant left the surface roads for a tollway. Even the tollway called the New Arden Parkway was heavily congested. Paying tolls also would not alleviate traffic for the Cathedral detectives. With his plan unsuccessful, Eddie returned to the clogged city route. Then the traffic signal at the intersection of South McKinley Street and W.H. Harrison Avenue had lost power, bringing traffic to a hesitant stop and go crawl. Likewise the traffic lights at Dressler and East 12th Avenue had suffered from a power outage, resulting in gridlock, which Lt. Knighton had to reroute to bypass.

After using its sirens and liberally using its horn, Eddie drove the PSUV through three red lights on Polk Parkway, making new friends each time. The lieutenant fought traffic along the next three streets before diving onto Perennial Parkway. With the greatest of efforts, Lt. Knighton dodged and weaved through traffic with the PSUV's sirens blaring. He thundered along Perennial Parkway as thunder could be heard overhead. Eddie was in full dodgem mode when entering Grand Cathedral Square. He sped through and around vehicles as they approached the Flockman and Bellweather building.

Eddie darted into the far right lane, hopped up the curb, and threw the PSUV into park. The police vehicle was blocking the curb lane, was on the curb, and obstructing part of the sidewalk. The lieutenant placed the vehicle next to a holographic ad pillar for some protection. It was parked at a severely slanted angle to suggest this was the location of an emergency visit. The lieutenant left the vehicle's police lights running on full blaze and left the PSUV in full illumination to serve as a beacon for reinforcements. Since there was no valet or parking droids to be seen, the mud tusslers were not harassed as they left the PSUV in this extremely awkward position.

The pair of detectives wasted no time or movements exiting the vehicle and preparing themselves. After swiftly unloading the robot, Oftenmarch dropped the MPAR onto the remaining unimpeded sidewalk. She did a quick check that her firearm and stunner were properly secured and then followed the lieutenant along the walkway. As Lt. Knighton approached the building, he turned on his copcam and indicated to Emily to do the same. Seeing his signal, Emily understood its meaning and astutely turned on her copcam as well. This time they also had the MPAR and its recording capabilities.

As the pair of detectives entered the lobby of the Flockman and Bellweather Building, the lights flickered a couple of times before returning to normal. The building's lobby was eerily silent and was occupied by only two people. A sparse crowd for a popular and normally busy luxury hotel slash premium business suites. Even stranger was the fact that nobody was at the front desk. No receptionist, no security officer, no valet attendant, and no concierge, there was absolutely nobody to be found working in the front lobby.

When the detectives reached the deserted front desk with their MPAR in tow, Lt. Knighton pressed the electronic bell for service. A pleasant electronic chiming could clearly be heard. As the detectives patiently waited, the building lights momentarily flickered another couple of times. The ornate plasma lights behind the front desk were having trouble with the unstable power as they struggled to reilluminate after each flicker. When nobody responded to the bell after about thirtysome seconds, Lt. Knighton firmly pressed the button to the service request e-bell again.

After another moment of silence and inactivity, Emily broke the ominous and eerie quiet. "Something's not right here, Eddie. This seems suspiciously abnormal." she deduced. The lieutenant shook his head in agreement.

The building power fluxuated for a third time as nobody responded to the front desk's e-bell. Eddie looked intently towards the glass front doors, seemingly lost in decision making. The police lights from their PSUV could be seen flashing through the building's front glass and reflecting on the lobby's side wall. Finished with waiting, Lt. Knighton decided to move. As he departed the lobby desk, he beckoned Emily to follow him. It was time to move, the detectives began to cross the lobby which drew the undivided attention of the only people in the lobby, two large males.

The two goonish men saw the detectives coming and moved to intercept them on their path through the lobby. The larger goonish man stood directly in front of Emily, blocking her path to the pair of lobby elevators. Detective Oftenmarch held up her CPD badge, identified herself as an officer, and began to alter her path to walk around the hulking man. However, the goonish man stepped in front of Emily, again blocking her path to the elevators. The second goonish man held his arms wide as he attempted to prevent Lt. Knighton from progressing through the lobby to the elevators. Eddie used a lobby chair as a blocker and began to slide around the goonlike man's position. The man hustled to reposition and to beat Eddie to the walkway to the elevators. The lieutenant also held up his badge and identified himself as a Cathedral Police detective. This did nothing to alter the second goon's blockade.

Emily was done changing her walking route. She sidestepped the larger goonish man and began to walk past him. As she was walking by him, the big goonie grabbed her by her left arm. As he tried to pull her back, Detective Oftenmarch brought her left foot down hard on the instep of the grabby goon's shin and ankle. He howled and threw a wild right cross in Emily's direction. Anticipating an attack, Emily swiftly and adeptly dodged the reckless punch. Being much faster that the goonie, she countered with a strong throat punch and a palm strike to his temple. He reeled backwards then prepared to charge.

Having seen the other goon grab Emily, Lt. Knighton kept some distance between himself and the second goonlike man as he drew his Phasepulser IX. Keeping the stunner aimed at the impeder, Eddie began to walk around him. The burly blocker continued to maneuver to stop Eddie from reaching the elevators. As the gorilla-like goonie's movements closed the distance between himself and Eddie, the lieutenant fired his Phasepulser IX and stunstruck the second goonish man in the chest, which staggered him. With his stunner still trained on the burly blocker, Lt. Knighton moved to a position where he was now closer to the elevators than his hinderer.

It was at this moment the large lummox made his bullrush at Detective Oftenmarch. The gigantic goon attempted to bearhug tackle her but again Emily was far too quick for him. She slipped his bullrush tackle with a sidestep and sly pivot spin. Avoiding the brutish tackle, Emily followed the dodge by pulling out her Phasepulser XII. With her stunner unholstered, the detective rapidly fired off a pair of streams. One struck the big brute harassing her and the other stuck the jerk impeding the lieutenant. The stunner streams from the new Phasepulser XII had a swift and decisive effect on both men. They tumbled to the ground where they made no efforts to rise and resume their blockage.

Both detectives quickly moved to handcuff the grounded goons. As the detectives were restraining the stunned stooges, the building's power went out in the time frame of fifteen to twenty seconds. As the power resumed, both floored fools were cuffed. Emily sprang to her feet and darted to the elevators, where she read floors 9 and 26 off their electronic displays. She promptly pressed the call buttons for the building's elevators. Neither elevator was moving according to their digital displays. Detective Oftenmarch traversed her steps to where the lieutenant was reading the bemoaning brutes their rights.

"One elevator is on floor 9 and this other one is at the midlobby on floor 26. Either the power interruptions have crippled them or they have been deliberately held on those floors because neither elevator is moving." Emily informed him as she watched the frozen elevator displays. The lieutenant nodded in understanding.

In a fifty-two story building, having no elevator access was a terrible scenario to overcome. Even for the most physically fit individual, climbing fifty flights of stairs would not equate to happy times. On the bright side, they now at least had a couple of possibilities for which floors to search for intruders. When they entered the building, they we looking at the prospect of searching floor by floor.

Coming through the front entrance, the Cathedral crisis response team had made their arrival. They entered damp due to the fact that it had started raining. Not looking particularly thrill as they entered, it was clear this was not a group of volunteers. The mud tusslers' MPAR unit, which had held its position by the front desk during the lobby fight, joined in with the soggy group as they passed the welcome station.

Leading the group was Sgt. LaShawndra LeRoyson, a familiar face from the 271st precinct. The sergeant was always extremely professional and helpful when she worked with them. Emily has glad to see LaShawndra in the team. LeRoyson was followed by an older male officer who looked to be a sexagenarian and near retirement age. Next to him, was a chubby out of breath officer with a sour expression on his face. The man was clearly not happy to be here. Next to the unhappy nondieting officer was a nervous looking young man with a rookie patch on his uniform. His pale expression showed he was unsure about being here. Behind them was a trio of old out of date droids in disrepair. The dilapidated droids showed signs of tarnished age and were moving jerkily. One of the archaic robots only had one arm. They each carried a pugil shocker stick, even the one-armed droid.

They were a ragtag bunch of law enforcement. If police dispatch had picked names out of a hat, they could not have come up with a more eclectic combination. The shabby state of the police droids, called Policebots, was the most concerning part of the crisis response team. Those Policebots did not look like they were capable of responding to any crisis. Eddie and Emily's MPAR looked to be more helpful.

"Crisis response team reporting for duty, lieutenant." Sgt. LeRoyson declared.

"LaShawndra, it's good to see a friendly face from the 271st. " Emily greeted.

"Where's the rest of you?" Lt. Knighton interrogated.

"We are it. This is tonight's response team." the older officer answered.

"Between the championship cage fight in town, the Granthum Grey Sox playing the Cathedral Bishops at the stadium, multiple poker nights, the Roaring Lion rock star concert, The Sapphire and Ruby Bouquet performing at the playhouse, and the dirigible races at the Cathedral Skyway, many police officers are off tonight." LaShawndra explained.

"The dirigible races will probably get postponed because of the stormy weather." the rookie hesitantly added.

"Not many officers are going to the playhouse tonight." the older officer grumpily commented.

The lights fluttered and the building's electricity went out for five seconds before returning. "Loss of power detected." voice the first droid. "Loss of power detected." echoed the second droid. "Fzzt..zzzz.. uurrrt." let out the third droid.

Looking at the older officer, Lt. Knighton pointed at the pair of prone preventers. "Detain them, please." he instructed.

"Between the empty lobby and these two unfriendly greeters, we have good reasons to believe the lycan masquerade killers are already here. Should we call for more backup?" Oftenmarch queried to the lieutenant. The building lights again flickered twice.

"Yes, but we don't wait." Lt. Knighton decided as he started for the stairs.

"I can do it, sergeant. I'll put out a three alarm level request for backup." the older officer offered, speaking to LaShawndra.

"Did you say lycan masquerade killers?" the rookie nervously asked.

"We know police protective services are on the premises. We also know the lycan masqueraders are hunting for a witness in CPD protection. We have strong suspicions that the murderers are already in the building and on the attack. Therefore, we must move quickly." Emily gave a summary.

"Partner with Barney and wait for the reinforcements in the lobby. Send them up as soon as they get here." Sgt. LeRoyson instructed the older officer.

"We start on nine." Eddie called out as he marched toward the stairway.

"We're not taking an elevator?" the dumb struck rookie questioned.

"The elevators are not moving and even if they were moving, neither one is reliable with the building's unstable power state." Oftenmarch explained.

Emily hustled to catch-up to the lieutenant and took the second position in the march. Next in the procession were a pair of dilapidated droids followed by LeShawndra. Shakily, the rookie followed after the sergeant. He followed close behind her like a shadow. Then the MPAR motored along in the parade. Finally, bringing up the rear of their ranks was the last decrepit droid. This eclectic squad of police officers began their march into action.

As they approached the door to the stairwell, the building's lights surged off and on yet again. The building's power was performing as unstable as a neovirtual cryptocurrency. This power surge triggered the Policebots' detection warnings again. "Loss of power detected." voiced the first droid. "Loss of power detected." echoed the second droid. "Bzzztt..eee... uurrrnn. " let out the third droid.

"Is the weather affecting the power or is someone messing with the power?" Emily pondered aloud.

"Incidental power fluctuations or deliberate sabotage attempts, either is going to cause us visibility troubles." Sgt. LeRoyson forecasted.

"We keep going." Lt. Knighton declared not breaking stride.

"Half a league, half a league, half a league onward." Emily recited.

When Eddie arrived at the door to the stairs, he found a locking mechanism on the door with a familiar minirobot making a familiar halt gesture. Recognizing the locking module and minirobot, Lt. Knighton knew what need to be done to quickly unlock the door.

"Geshuntit." the lieutenant instructed. The locking mechanism immediately disengaged, the minirobot gave his welcoming wave, and Eddie opened the door to the stairwell.

As he led the way through the door, Eddie adjusted his shoulder light. He had a suspicion he was going to need it. Emily held the door for LaShawndra, the rookie and the three Policebots. However, the MPAR halted as it approached the doorway. Nine flights of stairs was far too many to carry the robot, so Detective Oftenmarch elected to leave it behind. They had just got the robot back and they were going to have to do without it again.

The stairwell was dimly lit, cool, and unwelcoming. The concrete walls in the stairway were painted a dungeon gray and were completely undecorated. Beginning the dismal climb of the drab stairs, the law enforcement team travelled wordlessly. Their footfalls began to echo in the stairwell as they hiked upward. The metal hand railings were icy cold like the air conditioning was left unregulated in the chilly stairway. As they trudged upward the three raggedy robots began to fall behind the rest of the group. Emily had passed all three of the units in the first three flights. With each floor the officers climbed, the farther the down-trodden droids fell behind them. Policebots were not the fastest of stair walkers.

The stairwell climb was quite a workout. Who needed Jazzercise when you could just walk up staircases in a midscraper. Even though it did not take very long for them to climb to the ninth floor, it seemed to last forever as they ascended. Each step was more fun than the last. When they reached their destination, Emily was glad to see the number 9 displayed on the stairwell door.

When the group exited the stairway onto the ninth floor, they entered a long hallway that ran from the front of the building all the way to the back of the building. There was not any center aisle leading toward the main elevators from this hallway. Therefore, straight was not an option. After looking up and down the hall, the lieutenant decided to head toward the front of the building. The floor was serene and quiet and none of the suites in this hall had any coming or going activity.

Following the lieutenant, the group decided to stay together. Within the first twenty some steps, Emily had taken the lead. It seemed she was the least affected by the cardio workout. Everything remained quiet until the group reached the first T-junction. There was nothing to see down the first intersecting hall but Emily could definitely hear some odd noises. Satisfied there was nothing abnormal in this intersecting hall, Emily moved forward. The farther forward the detective walked, the louder the strange noises grew.

At the second T-junction of the hallway is where Detective Oftenmarch spotted the source of the noises. It was Lawtech Patrollers identical to the robotics the detectives had seen in the warehouse. They seemed to be guarding the service elevator. Emily moved slightly into the intersection of the hallways. As soon as she had done so the Patrollers switched from sentry positions to a more unified formation. The mechanical guards formed a staggered line similar to an old British musketeer firing line. Bringing their side stunners to the ready, the

Patrollers made ready for a serious defense. Eddie moved into the hall next to Emily and Sgt. LeRoyson stayed close to the far wall of the first hallway.

A pair of the Lawtech Patrollers in the front fired a pair of warning stunner streams into the ceiling of the hallway just above the detectives. The pair of detectives looked at each other in disbelief. Eddie raised his hands, palms outward, in a gesture of surrender. Oftenmarch took a step backwards to appear less threatening. Neither made any sudden or aggressive movements. None of that made any difference to the droids. A second pair of Lawtech Patrollers fired a pair of warning stunner streams into the ceiling of the hallway above the detectives. Bits of ceiling tile rained down on Eddie and Emily. This time the mud tusslers decided to take the opposite approach and drew their Phasepulsers to return salutations.

Firing several times each from their stunners, they sent a volley of stunner streams streaking down the hallway into the firing line of Lawtech Patrollers. A high percentage of the streams struck the sleek and shining row of robots. All the Phasepulser IX streams which struck the line of Lawbots were absorbed by the new advanced armor of the droids. The Patrollers were completely unfazed by those stun strikes. Only the Phasepulser XII, which Oftenmarch used, had any effect and that effect was to cause one of the Lawbots to fall out of its firing stance and onto its robotic knee joints. Then it toppled to the ground.

Following their predetermined programming, the Lawtech Patrollers returned fire. Flashes of stunner arcs erupted from the robots' side stunners, sending dozens of streams shooting back up the hallway toward the Cathedral Police officers. A blindingly bright collection of streams lit up the hall as the roaring rush of those stunner streams hurtled up the hallway. It was an unfriendly indoor fireworks display. Eddie and Emily took cover around one hallway corner as LaShawndra and the rookie took cover around the other hallway corner. The streams whizzed by them striking walls and toppling some artistic wall hangings. Although missing the police officers, the buzz and thump of the return streams were menacing.

Undissuaded, Lt. Knighton swiftly switched from his Phasepulser IX to his service pistol. Taking the cue from the lieutenant, Detective Oftenmarch rapidly switched from her Phasepulser XII to her Maxwell TriAlloy XL-2. Even though the Phasepulser XII was effective, she felt the gun would be even more effective. Since their opponents were droids, they could afford to risk deadly force. The sergeant was slow to make her weapon exchange and the rookie was still hunkered down in cover. Therefore, the pair of detectives returned fire on their own again. They popped around the corner, fired off two shots each, and then ducked back around the corner to safety. All four shots slammed Lawbots solidly. Bursting brightly, two droids dropped from their line and crashed awkwardly to the floor with clamorous clanks.

Predictably, the line of Lawtech Patrollers was reformed and the dutiful droids again returned fire. Again flashes of stunner arcs erupted from the Patrollers' stunners propelling dozens of streams soaring back up the hallway toward the Cathedral Police officers. A blindingly bright collection of streams lit up the hall as the roaring rush of those stunner streams hurtled up the hallway. It was another unfriendly interior fireworks display. Already under cover around the hallway corners, the Cathedral PD officers were clear of the parade of streams. Once again the streams whizzed by them striking walls but this time removing chunks of the corners of the walls. Bits of drywall and wood fragments came raining down on the law officers.

Thinking quickly, Emily handed her Phasepulser XII to Eddie so he could counterattack two handed. Being ambidextrous, the lieutenant was quite good at shooting double fisted. LaShawndra and the rookie were ready this time. The Cathedral Police came out guns blazing when they returned fire this time. Lt. Knighton fired the Phasepulser XII twice and his service pistol twice. Detective Oftenmarch discharged her TriAlloy pistol thrice. Both Sgt. LeRoyson and the rookie each shot their service weapons twice. While the intensity of their attack increased, the accuracy of their attack slightly decreased.

Five of the remaining ten upright Lawbots were struck and took damage. Three of the impacted robots plummeted to the ground, while one of the dinged droids sustained enough damage to be omitting a plume of smoke. The grounded robots were not only out of the fight, they were obstacles to the remaining battling bots. Not only were the standing Lawbots impeded in their attempts to reform a firing line, a couple of the droids had initiated a retreat. The bumbling bots were so disorganized and executing so sub optimally, the Cathedral Police foursome had plenty of time to take refuge.

Finally returning fire, the Lawtech Patrollers' counterattack was more subdued and lackluster compared to the prior two salvos of streams. This time the reeling robots discharged a half a dozen of stunner streams at the Catherdral police officers. The group of streams were not as bright and the roaring rush was diminished. It was definitely not a grand finale of fireworks. The streams hurled up the hallway, slammed into walls, and put several dents into the far back wall. The Lawbots collective firepower had dwindled from menacing to now being annoying.

The foursome of Cathedral police officers came out of cover, firing at full force. In contrast to the diminishing attack of the Lawbots, the police officers escalated their counterattack. Both Eddie and Emily emptied their weapons' magazines in return fire. With determination to win the fight, they spent their clips endeavoring to press their advantage. Sgt. LeRoyson shot her service pistol four times and the rookie took two more shots. The crack of gunfire echoed in the hallway as the Cathedral police attempted to conclude the ninth floor conflict.

Falling like bowling pins, the Lawtech Patrollers sustained heavy damage and massive robotic casualties. There was a great carnage of droid carcasses scattered across the hallway floor. The robotic firing line was obliterated; the defense of the freight elevator was shattered. Mechanical parts were mangled, electronic parts were eviscerated, and robots lay in ruins. A pair of retreating droids barely made it into the service elevator. One Lawbot stumbled into the elevator as the other Lawbot fell into the elevator with a loud thud. The elevator doors closed behind their faltering retreat and they disappeared from sight.

As the service elevator doors closed, the door to the stairs could be heard opening around the corner. As the last of the Lawbots departed, the old Policebots finally arrived on the ninth floor. The clomp of their mechanical footsteps could be heard. While the gunsmoke and robot death fumes cleared, Lt. Knighton handed Emily back her Phasepulser XII. Sgt. LeRoyson was helping the young rookie to recompose himself. Trudging along the front hallway, the outdated robots were coming to rejoin the group now that the conflict was finished. As the old Policebots approached, Detective Oftenmarch left the group to inspect the fallen Lawtech Patrollers. Quickly reloading her firearm, she proceeded nimbly down the hallway with caution.

Carefully, Emily slowed down at the hallway junction which led to the center hallway and the main pair of elevators. This passageway had access to the elevators. With her weapon at the ready as a precaution she approached the intersection of hallways. Using the inside corner of the walls as a shield, the detective scanned the center hallway. The hallway was deserted but Emily could see how the one elevator was blocked. Somebody or somebodies had dropped a steel plate over the threshold of the elevator, preventing the doors from closing. The elevator threshold was being treated like a roadway pothole. Satisfied the center hallway was safe, Oftenmarch continued down the hallway toward the downed droids.

Emily hopscotched through the downed droids, checking that each of them was out of commission. Her inspection was swift but scrupulous for each Lawbot. Satisfied they were all out of order, Emily reached down and collected one of the undamaged side stunners. The stunner read Lawtech Surestun Plus along its muzzle and was surprisingly light. After a cursory examination of the weapon, Emily tucked it into an inside coat pocket for future use.

"Clear." Oftenmarch called out.

Having followed Detective Oftenmarch, the lieutenant had walked to the intersection of the hallways. Where Emily had turned her attention towards the pummeled Patrollers, Lt. Knighton had turned his focus towards the main elevators. He was looking intently in their direction as his brow furrowed in thought. From the top of the hallway, Sgt. LeRoyson's police radio comm crackled before the voice of the older officer had broadcast.

"Sergeant, there is a private police company here.....What's your name again?.....the Greater Cathedral Crimestoppers. They want to speak to the officer in charge." he announced.

"Copy that." LaShawndra replied over the comm.

"A pair of patrolmen have also arrived on scene. They are securing the front entrance from the inside because there is a raging thunderstorm outside now." the older officer continued.

"Copy that." LaShawndra repeated over her comm. "You want to speak with the GCC, lieutenant?" she asked Eddie.

"Tell them, I'm up here." Lt. Knighton responded. The building's lights flickered.

"Guidry, tell the GCC the lieutenant's on floor nine. They should get up here if they want to chat with him." LaShanwndra translated over the radio.

"Roger that, over and out." Guidry ended transmission.

"Search the floor." Lt. Knighton ordered with urgency.

"Affirmative" one of the ramshackle robots voiced in confirmation.

"We will head to the last hallway." Sgt. LeRoyson indicated. The rookie followed her back up to the front hallway.

"I will take the back hallway." Emily volunteered. With that said she moved.

Darting to the end of the hall, Emily slid to the corner of the wall where she could view the short section of the back hallway. Nothing out of the ordinary was there. Emily pushed tight into the wall and cautiously peeked around the corner to peer across the rest of the back hallway. The overhead hallway lights flickered twice as the building's power continued to be temperamental. The hallway was empty of occupants, both of human and robot. At first glance all seemed normal but as Emily scanned further she noticed the second door on the back wall was damaged.

The detective stealthily snuck around the corner, moved along the hallway with her weapon at the ready, and took up position against the back wall to inspect the door closer. Dented, skewed, and unhinged to substantial degrees, the door was unable to be closed properly. Not only could the door not be closed properly, it was also too damaged to be secured by its locks. The detective noted the suite number on the door, 940. Slowly, Emily pushed the mistreated door open. It creaked and groaned with protest as it opened, giving considerable resistance.

Detective Oftenmarch swung into the room, staying low in a partial crouch. Staying in a baseball catcher's squat, Emily surveyed the suite. It was dark and quiet with no motion to be detected. Lightning flashes coming in from the large back windows illuminated the space briefly. From her survey, Emily could see it was a large open living area with a small kitchenette to the left, a staircase winding upward in the suite's midsection, and two open doors to the right side of the room. Both couches had been turned upside down, the big jumbo screen television had been smashed, and two card tables had been knocked over to the floor. Taking out the autotracker device, Oftenmarch used it to scan for life signs in the suite. After a few moments, the device read: 44 Fetch error, TCK not found %1A.

Emily clicked her radio broadcast button and with her signal synched with Eddie's radio she reported, "Evidence of violence in Suite 940, back hallway."

After a few moments of fumbling in the dark, Detective Oftenmarch found a light switch and turned on some lights in the suite. With some light shed on the situation, Emily could see the damage in the open living area was rather extensive. There were several sizable holes in both side walls, the kitchenette microwave was destroyed, several broken beer bottles laid on the kitchenette counter, a section of the living area carpet had been torn, several decorative vases had been shattered, a section of the staircase railing had been removed, and a recliner chair had been ripped and torn in three places.

Crossing the damage laden room, Emily maneuvered to the first open door on the right, avoiding debris and overturned furniture as she went. Rain pattering could be heard on the tall rear windows. Swiftly, Emily moved to the side of the doorway, then swung into the adjacent room weapon first. This explored room was a bedroom with an unslept bed and a half unpacked suitcase. Turning on the overhead light, Emily discovered the bedroom was tidy and untussled. Trying the autotracker again, Emily scanned for life signs in the room. The result displayed on the tracker was 44 Fetch error, TCK not found %2A. Abandoning the useless autotracker, Detective Oftenmarch checked the room efficiently and expediently for any hideaways. Finding nobody she moved to an inner door and silently slipped into the next room. As she expected, it was an attached bathroom.

With the shower curtain pulled back and no closet, the small bathroom gave an individual no place to conceal themselves. Once she had the lights on in the bathroom, Emily cleared it quickly. The bathroom lights flickered. Satisfied there was nothing to see here, Emily traversed her steps and double-timed it back to the main living area. When Detective Oftenmarch returned to the suite's main room, she saw Lt. Knighton was positioned against the door frame inspecting the suite.

"Thunder." the lieutenant stated.

"Flash." Emily replied.

"No, thunder." Eddie restated, pointing at the windows.

"Two-story suite, I think the witness and their protection detail must have made their escape upwards." Emily theorized. Lt. Knighton nodded in agreement.

"Call LaRoyson, please." Eddie requested as he surveyed the inner suite staircase.

Wasting no time, the detective speed into action to find the sergeant. Detective Oftenmarch moved double time across the suite's main area and swiftly exited Suite 940. Once out in the hallway, Emily had only taken a couple of steps when she spotted Sgt. LeRoyson coming around the corner into the back hallway of the ninth floor. The rookie was still tailing her.

"All clear this way, Emily." LaShawndra announced.

"There's signs of forced entry here at Suite 940. The suite's been trashed. The lieutenant wants us to gather there. It's a two-story suite and we have to search the upper floor next. What radio channel are you on, LaShawndra?" Emily detailed speaking speedily.

"Echo 14." Sgt. LeRoyson shared as she hustled down the back hall.

"Thank you, LaShawndra." Oftenmarch replied as she quickly adjusted her radio comm channel.

Reversing her recent rear hallway steps, Emily led the group back to Suite 940. None of the ancient slow moving Policebots were anywhere to be seen. As they moved along the back hall of the ninth floor, the power briefly went out before coming back on again. The Policebots voicing loss of power detected could be heard off in the distance somewhere in the halls of the ninth floor.

When the trio of police officers entered Suite 940, Lt. Knighton was at the doorway of the second open door to the room's right side. With the lights turned on, the lieutenant was surveying that adjacent room. He was displaying no reaction to whatever was to view in that room.

Upon seeing Emily return with the sergeant and the rookie, Eddie ended his inspection and motioned towards the staircase with a pointing finger.

Moving silently but swiftly, the group of law enforcers moved across the suite to the inner suite staircase. Lt. Knighton was first to reach the stairs and began his ascent with his service pistol at the ready. Second up the stairs, Detective Oftenmarch followed the lieutenant upward as she switched to her Phasepulser XII as her weapon of choice. She did not bother with the autotracker. Sgt. LeRoyson was third to climb the stairs to the suite's second floor. With her service weapon drawn, the sergeant stayed close to Emily as they climbed. Finally, the rookie reached the staircase. Last to start moving upward, the rookie was several steps behind the female officers and fell further behind them as they rose. He had no weapon unholstered and in hand.

The group climbed from the lighted lower level to the darkened upper floor. Lightning flashes through the upper-floor windows temporarily provided some light. Hallway lights also seemed to be peeking into the upstairs. When Lt. Knighton reached the top of the spiraling staircase, he slid onto the upper floor staying low and weapon aimed. Likewise entering the second level low to the floor, Emily silently slid in the opposite direction of Eddie with her Phasepulser XII in firing position. Sgt. LeRoyson professionally moved into the upper floor then took up a position to cover both detectives.

The main area of the suite's second floor was much tinier than on the first floor. The suite's upper floor was divided into several smaller rooms, each connecting to the floor's main area. Cautiously and catlike, Emily shadow-stepped from door to door on the second floor. Within thirty seconds, Eddie had the overhead lights active in the main area. Within a minute, Emily had the overhead lights in all the adjoining rooms going. The rookie had finally joined them on the upper level by that time. On the second floor, it was serenely vacant. Not a creature was stirring or moving around; there was absolutely nobody to be found. From the way the front door stood open and giving the lack of suite occupants, it appeared as through the killer's quarry had flown the coop. This was an encouraging discovery, there was still hope.

A pair of work shoes lay in the middle of the walkway, sloppily scattered just outside a doorway. Emily scooped the abandoned shoes from the floor one at a time. Carefully checking inside the shoes as she collected them, Emily found what she was looking to find. The discovery was worth the footwear's unpleasant odor. Inside the second retrieved shoe was a piece of paper with a handwritten note. On the shoe hidden paper, Mockingbird Lane was written in alternating black and dark green crayon. It was the same method of communication which Barrett Alexander had been using when he perished. With great interest, Eddie looked at Emily expectantly.

Recognizing that the note was in reference to a 1960s sitcom about a family of monsters, Emily believed she knew what the message meant. Knowing the address of that fictional monster family, Emily had an idea of where to go next. Their destination should be suite 1313, if her interpretation was correct.

"We have to go to the thirteenth floor." Emily declared.

"The kindergarten trail." Eddie commented with a frown.

"It is a bizarre way to communicate but it seems to work for Cathedral Special Police's witness protection division." Emily admitted.

"Claiming an elevator." Lt. Knighton revealed his intentions.

The suite lights flickered. "I will take the stairs, Eddie." Emily informed him.

"I can stay with Emily in case the power gives out completely." Sgt. LeRoyson suggested. Eddie nodded in agreement.

"Detectives Knighton and Oftenmarch moving to the thirteenth floor in pursuit of suspects." Emily reported over her police comm.

"Calvary call, 271st homicide." the lieutenant broadcasted into his police comm.

A pair of the Policebots showed up unpunctually to join the police huddle. Almost as soon as they arrived, the lieutenant took charge of them to go reclaim an elevator. Detective Oftenmarch and Sgt. LeRoyson headed off in the opposite direction with the rookie trailing them. Emily dashed through the halls, making her way back to the stairs at her best possible speed. Turning a corner, she encountered the last Policebot which was lumbering along the hall. Emily zoomed by the Policebot enroute to the stairs. Leaving the robot in her wake, Oftenmarch quickly raced to the stairs.

Upon entering the dimly lit stairway, the police squad was met with the same cool air and cold banisters they experienced earlier. As Emily led the way upward, she was more motivated than ever. The confrontation with the Patrollers had fueled her with a stronger passion to stop this villainy. The detective was soaring up the stairs, taking two steps per stride. Reaching the thirteenth floor, Emily was more driven than relieved.

Entering the thirteenth floor, the detective immediately took an inventory of her surroundings. The direction of trouble was not hard to determine. Big long gouges ran along one end of the hallway and loud bangs could be heard coming from that direction. Without hesitation, Emily sprinted in the direction of the commotion. Within seconds, she was down the hall and around the corner.

When she entered the next hallway, Emily instantly noticed three downed robotic sentries, each severely damaged beyond functionability. The artificial sentries were cylindrical robots with domed tops full of sensors and alarms. Robotic sentries were more often used by private law enforcement, but the Cathedral police department was beginning to also use the droids more often. From the wreckage of the robots, Emily could tell that two of them were stationed on either side of a suite door and the third was patrolling the hallway. The carnage of the third robot ran about thirty-feet along the passageway; most of the bot's important parts had been ground into the hallway carpet.

Avoiding the mashed-up debris of robotics, Emily hustled along the corridor towards the door with the damaged droids flanking its sides. Upon reaching the nearest destroyed sentry, the detective pulled the electronic mess off to the side and out of her way. The robot was so pulverized that Emily had no choice but to move it in several pieces. After clearing the robotic debris, she took up a position next to the partially open and partially damaged door. Sgt. LeRoyson had caught up to Emily and was now cleaning up the other robotic sentry on the opposite side of the door. It was equally as messy as the first.

Listening from her secure position, Emily could hear loud gunshots. Slowly and silently, she opened the door slightly wider. Remaining unnoticed, she could see wolf mask wearing intruders shooting their weapons towards a closed inner door. Firing repeatedly into a bedroom door until their gun was emptied, was the perpetrators' grand plan. It would be an understatement to say they were not having much success.

"Where's the rest of the ammo?" one masked man angrily asked aloud.

"You used it all, fool." another masquerader annoyingly answered.

Emily looked over at LaShawndra, who had taken up a secure position on the other side of the doorway, and quietly indicated three intruders and their current direction in the room by using hand gestures. The sergeant nodded in acknowledgment; she understood the charades. As the pair of female law enforcement personnel held their positions outside the suite door, the lieutenant and the rookie both arrived from opposite directions to join them. Lt. Knighton moved into a safe position next to Emily; the rookie did likewise next to LaShawndra.

"We control an elevator" Eddie informed Emily.

"Does the building's power know that?" Emily asked Eddie half in jest.

As if on queue, the building experienced another power fluctuation. Breaking a momentary silence, a couple more noisy gunshots erupted from within the suite followed by the clicking sound of an empty firearm. Staying low, the lieutenant snuck a peak into the room. With cat-like stealth, Eddie got into a position to observe the situation. After a brief recon, he pushed the door all the way open and swiftly returned to a fortified position out of the doorway. He gave Emily a signal to open a dialogue.

"J.D., give up this folly. We know it's Patrick, John-Paul, and you. We have evidence against the three of you; we have you boxed. Please, stop this madness." Emily pleaded.

"It's too late, Emily. You don't know them, what they are capable of doing, or what they will do to me." Fairbankers explained.

"Shut up, dude. Don't answer with her name." one of the other trainees called out.

"You're right, J.D. I don't know them but I know you and what you're capable of doing. I know the man who cared enough to rescue a pair of young ladies from being horrifically murdered on a cold moonlight night in a dark and cruel cemetery ritual." Emily responded.

"There are actions that cannot be undone. Crimes that run too deep. It is too late, Emily." J.D. replied.

"It does not matter what you have done as much as it matters what you will do. Today is a day of grace; today is a day of forgiveness. GOD will forgive you. Repent and give up this masquerade killing. It is written: *You are forgiving and good, O LORD, abounding in love to all who call to you.*" Emily reassured and persuaded.

"Psalm 86:5" Lt. Knighton stated.

"I'm scared, Emily. I don't want to go to jail; I don't want to be exposed as a villain." Fairbankers admitted.

"Fight the fear, take back the peace of a renewed clear conscience. Find the peace of choosing the seemingly tough path of redemption over the easy path of degradation. Now is a moment of redemption, a turning point. Take the path less travelled by, start fighting the good fight." Emily implored.

"I feel entrenched in this mission; I'm trapped in my transgressions and bound to fight with this team until the end." J.D. continued to explain.

"This is not the end, J.D. You have picked the wrong battle, served the wrong master, and allowed your pride to view surrendering and abandoning foolishness as failure. Make the right choice, now. Stop being a masked madman and come help the Cathedral Police. As the Bible says: *Create in me a pure heart, O GOD, and renew a steadfast spirit within me*." Oftenmarch counter explained.

"Psalm 51:10," Eddie declared.

"You make it sound so simple. It's not so simple. If we are captured, we are ruined." Fairbankers complained.

"We need you for us not against us, J.D. I need you to stop helping the villains and help me save people." Emily requested.

"It is a far, far better thing that I do, than I have ever done; it is a far, far more courageous act I take than I have ever dared." Fairbankers expressed aloud as he took off his wolf mask.

"What are you doing, J.D.?" John Paul exclaimed.

"Get back here, Fairbankers!" screamed Monkhouse.

"This is the right decision, J.D. You are doing great, just keep going." Emily encouraged.

J.D. walked out of the room with his mask off and his hands raised. The man had made his choice; he had picked his side. The wolf disguise had gone; a new conversion to sanguinity had come.

"I surrender. I surrender all." J.D. Fairbankers declared.

Sgt. LeRoyson pulled the surrendering trainee out of the doorway and off to the side into safety. The sergeant began arresting Fairbankers as Emily gave him a heartfelt hug.

"Thank you, J.D." Emily gratefully told him as LaShawndra began reading the apprehending trainee his rights. There were tears in both his and the detective's eyes.

There was a commotion coming from inside the suite. Oftenmarch pulled herself back into cover as the rookie took custody of Fairbankers now without a weapon. It sounded as if furniture was being moved inside the suite. It seemed like the other two trainees were preparing to resist. One battle was over but another battle appeared to just be beginning.

"I am not giving up. Come and get me, Princess. I'm no costumed robot or ridiculous clanker." Monkhouse screamed.

"We're in no position to fight." John-Paul protested to his cohort.

Monkhouse pulled out an odd looking and strangely shaped stunner. From behind the plush recliner where he was hiding, Monkhouse fired the bizarre weapon toward the entrance door to the suite and the police officers. His first shot sailed wide right and upward toward the ceiling. Chunks of plaster fell from where the stream struck. His second shot flew left and into the floor as Monkhouse had overcompensated.

"J.P., you idiot. This stupid stunner is rubbish." Monkhouse screamed some more.

"It's retractable, Patrick. You have to properly extend it." John-Paul explained from behind the plush recliner where he hid.

Monkhouse let loose another stunner stream which was just as lousy as the first two shots. Any adjustments he had made were made in vain. This shot sailed wide right and high into the ceiling again. Again plaster fell from the point of the stream's impact.

"Give yourselves up. You're trapped in the suite and have nowhere to run." Sgt. LeRoyson called from the side of the suite door.

Monkhouse threw the partially extended stunner across the suite in the direction of the entrance door. It landed about three feet short and skidded to a halt next to a broken round leg from a table. Staying hidden, Tuttle threw an empty fruit bowl at the entrance. It awkwardly struck the doorframe, shattering into pieces. Monkhouse angrily hollered in frustration as he fired his pistol. Two shots rang out before his weapon clicked, revealing it was empty. He had used all his ammunition on the suite's doors. Both wildly fired shots struck the suite wall just wide of the doorway. Neither shot did more than buy time and waste ammo.

"Do you have your revolver, J.P. ?" Monkhouse called wantingly.

"Are you kooky nuts? Of course I didn't bring my revolver. We were supposed to capture Ryerson, not shoot at cops." Tuttle answered staying well concealed.

While the pair of posing trainees were distracted, Emily spun around the corner of the doorway to shoot her Phasepulser XII twice. Keeping her stunner streams low, she fired toward the ground. Both streams travelled under the plush recliners as intended to strike both trainees in their semi-exposed feet. Both streams struck the lower extremities of the traitorous trainees causing them to stumble.

In a fit of rage, Monkhouse struggled to his feet and charged toward the main suite entrance. Removing his bolt stunner, the mad masquerader raced forward in a rush toward Oftenmarch. As Monkhouse made his mad dash for her, Emily calmly pulled out the Lawtech SureStun Plus from her inner white coat pocket. Exposing himself in his blind rage blitz, Monkhouse made a critical mistake. Oftenmarch fired the LawTech SureStun Plus accurately at the approaching rusher. The stunner stream struck Monkhouse squarely in the chest, lifting him off his feet. He soared backwards and crashed to the floor with all his rage momentum taken from him.

Eddie swung into the doorway to fire a pair of Phasepulser IX streams in trainee Tuttle's direction. One of the stunner streams slammed into the recliner while the second stream skidded off the floor. Either stunned or staying out of sight, John-Paul stayed prone behind the recliner, neither resisting nor retaliating.

Sgt. LeRoyson sprinted past the detectives and dashed into the suite. Following the sergeant was a clanky old Policebot which gangly gallomped into the room. The sergeant and robot pair pounced on the prone trainee Monkhouse. Poking him with its stunner stick, the dated droid was preventing Monkhouse from rising to his feet. Unable to recover from his stunning, Monkhouse began to thrash desperately against the law enforcement piled on top of him. The trio began to tussle in a collective pile on the floor. Struggling to arrest the trainee, the police fiercely fought the resisting Monkhouse.

As the group wrestled on the ground, Lt. Knighton rushed into the room with his Phasepulser IX at the ready. The lieutenant hustled over to where John-Paul was laying behind a plush recliner. Rounding the protective furniture, Eddie moved toward the other prone trainee. The lieutenant moved in to detain Tuttle and if necessary restun him. John-Paul showed no signs of resisting.

"I'm not a killer, I am an electronics expert." John-Paul meekly told Lt. Knighton as he lay on the ground.

While Sgt. LeRoyson and her assisting droid fought to restrain Monkhouse, Lt. Knighton began apprehending unresistant Tuttle. Emily stayed by the door covering the officers inside the suite and keeping an eye on Fairbankers simultaneously. Next to the remorsefully detained, stood the rookie officer. The rookie was content to guard the docile and arrested Fairbankers. Oftenmarch held her position dutifully with the Lawtech SureStun Plus also at the ready.

Within seconds, Lt. Knighton had John-Paul arrested and was reading him his new Miranda rights. The arrest of Monkhouse was taking longer as the grappling and struggling continued. The Policebot had twice more given Monkhouse a helping of its stun stick. Screaming in rage, the trainee only seemed to fight more with each stun. Trusting J.D. would stay put, Emily strode over to the scuffle. Reacting briskly, Oftenmarch grabbed Monkhouse's flailing right arm. With a quick twist of his arm, Emily repositioned the trainee. Then she put her knee into his back and forcefully pinned him to the floor with the sergeant's help. His right arm was now pinned behind his back. As he was held in place, Sgt. LeRoyson cuffed him and read him his new Miranda rights.

As Sgt. LeRoyson hauled the hollering trainee Monkhouse away, Lt. Knighton motioned for Tuttle, now maskless, to follow in the evacuation process. Obediently, trainee Tuttle quietly trotted out of the suite. The Policebot escorted him out of the room. With the suite now clear of lycan masqueraders, the lieutenant knocked three times on the well-abused and shot up door. There was no answer to his first attempt. So Eddie tried another three more rhythmic knocks.

"Dotson, Brownsides, It's Knighton and Oftenmarch. We're here at the Wing and Ring tower. We're here to help." Emily shouted through the busted door.

Barefoot and wearing a white pizza sauce stained tee shirt and holey jeans, a medium height man with untidy hair hesitantly came out of the room. Holding a beer bottle but no weapon, the man did not come out to fight. His expression changed from apprehensive to relieved as he slowly exited the side room. His mouth widened into a broad smile as he scanned the suite. His shoulders relaxed as he stood a little taller.

"Working hard, Bobevvins." Eddie asked the man.

"Steady Eddie, you are a welcoming sight for once in your life." Bobevvins replied.

Brownsides exited the room behind Bobevvins. He also was not carrying a weapon but at least he was wearing a clean shirt and shoes. Unlike Bobevvins, he did look like he was coming out to fight with clenched fists. Like Bobbevvins, his demeanor changed when he saw the homicide detectives. He unclenched his fists and slackened his stance.

"Hey, you're the cops that Donny Boy knows. The mud tusslers, that's what he calls you." Brownsides recalled in relief.

"The Wing and Ring tower, we got your reference, Reggie." Emily expounded.

"Glad somebody in the Cathedral PD is paying attention. I was beginning to think we were left on our own here." Brownsides shared.

"You called for backup?" Lt. Knighton asked, straightening his shirt collar.

"About ten minutes ago but that's just an estimate since I left my watch downstairs. Had to exit in a hurry. We put out a distress request for backup as we changed floors. We didn't get any response from our request so we were afraid nobody was coming." Bobevvins recounted as he moved farther into the main area.

"I have a bad feeling that your request was blocked. These suspects are capable of some skullduggery." Emily speculated, looking towards Tuttle now under guard with the sergeant in the hallway.

"We had the same bad feeling when we did not hear back from Dotson." Brownsides shared also moving farther into the main area.

"Dotson's not with you? Did he get injured? Where is he?" Oftenmarch rattled off questions with concern.

"He's farther up the tower guarding the gorgeous girl." Brownsides responded.

"The boss assigned him to the supermodel as miss good looking is a VIP witness. Seems she is a very popular person" Bobevvins added.

"Who are you guarding?" Lt. Knighton asked the guardian police.

"Some bloke named Ryerson." Bobevvins answered.

"Some little scrawny dude named Ryerson." Brownsides also answered.

"Zeke Ryerson? How is he?" Emily wondered.

"Actually, I am quite fine now. Thank you." a quiet little man spoke from behind the adjoining now damaged door.

"Arrest Liarson." Eddie said to Emily, pointing to Ryerson.

"But I have an immunity agreement with the Cathedral PD's high commissioner's office. They guaranteed me that if I helped them then I would not be arrested for any involvement." Ryerson stammered.

"That would be your brother." Lt. Knighton corrected.

"If Steady Eddie says you're a criminal, chances are good you are a criminal." Bobevvins told Ryerson, who stayed behind the door.

"Maybe I'm not the twin you think I am, detective." Ryerson riddled.

"And maybe you're still as guilty as your brother." Bobevvins reasoned.

"Maybe your lies lose immunity." Knighton riddled in return.

Emily called toward the main entrance of the suite, "J.D., which Ryerson brother is this one, do you know?".

The rookie had brought Fairbankers into the doorway, keeping him close in custody. "We don't know, Emily. They were supposed to be together on Friday night but they were not. We don't know which is which." Fairbankers explained.

"Shut up, JD." Monkhouse exclaimed. The Policebot poked Patrick with its stunner stick.

"I have immunity; I have cooperated." Ryerson protested.

"Were you going for the young lady next?" Emily interrogated Fairbankers.

"The pair of leaders we reported to have gone higher up the building to get the main target, a young woman who saw them during the DA's murder. Witness protection shuffles rooms every night so finding the occupied suite might take them time which means you still have a chance to stop them. However, they have a pair of lunatics with them tonight, scary dudes who look like a werewolves." Fairbankers divulged.

"Dotson and the state appointed agent are up on the 32nd floor." Brownsides offered.

"Donny Boy is the best there is in the business. Wolfman or no wolfman, he will protect the witness." Bobevvins confidently said.

"Stay here, you'll never make it past the midlobby." Tuttle offered while arrested.

"We cannot delay." Eddie declared.

"Ryerson twin, you are under arrest." Emily stated. She pulled out her second and last pair of handcuffs and began arresting Ryerson. He whined and protested the entire time she read him his new Miranda rights. Oftenmarch did not dawdle or pause to debate in her duty, the mud tusslers had to keep moving as there was more work for them to do in the Flockman and Bellweather building this stormy evening.

Chapter 18

Lycan Attack

Knighton and Oftenmarch left Sgt. LeRoyson and the rookie on the thirteenth floor to hold the federal trainee segment of the lycan masquerade killers in custody. Also remaining on the thirteenth floor, Bobbevvins both held and guarded Ryerson, whichever brother he may be. Wishing to help Donny Boy, Brownsides volunteered to escort the detectives to the appropriate suite on the 32nd floor. To aid in the prisoner overwatch, the lieutenant decided to leave one of the old Policebots with the sergeant. As for the pair of aged Policebots reserving and securing the elevator, Lt. Knighton drafted them to aid in the efforts to stop the rest of the lycan masquerade killers. If anyone from the Greater Cathedral Crimefighters or anyone from the Cathedral Police Department arrived as backup on floor thirteen, the lieutenant requested that Sgt. LeRoyson contact him over the police comm.

With little discussion and no real plan established, Brownsides, two battered bots, and the mud tusslers boarded the acquired main elevator and rode it to its uppermost floor, the midlobby on floor twenty-six. Risking being stuck in an unpowered elevator, the group gambled on an uninterrupted trip to the sky lobby as the elevator was their fastest option. Since the Bellweather and Flockman Building did not have an express elevator, it was unusual for it to have a sky lobby. But that was the city of Cathedral, full of the unusual. Quietly riding the elevator, the human portion of the group hoped for continuous power as they prepared for the unexpected once the elevator doors opened on the twenty-sixth floor.

Taking a knee as the elevator rose, Emily broke the silence to say a prayer. "Dear LORD, help us to live this moment in our lives well. Show us the way we should go, for to you, LORD, we entrust our lives. Help us to love, serve, and protect others. Let us act not out of our own strength but out of your love and wisdom. May Your WORD be a lamp onto our feet and a light onto our path. May we love YOU with our whole heart; may we love others as we love ourselves. I pray we can protect those who need protecting and prevent those who choose folly from harming others in their mistakes. In Your mighty name we pray. Amen." Emily prayed.

"Amen." Eddie supported.

As the prayer concluded the elevator came to a stop with its digital display showing floor twenty-six. As the doors to the elevator slid open, the one-armed robot immediately exited to enter the building's midlobby. The second Policebot also quickly departed the elevator just behind the first Policebot. Once the Policebots had exited the elevator, Emily had a clearer view of the sky lobby. It was smaller and less ornate than the building's main ground lobby. The midlobby was also cleaner and its carpeting seemed less worn by foot traffic than the main lobby. Having a small coffee kiosk, a super sub vending machine, several oval dining tables, and a Cathedral news monitor, the midlobby was set up more as a gathering area than a waiting area. The half of the floor visible from the elevator was completely open. There were no suites to be seen on this floor.

Detective Oftenmarch swept into the lobby with her Phasepulser XII at the ready. Lt. Knighton followed her closely into the open area with his Phasepulser IX also posed to fire. Before special police officer Brownsides exited the elevator as the rear guard, Eddie indicated for him to hit the ground floor button to send the elevator back down to the main lobby for possible reinforcements. After having done so, Brownsides joined them in the midlobby. Emily began to carefully inspect the lobby area for any danger. The lobby's overhead lights spun in a continuous clockwise circle, spreading light in a swirling pattern. The building's recent unstable power had caused havoc with some of the lights as they were having trouble rotating. As Emily swept her focus across the midlobby, she noticed that a metal plate was placed over the second elevator's threshold, exactly as what had been done to the first elevator on the ninth floor. Covering the elevator entryway, the big metal plate prevented the elevator doors from closing.

Also noticing the obstructive metal plate, the lieutenant was drafting Officer Brownsides and the one-armed robot into helping him shift the plate off the elevator. As the lieutenant worked on that strenuous task, Emily resumed her patrol of the sky lobby. She began to maneuver around the corner of the inner wall to observe the other half of the lobby. Moving along the inner wall and using it as protection, Emily continued to inspect the lobby area for any danger. The sky lobby had a now closed soup, salad, and suds kiosk in this section she was observing. Several lobby tables had discarded coffee cups and abandoned food containers sitting cluttered on the tabletops. Candy wrappers and unwanted brochures of city attractions were comingled with some of the containers.

Emily had gone about one hundred and twenty degrees around the lobby and had arrived at a second inner wall corner when she began hearing strange noises. Taking up a defensive position at the corner, the detective peered around the corner into the main area of the other half of the sky lobby. This half of the lobby was not visible when exiting the elevator. In the middle of this section of the sky lobby was an unmanned information kiosk. Currently, the automated information desk had a sign indicating it was out of order. Although unoperational, the kiosk had a nice billboard full of local Cathedral attractions and restaurants. That informative billboard unfortunately also obscured some of Emily's vision of the sky lobby.

Patrolling this section of the lobby, in an intersecting weave pattern of a sentry march, were the second strangest robots Emily had ever seen. The odd robots were translucent and seemed to have a gelatinous shell which jiggled as they moved. Being able to see through their jellylike exterior, Emily could observe their thin metallic skeletal interior. Their visible metal framework had several series of wires running along and around it, like an entangled bird's nest. Each very slender robot was roughly seven feet tall. Their long strides made up for their slow mechanical movements. The robots looked like long cylindrical blocks of solidified jelly walking around the midlobby. There was a unique muffled hum of motors and a dampened clicking of gears emanating from the jellybots. It was like the gelatinous shells muted the noises from the machinery.

These bizarre bots appeared to be guarding the pair of elevators which travelled upward to the highest floors of the building. The patrolling gelatin robots did not carry any weapons. Their back and forth patrol route ran directly in front of the elevator doors. From her position around the corner, Emily did not receive any responses from the jellybots which suggested they detected her presence. They continued their sentry duties as if she was invisible or she had been assessed harmless. Emily was attempting to formulate a plan of action when an unanticipated action set things in motion.

From around the other interior corner on the other side of the sky lobby, the two-armed Policebot had charged into the open area directly towards the gelatinous robots on guard duty. Emily thought the old robot would be helping the lieutenant remove the metal plate off the elevator threshold but obviously that was not the case. The old robot was on the mechanical move to confront the odd robots. It came up to the jellybots swinging its electrified stunner stick.

At first the bizarre looking jellybots paid no attention to the charging old Policebot. However, as its proximity grew closer, their detection grew focused. As the Policebot attempted to strike them with its stunner stick, the odd jellybots scattered adeptly, avoiding the swinging electric tipped pugil. Several of them swiftly scrambled to reposition themselves away from the attacking droid. Sadly, the old Policebot looked like it was swatting at flies as it swung and missed its targets repeatedly.

Beginning to have patches of swirling glow flow from within their gelatinous material, several jellybots seemed to be in a state of flux. Forming around their inner metal framework and spreading into the jelly, current seemed to be generating. Streaks of darker color ran across their gelatinous exteriors and surged outward along their arms. Some type of electric pulse was flowing through their jellylike material and building up in the gelatinous portion of their arms. The strange robots extended their arms and held up their jellybot palms out flat and upward. Bursts of streams erupted from three of the jellybots' palms. Within seconds the lightning quick stunner waves struck the old Policebot. The stunning strikes spun the Policebot around like an old fashioned top. Round and round the overmatched old robot whirled. Dizzied from stunner strikes, the Policebot staggered a step then crumbled to the floor, dropping its stunner stick as it fell. Laying in a heap on the ground the Policebot emitted some sad sparking. Its shielding was no match for the strength of the jellybots' intense stunning power.

Witnessing the stunner streams emanate from their thin metal skeleton and gelatinous bodies, Emily knew why the jellybots carried no weapons. The detective also did not see a way to walk to the elevators without getting stunned. Also seeing the damage inflicted on the aggressive Policebot, the detective knew she could not risk either a direct assault or a prolonged stunner stream battle. Pulling out the Lawtech SureStun Plus, Emily also made ready the Phasepulser XII as she prepared to fire both stunners at once. As she promptly prepared, Lt. Knighton quietly came up next to her. Suppressing her startlement from his stealthy appearance, Emily kept her cool. Giving him a halt signal, Emily mouthed the words: more droids. Understanding her, Eddie unholstered his service weapon and got ready to fight. For the lieutenant, robots did not qualify for the capture before kill CPD policy.

As several of the jellybots circled the fallen Policebot with their focus there, Detective Oftenmarch took the opportunity to make her move. Bouncing off the corner, Emily positioned herself in a semi-crouch and began her dual stunner attack. The lieutenant came around the corner behind her and moved into the Weaver stance. The mud tusslers began their attack with a full measure of force and determination.

The pair of detectives fired off a flurry of shots at the gelatinous hide robots guarding the sky lobby's elevators. Their barrage caught the guarding robots off guard. Lt. Knighton fired off a half a dozen shots, all of which were accurate. Two jellybots were struck by two bullets each and two jellybots were each struck once. Detective Oftenmarch fired off fourteen stunner streams, six streams from the Phasepulser XII which exhausted its charge and eight streams from the Lawtech stunner which likewise spent its available charge.

Absorbed by the jellybot's gelatinous material like ballistic gel, the bullets from the lieutenant's pistol had no effect on the odd robots. Likewise all the stunner streams from the Phasepulser XII had no effect on the jellybots. All three robots struck by the Phasepulser streams were unphased; they simply absorbed the stuns. However, the stunner streams from the Lawtech SureStun Plus had amazing results on the jellybots. It was like the Lawtech stunner was designed to work against the jellybots. Four jellybots, each hit with a pair of Lawtech streams, shook violently like they were being electrocuted. Bits of their gelatinous hide began to melt off of their roboskeletal structure where the streams had knifed through the jellylike material. The four afflicted robots struggled and staggered for a moment, then dropped like dominoes onto the midlobby floor. Eliminating each strange robot its streams stuck, the Lawtech stunner exploited vulnerabilities in the jellybots in its domination over them.

Observing several jellybots develop darker patches in their gelatinous material and having witnessed this phenomenon minutes ago, Detective Oftenmarch knew it was time to move. Swiftly retucking herself around the inside wall corner, Emily took cover. Taking his cue from Emily, Eddie backpedaled as he also took refuge around the corner. No sooner had the lieutenant moved out of the line of fire, a barrage of stunner streams sailed past their previous position. Stunner streams saturated the sky lobby like wind driven rain. Stream after stream struck walls, tables, and windows. The mud tusslers were caught in a stunner stream storm that shook the walls and ground as the streams kept coming and striking hard.

"What in the wide world is going on over there?" Brownsides bellowed from the other side of the midlobby. Neither of the under siege detectives answered him. Stunner streams continued to streak across the sky lobby.

Holding position as the onslaught persisted, Emily waited for the Lawtech stunner to regain a full charge. As the detectives stayed behind cover, the streams kept coming. The persistent counterstrike of streams seemed to be endless as the jellybots maintained their assault of stunning shots. It was beginning to feel like the detectives would be pinned down and unable to move farther up the building when the jellybots blundered. As they continuously fired, the jellybots had moved forward in the detectives' direction. With each stunner shot, the jellybots moved closer to the detectives. As the Lawtech stunner reached full charge, the lead jellybot moved into Emily's line of sight and line of fire. As soon as the robot came into her vision, Emily fired the Lawtech stunner.

The jellybot was struck at such close proximity to the stunner that it was blown off its robotic feet. It flew several feet backward in the air before smashing to the ground. It was a short trip but an electric one. The next jellybot to come into Emily's line of stunner fire received the exact same treatment. This second jellybot was struck point blank with the Lawtech SureStun Plus and driven backwards into a short flight which culminated in a crash landing next to its fallen robotic mate.

Fortunately for the Cathedral Police Department detectives, the strange jellybots were poorly programmed as their digital decision processing did not improve. Making the exact same mistake as the first pair of jellybots, the next pair of jellybots presented themselves as close range targets. Capitalizing on the odd robots' flawed artificial intelligence, or software stupidity, Emily took full advantage by greeting both jellybots with a Lawtech stunner produced stream. Both jellybots received a full blast of stunner stream which knocked them over like bowling pins. The halfwit programmed robots were presenting themselves as easy targets one at a time. Emily was gratefully eliminating the electrical idiots one by one. The pile of destroyed gelatinous robots was growing by the stunner shot.

The next three jellybots all came around the corner simultaneously. Detective Oftenmarch could only manage to fire at one of the three jellybots. The targeted robot's sacrifice allowed the other two jellybots to get into melee range. Blasted backwards, the stunner struck jellybot collapsed. The next jellybot engaged Lt. Knighton at close range, attempting to shock him with an electrified gelatinous arm. Eddie blocked the sparking arm with his drawn Phasepulser IX. The Cathedral PD issued stunner let out a loud popping noise as it flew out of the lieutenant's hand. He let out a curse before placing his service pistol against the jellybot. Firing his weapon directly into the jellybot, Eddie pinpointed his attack to one concentrated spot. Pressing hard against the strange robot as he discharged his weapon, the lieutenant sent bits of jellylike material flying everywhere. It took three shots before the stubborn robot went down and decommissioned.

The third jellybot attempted to shock Emily with its now electrified arm. Emily dexterously dodged the electric extremity and the jellybot bashed the wall instead. Whirling around for a second try, the strange robot swung its sparking arm at Emily again. Reacting quickly, the detective swiftly slipped out of the path of the dangerous arm. The jellybot's second melee attack struck nothing but air, it was a complete whiff. Emily blasted the attacking jellybot with a stream from the Lawtech stunner. Too close to Emily for its own safety, the jellybot was stunner streamed into the middle of next month. It was launched several inches high and several yards outward. Doing a pirouette in its miniflight, the rotating robot failed to gracefully land as it plummeted to the floor in a wreckage. Its spin sent some gelatinous material flying; its crash sent chunks of gelatinous material splattering.

Covered in sticky jellylike material, Detective Oftenmarch rounded the corner, staying low. One leg elongated to her side and one leg tucked in a squat, Emily stayed below an oncoming stunner stream. The whizzing stream sailed wide and over her head. She was now one on one with the lone remaining jellybot. From a shooting stance, Emily emptied the Lawtech SureStun Plus's charge on this last jellybot. A pair of stunner shots tore through the rear robot, punching deep into his gelatinous body reaching its circuitry. Bits of jellylike material were scorched away by the stream, exposing vital circuits. Shaking violently the robot arced twice before pitching clumsily to the floor. Landing with a thud, the last jellybot still vibrated from the effects of the stunning. It took a moment before the robot let out a sad whining noise and went still.

Looking miserable and covered in a sticky jellyesque substance, Lt. Knighton surveyed the sky lobby littered with damaged and destroyed droids. The floor was bathed in robotic waste products. The air was thick with smoke from fried electronic components. Eddie shook his head in disbelief. "The absurdity grows." he said aloud to nobody in particular.

"It sounds like a war zone over there." Brownsides commented as he half carried half dragged the metal plate previously blocking the elevator with the assistance of the one-armed Policebot. "It is a war zone. What a mess!" he continued, seeing some of the fallen robots and the damage to the sky lobby.

"Nrr.. ittzzzch. ... rrrrrck." voiced the Policebot as they passed a downed droid.

"This plate is heavy, like a lump of lead. Couldn't we at least get a two-armed robot to help carry this boat anchor?" complained Brownsides.

"Sure, take your pick." Eddie responded, pointing to all the prone and pummeled two-armed robots scattered across the midlobby floor.

"Hilarious, lieutenant. You're a funny guy." Brownsides retorted still hauling the steel plate with the one-armed droid's help. They were heading for the elevators to the upper levels.

Also covered in tacky gelatinous bits, Emily moved over to the pair of elevators for the upper floors. These two previously guarded elevators ran to the higher floors in the Flockman and Bellweather building. After pressing the call button for an elevator ride, she looked up expectantly at the elevators' digital floor displays. Seconds passed but neither display diminished in value but remained stubbornly fixed on their current floors. As she continued to wait, Detective Oftenmarch made another visual inspection of the sky lobby. It appeared to her that the building's freight elevator did not stop on this floor. Neither elevator was descending after her second survey of the lobby.

"These elevators are stopped on floors 32 and 38. It looks like we are back to taking the stairs." Emily informed the others.

"What's on 38, Brownsides?" Eddie asked the protection detail officer as he retrieved his blackened and broken Phasepulser IX.

"Nothing Cathedral PD uses. The last safehouse rented in this tower is on floor 36. The Cathedral PD cannot afford to rent any suites above that level." Brownsides responded.

"These elevators are labelled to go as high as the fortieth floor. I think the top twelve floors would all be penthouse suites, deluxe luxury rooms. That would leave us with eight floors to search if they are not in the 32nd floor suite." Emily calculated.

"All the options we were using are on the 32nd floor, three suites rotating every night. One is the safehouse, one is the reserve, and one is the decoy. Then they would switch roles the next night." Brownsides explained as he dropped the steel plate by the elevators.

"Rrrr. . tck. . . aaeeee." the one-armed bot voiced as the plate fell from its robotic grasp.

"Thirty-two it is." Lt. Knighton decided.

After handing the Lawtech SureStun Plus to the lieutenant to replace his fried service stunner, Emily led the way across the mid-sky lobby to the stairs located on the far wall. The detective moved quickly across the open space to the door for the upper building staircase. Noticing the lobby had slimline microlense video security cameras along the edges of the ceiling, Emily was curious if they were actively recording. Each security camera had a flashing red light next to it. She was unsure if that meant they were recording or if that meant they were broken.

When Emily arrived at the door to the stairs, she found a locking mechanism on the door with a familiar mini-robot making an all too familiar halt gesture. Recognizing the locking module and mini-robot, Emily knew what need to be done to quickly unlock the door.

"Geshuntit." the detective instructed. The locking mechanism immediately disengaged, the mini-robot gave his welcoming wave, and Emily opened the door to the stairwell.

Back into the cool stairwell and icy metal rails for a third time, it was becoming familiar surroundings for the mud tusslers. Once again, the group of law enforcement was trudging up the Flockman and Bellweather building towards trouble. It was becoming the theme of the evening. With renewed determination, Emily set a quicker upward pace, wanting to assist anyone in the lycan masqueraders' crosshairs. As the group climbed the stairs, the old one-armed Policebot fell further behind the officers. It was left in their vertical dust.

Exiting the barren stairwell and the echoes of their footsteps, the three Cathedral officers entered the 32nd floor. Unlike the resonant stairway, the 32nd floor was quiet, actually it was too quiet. Detective Oftenmarch knew they would be sent among the wolves, in this case werewolves, but her hope remained that they had enough shrewdness to avoid being devoured. The time had come to find out if the mud tusslers were on tonight's menu. Some of the overhead hallway lights had been destroyed or physically damaged, reducing the amount of light in the hallway. Fortunately, there was still enough visibility to see a significant distance down the hallway in each direction.

Cautiously, Emily stepped into the dim hallway. keeping her Phasepulser XII drawn and her head on a swivel. Lt. Knighton followed closely, keeping the homicide detectives in a tight formation. Brownsides kept some distance from the detectives and he moved quickly to his left to begin leading the way to the suite being used as a safe location. The group had to dodge bits of glass and light bulbs laying across the hallway carpet. Motivated to help Dotson, Brownsides moved rapidly with purpose along the 32nd floor hallway. In his brisk hustle, he had pulled several feet ahead of the detectives as he reached the end of the hallway.

Appearing quickly and quietly from around the corner, a massive hairy man dressed as a werewolf descended upon Brownsides in an instant. Officer Brownsides was not a small man but he was dwarfed by his assailant. Being struck by three rapidly consecutive blows, Brownsides was rocked backwards and dropped his stunner. The surprised expression on Brownsides' face showed how unprepared he was for this unprovoked attack. Stumbling backwards, the security officer raised his arms to a defensive guard position. Brownsides readied himself for yet another strong strike which did not come.

Upon seeing the surprise attack on Brownsides, Emily fired her Phasepulser XII in rapid response. The accurately fired stunner stream briefly halted the masked assaulter's attack. All the aggression was removed from his attempted thrown punch causing it to be negated. The masked assailant was forced to reset his attack. The pause gave Brownsides an opportunity to counter the attack against him. Using the opportunity, Brownsides decided to clench his attacker and began to grapple with the masked attacker. Unfortunately, the grapple between Brownsides and the lycan masked assailant put them in very close proximity, too close in proximity for Emily to fire another stunner stream. The interlocked men were now one intertwined target, taking away the option to fire a stunner stream from the detectives. The risk of hitting Brownsides was far too great.

Both large men struggled mightily to gain an advantage over the other large man. As the big men wrestled, Emily rushed forward to get a better stunning shot. Both big men were struggling and straining against each other's might. As the brutish brawl continued, the lycan masked wrestler threw Brownsides up into the wall. Crashing violently into the hallway wall, Brownsides left two massive dents in the wall. One big dent was from his head and one big dent was from his back and left shoulder. Shaken but not defeated, Brownsides spun the masked attacker around and returned the wall slam.

Crashing brutally against the hallway wall, the lycan masquerader grunted angrily, then went into a rage. The madman left a third hole in the hallway wall. Pulling Brownsides and all his mass off his feet, the raging lycan masquerader whirled the police officer around to drive him head first into the wall. The impact of Brownsides' head with the wall was loud. Staggered from forcefully headbutting the wall, Brownsides fell to his knees. Since the protection officer had dropped to his knees, Emily was able to fire a second stunning shot at the disentangled villain. This second stream struck the lycan masquerader squarely in the side of his head.

With a howl of rage, the lycan masquerade killer stumbled once, then recklessly charged towards Oftenmarch. In her attempt to help Brownsides, Emily had rushed forward enough that the lycan disguised brawler only needed a few rampaging steps to reach her. The beastman attempted an overhead strike followed by a full force shoulder ram. Reacting quickly, Emily leaned out of the path of the downward punch and then nimbly pivoted around the oncoming bull charge. As the lycan masquerader rumbled past her, Emily twirled quickly and then drove her right elbow into the back of the lycan berserker's head.

The skull strike caused the lycan charger to stumble forward off balance, where Lt. Knighton punched him square in the face. As blood trickled down his hairy mask, the criminal regained his footing and threw a counter punch in the lieutenant's direction. His furry fist slammed through Eddie's block and glanced off the side of the lieutenant's chin. This partial blow was enough to drive Eddie flat-footed which allowed the hairy brute to violently shove the lieutenant to the ground. Push off his feet from the forceful shove, Eddie flew airborne before crashing to the ground, skidding a couple of times. Like a hockey player being blind-side bodychecked, the lieutenant was dropped.

As Lt. Knighton smashed forcefully to the floor, Detective Oftenmarch fired a third stunner stream from her Phasepulser XII. This well aimed stream struck the lycan brawler in the back, causing him to tense in place. Emily followed the stunner stream with a roundhouse kick to the big villain's side abdomen. He showed no reaction to her boot strike. As he turned in Emily's direction, Eddie kicked the brute in the side of the knee from where he laid on the ground. In retalia-tion, the masked madman tried to stomp on Eddie as he simultaneously attempted to roundhouse punch Emily. His dual attack failed on both fronts. As the lieutenant rolled away from the barbaric foot stomp, Detective Oftenmarch took a backstep and did a side lean to dodge the brutishly big swing.

As Emily back pedaled to avoid additional punches, Brownsides charged past her to attack the lycan masquerader. He was a blur as he passed by her. The two large men began exchanging massively aggressive punches. After the first couple of punches, the fight was going well for Brownsides. The fight took a turn for the worse as the next two or three fists flew. Getting powerfully struck in the jaw, Brownsides staggered backwards and fell over Lt. Knighton as the lieutenant was in the process of getting to his feet. Both men toppled to the hallway floor very ungracefully.

Firing a fourth stunner stream from her Phasepulser XII, the detective attempted to subdue the lycan crazed lunatic again. The stream struck the madman squarely in the back again but did nothing to subdue him. With angry yells the massive madman spun around and charged at Emily again. Prepared for the berserker's attacks this time, Emily performed an uke nagashi tenkan on his punch and charge attack. The masked brawler was redirected past the detective without inflicting any damage. Fueled by hostility, the brute sent a wild sideswipe at Emily after he had bypassed her, which missed her by a wide margin. The maniac came back towards the detective, sending a jab to the gut in her direction. Emily executed a kokyunage, or breathe throw, sending the assailant tumbling to the floor.

As the lycan disguised assailant sprang to his feet and looked to pounce for more fighting, the lieutenant fired the Lawtech SureStun Plus from a shooting stance on his knees. The stunning stream from the Lawtech stunner took the fight out of the lycan masquerade killer as he crumpled to the floor. Once the madman fell, Emily moved quickly to pin his arm behind his back and put her knee forcibly into his back. Lt. Knighton rushed over to the pinned villain as he removed his double clasped and double linked tri-steel Promans handcuffs. This was the pair of heavy duty restraints the lieutenant used on seriously violent criminals. Eddie wasted no time putting the heavy duty restraints on the lycan disguised villain who was beginning to squirm mid-cuffing. After the lieutenant had finished cuffing the criminal, the crazy man began resisting more vigorously. Lt. Knighton restunned the madman with the Lawtech SureStun Plus at close range.

"Check on Brownsides, please." Eddie asked Emiily as he pulled out a pair of oversized plastic zip ties.

"We cannot keep fighting werewolf wackos in hand-to-hand combat. We have got to come up with a better plan, Eddie." Emily reasoned. She moved over to where Brownsides lay on the floor.

"Working on it." Eddie replied as he zip tied the lycan looney's legs.

The stairway door opened as Emily knelt beside Brownsides. Dutifully marching onward, the one-armed rundown old Policebot entered the 32nd floor hallway. After noting the arrival of the old robot, Emily turned her attention to Brownsides. Detective Oftenmarch looked into the face of the prone police officer. His eyes were glazed over in a dazed look. Her best guess was that he was concussed. His forehead was bruised and he had a cut on his lower lip. As the Policebot mechanically trudged loudly down the hall, Emily took out a handkerchief from her white jacket pocket and began to stop the bleeding from Brownsides' lip. This task became more difficult as the officer started moving and then shifted to speak.

"Suite 3216." he whispered weakly to her.

"Don't worry about that, Reggie. You just try to stay awake." Emily tried to calm the concussed officer. Oftenmarch took off her scarf and placed it under the beaten cop's head. As Emily tried to aid Brownsides, Eddie zip tied the werewolf's feet.

"Help Dotson." Brownsides softly requested, still looking fuzzy eyed.

"We have not forgotten about Donny or what we are here to do. Don't worry about that now." Emily reassured him as she searched through her pockets for some smelling salts or maybe at least a strong breath mint. She was coming up with nothing helpful.

While searching her pockets, the detective noticed dark domes over the hallway security cameras with adjacent flashing red lights. Emily still wondered if that meant the cameras were working or malfunctioning. The one-armed Policebot was moving down the hallway at a progressively sluggish rate like it was running low on power. Two loud bangs could be heard further off on the floor. It sounded like something being struck by a sledgehammer. Emily looked at Eddie; he returned her look. Their exchanged look told each other they both knew the situation. They needed help but did not have the luxury of time to wait for it.

Detective Oftenmarch activated her police radio as she tried to help Brownsides reposition himself. "Officers urgently need assistance on the 32nd floor of the Flockman and Bellweather building. If you can hear this transmission, then please come sooner rather than later." she broadcast.

"Thirty-four eighteen needed." Lt. Knighton followed with another broadcast.

"Reggie, the lieutenant and I have to move. You stay put but stay awake. Sing karaoke, recite Cathedral police procedures aloud, or shout curse words. Whatever you need to do to stay awake. Nod if you understand.", Emily ordered Brownsides as she gave him an ammonia inhalant wipe from her pop minikit and a lemon flavored gummy. He nodded affirmatively.

"Neee.... uurrhh... oooeeee" voiced the Policebot approaching the officers.

"Suite 3216." Oftenmarch called to Knighton.

"No half measures now." Knighton replied with his service pistol armed and ready. The lieutenant had zip tied the lycan suspect's legs a second time.

Moving with renewed urgency, the mud tusslers hustled around the corner and into the next hallway. The low powered old Policebot tried to follow them but was quickly straggling behind again. As the detectives quickly travelled down the hallway, the loud hammering noise started again, this time it was growing louder and closer. As they passed suites, the suite numbers ascended. This hallway had more broken overhead lights and less luminescence than the previous hallway. The detectives were navigating more by sheer determination rather than visibility. With police officers and a witness in distress ahead of them and an injured officer behind them, the mud tusslers needed to make haste.

Faster on foot than Eddie, Emily reached the door to suite 3216 first. The suite door had been pummeled off its hinges. Any finesse and sophistication used on previous crimes by the lycan masquerade killers had been abandoned. It appeared like a battering ram had been used to penetrate this substantial suite door. Severely dented and destroyed, the entrance door to the suite lay on the floor just inside the suite. Too mangled to be reused, it was difficult to believe the misshapen mess was ever a door.

As Detective Oftenmarch stepped over the damaged door and into Suite 3216, a cry for help could be heard coming from a nearby hallway on the 32nd floor. Lt. Knighton detoured to investigate the call for aid as Emily continued into the obviously trespassed suite and clearly breached safehouse. In contrast to the dimly lit hallways, all the suite's ornate overhead lights were shining brightly.

The detective began to search the luxury suite for intruders or signs of a struggle. Scanning the suite's main living area and adjacent kitchenette, Emily saw no indication of either one. This section of the suite was vacant and actually quite tidy. It displayed neither signs of an intruder nor any signs of panicked fleeing from an intrusion. Emily began moving across the pristine main living area continuing to look for anything suggesting trouble. In addition to being bright, the luxury suite was also quite silent. No banging, no rapping, no running footsteps, and no cries of distress. It was quiet in the deluxe suite; it was eerily too quiet.

As Detective Oftenmarch moved through the suite's main area, suddenly the calm trouble free environment ceased to exist. From out of a back dark hallway entrance appeared a lycan masquerader. The wannabe werewolf crept silently out of the shadows into the light of the suite's main quarters. With a menacing look, the beastly brute stared intently at the detective. Intimidation was the masquerader's initial move, making a deep low guttural growl. Directing his scowl and growl at Emily, it was clear the villain had ill intentions.

A thought too profound to be her own crossed Emily's mind. This was not a werewolf; this was a fear tactic. "Bad news, hairball. Fear of insanity did not keep me away. Sanity has found you and found you lacking." Emily told the lycan masquerader.

The threatening werewolf pretender sprang into action as he dashed in Emily's direction. As the raging faux wolfman charged, Emily fired her Phasepulser XII three times. All three shots struck the oncoming madman but to no effect. Three stunner strikes did not even slow the lycan masquerader down, he maintained his attacking run. Emily spun away from his initial clothesline attempt. The lycan masquerader continued his assault with a pair of punches. After deflecting and blocking aside the first powerful punch with a firm arm bar defense, Emily bounce stepped away and leaned out of the path of the second propelled punch. The aggressive assailant threw an additional two-punch combo at the detective. The detective blocked the first flying fist with both her arms in a strong guard. Emily sidestepped the second strike then hooked his arm and performed an Aikido toss. This sent the masked brawler tumbling to the floor.

After colliding with a recliner mid-tumble, the lycan masquerader sprang back to his feet with great agility. The wolfman, with power and quick reflexes, surprisingly launched himself back towards Emily. Ramming her with a shoulder bash, the lycan masquerader sent her off her feet and airborne. Detective Oftenmarch crashed to the suite's plush carpeted floor before gracefully barrel rolling to her knees. From her knees, Emily drew her Trialloy Max5 pistol with lightning quickness. The detective fired a shot in the fake lycan's direction, which forced the assailant to dive for cover.

Once the crazy man had taken cover, he grabbed a nearby lamp and threw it at Emily in return fire. Emily easily dodged the hurled object and it smashed to pieces against the wall. After the hurled lamp had smashed, the lycanish brute had flipped up a loveseat and sent it tumbling end over end in Emily's direction. The mistreated loveseat came summersaulting quickly at the detective, so quickly she had little time to react. Emily sprang sideways to elude the awkwardly pitched loveseat which caused her to be in an off-balance stance. As the loveseat knocked over a modern design floor lamp and crashed into the wall with a loud thump, the detective became distracted as she struggled to maintain her balance. The impact of the loveseat left a huge gash in the wall. Taking advantage of this result, the lycan masquerader sprang into action as he made another attack. With fast strides fueled by rage, the lycan brawler charged the detective again. Ramming her with his shoulder, the lycan brawler sent her soaring. Slamming hard into the same suite wall as the loveseat, Emily fumbled her pistol and felt pain in her left arm and shoulder. Her firearm fell to the ground and slid annoyingly out of reach.

Gunfire could be heard in the hallway. Pain could be felt throughout Emily's left extremity. The lycan disguised criminal threw a forceful punch at Emily attempting to end their combat. Despite the aches in her left arm, Detective Oftenmarch still had her catlike reflexes. Moving from the wall, she avoided the punch and the battling brute struck the wall with his fist. His strike added to the damage to the poor suite wall.

From over her radio, Eddie's voice could be heard. "Officer down. Ambulance required." he had radioed.

Recovering from punching the wall, the lycan masquerade killer pulled out a long slender knife. He approached Emily with a wicked toothy grin. Abruptly the wannabe wolfman pounced, he tried to violently stab her but Emily deftly dodged the straight forth attack. With an Aikido maneuver, the detective wrist locked the aggressor and twisted his wrist and hand, causing the knife to fall from his grip. Once the dispossessed knife had landed on the floor, Emily kicked it far away. The blade disappeared under an entertainment center across the room. Outraged, the beast grabbed her hair and pulled her head cruelly back. The lycan masquerader opened his mouth wide as he prepared to get closer in an attempt to bite her. Again with catlike reflexes, Emily drew her Phasepulser XII and shot him at point blank range in his masked face before he could get close enough to bite. The phony lycan howled in pain and released his grip on her hair. As soon as the brute had let go, Emily kicked him in his private region and rang his chimes soundly. She had rung his personal chimes but good. With a whimper, the fake werewolf fell to his knees, holding his abused parts.

More gunfire could be heard coming from the hallway. This round of shooting seemed to be nearer to the suite then the previous shots. There was clearly another confrontation occurring nearby on the 32rd floor. Occupied with her own problems, Emily had to leave whatever was happening outside the suite for the lieutenant to sort. If anyone could hold their own in that struggle, then it would be Steady Eddie.

As the lycan masquerader knelt in agony, Emily pulled out the pair of restraints she had borrowed from Brownsides. Before the detective could apply the restraints, the wannabe werewolf lashed out in hostile desperation. His unexpected strike only grazed Emily's side abdomen as Emily's reflexes were still working wonderfully. The foolish fiend stood up and lunged to grab the detective. Emily applied another wristlock, then performed a kotegaeshi throw. She lost hold of the handcuffs to perform the maneuver. Flopping to the floor like a crash test dummy only seemed to anger the brute. The wannabe werewolf scrambled to his feet and attacked again. This time the brute leaped at the detective. Emily caught the assailant mid-movement and executed a koshinage throw. Again the lycan masquerader was thrown to the floor, where the goon forcefully landed extremely inelegantly. Detective Oftenmarch followed the throw with a downward boot stomp, which landed powerfully into the prone pretender.

Moving rapidly, the detective located the dropped handcuffs and scooped them up from the floor. Emily swiftly descended upon the battered brute and applied a khecksinagwa hold before the wannabe werewolf attempted to resist again. Without hesitation or reservation, Detective Oftenmarch expediently secured the handcuffs on the wolfish criminal. As Emily restrained the masquerader, Lt. Knighton entered the suite assisting a medium sized injured fellow. The lieutenant's newfound companion was very pale, possibly due to blood loss, and was wearing a U.S. Marshals windbreaker.

"We are on the defensive" the lieutenant called to her as he took up a secure position against the wall by the door. Eddie began rapidly reloading his firearm.

Once the wannabe werewolf was restrained, Emily pulled the wolf mask off the defeated villain to reveal their identity. It was Diego Lowendowski, the Cathedral Police Department union representative. He had been masquerading as both a werewolf and a friend of the police. Detective Oftenmarch read the former lycan masquerader his new revised Miranda rights.

"I am guessing a safe path to the elevators has been cut-off." Emily speculated.

Eddie shook his head in the affirmative as he kept watch by the door. The man with the marshal's jacket had dropped down and was sitting on the floor against the wall. He appeared to be in pain.

"Find the witness. Hurry, Emily." Eddie urgently requested.

Emily hurriedly pulled the waistbelt out of the white trench coat she was wearing and promptly used it to bind Lowendowski's feet. With the belt secured tightly, the detective hastily located and collected both her fumbled Phasepulser XI stunner and her dropped TriAlloy Maxwell XL-2 weapon. Once collected, Detective Oftenmarch hustled out of the main living area and through the rear doorway leading into the back area.

The doorway ushered into a dark narrow hallway. This hallway was full of wall art and chestnut doors. A pair of tall chestnut doors were closed and a pair of lofty wooden doors were left open. Dashing from door to door, Emily peered into the rooms behind the open doors and opened the closed doors to do likewise into those rooms. It was not until the last room along the hall did something noteworthy gain her attention.

Light peering out from under an inner door displayed signs of occupancy. The room itself was a master suite bedroom and also looked like a tornado had passed through it. With clothes scattered everywhere, the bedroom's level of tidiness was poor. With the double bed, dresser, and a pair of chests shifted strangely about the room, the bedroom's level of navigability was also poor. An upturned suitcase, a pair of knocked over chairs, and a broken luggage rack all showed signs of a struggle. This was definitely where the lycan masked Lowendowski had been prior to their encounter. Emily swiftly navigated the chaotic room and approached the door shrouding light. Several gashes and dents could be seen in the door once she stood next to it.

With a knock on the damaged door Emily called, "No more huffing and puffing. I'm not here to blow the house down. My name is Detective Emily Oftenmarch with the Cathedral Police Department and I'm here to help."

Silence was returned in reply before the door slowly opened. It opened to reveal a sad and troubling sight. Behind the door knelt a very wounded Officer Donny Dotson. The man was bleeding from multiple claw and stab wounds. He looked at Emily with an exhausted expression of relief and a small smile of hope. Before Oftenmarch could fully assess the extent of his wounds, Dotson fell sideways onto the floor too hurt to sentry on. The powerhouse police officer had held the defense at a steep and heavy price.

"Second officer down, immediate medical assistance required at the Flockman and Bellweather Building." Emily urgently radioed.

"This is third north central Cathedral dispatch. Please repeat your last request." a reply came over the comm.

"Second officer down, immediate medical assistance is needed on the 32nd floor of the Flockman and Bellweather Building." Emily repeated with more urgency.

Emily stepped into what seemed to be a midsize luxury bathroom. With the vast majority of her attention on Officer Dotson, the detective did not observe any details of the bathroom. The room contained lots of bath towels and that was all Emily cared about at the moment. As Emily grabbed a stack of nearby towels to use as bandages, she did observe a young lady cowering in the bathroom corner.

The young female was barefoot and wearing tight yoga pants and a red hooded sweatshirt which read Cathedral State University across the chest. Despite wearing the bulky sweatshirt, it was still apparent the young lady was quite buxom. She had a bright red throw blanket wrapped around her and was wearing both a bracelet and an anklet with red heart shaped jewels. She was also wearing a long sparkly necklace full of glitter over her sweatshirt. At the end of the necklace were three rings full of bling. Each bedazzled ring connected to a cell phone cover, one cover for each of her three phones. One phone cover was pink, one was white with bright red hearts, and the last cover had Greetings Princess themed artwork. Tears were streaming down her face, causing her make-up to run. Her tear stained face and melancholy eyes looked up at Emily.

"What's your name, young lady?" Oftenmarch inquired as she began applying towels to stop the wounds of Donny from bleeding.

"Tricia. Am I going to die?" the red hooded lady shakily counter-queried. She had a look of absolute dread on her face and predominant panic showing in her wide open eyes.

"No, you're going to run. We need to run, Tricia. Please set your phones aside. There is glass on the hallway carpet so you need shoes for running." Emily explained, still attending to Dotson's wounds. She held towels to his chest, then took Donny's left hand and put it on the towel prompting him to press.

"I only have high heeled dress shoes with me." Tricia revealed.

Oftenmarch did a quick comparison of foot sizes in the room. Her boots were at least one size too small for the witness and Donny's boots were at least ten sizes too large for the witness. There was no third, just right, option.

"Do you have any bedroom slippers packed?" Emily hoped as she tied two towels together then circumwrapped the towels around Donny's waist.

"No, but I do have my floppies." Tricia remembered.

"Those will have to do. If they are in the bedroom next door, then please go get them quickly." Emily decided while putting pressure on the tied towels, then tightly tying them in place.

"But the big bad men are out there. They look like werewolves." Tricia protested with a sob.

"Two big buffoons have been arrested and my partner is guarding the suite entrance with his favorite gun. You will be fine but we cannot delay. We have a limited window of opportunity and we must take it." Oftenmarch explained as she wrapped a towel tightly around Dotson's right arm and tucked it neatly in place.

Tricia nodded in understanding but said, "I'm scared. I'm really scared."

"Use that fear as motivation, Tricia. The faster you find your shoes the sooner we can go." Emily encouraged her. The detective was using a larger bath towel to wrap over the wounded officer's right shoulder.

"Ok, I guess." Tricia responded hesitantly as she got up and left the bathroom, leaving behind the throw blanket laying on the floor.

"Donny, you fight on. We have to run but that doesn't give you permission to be done. Stay strong and sentry on, my friend." Emily motivated as she tightly tucked the over shoulder towel to secure it.

"Save her, Emily." Dotson quickly replied.

"That's what Eddie and I are here to do. You hang in there." Emily returned. Gunshots coming from the front of the suite could be heard. Three shots in total. "That's my queue, Donny. I have to go." Emily concluded as she reached over and grabbed the throw blanket. Emily wrapped it around Dotson for warmth. Then she sprang up and out of the bathroom. This was the second time she had to leave an injured officer alone on the 32nd floor of the Flockman and Bellweather Building, and Emily was disliking this troublesome trend more and more.

When Detective Oftenmarch returned to the cluttered bedroom, it was somehow in a more disheveled state than it had previously been. Unbelievably, Tricia had managed to make the room even messier. Running around in a panic, the young lady only had one flip-flop in her hand and none on her feet. Keeping composure for the both of them, Emily calmly moved over to a massive pile of clothing. Swiftly sifting through the jumbled mess, the detective spotted a flip-flop in about twenty seconds. With the footwear now in her possession, Emily quickly collected Tricia and gave her the flip-flop.

Flip-flops on foot, they began their dash from the lycan masqueraders' attacks and the 32nd floor of the Flockman and Bellweather Building. The back hallway went by in a blur, Emily led the dash into the main area of the suite. Lowendowski was going berserk trying to get free, the U.S. marshal had not moved, and Lt. Knighton was still standing guard at the door with his firearm at the ready. Emily rushed into the room, pulled out her Phasepulser XI midrun, and stunned Lowendowski as she passed him. This took some of the fight out of him. The detective raced to the guarded door with the witness, who avoided going near

Lowendowski, not too far behind her. Once at the door next to Eddie, they paused their run for the exit.

"We're ready to run for the stairs. Could you provide some covering fire?" Emily asked Eddie as she took a defensive position next to him.

"You're pulling the goalie?" Eddie replied.

"Pulling the team off the ice, it's melting under our feet." Emily retorted.

"Go now." the lieutenant called as he led the way into the hall. With his pistol ready, Eddie took a blocking position.

Emily ran past him and started the sprint towards freedom. Tricia was two steps behind her, eager to get away but hesitant about entering the hallway. Once Emily was in the hall, she saw what looked like a lycan out of a horror movie. The werewolf looked too realistic and very intimidating. The beastman was aggressively fighting with the Policebot and the one-armed Policebot was getting brutalized by the brute. The lycan masquerader had stolen the droid's stunnerstick and was beating the poor Policebot with its own stunnerstick. As a result of the abuse the Policebot was taking, there was now an opportunity to escape. After verifying Tricia was following her, Detective Oftenmarch took advantage of this opportunity.

Emily dashed down the hallway at top speed away from the vicious lycan and towards the hall with the stairway entrance. She sprinted down the hallway quickly passing by suites, broken lights, and damaged walls. Emily rounded the corner and accelerated like a baserunner rounding third and heading for home. The detective glanced over her shoulder as she turned, Tricia had fallen about two suites behind her, but was still running freely.

Around the turn, Emily saw Brownsides slumped against the wall, and then clear hallway all the way to the stairs and to the end of the dimly lit corridor. Just as it looked like they had a chance at an unobstructed path to escape via the stairs, a shadowy figure emerged at the far end of the hallway. Emily's heart sank as another out of a horror movie scary lycan appeared at the end of the hall. The brute was fierce looking and was bounding straight for them. Doubling her determination, Emily increased her pace and pulled out her Maxwell XL-2.

Moving past Brownsides, Detective Oftenmarch raced along the hallway with her weapon at the ready. "Halt, Cathedral Police. Remain where you are!" she shouted.

The charging lycan neither halted nor remained where he was, so Emily fired off a pair of shots from her TriAlloy gun. Both shots struck the wild werewolf in the torso but neither slowed him down, not even a little. The accurately placed gunshots seemed to have absolutely no effect on the brute. Still not halting, the wild werewolf continued to charge. This beastman must have been wearing some type of bulletproof armor. Emily sprinted around the captured lycan masquerader squirming on the ground. Tricia, who had just turned the corner, screamed from behind Emily.

Still determined, Detective Oftenmarch continued forward, hoping to reach the doors to the stairway first. From the door maybe she could take up a defensive position allowing the witness to escape. As Emily dashed, she fired another two shots from her Maxwell XL-2 weapon hoping to slow down the wild werewolf. Aiming lower, Emily placed both shots into the beastman's upper thighs. Unfortunately, this pair of accurate shots also failed to stop or phase the wild werewolf. He continued to charge forward unaffected and unafflicted.

Emily continued to run and shoot, being committed to the get off the 32nd floor plan. Firing a half a dozen more shots at the wild werewolf as she rushed forward, the detective was getting closer and closer to the lycan masquerader with each shot. Each shot struck the brute, failing to hurt him or even slow him. Within seconds Emily had won the race to the stairway door only to find herself within striking distance of the lycan. Emily had not reached the door quickly enough to have a defense prepared.

The wild werewolf launched a backhanded strike as he reached the detective. For as fast as Emily was she was not fast enough to dodge this lightning quick strike. Being struck brutally in the face, Detective Oftenmarch staggered backwards stunned. Following his mean backhand, the werewolf plowed into Emily, sending her flying off her feet. After she flew backwards, the detective crashed to the floor, now both stunned and dazed. Emily hit the hallway floor with force.

As she lay on the floor in a fog, Emily struggled to focus and recollect herself. Lt. Knighton jumped over her as he fired his weapon. Her surroundings seemed muffled as the lieutenant came to her defense. She didn't hear the gunshots. The world seemed to go blurry and her movements felt like slow motion. As Eddie fought the lycan, Emily fought fuzziness. Struggling to recover, thoughts came rushing through her muttled mind.

Hello failure my old friend, I have fallen once again

Fought as hard as anyone, just to find I've been undone

My many faults are crushing, as the aching pain keeps rushing

The tide turned in mere moments, an attack on innocents

The wolf howls in victory, triumph taking all glory

In the midst of my despair, comes a hope beyond compare

I just needed to recall, who it is that's LORD of all

The loving GOD Almighty, great in power and mercy

People live without weeping, children held in safe keeping

In HIS grace I cannot fall, knowing who is LORD of all

My defeat has been erased, in HIS love I've been embraced

Countless sing in robes of white, their voices rise in delight

Words of prophets still remain, there not mundane or insane

Peace comes to all HE's loven, it is the sound of heaven

Bursting through the stairwell doorway came a muscular man. Looking like a bouncer at a night club, the shaven headed man acted like a knight in shining armor. He charged directly at the wild werewolf and drove the beastman backwards. Following the muscleman, came fellow 271st precinct homicide detectives Murkendale and Cole. They rushed into the hallway and provided re-enforcements against the wild werewolf. As the beastman was getting overrun, Detective Valdez-Scantling came barreling into the hallway to join the feverish fight. Following Theo were detectives Maxson and Coventry. As Coventry rushed to join the escalating fight, Detective Maxson noticed Emily struggling to get to her feet. He hurried over to help her up. With a helping hand, Oftenmarch was able to get to her feet.

As she wiped blood from her bleeding lip, Emily spoke to Detective Maxson. "Mark, please help get the young lady to safety and off this floor." Emily pleaded as she pointed to Tricia. Tricia had gone over to huddle next to Officer Brownsides. She was using him as a shield to hide behind. Tricia was staying well away from the handcuffed lycan masquerader.

"I'm on it, Emily." Maxson reassured her then dashed off to help Tricia.

"It had to be all the way up on the 32nd floor and it had to be after hours. You and the lieutenant need to pick better times and places to need help." Valdez-Scantling complained as he stood next to Emily, now steady on her feet.

"Theo, there's another lycan lunatic down the hallway and to the right. This nightmare's not over yet." Oftenmarch urgently informed her co-worker.

"The fool arrested on the floor?" Theo asked.

"No, the wild and free fool around the corner." Emily answered still with urgency.

"Covie, we have another perp to catch. Let's get on this so we can go home." Valdez-Scantling called to Detective Coventry.

Coventry was helping restrain the other wild werewolf. He was on top of a pile which included a buff rescuer, two homicide detectives, and Lt. Knighton, all of whom were on top of a wild werewolf. As hard as the crazed wannabe werewolf fought, he was outmanned and overmatched. Detective Coventry left what looked like a rugby match and hustled to follow Theo down the hallway Emily had just raced up moments earlier.

Emily took a moment to compose herself. On one side of her the wild werewolf was being arrested. On the other side of her Maxson was helping Tricia to her feet. Theo had stopped to briefly chat with the voluptuous Tricia in her red hooded sweatshirt. Just now realizing she had fumbled her gun on her crash landing, Emily saw it on the hallway floor. Scooping it off the ground quickly, Oftenmarch holstered her weapon. Then straightening her dislodged and crooked copcam back into an orderly position, Emily started towards Maxson and Tricia.

That's when the last wild werewolf suddenly appeared at the top of the hallway. The beastman had dashed past Valdez-Scantling and Coventry before either surprised man could react. Brownsides stuck out an arm in an attempt to trip the brute but was too slow in his reactions. Tricia's scream alerted Detective Maxson and he was able to unholster his service pistol and fire one shot at the wild werewolf. The gunshot did no damage to the lunatic but it did distract him enough that he did not see Emily's stunner coming. Oftenmarch pulled out her Phasepulser XI and threw it at the crazy cretin. Hitting the unsuspecting wannabe werewolf in the face, the Phasepulser XI made a cracking sound when it struck.

Being struck in the face with a hurled stunner disoriented the wild werewolf. He was no longer on the offensive. As the beastman hesitated, Valdez-Scantling and Coventry charged towards him. Detective Maxson aimed his weapon at the brute and Emily got in front of Tricia to act as an obstacle. The lunatic lycan had lost his advantage and was now injured from the flung Phasepulser.

Being surrounded and now bleeding through his lycan mask, the wildman came to a decision. Seeing a pair of shackled masqueraders from his pack of wolves helped expedite his decision. Realizing he was now a lone wolf, he decided to flee and flee he did. As suddenly as he appeared in the hallway was how suddenly he began his departure. As fast as he advanced was also how quickly he retreated. The lycan masquerader ran away from Valdez-Scantling, Coventry, and Maxson. Emily prepared to guard Tricia so she was unprepared for the wannabe werewolf to run past them and for the stairs. The beastman darted for the door to the stairs. Before any of the men who had now detained the first lycan miscreant could react, the second lycan miscreant had run through the doorway and into the stairway.

Emily instinctively gave chase; she gave chase without a second thought. Seeing the detective go after the wannabe werewolf, the strongman also gave pursuit. As they entered the stairway, footsteps could be heard coming from below them. Cathedral police officers were coming up the stairs in numbers, forcing the wild werewolf to go further up the stairs. In desperation he began ascending the staircase to higher floors. Emily raced after him with the muscled man following her in support.

Higher and higher they climbed; faster and faster they raced. With each level of the building zipping by as quickly as the last one, the chase was reaching new heights. Emily had to give the lycan masquerader credit, he was in great physical fitness. However, Oftenmarch was in better shape and was gaining ground, or stairs, on the wild werewolf as they raced upward. With each floor they rose, the detective closed the distance between them. Since he could not outrun her on the incline, the beastman stopped ascending the stairs on the 38th floor. He rushed through the stairway door and onto the 38th floor.

The 38th floor was a maintenance level with wide open areas and wire cages containing utility equipment. Much of this level was a restricted area and caged in to prevent unauthorized entry. This floor was also a dusty and musty space with hung sheets of plastic being used as dividers. Emily was even quicker and faster on foot than the wild werewolf when on level ground. Very quickly once on the 38th floor, Emily tackled the brute from behind with a diving, shoulder driving technique. The strong-man came to her assistance within seconds. He had the strength to wrestle the wild werewolf fully to the ground. Moments later two Cathedral Police Officers joined them in restraining the last crazy beastman.

From her position in the pile, Emily could feel the strength of the werewolf and the counter might of the broad-shouldered hero. The good guys had more restraining arms then the lunatic had resisting arms and they were using that fact to their advantage. With the wild werewolf now being overwhelmed, Oftenmarch removed herself from the fray. Tired of tussling with crazy people disguised as lycans, Emily was happy to end her contribution to the wrestling match. The last madman was on the losing end of the 38th floor scuffle.

The Flockman and Bellweather Building narrowed on the 38th floor. Because of this architectural design, a section of the rooftop could be seen outside the windows on the near wall. The windows on this wall were so big and numerous that they ran the length and heigh of the wall. As the wild werewolf was being arrested, Emily walked over to the windows. She could not believe her eyes.

Outside on the rooftop stood a massive ferocious looking lycan. A creature with big sharp teeth and massive muscles. It had the full appearance of a science fiction nightmare werewolf. This creature glared menacingly at Oftenmarch for a long moment, then suddenly ran towards the edge of the building. The lycan unexpectedly made a leap from the roof towards the roof of the adjacent building. Forcefully launching itself upward and outward, the lycanesque creature seemed to have jumped so tremendously well that it was going to make the leap between buildings. It was covering the distance between buildings so effectively, the unmakeable jump suddenly seemed remarkable achievable. But then in mid-jump, the creature struck a passing advertisement drone causing it to pitch sideways and lose all forward momentum. Striking the ad drone forcefully hard, the creature's jump went from a graceful outward arc to an awkwardly downward sprawling plunge. The lycanesque creature began to plummet earthward as gravity took over, accelerating his downward momentum. Soundlessly, the creature fell out of sight and into the night.

Emily closed her eyes and quietly remembered songs from Psalm 46:10.

There is a river whose streams make glad the city of God, Where the Most High makes his home. God is within her, she will not fall; God will help her at break of day. Nations are in uproar, kingdoms fall; he lifts his voice, the earth melts.

The Lord Almighty is with us; the God of Jacob is our fortress. He is in our midst we will not be moved. He will be our help when the day is new. He's our refuge.

Come and see what the Lord has done, the desolations he has brought on the earth. He makes wars cease to the ends of the earth. He breaks the bow and shatters the spear; he burns the shields with fire. He makes wars cease. With the power of His voice weapons shatter. Weapons shatter with one word. See the nations rage see the kingdoms fall but the Lord of Hosts He is with us all. He's our refuge.

He says, "Be still, and know that I am God; I will be exalted among the nations, I will be exalted in the earth." Be still and know He is God. Be still and know He is God.

Though the earth gives way. Though the mountains move. Though the waters roar we will cling to You. God our refuge. You're our refuge

Be still and know He is God. Be still and know He is God.

Chapter 19

The Lycans' Master

As Emily contemplatively looked out the window of the 38th floor of the Flockman and Bellweather building in north midtown Cathedral, the storm had passed and the skies were clear now. Emily wondered if she had really seen a rooftop werewolf or if she had imagined the whole bizarre lycan scene. The whole thing had been surreal. Again a thought too profound to be her own thought came to her: have peace and do not be troubled. Then she remembered John 14:27, *Peace I leave with you; my peace I give you. I do not give to you as the world gives. Do not let your hearts be troubled and do not be afraid.*

Breaking her moment of silence, the bouncer looking strong man approached her and said, "My employers described this job correctly. They said to protect the lady detective so she could protect everyone else. My employers could not have been better with their instructions."

"Hello, my name is Detective Emily Oftenmarch. Thank you for coming to the rescue. What is your name? And did the old professor send you?" Emily greeted, thanked, and asked turning towards the man.

"My name is Jeremiah Jefferson. Nice to meet you, detective. I'm a bodyguard with my own company called Quality LifeShield. I was hired by a pair of retired judges living in a retirement home in Florida, who asked for anonymity. The judges had indicated that you had called for aid. They paid me well to drive immediately to Cathedral to protect you. And the last thing they told me was to be prepared for anything once I arrived. They were right." the bodyguard named Jeremiah explained.

Lt. Knighton, who had run up the stairs to the thirty-eighth floor, had been observing the arrest of the last lycan masquerader as four Cathedral police officers literally carried the crazy man away. The wild wannabe kicked, struggled, and howled all the way to the elevators. Eddie walked over to Emily and the bodyguard now that the arrest was done.

421

"Emily, we still have work." the lieutenant quietly reminded her.

"Eddie, this is Jeremiah. Jeremiah, this is Lt. Knighton." Emily gave introductions.

"Good evening, lieutenant." the tough guy Jeremiah greeted.

"An answer to a call." Eddie speculated correctly.

"A hero who came to the rescue." Emily countered.

"Good evening, mister hero." the lieutenant greeted.

"Eddie, I've had a thought just now. Humor me for a moment. I've read my share of vampire fiction in my youth. In fictional lore, vampires enslaved lycans to serve as their guardians in the daylight. As I recall the stories, the lycans were made to serve their vampire masters. They were kept close in order to guard the vampires during the day and to serve their masters during the night. This got me to thinking it may be possible, with this many lycan masqueraders on this crime, that their master could be nearby. These criminals like to mimic werewolves. Maybe they pattern their villainy in other aspects of fiction." Oftenmarch theorized.

"You think they're hired henchmen. You think their employer is close by." Jeremiah followed along.

"Begs the question where." Lt. Knighton pondered.

"Still working on that part." Emily admitted.

"Cowards can be hard to find." Jeremiah interjected.

"Could you give me until we find out how Officers Brownsides and Dotson are doing?" Emily requested.

"Seems fair." Eddie agreed.

"Lieutenant, what should we do with the pretty young lady?" Detective Maxson asked over the radio.

"Protocol nineteen." Eddie replied over the radio.

"Have to admit, I don't remember protocol nineteen." Maxson returned after a pause of radio silence.

"Don't advertise." the lieutenant answered.

Emily held out her hand and Eddie lent her his radio. Without a word the two partners communicated. "Please take her to the floor of Theo's favorite number and we will meet you there, Mark." Oftenmarch added, then returned the radio to Eddie.

"Roger that." Maxson confirmed.

"I wonder why the bad wolf ran to this floor?" Jeremiah puzzled looking around the mostly empty maintenance level.

"He knew they had the elevator emergency stopped on this floor, the 38th. He thought he could run upstairs away from the pursuit and then ride the waiting elevator back to the 26th floor and try to escape from there." Emily reasoned.

"We still have work." the lieutenant solemnly repeated.

That was Detective Oftenmarch's cue to follow him back to the 32rd floor. Emily took one last look out of the 38th floor windows onto the roof outside and all she saw was a pair of ghastly gargoyles made of stone. There were no more lycans to be seen. As she began walking toward the exit, Emily discovered she still had a trickle of blood coming from her lip. Her left arm and shoulder were starting to hurt. This evening the detective had done enough werewolf battling to last her a lifetime.

The trio took the stairs back to the 32nd floor. It was much easier and, in this case, much less stressful going down the flights of stairs than it had been going up them. The stairway lights seemed brighter, but maybe that was a result of having a brighter mood. In quick time they were back on the infamous 32nd floor of the Flockman and Bellweather Building. The floor was full of police activity now. Murkendale was waiting for them when they arrived on the 32nd floor.

"We knew the two of you were in the building when we saw two large men arrested in the lobby, a hallway of hammered halfbots on floor nine, a group of unmasked miscreants on the thirteenth floor, and a big jelly mess of a massacre in the sky lobby. It was definitely a trail which could only be left by the pair of you." Murkendale told them.

"Glad we're noteworthy." Eddie replied.

Full of Cathedral police officers now, the 32nd floor of the Flockman and Bellweather Building seemed like an entirely different site from just minutes ago. Charging wild werewolves had been replaced by law enforcement foot traffic. The lunatic lycan portrayer had been taken away and police had the shackled lycan masquerade killer surrounded. A pair of paramedics were treating Brownsides, who appeared much improved and in happier spirits. Someone called out that both elevators were available now. This definitely was a happier, cheerier 32nd floor and Emily liked it much better now.

"The pretty young witness had told us that the other perp and more wounded officers were in suite 3216. I have been sending personnel that way. Darrius and a pair of officers took the first wierdo to our squad van." Murkendale updated them.

"Officer Donny Dotson is quite seriously wounded in the bathroom of suite 3216. Have any paramedics been sent there?" Emily inquired with concern.

"I will go check on him now and, if necessary, will make sure somebody helps him." a passing police officer volunteered.

"I think somebody is already helping him. I think they are." Murkendale speculated.

"We need to make sure." Eddie stated. Hearing this, the volunteering officer ran off to go check on Dotson.

"Suite 3216 should be our next stop. We might be able to help or find some additional evidence to collect." Emily indicated. The lieutenant nodded in agreement.

As they walked down the hallway towards suite 3216, the group of law enforcement officers and the bodyguard passed the arrested lycan masquerader. A pair of patrol officers were around him idly watching another officer as she was working on removing the wolf mask. The lycan themed head wear was proving to be difficult to remove. After roughly manipulating and struggling with the wolf mask, the officer was finally able to remove it to reveal the identity of the masquerader. The lycan masquerader looked familiar to Detective Oftenmarch as she watched with interest. With some recollecting, Emily finally remembered who this masquerader was and where she had seen him. He was Kajay Malgrave, one of the poker players she had encountered on the fourth floor of the Great Getaway last Friday. It had taken Oftenmarch a moment to recall his semi-familiar face. Once Emily remembered, she paused to take out her complink and to take a picture of the arrested maniac without his mask.

"Do you know this man?" Murkendale asked, noticing her picture taking.

"I recognize this man, Ken. He is a poker player who likes high stakes games. Think his name is Kajay,...Kajay Malgrave." Emily's memory had improved.

"You'll be sorry for this outrage. You've stopped what needed to be done." Kajay screamed.

425

"It appears gambling is not his only bad habit." Murkendale replied.

"Police corruption must be stopped. You're all evil demons of injustice." Malgrave continued to shout as he was being removed from the hallway.

With the picture taken, Emily started walking the hall again, ignoring Malgrave's rants. "The other lycan masquerader we unmasked was Diego Lowendowski, the local Cathedral PD union representative." Oftenmarch updated Murkendale.

"Union dues hard at work." Eddie suggested.

"That does not make me feel very well represented." Murkendale admitted.

An idea came to Emily as she was heading to suite 3216. The unmasking of the poker player gave her the delayed idea. The masquerader's boss could be at a high stakes, no limit poker game somewhere close to this location. Luckily, Emily knew someone who knew where and when such poker games where held, her brother Seventh. Seventh was knowledgeable in subjects most people would find unuseful but not Emily. She often found her brother's obscure knowledge extremely helpful. Oftenmarch decided to give her brother a call as the group approached Suite 3216.

The detectives and the bodyguard continued their journey to suite 3216. They travelled around the hallway corner, into the next hallway, and passed two police officers trying to salvage what was left of the poor one-armed Policebot. While walking, Emily began searching through her pockets and all her police electronics to find her personal cell phone. Lowendowski was being dragged out of the suite by three uniformed police officers as they approached the suite. Pausing her phone search, Emily took a picture of him with her police complink as he was being dragged away. He scowled for the camera with his very best scowl. The unmasked lycan masquerader was clearly unhappy. Unlike his lycanesque cohort, Lowendowski remained silent as he was being hauled away.

As Lt. Knighon and Detective Murkendale entered suite 3216, Emily found her personal cell phone. Hanging back to call her brother, she let her homicide division teammates check on Officer Dotson. Jeremiah stayed with Emily, not letting her out of his sight. Before dialing, Oftenmarch remembered that Lowendowski's knife had slide underneath the large entertainment center during their confrontation. Emily abruptly hustled into the suite with a confused Jeremiah following her. Everything had happened so quickly when the masqueraders were on the loose that Oftenmarch was now trying to catch up on some procedural police work.

"Ken, do you have an evidence bag I could use." Emily called to her fellow detective once inside the suite. She was just remembering she had left the MPAR thirty-two floors below back in the lobby.

"Yes, Emily. I have a couple of evidence bags I can give you. Take two, they're kind of small." Murkendale turned to reply while reaching into his pockets.

Emily postponed her phone call to her brother to instead collect any evidence bags from Murkendale. She wanted to call her brother, check on Officer Dotson, and log the potential murder weapon into evidence all at the same time. Dutifully, she opted for collecting evidence first.

"Thank you, Ken." Oftenmarch thanked as she hustled over to get the bags.

The detective noticed a paramedic was looking at the US marshal as she prepared to collect the lost knife. The marshal seemed to be in some discomfort and the paramedic was working diligently to aid them. While the paramedic worked quietly, the marshal suffered silently off to the side of the room.

Now that she had evidence bags, Emily went to get a collection glove. Discovering her pocketed collection kit was open and only a partial kit, Emily found only one latex glove. After putting the lone glove on her right hand and spraying with the little portion of sealant remaining in the kit, Emily went for the knife. The entertainment center held too many electronics to pick-up the unit and it was a very tight squeeze to get under the unit. Opting for the under approach, Emily then climbed under the luxury suite's ridiculously large entertainment center to retrieve the lycan masquerader's knife. It took the detective three tries to get the right spot and enough reach to burrow under the big entertainment center to retrieve the knife. Jeremiah watched with curiosity.

Once obtained, the knife went directly into an evidence bag. Emily scrambled out from under the entertainment center. Glad to be out from under the unit, Emily examined the bagged knife. Jeremiah whistled when he saw the knife. The weapon looked long and nasty, like the type of knife that could only be used for dangerous and dirty deeds. As Emily examined it, the knife poked a hole in the evidence bag and she ended up having to double bag the dangerous weapon. Placing the first evidence bag into a second evidence bag, Emily was far more cautious with the bagged knife now.

As Emily labeled the two bagged knife, Detective Murkendale dashed across the suite and into the hallway. His shouts for paramedics could be heard throughout the whole floor. He had been in such a rush, the detective had not noticed that he ran right past a paramedic, the one treating the U.S marshal.

"Would you be available to help an officer with multiple stab wounds?" Emily politely asked the paramedic.

"What size stab wounds?" the paramedic questioned.

"The officer was stabbed with this blade." Emily answered while holding up the double bagged knife for the paramedic to see.

"I'll get to work immediately." the paramedic returned then stood.

"The victim's back in the far rear bathroom." Emily indicated.

Detective Murkendale returned to the suite followed by another paramedic. "Follow me." he instructed as he crossed the main suite area.

Both paramedics obediently followed him into the back of the suite. Each paramedic matched Murkendale's urgent stride. Once the paramedics had left the main area to go help Officer Dotson, Emily decided it was time to call her brother.

For the second time, Emily searched through her pockets for her personal cell phone. This search was much shorter since her phone was recently pocketed. After bringing up her brother on speed dial, Emily called Seventh. The phone rang several times before he answered.

"Not a good time, E. I'm at work." he greeted.

"Sorry to bother you, Seventh, but I have a question for you." Emily replied.

"I'm stocking shelves for the A&P supercenter so you have to make it quick." Seventh shortly told his sister.

"Is Sarah hosting a poker game tonight in Cathedral, specifically one for Cathedral police or one in the Grand Cathedral Square area?" Emily asked her question.

Seventh sighed. "How do you know so often? It's like the clandestine poker games call to you. E, come find me they say." he jested.

"It could be important, Seventh." Emily added.

"There is a police friendly game on Perennial Parkway tonight. It's an Arden style no limit hold 'em game in the Double Deluxe Hotel. Sarah's going to know anyway, but you didn't hear that from me. I have to get back to work. Good night, E.", Seventh responded and concluded by disconnecting from the call.

Oftenmarch knew a little about old Arden style hold 'em poker. There were two small blinds to go along with the big blind. Three cards were shown on the flop as normal but then two cards were shown on the turn instead of the usual single card. Before the river card was displayed, two cards were burned instead of the usual single card. The river card was also known as 6th street in Arden style poker. After sixth street was revealed, players could no longer check. It was bet, call, or fold only. Finally, the etiquette for buying back into the game was to also buy a round of drinks for everyone at the table.

Emily also knew a little about the Double Deluxe Hotel. The original hotel owner was a drug dealer and a shrewd swindler. He used his grand hotel for all types of illegal activity. About fifteen years ago, a police raid on the hotel one fateful night led to a massive gunfight. Five Cathedral police officers, twelve criminals exchanging fire with the police, and the hotel owner himself were all slain in the altercation. Having made not only the local news but also the national news, the Double Deluxe Hotel's gunfight become well known. Books were written on the hotel and the gunfight on its premises. The Double Deluxe Hotel became somewhat of a tourist attraction. A couple of movie scenes were even filmed in the hotel.

The lieutenant returned from checking on Dotson. Eddie had blood on his shirt and pants. Clearly upset, the lieutenant also looked extremely tired. He was slowly making his way over to Emily. Seeing the blood on Eddie reminded Emily that she still had blood trickling from the corner of her mouth caused by the lycan's strike. Fishing out a tissue from one of her many pockets, Emily mopped some blood from her lip. The detective was hoping that Eddie would still be willing to entertain her theory.

"How is Dotson doing?" Emily sought with concern.

"Holding strong." Eddie responded.

"Found out there is a poker game for the Cathedral PD in the neighborhood. I think the werewolf puppeteer could be at the game." Oftenmarch shared her suspicions.

"You want a peek." the lieutenant hazarded a guess.

"I think it's worth a look. We may find an ace up somebody's sleeve." Emily expressed.

Either out of curiosity or the desire to appease his partner, Lt. Knighton relented and agreed to Emily's request. After dropping Jeremiah off to help guard Tricia on the floor the 271st was keeping secret, the mud tusslers rode an elevator back to the ground floor. Now filled with private law enforcement and emergency personnel, the lobby was bustling with activity. It was the exact opposite as it had been when Eddie and Emily had first arrived. The crisis response team had taken away the two lobby antagonists and were no longer present but their MPAR was still there idling lonely in a corner. The detectives weaved their way through the crowd, left the MPAR behind humming away unused, and exited the Flockman and Bellweather building.

Returning to the city streets, the environment around the Flockman and Bellweather Building had changed significantly. On the now rain soaked pavement, dozens of CSPs guarded the building and four police squad cars barricaded the perimeter of the building. Among the police cars were now also two ambulances and a rescue paramedic van. Their PSUV was also surrounded by two more patrol vehicles. The detectives navigated their way through the new arrivals to head for the Double Deluxe Hotel. As they passed the Flockman and Bellweather building, Emily looked down the service drive between the midscrapers. There were no lycans lying on the ground, there was no police activity to suggest a victim fell from the building heights. Was the lycan in her imagination? Did she have a hallucination? Had she had a vision or seen a symbolic visualization? No answers came to the detective. So Emily thought to herself to trust GOD when you can't trust what you see. Trust the LORD when you can't trust your eyes.

It was a brief walk to the hotel and the pair of detectives arrived in quick time. The first twenty-some floors of the building were more traditional looking architecture. Above that portion of the hotel were twin cylindrical towers with full glass fronts facing Perennial Parkway. The twin cylindrical structures were staggered, with one being positioned to the left and forward while the other was positioned to the right and set back. These twin structures stretched upwards for twenty-some floors. Both towers, full of deluxe suites, reflected the surrounding bright lights of Cathedral extremely well.

A section of the ground floor had a club, called the White Flamingo Lounge, which was separate from the hotel. The White Flamingo had its own street entrance and an entrance from the hotel to give hotel guests easy access to the club. Booming music and bright flashing aqua, orange, fuchsia, and flamingo colored lights came from the crowded lounge. Pockets of laughter overcoming the loud music could also be heard from the White Flamingo. Patrons of the club were having a joyous Monday night.

The luxury hotel itself was quieter and more subdued. With wide double glass doors full of neon art decorated on them, the front entrance of the Double Deluxe Hotel was ostentatious. Matching the front entrance, the lobby of the hotel was just as flashy and full of neon lights. Stationed at the front lobby desk was a two headed droid. Full of chrome and flashing lights, this droid was also quite ornate. The pair of detectives made their way to the lobby desk and the awaiting two headed droid.

The programmed for politeness desk droid greeted the detectives, "Welcome to the Double Deluxe Hotel. How may we help you?"

Emily displayed her badge for the droid to autoscan then stated, "We are here for the poker game."

"Officially, there is no poker game on this premises. If you were to look for a game then you could go seeking on the eighth floor." the droid monotoned its programmed answer.

"Guess we will go seeking." Emily decided.

"Sorry, I could not be of more help. Have a pleasant evening." the second head of the two headed droid digivoiced.

432

The pair of detectives walked over to the main elevators. Their path was not impeded by goons, the building lights never flickered, and the elevators were available on the ground floor. Things were very different from the Flockman and Bellweather Building. When the elevator doors opened, the detectives were greeted by another two headed droid working the elevator. Just as shiny and bright as the desk droid, this robot also greeted the detectives with similar programmed politeness as they entered the elevator.

"Good evening and welcome to the Double Deluxe Hotel. What level would you like?" the droid dutifully asked.

"Eighth floor, please." Emily replied.

"Eighth wants the eighth." Eddie said to himself.

They rode the elevator in uninterrupted silence until the droid announced the eighth floor and the doors smoothly opened. Revealed was the hallway of the hotel's eighth floor. Plain and simple were the halls of this floor, very much in contrast to the building's lobby and entrance. Confetti was strewn along the hallway carpet. The elevator's two headed droid bid the detectives a good evening as they exited. Once off the elevator, the detectives followed the confetti like breadcrumbs in the fairy tale of Hansel and Gretel. Following the trail of confetti down the hall, around a corner, and to a set of pristine suite doors, the detectives had no trouble finding what they sought. Emily pressed the illuminated suite buzzer next to the doors. An expected reply came from the suite intercom, one that Detective Oftenmarch had heard in the past.

"Name and password please." the auto assistant voiced.

Emily held up her badge to allow the automated system to scan her credentials. "Detective Emily Oftenmarch, Cathedral Police." she told the door electronics.

"One moment please." voiced the e-assistant.

It was a rather long moment. It was almost as if they were neither expected nor had the correct password. Emily had forgotten to ask her brother for that piece of information and didn't want to bother him at work again. Eventually, Sandra Silvers came to the suite doors to greet them but she did not seem at all pleased to see them.

Sandra had on a lovely violet and black evening dress and several pieces of sparkling silver jewelry. There were silver flecks throughout her dress which reflected the light quite pleasantly and paired well with her jewelry. Her hair was neat and tidy, done up in a lovely decorated bun. She had an elegant and radiant appearance but, in contrast, a stern and serious expression on her face.

"Your brother's not here tonight, Emily." Sandra began matter of factly.

"I am aware of that, Sandra." Emily explained.

"And you really should not be here tonight either." Sandra continued less than welcoming, but keeping her tone pleasant.

"This is important, Sandra. My partner, Lt. Knighton, and I are here in an investigative capacity. We need a quick look around to see all the Cathedral law enforcement who are here tonight." Emily explained further.

"No, you really don't." Sandra rejected the idea.

"Sandra, I don't care about gambling licenses, city gambling ordinances, interstate gaming laws, or income taxes. There are mask wearing murders going around this city killing people and we are trying to put a stop to it." Emily stated her reason for wanting to intrude.

"And you think spying on off duty cops will achieve this." Sandra doubtfully replied.

"I believe there is a wayward police officer hiding among the poker players pretending to be here just to gamble." Emily responded.

"And what if everybody who is here is simply here just to hypothetically gamble?" Sandra countered.

"Then we won't find who we are looking for and be on our way." Emily indicated.

"This whole request seems absurd." Sandra expressed with little cheeriness.

"Do you think I would upset you and risk my brother not being welcome to work for you again just for the fun of it or for a laugh?" Emily posed to make a point.

While Emily was in the middle of her question, Lt. Knighton walked up to the suite doors. He next gave Sandra an affectionate hug and then said, "Thank you, young lady."

The lieutenant then walked past her in the doorway and into the suite. Both as Eddie passed by her and long after he had gone into the suite, Sandra just stood there with a shocked and dumbfounded look on her face. He had caught her completely unprepared for his actions. Sandra seemed unsure if she should chase Eddie or remain at the door debating with Emily. She started to leave the door then stopped three separate times.

"Did he just....did your partner just....just...." Sandra stammered in her shock.

"Decide for you? Yes, Sandra." Emily finished for her. "Can I come in now?"

"You might as well. Your partner has already invited himself inside." Sandra indignantly concluded.

"Thank you, Sandra. I do plan on being quickly finished with an unobtrusive survey over the room of glad tidings." Emily promised as she hustled into the suite before Sandra changed her mind.

Inside the room was a medium sized entranceway which served as a nice cloak room. Coat racks, vending machines, and a money for chips exchange booth were blocking the entryway to the main area. On the right side of this receiving room was a long narrow front hallway. Tidy and full of tasteful decorations, the hallway led to another medium sized room. That well decorated room seemed to be some type of lounge with a pair of large screen televisions. That room also had a small table with decanters, bottles of booze, and several drinking glasses. The lieutenant was standing next to that table helping himself to some alcohol. Emily hustled over to Lt. Knighton with a quizzical look on her face.

"I needed a drink." Eddie explained.

"But you don't drink, Eddie." Emily replied in puzzlement.

"Tonight, I do." the lieutenant indicated.

Next to the unoccupied lounge was a large open area which was clearly the main hotel room. This open space was where all the gambling was happening. The room was filled with merry people without a care in the world. It was packed with happy people having the time of their lives. Their night was still young and still full of possibilities.

The main hotel room had been decorated like the floor of a casino, full of bright lights and opportunities to purchase alcohol. There were slot machines with flashing lights sitting in a designated section of the hotel room lined up against the wall. Nobody was currently playing any of the attention beckoning machines. To the near side of the main room, the kitchenette had been converted into a bar. Full of bottles, growlers, fruit, glasses, and more bottles, the kitchenette turned casino bar even had its own barman. He was a flashy dressed man with an eager to server look on his friendly face. All the typical furniture one would usually find in a Double Deluxe hotel suite's central room had been removed. In the place of the usual deluxe hotel furnishings were gaming tables and chairs set-up across almost the entire room. Every table was full of poker chips, playing cards, empty drinking glasses, cocktails, coasters, and hookahs. Every seat at every table was occupied by either a dealer or, mostly, by card players.

Young ladies in short skirts and small shirts were travelling between tables selling alcoholic beverages and snacks from tiny round trays. The players were buying these items with poker chips not yet committed to pots. All the simultaneous conversations from the players made for a cacophony of voices filling the room. The overall mood of the crowded room was jovial. Again, it seemed the night was still young and still full of promise. Every curtain in the room was drawn shut and ambient lighting was placed throughout the room of gamblers. Chips were on the move, cards were being swiftly dealt, drinks were being liberally consumed, and conversations were flowing across the casino converted room.

In general, a grand time was being had by the poker players as Detective Oftenmarch watched quietly from the hallway entrance. Unnoticed, she silently observed the happy poker partakers as she tried to read their nonverbal communications like she was playing in multiple poker games at once. In the far corner of the room by the entrance to the back rooms, presumably the bathroom and bedrooms to the suite, a man stood at attention like he was on guard duty. This sentry-like man stood still with a blank expression on his face. He was the only person in the room to look in Emily's direction. The two of them made eye contact and they had about a fifteen-second staring competition before his attention moved elsewhere. For a moment Emily thought she saw a tall dark figure in the corner of the room but after a second look she saw nothing there. Detective Oftenmarch made a mental note, then continued to earnestly survey the room full of frivolity.

"Do you see what I see?" Emily asked Eddie.

"Poor usage of earned wages." Eddie offered in answer.

"A man out of place, mis-stacking his chips, then betting out of turn, and still has no drink." Emily quietly commented almost to herself.

An older man from one of the nearest tables to the hall entrance rose from his seat unsteadily and started walking away towards the kitchenette turned bar. He staggered when he first rose from his chair, swayed his first couple of steps, but then he found his footing. As he made his way around the gaming tables and towards the bar, the older man recognized the lieutenant.

"Steady Eddie, how are you, you sad predictable man?" the seemingly intoxicated man said in greeting.

"Working." the lieutenant grunted.

"I didn't know you were a big poker player, Eddie. Although, you certainly have a great poker face." the inebriated man boisterously stated.

"Prefer playing pinochle." Eddie quietly admitted.

"You have a way of bluffing suspects into confessions. Are you here tonight to try your luck with police officers?" the jolly greeter wondered with a wide grin.

"Just here for the alcohol." Lt. Knighton responded, still holding his drink.

"Wouldn't have predicted that." the older man said in shock.

Emily paused her scrutiny of the hotel room turned casino to focus on the chatting man. She recognized him as Sgt. Jack Flanniham, an old school officer out of the 99th precinct who went by the nickname Cincinnati. "Good evening, Jack. Don't mind Lt. Knighton and me. We're just having a look around. Checking things out." Emily counter greeted.

"Doing a little peek-a-boo. Having a quick looky-loo." the old fashion officer replied with a grin.

"How's lady luck treating you?" Eddied asked the sergeant.

"I got pot committed on a great hand, went all in, and ran into a monster of a hand. Went bust early so I decided to go get a few drinks." Flanniham admitted.

"Poker can be cruel sometimes." Emily comforted before returning to watching the room of card players.

"You're the pretty young detective that Hedra trained. I remember pretty faces. You're doing the old Shippendarrow stare, observe the crowd for oddities and inconsistencies. Strange seeing a beautiful lady doing his move." Flanniham commented.

"Immitation is the best form of flattery." Emily expressed.

"Shippendarrow was crazy like a fox but odd as a clean Cathedral street. How's the old detective's unique technique working for you?" Flanniham wondered with curiosity.

"She sees a misplaced man." Eddie divulged.

"Does she now. Thinks she found a wolf among the sheep, does she?" Flanniham stated with renewed interest.

"I'm not as good at observing as Hedra was but I do remember some of his guidelines of watching properly. Observe, don't just look. To gather information, you need to observe. If at first you don't observe, then observe again. He also liked to say Confucius said three things cannot long be hidden: the sun, the moon, and the truth." Emily recalled.

"And you believe you see someone who does not belong here tonight?" Flanniham wondered still curious.

"It's more like I see someone who's primary reason for being here tonight is not to play poker. Everyone else in the room playing poker is using their chips in a normal fashion. They have their lower value chips, the ones used for antes, blinds, and early bets, located on top of stacks or loose to the side for easy access. They have those value chips somewhere accessible; some have them in hand ready. Those players have their higher value chips stacked in reserve in back stacks or at the bottom of stacks of chips. However, the man at the table four rows deep, third from the right, and at the six o'clock position next to Captain Wesslemont is doing the exact opposite with his chips. He has his lower value chips buried and not ready to play. He has his higher value chips intermixed in values and out towards the front. His neighbor to the other side of him had to ante for him in the last hand. Finally, it also seems like he is paying very little attention to the betting, things like how much to raise and how much to call." Oftenmarch presented her observations.

"Interesting. That's Chief Anton Chinchinocippi of the 219th precinct and uncle of the Cathedral Police Commissioner-at-large, Harold Chinchinocippi." revealed Flanniham.

"This proves nothing, Emily." Eddie reasoned with her.

"True, Eddie, but it tells us a lot. What we observe here could point us in the direction we need to be looking. We now have an idea of who may be involved and how high up the law enforcement beanstalk the rotten parasite grows." Emily countered.

"Maybe he's just a lousy card player." the sergeant challenged.

"Cincinnati makes a good point." Lt. Knighton agreed.

"Let's do an experiment then." Emily decided.

Detective Oftenmarch stealthily approached the nearest cocktail waitress. The scantily dressed young lady was available and greeted Emily pleasantly. Upon Emily's request, the young lady handed the detective a cocktail napkin. Once in possession of the napkin, Emily took out a pen from her inside pocket and began composing a note. She wrote on the cocktail napkin the following: *The lycan masquerade killers are officially done. No more killing. No more masquerading.*

Quietly, Emily handed the nifty nameless napkin note back to the young lady serving refreshments along with some money. The Cathedral detective politely asked the charming waitress to deliver the hand-written message to the 219th precinct chief while keeping the note's author anonymous. Happy to help, the young waitress headed over to the police chief's table to deliver the agitating news. Detective Oftenmarch silently slipped back to the front hallway entrance, remaining unnoticed by the room of happy go lucky poker players where she waited for the police chief's reaction to her message.

When the kind attractive waitress approached the halfhearted poker-playing police chief, he was all smiles and charm. The police chief flirted with the waitress, gave her a higher value poker chip as a tip, and accepted the napkin with the message with a wide radiant grin on his face. He appeared to be expecting some news and from his cheery demeanor that expected news was meant to be encouraging news. The police chief Chinchinocippi continued to flirt with the pretty waitress until she moved on to the next table to sell more booze. Only after the lovely waitress had departed did Anton Chinchinocippi read the note on the napkin. His big smile instantly disappeared from his face. It was replaced by a stern serious expression as he stared at the message. His cheery presence vanished to be replaced by a somber posture.

Slowly, the police chief began to look around the room toward the front entrance like he was searching for the note's origin. As his gaze fell upon the mud tusslers, his focus remained with them. Anton Chinchinocippi glared at them disapprovingly like he was convinced he had found the note's authors. A nasty wolfish baring of the teeth expression formed on his face. His brow furrowed and his eyes squinted in a loathing expression of dislike and hatred. He held his malevolent gaze upon them for about a minute before he went back to half-heartedly playing poker.

"Finally, we found a wolf." Lt. Knighton commented, then headed towards the door.

"You and mini-Shippendarrow are fun, Eddie. You found your suspect and provoked a hostile reaction like a magic trick. What did you write to get such a nasty look?" Flanniham said with enjoyment.

"I wrote the truth, the lycan masquerade killers are finished." Emily divulged.

"You certainly rained on his poker parade." Flanniham stated with a chuckle.

"We are in for stormy weather, Cincinnati. It's Cathedral police corruption cleansing season. Stay calm and civic duty on." Emily replied, then followed the lieutenant towards the exit.

"Happy house cleaning, mini-Shippendarrow." Flanniham merrily called after her.

Chapter 20

Interrogation of Three

Events began unfolding quickly after the apprehension of the lycan masqueraders. Lt. Knighton took two of the federal trainees back to the 271st precinct for booking and interrogation. Detectives Cole and Murkendale took Diego Lowendowski to the 271st precinct for the same process. A pair of police officers from the 38th precinct assisted in taking Kajay Malgrave to the 271st precinct also for the same process. Detective Coventry took the third federal trainee back to their home precinct for the same reason. The lieutenant wanted as many of the masquerade killers as possible at the 271st precinct to be questioned by the mud tusslers. Finally, Detectives Valdez-Scantling and Maxson brought the witness secretly back to the 271st precinct through a secure rear entrance. The plan was to have her identify the district attorney's murderer, then get her to a new hideaway for safe guarding. Officer Binbevvins accompanied them to help protect the frightened female witness. In all the turmoil of the aftermath from the events at the Flockman and Bellweather building, Ryerson had been arrested and taken to another Cathedral precinct. Already processed at the other precinct, he was not transferred to the 271st precinct until a couple of hours later.

Neither hardcore werewolf wannabe was taken to the 271st precinct. The measures taken by the lunatic lycan pretenders in their werewolf transformations were so extreme, which included drugs and genome alterations, that they needed to stay in a hospital overnight for observation. Not in just any hospital either, they had to be taken to the intensive care unit of Grand Cathedral General where they could be diagnosed and treated by several specialists. Currently, both were heavily chained to a hospital bed as they were being dewolved.

Detective Oftenmarch hitched a ride with a police officer from the 117th precinct who had responded to the urgent messages of distress. Accompanied by her new heroic bodyguard, Jeremiah Jefferson, Emily returned to the Wallace-Franklin Building. Emily had been upset with herself for not collecting the out of business sign for Moonlight Security earlier in the day. She was cursing herself the entire trip to get it. On at the Wallace-Franklin Building, she raced up to the eighth floor with an evidence bag. Returning to the empty suite of Moonlight Security, Emily took a picture of the out of business sign and immediately bagged it into evidence. She noted the new company Evereyes, Inc. was a division of Middleton, AJC, and Hoyt Enterprises. Emily now believed AJC stood for Anton J. Chinchinnocippi.

This side trip had caused her to be the last 271st precinct homicide detective from the Flockman and Bellweather building to return to their home base. When Emily arrived at her home precinct, Detective Maxon and a pair of Cathedral patrol officers had already sent out a dozen CSPs around the precinct. This had the police precinct looking like the location of a crime scene rather than her home precinct. Upon her tardy arrival, Lt. Knighton politely reminded her to focus on the homicides committed by the lycan masquerade killers and let others worry about the corruption in the ranks of the Cathedral Police Department.

While Emily was retrieving the possibly implicating sign, assignments for this case had been delegated. The lieutenant did some macromanaging, which he rarely did. Leaving Weibei and Jasper available to respond to calls, he assigned Murkendale and Cole to interview Malgrave, asked Maxson to take evidence to the house of higher learning, and gave Vallen-Scantling the task of having the witness Trudy identify the DA's murder from a serious of line-ups. Theo was still upset about missing the rest of burger night at Crazy Skeeters. Eddie was still apathetic about burger night.

The pressing task pending for the mud tusslers was to interview the young federal trainees. Emily was rather intrigued as to how the secretive trio would answers their upcoming questions. The ordeal at the Flockman and Bellweather building had drained Emily of a lot of her energy. As the detective prepared for the interrogations, she started to get her second wind. Some ready-made snack food for dinner had helped. After a limited transition period, Emily made her way towards the interrogation rooms. The comfort level of the environment deteriorated the closer she got to her destination.

In the 271st precinct homicide department, the interrogation rooms were vastly different from the rest of the department. The office bullpen and witness meeting rooms had high ceilings and brightly painted walls. In contrast the interrogation rooms had low ceilings and dull bland walls. The precinct's meeting rooms had comfortable chairs, as opposed to the interrogation rooms' basic uncushioned seats. The office bullpen was a spacious area full of activity where the interrogation rooms were small dingy rooms only used for questioning. The bullpen and meeting rooms were full of tall windows and were well illuminated. In contrast, the dimly lit interrogation rooms had no windows, only a one-way mirror used for outside observation.

Right from the start of the interviewing process, there was a change in the demeanor of the suspects which was very different from the Flockman and Bellweather building. The now captured and humiliated Federal trainees had become extremely cooperative as apprehended suspects facing serious trouble. Perhaps this was because they hoped being cooperative would get them out of serious trouble. Perhaps this was because they knew FDILE, the Federal Department of Improved Law Enforcement, would protect them so they might as well cooperate. Perhaps they had come to their senses and decided cooperation was the right thing to do.

One at a time, Eddie and Emily interviewed the trio of trainees, asking each of them the same set of questions. They wanted to see how similar or different their responses would be to the exact same questions. Therefore, the detectives used a script of questions which was used for all three interviews.

"How did you become involved?" Eddie began each interrogation.

Fairbankers: Two weeks ago in a training class in West Cathedral, our instructor asked us if we wanted to earn some extra money. He said it would be good experience and good pay. The work was described to us as low risk undercover work.

Tuttle: We were attending a Federal training course in the area. The class professor offered us some work. It was an opportunity to gain some experience and earn some spending. Our teacher informed us it would be simple and safe work undercover.

Monkhouse: We had a boring training class somewhere in West Cathedral. The teacher told us there were well paying jobs available. There wasn't much to do in the area where the training class was held and the job sounded exciting, so why not. Getting paid to do something interesting was better than sitting around doing nothing.

"Who was your instructor?" Eddie asked next.

Fairbankers: Special Agent Lessendyke.

Tuttle: Senior Special Agent Boris Lessendyke.

Monkhouse: Some old retired dude named Lessendyke.

"What was your first job?" Eddie continued to question.

Fairbankers: We were doing surveillance. We were watching what we were told were crooked Cathedral police officers. We were logging times of cops coming and going from an apartment building somewhere in Harrision Heights. Not sure how many of them were actually policemen, but there were a number of people coming and going.

Tuttle: The job was to stake out an apartment building that was allegedly a meeting place for dirty police officers. It was a lot of watching people come and go then writing down times in a handwritten log, very old school.

Monkhouse: Extremely boring, it was to sleep in a car while watching people come and go from an apartment building. It was more boring than class but at least the pay was better.

"How did you go from having a job from an instructor doing surveillance to wearing werewolf masks and attacking people?" Emily puzzled.

Fairbankers: The work progressively got stranger. We started researching people in witness protection with the Cathedral PD. Then we were given wolf masks to scare people. Next thing I knew we were sent to pick up those nasty big wolves, told to babysit them, and then ordered to deliver the pack of wolves to the bottling plant in New Terranceville. But we didn't attack anyone; we never attacked anyone.

Tuttle: FIrst it was just research and surveillance. Next they asked me to do some technical work like robotics repair and encryption breaking programs. It wasn't until we started getting wolf masks and were told to pick up wilderbeast wolves that the job turned cruel and bizarre. The attacks at the bottling plant was not me, detectives. I never attacked anybody.

Monkhouse: It all changed when we were given the Halloween werewolf masks. Then the jobs went from boring but normal to absolutely ridiculous but at least interesting. At first we were just scaring people. Just be seen and look frightening kind of thing. Then we had to pick up, hold, and deliver those stupid giant wolves. Hated those beasts. Worst job I have ever had, those beasts were a pain in the rear to keep in order.

"The lycan masquerade killers were all over the news. Every day some form of Cathedral media was discussing werewolf masked killers. Didn't receiving the wolf masks concern you or trigger an internal alarm?" Emily questioned.

Fairbankers: We thought we were being sent undercover. We thought we were posing as low level henchmen in order to infiltrate the gang or group working for crooked cops. We would play our role until we had enough evidence to arrest either the leader of the lycan killers or the leader of the witness scaring gang. Our part was minor and non-lethal. Delivering drugged wolves to a bottling plant was actually far stranger and more concerning than the masks.

Tuttle: It was suppose to be an undercover assignment. The plan was to catch copycat werewolf themed criminals. The assignment seemed like we were gathering evidence against a wolf themed criminal syndicate. We figured the masks both hid the criminals' identities and promoted their fear induced criminal business of scaring witnesses. It did not make sense for this to be cold blooded killers who were shipping big wolves to their crime scene. We had no idea this was part of the lycan masquerade killings; that seemed mental.

Monkhouse: The whole wear the mask request seemed ridiculous. The whole scare this person routine seemed childish. We were told we were going undercover as newbie henchmen and smugglers. I thought the dire wolf masks were a joke, like the part time rookies were receiving a stupid hazing. A let's see if they actually wear them kind of prank.

"Where'd the megawolves come from?" Eddie inquired.

Fairbankers: An unused distribution center in Harrison Heights. It was a sad unkempt area. We followed a carnival truck to the pick-up location. We had to travel down several back alleys to get to the pick-up point.

Tuttle: Some rundown shipping warehouse in the suburbs. We followed some wacky carnival truck to the pickup location, an abandoned warehouse. Don't remember the address. Will never forget how rank the area smelt.

Monkhouse: We followed some crazy carnival truck to the location of the pick-up. We got the wilder beast from a weird bloke dressed like a witch doctor in an abandoned building.

"Who dumpstered the megawolves?" the lieutenant interrogated further.

Fairbankers: So you did find those dead wolves. That's not a surprise to me, you are very good detectives. Patrick and I got rid of the dead wolves into the construction dumpster in West Cathedral. We did not know what else to do with the carcasses.

Tuttle: I had a feeling you found the wolves we discarded in the trash when I saw the Breakfast and Brew bags Detective Oftenmarch brought to the precinct this morning. Fairbankers and Monkhouse pitched the dead beasts while I purchased the food.

Monkhouse: You found those stupid wolves, guess Johnny P. was right about his suspicions. J.D. and I got rid of the dead wolves. The other wolves were fighting over them and their bodies were starting to stink. We chucked them the first opportunity we could find.

"Who killed the dumped wolves?" Eddie questioned onward.

Fairbankers: Monkhouse got violent with them, too violent. He was trying to keep them in line, keep them from fighting. He took disciplining them too far.

Tuttle: Patrick killed them with his bolt stunner and knife. He was trying to subdue them and things got out of control. Things got crazy out of control.

Monkhouse: I did. They gave me no choice. Those wolves were super aggressive and difficult to control. They kept fighting each other. I was trying to restore order and had to get too forceful with a pair of the drug raging biters.

"Was Conglomerate Warehouses in Cathedral the planned staging area for the bottling plant invasion or was that also an ad lib due to unruly megawolves?" Detective Oftenmarch wondered.

Fairbankers: We were ordered to go to the Conglomerate Warehouses. The plan was to prep the wolves to be delivered in the early morning hours of the next day, but things did not go as planned.

Tuttle: The plan was to take the wolves to the warehouse so that syndicate's experienced members could assess them and get the wilder beasts ready for action.

Monkhouse: The plan was always to stop at the warehouse. It was supposed to be a brief stay to make ready the stupid wolves. The fools calling the shots were no more prepared to deal with those beasts than we were.

"How did former Officer Brahmson get murdered in warehouse D505? Emily asked with a serious expression.

Fairbankers: No one was meant to get hurt, nobody was supposed to know we were there. He came into the warehouse while we were trying to feed the wolves. Things were so chaotic with the animals, nobody noticed him at first. When he approached us with questions, Lowendowski got into an argument with him that turned violent. We are talking too violent, too quickly. In a blink of the eye, the man was dead.

Tuttle: It was feeding time at the wolf warehouse of horrors. The wolves were hard enough to herd just to watch, then adding food to the situation made it ten times harder. They went crazy when they smelled food like they were always super hungry. We could neither feed them enough nor feed them fast enough. One second we were trying to feed wolves, the next second a security guard was asking us what we thought we were doing. The conversation escalated quickly into a fight, very quickly. Then the fight turned deadly.

Monkhouse: Dude showed up as the wolves were fighting over food. He obviously didn't like us being there or that we brought a pack of nasty wolves to set loose in the warehouse. Wolves were too busy eating to take notice of him, but Lowendowski got in his face. He told the guard to mind his own business and take a hike. That didn't go over well with the guard and a fight broke out. The fight escalated quickly and ending abruptly with the guard's death.

"Who killed Brahmson?" Eddie asked directly.

Fairbankers: Lowendowski killed him. At first, it was a fist fight but then things escalated. Lowendowski pulled out a knife and the guard tried to draw his stunner. Lowendowski stabbed the man before he could use the stunner. I recorded the fight on my maxcell phone; I still have the recording of it.

Tuttle: Lowendowski did. Rude dude went crazy when the security guard showed up. First, he yelled like a banshee. Then he started throwing punches at the guard. Next thing I knew, Lowendowski had pulled a knife and had stabbed the man. Whole thing happened super fast, ridiculously fast. I had a robot camera running at the time because I happened to be working on a bot. So I have the whole altercation on a recording. I have a video of the whole surreal thing.

Monkhouse: That Lowendowski idiot killed him. He got ridiculously brutal and butchered the guard for no reason. There were four of us, we could have overpowered the guard and tied him up long enough to get lost. That hot-head maniac, Lowendowski, went homicidal.

"Would you testify to that?" Lt. Knighton inquired seriously.

Fairbankers: Yes, I would.

Tuttle: Absolutely.

Monkhouse: Gladly.

"So you left the man for dead and switched warehouses, is that correct?" Emily inquired with a tone of disapproval every time.

Fairbankers: We didn't want to leave him. Killing the man was never part of the plan. Lowendowski ordered us to switch warehouses. He just wanted to hide until that evening ended then leave, but the plant scare tactic got postponed a day. The postponement prevented us from reporting to our superior for over a day.

Tuttle: We didn't see our instructor, Lessendyke, who was also our boss, again until after the bottling plant fiasco. We told Lessendyke about the murder as soon as we saw him and he told us he would take care of it.

Monkhouse: Wasn't much we could do for the man. Before we could intervene, it was too late for him. The wolf delivery was unexpectantly postponed a day, so we were stuck babysitting the nasty wolves another day and we did not have a chance to report the murder to our boss.

"Who masked the Lawtech Patroller?" Eddie changed subjects with this question.

Fairbankers: That was me. Somebody didn't show up to get their mask that evening, someone Lowendowski referred to as Mitchy Moe. I was bored so I wandered over to the LawTech side of the warehouse. While I was looking at the robots, I put the mask on one of them as a prank. After the horrible murder and quick departure, I forgot about the mask.

Tuttle: Probably J.D. He was the only person to go over to the LawTech side of the first warehouse.

Monkhouse: That sounds like the kind of stupid nonsense that Fairbankers would do. I had no idea he had done that.

"Why camp next door?" Eddie requested.

Fairbankers: The plan was to only be at the warehouse until early Thursday morning. We did not know where else to take the wolves as they were difficult to control. We thought we could use the abandoned warehouse next door for just the day then prepare to move the following early morning, but all the plans were postponed for a day. Our expectations were never to camp for almost two days with the nasty beasts at that creepy abandoned warehouse.

Tuttle: What a disaster the whole staging the wolves plan was from the beginning. When security discovered us with the wolves, there was no plan B at the ready. We ended up improvising in panic and that's how we ended up camping next door, as you put it. Lowendowski told us to stay put and keep out of security's attention. When the whole plan was delayed a day, we ended up babysitting the mean wolves for days.

Monkhouse: Lowendowski didn't know what to do or where else to go. The empty warehouse next door was convenient, so we used it. It was lucky security never properly canvassed the area or they would have easily found us. It was unlucky that the entire mission was delayed until late Thursday night. That's why we were forced to camp next door. That's why we had to be sitters for the snappers. Terrible experience from start to finish.

"What about the crazy robot?" Lt. Knighton wondered.

Fairbankers: Tuttle was playing with that robot. I only helped him a little because it was boring babysitting drugged wolves. I have no idea what he was doing or why he had to do it in the abandoned warehouse.

Tuttle: That was a project given to me, I am the robotics expert in the group. The assignment was to look over a prototype droid that was to be used in future operations. It was received in the same shipment as the wilder beasts. I only meant to inspect it, but when we got stuck in the warehouse for so long I just kind of kept going. Before I realized it, the whole project was on the warehouse floor. Guess I got carried away. In the end, I ran out of time to put any of it away.

Monkhouse: That's the kind of stupid nonsense that Tuttle does, he takes out the entire erector set, spreads it across the floor, and leaves the whole mess behind. I knew he was going to do that.

"Let's discuss the bottling plant." Eddie changed subjects.

Fairbankers: Sure.

Tuttle: What do you want to know?

Monkhouse: Whatever.

"What was your plant assignment?" Eddie questioned onward.

Fairbankers: We had our undercover assignment and we had our instructions from the masked criminals. Our undercover assignment was to find Zeke Ryerson for the Federal Department of Improved Law Enforcement. FDILE wanted us to deliver a message to Ryerson, who was an employee at the bottling plant. The department wanted him to provide the evidence he had promised in exchange for non-prosecution and they were tired of waiting. As for the assignment from the mad criminals, they wanted us to deliver the wild wolves. We were to set the viscous beasts free to cause as much disorder and fear as possible. Those assignments seemed unrelated at the time, but reflecting on things I now believe the target of both jobs was the same person, Ryerson. One group wanted to scare him with a warning and the other group wanted to scare him with wicked wolves and violence.

Tuttle: There were dual tasks for the bottling plant visit. There was a real or official federal police assignment from our instructor, and then there was the job the lycan themed syndicate had given us. Our actual task at the bottling plant was to contact a witness who happened to work at the plant and stealthily deliver a times up to testify message to him. I think his name was Ryerson. Our secondary task was to work the undercover assignment, which had us delivering chaos and terror to the bottling plant in the form of wicked wolves. Both objectives happened to align with the one location being the bottling plant.

Monkhouse: Basically the job was to deliver those stupid nasty wolves to the masked lunatics at the bottling plant in New Terranceville. We were giving them their shipment of horror to terrorize the bottling plant. It seemed like they didn't mind harassing the whole staff and plant, but their main target was supposed to be one specific employee. They were out to scare and hurt one specific person and anyone they scared or killed in the process was a bonus for them. Oddly enough, there was a reluctant federal witness, named Ryerson, who was reluctant to give evidence and who worked at the plant who may or may not have been that target. The Federal law department had also asked us to give him a message should we find him at the plant during our assignment.

"Did you speak with Ryerson?" the lieutenant wondered.

Fairbankers: Unfortunately, no. Once we arrived onsite, Patrick released the crazed wolves with the help of one of the masked criminals and there was nothing but mayhem after that point. Neither masked criminal acted sanely either. They both charged into the plant behind the wolves, chasing after people seemingly at random, howling all the way. The whole situation was nuts, unbelievable nuts. The loading dock emptied in a hurry and we were left there on our own. There was nobody left for us to speak with in the area.

Tuttle: The wild wolves were released very quickly. I had barely got the truck into park when the unloading process had already begun. By the time I got into the loading dock, the brutes were already released. Malgrave was chanting some bizarre language and Lowendowski was wolf calling as I arrived on the scene. As soon as all the wolves were released, they went on a rampage and Malgrave followed them swinging what looked like a machete. Lowendowski was not far behind him carrying a nasty knife. Those two combination of things immediately scared everyone working at the plant far away from our location in the loading dock. We never spoke to anyone, not a soul, at the bottling plant that gruesome night.

Monkhouse: No sooner had we delivered the ridiculous wolves, we found the loading dock cleared out. Wolves were chasing people, masked villains were chasing wolves, and alarms were sounding. The loading area had become an evacuation zone. Every plant worker had run for their life. I briefly looked in the area around the loading docks for any employees. Jeremy, Johnny P, and myself never saw Ryerson after that horror act, yet alone speak with him.

"Who murdered the poor men working at the Incanncennio bottling plant that night?" Emily asked the important question.

Fairbankers: It was Diego Lowendowski who did all the killing at the bottling plant that night. If setting drugged wolves loose in the plant would be considered crazy, then setting Lowendowski loose into the

457

plant was lunacy. Lowendowski's behavior after the wicked wolves were freed was completely homicidal insanity. He began shouting like a raging maniac, then chased after people brandishing a terrifying knife and then began howling like a mad werewolf. I had my mini-zoom drone with me and immediately launched it to follow that lunatic. Lowendowski chased down and stabbed two injured people, both injured by the savage wolves. Both murderous attacks were captured on video by the mini-zoom drone.

Tuttle: Malgrave and Lowendowski both had murderous intents that night. They chased after people with weapons in hand following in the wake of the wild wolves. They ran in separate directions, so I would speculate they each committed a murder. I followed Malgrave briefly but lost him when a stupid wolf tried to attack me. After I used my stunner on it and it ran off, Malgrave was nowhere to be seen. J.D. sent out a mini-zoom drone after the masked madmen and Patrick followed Lowendowski, so J.D. and Patrick might know better than me.

Monkhouse: I went into the plant looking for the reluctant witness. In my brief travels I did not see Malgrave, but I saw Lowendowski a couple of times. At first he was chasing after people with a wicked looking blade. The second time I saw him he was standing over a man covered in blood howling like a crazed werewolf. At least one of the murders was committed by Diego Lowendowski at that moment.

"Did you witness either murder?" Eddie wanted confirmation.

Fairbankers: I have video recordings from my mini-zoom drone of Diego Lowendowski committing both murders. It's concrete evidence against him.

Tuttle: Sadly, I did not. Though I believe J.D. has the murders on video. He should be able to help you there.

Monkhouse: I saw Diego Lowendowski remove a knife from a fallen bloodied victim. Personally saw him concluding his kill.

"With their masks being worn, how could you tell Lowendowski and Malgrave apart? How could you know which one was which at any given time?" Detective Oftenmarch puzzled.

Fairbankers: Malgrave had war paint on the clothing over his arms and chest.

Tuttle: Malgrave is at least six inches taller than Lowendowski.

Monkhouse: Lowendowski wore combat boots and had proper tactical gear. He was also shorter. Malgrave was a nutter wearing paint, sneakers, and dirty cargo pants.

"Now three unreported murders. Explain." Eddie challenged.

Fairbankers: We were unsure what to do. Being undercover when the murders occurred put us in an awkward spot. The expectation was we would be uncovering police corruption and extreme scare tactics to intimidate individuals. The prospect of multiple murders was never discussed by our boss. If we arrested Lowendowski and Malgrave, then we would never learn for whom they worked. In the end, the best we could manage was informing our boss once the bottling plant assignment was complete.

Tuttle: With no experience in covert assignments, the three of us had no idea how to handle the murders. We needed better instructions from our superiors prior to the bottling plant assignment. We thought staying undercover until we could speak with our boss after the assignment was the best plan. We thought they would handle the situation. There didn't seem like any other good options.

Monkhouse: The murders were reported to FDILE as soon as we were able. It was not possible to complete the undercover assignment if we interrupted events mid-assignment to make arrests. The masked killers were never getting away with their crimes; FDILE assured us that the department had everything under control.

"Why leave the megawolves?" Lt. Knighton wondered.

Fairbankers: With security alarms going off and overhead announcements being made that the police were on the way, there was no time to collect the crazed beasts. We would have needed hours to round up that lot of wild wolves. The masked maniacs plan for the bottling plant was absurd from the start. I honestly don't know how they thought they were every going to get the wolves removed from the plant.

Tuttle: The intrusion was so loud and alarm triggering, it was sure to attract every police officer on duty in the area. The window of time required to gather that pack of wandering wolves would have kept us onsite well past the arrival of the police. Even without the time restriction, herding that pack of wild beasts would have been a monumental task. There was no other option but to leave the wolves.

Monkhouse: Even the idiots, Lowendowski and Malgrave, knew we had to leave the stupid wolves behind. The whole fiasco was blatant and obvious, they might as well have called the police before breaking into the plant. After all the nonsense, there was no way to collect the wolves and not get caught. I think it was their plan all along to leave the nasty nashers at the bottling plant. It was a rude parting gesture or a how do you like me now move.

"Why the 271st precinct assignment?" the lieutenant interrogated further.

Fairbankers: We were supposed to monitor your investigation of the bottling plant murders and guide you in the correct direction if or when necessary. The hope of FDILE was that the Cathedral PD would solve the homicides and we could focus on the assignments of contacting Ryerson and stopping the werewolfish terrorism. FDILE only wanted us to intervene if the murders appeared to be going unsolved. Our boss thought that following your murder investigations would help us discover the head of the werewolves.

Tuttle: The scenario our superior gave us was never this complicated. Things got worse and worse as we progressed in our assignment. There weren't supposed to be multiple murders, there wasn't supposed to be all this violence. Reporting on the werewolf activity and establishing who they were working for is all we were supposed to be doing. We were put in the 271st precinct to find out more about who was in charge of the werewolves by observing your homicide Investigations.

Monkhouse: I was supposed to get assigned to you, lieutenant. However, your captain interfered and made the assignments himself. FDILE thought you would be investigating the murders at the bottling plant, lieutenant. My orders were to figure out who was giving the werewolves their marching orders through your investigation. Instead, J.D. got assigned to you and you were taken off the bottling plant murders. Nothing went to plan and things went downhill. Fairbankers was not supposed to fall in love with you, Oftenmarch. He was supposed to put you back on the werewolves' trail, not try to become your knight in shining armor.

"What was the plan at Superior Private Eyes?" Emily asked the next question.

Fairbankers: The criminals told us they were looking for Ryerson, but we did not know the man was already in police protection. FDILE wanted us to contact Ryerson and inform him that he was out of time to produce the evidence he promised. The department did not inform us that Ryerson was already working with the authorities for the city of Cathedral. I also got the impression the criminals were searching for someone else, someone important, but they would not admit to this nor disclose who that might be. John-Paul was supposed to get into the security company's database and video surveillance recordings to locate where Ryerson was hiding.

Tuttle: Monkhouse blames me but the alarm going off was not my fault. Malgrave was supposed to deactivate their security system, not knock out most of their power. That idiot both advertised our presence and put us in the dark to work. My initial plan was to find Ryerson's location, keep that information vague, and try to figure out who the other person the werewolf clan was looking for. But once our presence was known, it was hard to figure out the whos, whats, and whys of the videos with limited time and light. We had to rush to get what video we could and make a quick escape.

Monkhouse: That was mostly Tuttle's mess. He was supposed to discretely find Ryerson's location and the hell with the whereabouts of anybody else the villains wanted to know. We almost got caught trespassing while he was monkeying around with his database searches. I have no idea who the second person was that they wanted to find. All I know is that they really, really wanted to find that person. In the end, we were just lucky to get out of that place uncaptured.

"And then Flockman and Bellweather?" Eddie questioned onward.

Fairbankers: We just wanted to contact Ryerson. The plan was just to get to him and pretend to scare him. Once we reached him, the plan was to discretely pass FDILE's times up message to him. That is why we volunteered to go after Ryerson in the Flockman and Bellweather building. We had no idea he was in Cathedral police protection or that his life was in danger. FDILE only told us that he was a former associate of the terrorists and he was supposed to be giving evidence against his former teammates to FDILE.

Tuttle: Our task was to tell Ryerson his agreement with FDILE was expiring. All the robot forces nonsense and the additional werewolves was a surprise to us when we arrived at the building. FDILE did not clue us in or have any intel on what the werewolves were planning on doing in the Flockman and Bellweather building. We just knew they wanted to know where Ryerson and another person were hiding. We were focused on contacting Ryerson. We had no idea the bad guys were going to go on a rampage in the building.

Monkhouse: I was going to scare the poop out of Ryerson, not for the criminals but for FDILE. He was a lying untrustworthy creep who probably had no intention of helping FDILE. It seemed pretty apparent when we gathered with the villains that they were out to kill in the Flockman and Bellweather building. The best we could do was pretend to attack Ryerson and send him a message from FDILE. I was hoping to smack him around a little but keep him alive. Between the robots and the madmen, we had no chance to help whoever their other target was.

"Didn't it ever occur to you that it might be a good idea to come talk to us as your FDILE assignment deteriorated?" Emily challenged.

Fairbankers: We had discussed that as a group but decided, mostly Monkhouse, to continue with our instructions. What to share, how much to share, when to share were all things we had no experience with and no concept of best practice. We were left pretty much in the dark in a situation that was extremely dark to begin with.

Tuttle: We had no idea what we should do. We had discussed things with our FDILE supervisor and we were encouraged to keep undercover and silent. In hindsight, it was probably a better idea to share things with the Cathedral PD. At the time, it seemed alright to stay hidden.

Monkhouse: We worked for FDILE, not the Cathedral PD. We had no idea who could be trusted in a corrupt unscrupulous organization.

With the interviews of identical questions for the trainees completed, Eddie and Emily turned their attention to Diego Lowendowski. Being unfamiliar with lycan masqueradering behavior, their approach was going to be more adaptive and reactive to the suspect. A lot depended on Lowendowski's level of involvement and what answers the detectives received. This was Eddie and Emily's plan going into the interrogation. However, this interview was never going to go to plan.

In contrast to the trio of trainees, the apprehended police union representative was not in the sharing mood. He was sullen and silent.

The pair of detectives' interview with DIego Lowendowski was entirely different as a result. Lowendowski would not speak with them. He would only say one word: lawyer. After refusing to converse with them and requesting a lawyer, he was informed by the pair of detectives that he was being charged. That list of charges was read to him by Emily. She informed Lowendowski he was being charged with the Incannncennio bottling plant murders, the murder of Kenneth Brahmson, the attempted murder of Tricia Kawowski, and conspiracy to commit murder against the former district attorney.

He remained silent through the list of charges and then submissively was led away back to a holding cell by a pair of Cathedral patrol officers. Lowendowski dutifully fell in line like a good soldier protecting any superiors. It was difficult for the detectives to tell if Lowendowski believed his superiors would rescue him from the charges or if Lowendowski believed his superiors would reward him for his silence. One fact was clear: He was not talking. The man was exercising his right to remain silent.

Following this unproductive interrogation, Emily and the lieutenant left the bleak room to head for the common area of the 271st homicide division. Taking a moment to make mental notes and collect their thoughts, the pair of detectives walked in silence. They both had much to think about and mull over.

Lt. Knighton and Detective Oftenmarch met up with detectives Murkendale and Cole in the break room area just outside interrogation. Once together, they began discussing the case with each other. This surreal situation was a tangled mess, one that needed deep deliberation. Their discussion began with the three Federal trainees.

"Do we believe them?" Emily asked the lieutenant.

"Some." Eddie considered with a frown.

"Guiltier than they say but less nefarious than they seem." Murkendale conjectured. The lieutenant nodded in agreement.

"They could be charged with four counts of criminal trespass and three counts of vandalism. They let three murders go unreported. They took intellectual property from Private Eyes. They trafficked in illegal growth hormones and megawolves. Finally, they went after a witness in police protection. All this was done under the guise of working undercover for the Federal Department of Improved Law Enforcement. How do we handle this, Eddie?" Emily riddled in depth.

"What is FDILE doing working investigations? They are a training department." Murkendale wondered.

"Should we call Fiddle and give them a chance to confess their sins?" Cole offered.

"Charge them. Let Fiddle absolve." Lt. Knighton decided.

"Here is the next dilemma. Binbevvins told me that Zeke Ryerson made a deal with the Cathedral Police Department to testify against his brother Zack. But fingerprints indicate it is not Zeke Ryerson that was in protective custody. The fingerprints match Zack Ryerson from his criminal arrest records in our database." Murkendale laid out the problem.

"High Commissioner Harden admitted to us that Zeke Ryerson was supposed to be assisting the Cathedral Police. That confirms Binbevvins statement. The trainees told us that Zeke Ryerson was also giving evidence to FDILE in exchange for non-prosecution. The trainees were supposed to give Zeke a message at the Incanncennio bottling plant where he works. The lycan masquerade killers also appear to have been after Zeke Ryerson the night of the plant invasion. However, it seems that it was Zack Ryerson they both were trying to get to tonight at the Flockman and Bellweather Building." Oftenmarch shared in length.

"This is why Fiddle shouldn't fiddle." Darius mused.

"Malgrave confessed to Cole and I that they were after Zeke Ryerson. That's confirmed. The question becomes why were they attacking Zack Ryerson and how did he get into police protection?" Murkendale puzzled.

"They have their brothers confused." Cole speculated.

"Zack is posing as Zeke." Knighton answered.

"Neither the Cathedral PD nor the lycan masquerade killers knew Zack did the old switch-a-roo it seems. Maybe Fiddle didn't know it either." Darius suggested.

"Why did the high commissioner's office give assignments and protection to Zeke Ryerson?" Murkendale asked.

"Zeke recooked the police data." Lt. Knighton disclosed.

"Zeke Ryerson appears to be the lead computer cracker who falsified the Cathedral PD's arrest and conviction statistics. The high commissioner's office was giving him an opportunity to name names and to help catch any possible successors to himself. He turned informant, or stoolie, in exchange for lenience and protection." Emily explained.

"How does Zack fit into all this?" Cole puzzled.

"Zeke was working for Zack." Eddie postulated.

"Zack Ryerson has the criminal record; Zack has the criminal contacts. He is the one more likely to get involved in fraud and tampering with police records. So you're thinking Zack was the ring leader." Kenneth replied.

"Then Zeke gets caught." Lt. Knighton continued.

"Zack was too clever to get caught." Oftenmarch added.

"So Zeke was just the computer geek. He was not villain suave enough to avoid getting caught. Zack, on the other hand, had enough criminal experience to avoid detection. He gets away. So the captured computer nerd agrees to betray his criminal brother to avoid jail time." Cole continued the thought.

"Why stop talking to FDILE?" Eddie asked the important question.

"Because Zack did not know about that betrayal. He only discovered the sellout to the Cathedral police." Murkendale filled in the response.

"What made you suspect Zack had switched with his brother?" Emily asked.

"Choosing lycanphobic bluff over sanctuary." Eddie answered.

"His story at the bottling plant about the lycans intercepting his phone calls and being everywhere." Emily recalled.

"That's the one." Eddie confirmed.

"That makes sense, Eddie. Zeke agrees to incriminate his brother to the Cathedral Police Department. Zack discovers this fact, so he assumes the identity of his brother, Zeke Ryerson. He was feigning turning states evidence against himself, pretending to be his brother giving evidence on a sibling. Neither the FDILE nor the lycan masquerade killers knew that Zack Ryerson was pretending to be his brother. None of the plant intruders could tell the brothers apart. The trainees were sent on the bottling plant assignment to give Ryerson a message. That message was that the agency was done waiting on the evidence he had promised and that the offer for immunity was about to expire. FDILE hadn't received the evidence probably because Zack had never known about Zeke's federal deal. Furthermore, the trainees failed to speak with him that night so he still may not know. The lycan masquerade killers, Lowendowski and Kajay, went into the bottling plant to eliminate Zeke Ryerson or at least scare the police cooperation out of him to prevent him from incriminating his brother Zack and more importantly their employers. Zack then decides it is a bad idea to portray his brother, so instead of seeking police protection from us he tells us some convoluted and ridiculous story. At that point, Zack was most likely planning on running away. Then at some point he changes his mind. Perhaps it was when Mitchell Moe Gertzin gunned down former officer Barrett Alexander. Whatever the reason, Zack decides to go back to pretending to be his brother and seeks police protection. Therefore, he is the Ryerson twin we find under duress in witness protection at the Flockman and Bellweather Building." Emily tells the sad tale of the Ryerson twins.

"Complexity with stupidity, bad combination." Eddie commented.

"If it quacks like a duck then you call it a duck. If the fingerprints match Zack Ryerson, then we have Zack Ryerson in custody." Cole simplified.

"With an active warrant for his arrest." Murkendale expounded.

"We could also charge him with perjury, witness tampering, and false impersonation." Oftenmarch reasoned.

"Next question is where in the world is Zeke Ryerson?" Murkendale wondered.

"Dead, on the run, gone into hiding, or some other law enforcement agency has him secretly under protection." Cole listed several possibilities.

"All possible, none of them good." Emily expressed.

"Then we have Kajay Malgrave to discuss. Malgrave claims that he is not a murderer. His job apparently was merely to frighten people. According to himself, he administered scare tactics to stop weak willed people from hindering strong leaders in their uncompromising lawful pursuits. He was saving justice." Murkendale relayed.

"He's on a mission for a League of Superior Leaders to forge a better legal system. The man explained to us that he needed to take drastic measures to reclaim proper law and order in this cruelly corrupt city." Darius added.

"What a hero." Lt. Knighton stated with strong sarcasm.

"Did you charge Lowendowski with murder? And if so, with what evidence?" Murkendale asked his fellow detectives.

"Yes, Lowendowski has been charged with murder. We have him in possession of a wolf mask and the murder weapon. Hopefully we will have confirmation on the weapon soon. Then we have the testimony of the three trainees, two of which also claim to have video recordings of a murder. So Lowendowski was recorded on video committing the act of murder." Emily explained.

"Twice on video murdering Brahmson." Eddie expounded.

"The reason I ask is because we do not have any physical evidence against Malgrave for the act of murder. What should we charge him with in regards to the murders?" Murkendale queried.

"We might as well charge him with murder. He may confess to a murder in the end. Tell us how he did it for the greater good." Cole suggested.

"Attempted, accessory, conspiracy to commit" Lt. Knighton listed.

Half running, half walking Detective Vallens-Scantling entered the break area. Looking flustered, he was hustling, which was rare for him, like there was something urgent on his agenda. When Theo saw the lieutenant, he came to an abrupt stop and then seemed slightly relieved.

"We have a problem, lieutenant." Vallens-Scantling informed Eddie.

"Not burger night lamenting again." Eddie sighed.

"No, sir. We have a real problem, lieutenant." Theo replied.

Chapter 21

Seeking and Dreaming

In six line-ups of a half-dozen people each, which included Lowendowski, Malgrave, Fairbankers, Monkhouse, Tuttle, several police officers in plain clothes, and a couple of red herrings, the young witness to the district attorney's murder could not identify the murderer. Lowendowski and Malgrave were each put in two separate line-ups, giving Tricia the witness a second chance to identify either of them. To quote Theo, sugar plums does not see the mad wolf killer in any of the line-ups. Then having been given multiple books of mugshots, Tricia also did not identify anyone as the murderer of the district attorney. She was consistent and resolute that nobody she had been shown during the process was the murderer, or the killer, she witnessed. She was consistent and resolute in providing inconclusively uncertain results.

It was this development which brought Valens-Scantling, whom with Detective Maxson were orchestrating the line-ups and book viewings, to the lieutenant with bad news. Reaching an impasse, the detective brought this bad news to the lieutenant with considerable frustration. After a few seconds of contemplation, Lt. Knighton decided to allow Theo and Mark to go home and gave the job of working with the witness to Emily. Detective Valens-Scantling was delighted with that decision. Detectives Murkendale and Coles, who referred to Emily as the discovery queen, were not at all surprised by this decision. They both simultaneously announced that this was a job for the discovery queen. Detective Oftenmarch simply accepted the decision, figuring she was going to have to work a late night anyway.

With her new assignment, Detective Oftenmarch quickly got to work. While Lt. Knighton and Detective Murkendale re-interviewed Kajay Malgrave, Emily began collecting materials to create a new book of headshots. Having performed this improv task several times in the past, she had a stash of supplies squirrelled away. Using her hidden talent for arts and crafts, Detective Oftenmarch rapidly cobbled together a piece-meal book of headshots relevant to this specific case. She jury-rigged together the book by collecting from multiple sources. She used head-shots from the Cathedral Police Department's annual yearbook, a game program for the New Carnelian Knights, a program from a Chatham Hills playhouse production, a preview for a local cooking competition, a flyer filled with volunteers for a non-profit fund raising organization, an old outdated realty advert with a pair of realtors, a pamphlet with photos of Blueline Product Corporation's board of directors, and leftover cam-paign leaflets from last spring's Cathedral primary elections. Emily com-bined those photos with several existing mugshots from the Cathedral Police Department's arrest records to create the eclectic booklet. The quick creation made for an odd variety of photographs, but did the job of camouflaging potential suspects among people innocent of killing the district attorney. It was heartbreaking for Emily to be adding pictures of members of the Cathedral law enforcement as viable suspects to her makeshift booklet.

With her expedited and improvised book of headshots completed in record time, Detective Oftenmarch rushed over to the section of the floor which held the interview and meeting rooms. A new surprise greeted her when Emily reached those rooms. Outside of each of the meeting and interview rooms was a pair of robosentries. Each room's door was flanked with a robosentry on either side of it. Standing guard, the robosentries were stationed outside each room to disguise which meeting and interview room the very important witness was occupying. Each sleek robosentry had its flashing lights and scanners on full acti-vation, making for an impressive display in the 271st police precinct's corridor. With CSPs posted outside the precinct and robosentries placed at each entrance to the meeting and interview rooms, the Cathedral PD was making an all out effort to protect Tricia.

Having been informed by Detective Vallens-Scantling which room number housed the waiting witness, Emily knew which protected pas-sage to pick. She allowed the robosentries to scan her badge; then the robots in return allowed her to enter the room. Upon entering the room, Emily was greeted with another surprise. The homicide detective expected to see Jeremiah and Officer Binbevvins but she did not expect to see a new pair of federal marshals. Each federal marshal sat in a chair in separate corners of the room with their federal badged credentials prominently displayed and showing serious expressions on their faces.

Jeremiah was standing near the door where he assumed a guard position. Officer Binbevvins was sitting slouched back in a chair against the wall looking morose. He did not appear to be in a guardian position. Tricia sat at the oval wooden table in the center of the meeting and interview room. The young lady had traded her red Cathedral State University sweatshirt for a low-cut white tank top with an unbuttoned white crosswoven sweater as a covering. She still had on the necklace of three cell phones and was currently typing on one of the bedazzled phones. Tricia had pulled her hair back and into a neat ponytail. She was barefoot again and the young witness looked tired and upset. Although for someone who had just been the target of a lycan masquerade attack, Tricia also did appear well groomed and composed.

At first the young lady took no notice of the entering detective as all of her interest remained on her shiny phone. That blissful phone was all that mattered to her as the bedazzled device held her undivided attention. However, when Emily spoke, Tricia's head popped up and away from her sparkly phone and her focus immediately locked onto Emily.

"Hello again, Tricia. Allow me to introduce myself again. I am Detective Emily Oftenmarch. This night has brought us together again. This time under a much less stressful situation." Emily greeted.

"It's you. You're that supermodel cop who charged that terrible werewolf like a comic book superhero. That was mega crazy." Tricia expressed.

"The members of the Cathedral Police Department do the best they can to serve and protect the public. Sometimes we are mega crazy." Emily replied as she sat down next to Tricia at the oval wooden table.

"You're too pretty to be a cop. If I hadn't seen you fight those horrible werewolves, I would have totally thought you were an actress pretending to be a cop." Tricia told Emily.

"I'll take that as a compliment. Thank you. Unfortunately, I am not too pretty to work overtime and, unfortunately, beauty is not what brings us together here tonight. You and I have a task to complete; you and I have a murderer to identify. To accomplish this task, I have put together a book of pictures. We would like you to look through this book and tell us if you recognize the district attorney's murderer amidst these pictures." Emily explained. The detective slid the homemade booklet across the table.

"Not this again. I am now sorry I ever got involved with the important lawyer politician. At first, it was fun to get paid to dress up and go to fancy parties. Then the gifts he would give me made it even better. I was getting paid, getting nice gifts, and getting special attention. Triple score. Then he was killed on that terrible night by that psycho creep and everything has been totally awful for me ever since. Death threats, chased by werewolves, can't go out dancing, been told by the police to hide in nasty hotel rooms with lousy room service and smelly policemen, and I am not allowed to update my star-video accounts. It's been a complete nightmare. Now, I can't even get a good night's sleep. This completely stinks." Tricia complained at length.

"Let's try to identify the murderer. Then the Cathedral Police Department can arrest him and get you back to your happy life. Let's work on making this a forgotten memory for you. Let's put the bad guy in jail and put this behind us." Emily encouraged.

"So this is like the mobile comp app Pick a punk, only I pick the killer instead." Tricia looked for clarification.

"I am not familiar with that app but that sounds about right. You look through the book of pictures until you see the person who killed the district attorney, then you pick them." Emily reinforced.

Tricia reluctantly took the makeshift booklet from the oval wooden table with a heavy sigh. "Would it be possible to get an energy smoothie or a sweet sugar slushie?" Tricia requested.

Oftenmarch and Binbevvins exchanged looks. "Protective services won't pay for anything like that. This is your home base, detective, so it would be your treat." Binbevvins deflected the request.

"I know the 271st precinct doesn't stock those types of beverages. We only have coffee, synthetic coffee, and iced tea in the break room. I am going to have to figure out where to get that type of beverage." Emily admitted.

"We've got this. This can be Uncle Sam's treat. I know a reliable delivery service and a nearby place that makes great super smoothies.", the federal marshal in the right corner seat offered, pulling out their deluxe complink. "What flavor do you want?".

"Strawberry, double sugarberry, dreamfruit delight with a cherry." Tricia quickly answered with excitement.

"The usual for me, please." replied the federal marshal seated in the left corner of the room.

"Can we all get in on this refreshment opportunity?" Binbevvins asked.

"Sure. Drinks for everyone in the room." the federal agent graciously returned.

"If they have anything with chocolate then put me down for that." Binbevvins accepted without hesitation.

"None for me, thank you." Jeremiah declined.

"How about you, pretty detective?" the federal marshal asked as they were typing and taping on their deluxe complink.

"Do they sell any drinks that make a bad day go away?" Emily hoped.

"Sadly, they do not." the first federal marshal replied.

"You would need the state liquor store for that beverage, detective." the other federal marshal added.

"Get her the same as me." Tricia responded while looking through the booklet with renewed enthusiasm at the prospect of a nice beverage forthcoming.

"Please and thank you. This is very kind of you." Emily thanked then added, "And Uncle Sam."

"If I could find a cute guy and go to a mag party or a rad club after this, then this night would go from sad and tragic to ultra dreamy" Tricia commented.

"I hear you there, Tricia. My cute guy is probably heading to bed and our mag party ended hours ago." Emily sadly shared.

"I'm a cute guy and we can have a party right here." Binbevvins exclaimed.

"Sorry, no you are not and no we cannot. Lame." Tricia countered as she flipped a page in the booklet. One of the federal marshals chuckled and Jeremiah let out a laugh.

"My mag party and rad clubbing days are behind me, far behind me." the federal marshal not on the complink shared.

"I would settle for a cold beer and a good ballgame with no phone calls." the federal marshal on the complink shared.

"Hate to be a buzzkill, but there will be no parties in our future until a murderer is identified and captured." Binbevvins dampened the mood as he shifted his chair away from the office wall and closer to the center table.

"I wish I could hide in the dark until this whole nightmare was done." Tricia glumly wished as she looked at the booklet.

"We are better off in the light. As JESUS said in John 12: 46 *I have come into the world as a light, so that no one who believes in ME should stay in darkness.* It's the murderer who wants to hide in the dark. We want to shine a light on them and expose them. We need to remember John 1: 4-5 *In HIM was life, and that life was the light of all mankind. The light shines in the darkness, and the darkness has not overcome it.*" Emily shared.

"Is this a good time to talk about GOD?" Binbevvins inquired skeptically.

"Any time is a good time to talk about GOD." Emily emphasized. One of the federal marshals chuckled and Jeremiah concurred with an Amen.

"There are maniacs trying to hurt this young woman and we don't even know the killer's identity to the murder she witnessed. Several Cathedral PD officers have already been seriously hurt. We are in a precarious situation; we are in need of answers and action. It is a time of desperation." Binbevvins reminded.

"This would be the best time to talk about GOD. In troubled times, we have a loving FATHER in heaven who will help us. As it says in Hebrews 4: 16, *Let us then approach God's throne of grace with confidence, so that we may receive mercy and find grace to help us in our time of need.*" Emily replied.

"This is certainly a time of need." the US marshal not ordering drinks suggested.

"Why would we be seeking mercy and grace?" Binbevvins questioned.

"In Romans 3:23 it states, *for all have sinned and fall short of the glory of God.* There is a massive gap between sinful people and the HOLY

LORD. A big gap we cannot cross or fill to get to heaven. You are far removed from GOD and could never get to heaven on your own. You cannot earn it; you cannot discern it. You cannot achieve it; you cannot conceive it. You cannot cross the vast chasm of death, despair, and destruction between yourself and heaven." Emily explained.

"Mega bummer." Tricia commented as she turned another page in the makeshift photo booklet.

"So it is not possible to get to heaven then." Binbevvins surmised.

"With GOD all things are possible. Luke 1:37 says, *For nothing is impossible with GOD.* JESUS said in Mark 19:26, *With man this is impossible, but with GOD all things are possible.* We need JESUS to get to heaven. According to Romans 6:23, *For the wages of sin is death, but the gift of God is eternal life in Christ Jesus our Lord.* JESUS paid for our sins, HE supplied us with our only path to heaven and GOD. JESUS died in our place. He made a way between the HOLY and the unworthy, gave us hope where there was none, and bridged the uncrossable. JESUS's death on the cross crossed the vast chasm of death, doom, and destruction between ourselves and GOD." Emily expounded.

"A true gift indeed." Jeremiah commented as he stood sentry by the door.

"I like shiny gifts." Tricia shared as she turned another page in the booklet.

"The wonderful thing about gifts is that they are free. A gift is given without payment. JESUS paid the heavy cost for our sins. We did nothing and can do nothing to deserve this awesome gift. This wonderous gift of eternal life in paradise. We have been cleansed and renewed or made shiny thanks to the love of GOD. As it is written in Titus 3:4-5, *But when the kindness and love of GOD our SAVIOR appeared, he saved us, not because of righteous things we had done, but because of HIS mercy. HE saved us through the washing of rebirth and renewal by the HOLY SPIRIT.*" Emily gladly revealed.

"So how do you receive this awesome gift?" Binbevvins inquired with skepticism.

"That would certainly be worth knowing." an US marshal agreed.

"In says in Romans 10:9-10, *If you declare with your mouth, 'Jesus is Lord,' and believe in your heart that God raised him from the dead, you will be saved. For it is with your heart that you believe and are justified, and it is with your mouth that you profess your faith and are saved.* Therefore, trust in the LORD. Trust that JESUS is who HE said HE is, trust what JESUS has done for you. Speak it, believe it, and live it. Trust JESUS when he says HE is the way to heaven. As it is written in John 14:6, *Jesus answered, "I am the way and the truth and the life. No one comes to the Father except through me."* Emily told the truth.

Tricia turned another page of the makeshift book of headshots. "Sounds great to me." she admitted mildly.

"You say GOD loves us but horrible events happen every day. People are suffering, people are dying, and people are in misery. Where is GOD's love for those people? The world lives in fear and uncertainty, where is the love of GOD for the world. Where is the love for a world so badly in need of it?" Binbevvins debated.

"There are many people who feel this way. GOD has always loved us, HE loved us first, and HE always will. Romans 5:8 declares: *But God demonstrates his own love for us in this: While we were still sinners, Christ died for us.* GOD loves us so much HE allowed HIS only SON to be cruelly beaten and brutally crucified so that we could be saved. Displaying great love for us, GOD endured great anguish and agony watching HIS SON be killed to pay for our sins. GOD continues to love us and will be faithful for all eternity. GOD said in Jeremiah 31:3, *'I have loved you with an everlasting love'.* HE loves us in both word and deed. It reads in Mark 10:45, *For even the SON of MAN did not come to be served, but to serve, and to give HIS life as a ransom for many.* CHRIST painfully suffocated so that we may freely breathe. Through HIS agony we are saved. From HIS service we are blessed. Because of HIS love we have hope." Emily responded.

The room became very quieted. There was a hushed silence in the room for a while. The silence was broken by Tricia who abruptly erupted in elation.

"This is him. This is so him." Tricia exclaimed while enthusiastically pointing to a photo in the improvised booklet.

Containing her eager anticipation, Emily calmly observed the photo Tricia was excitedly indicating with a pair of pointing fingers. "Not to be annoying but are you absolutely positive, Tricia. Please have a closer second look." Emily sought verification.

"Hundo P, this is the killer." Tricia confidently confirmed.

As Binbevvins looked at the selected photo he let out a chuckle. "Unbelievable." he said in disgust.

"Does that mean one hundred percent?" one of the agents asked in confusion.

"There is a man two pages back who could look similar. Are you positive it is this man and not that man?" Emily re-inquired while turning pages in the booklet and then pointed to two pictures.

"Not that man, he looks old and creepy. Where this guy has that I want to be loved look. I remember thinking he was too good looking to be a killer. But he is the killer." Tricia re-identified the same man.

"Explain the want to be loved look." Binbevvins requested with a sly smile.

"Never mind that. Since you are confident with this identification, then I am satisfied. Please sign your name under his photo and the Cathedral PD will move forward with this case. Thank you very much for your assistance, Tricia. This is extremely helpful. You have earned both your drink and my drink." Emily gratefully thanked Tricia.

One of the US marshals came over to have a peek at the identified photograph. "So much trouble over one misguided man." the marshal commented.

As Tricia signed, Emily turned to Jeremiah. "Jeremiah, could you help keep watch over Tricia until tomorrow morning please? We could use your help a little while longer." she requested of the bodyguard.

"I can assist until noon tomorrow, then I have another job to get to." Jeremiah told her.

"Thank you for all your help, Jeremiah. You have come to our aid in a great time of need and I am truly grateful for all you have done." Emily thanked the bodyguard as Tricia finished signing the booklet where the detective had indicated.

"I was glad to help and I hope to meet you again, Emily. Only next time under better circumstances." the bodyguard replied.

"Does this mean this suckfest is over? Will I get my life back?" Tricia wondered now finished signing.

Once Tricia had signed the booklet, Emily collected it. "We are one step closer to getting this resolved. Thank you for your bravery, Tricia." Emily replied. With that said, the detective sprang from her seat and rushed out of the room.

Detective Oftenmarch hustled back to her desk and began working on her primary work computer. She attempted to start up the program KIMMIE and then begin a database search on the identified suspect. However, KIMMIE was not available because it was mid-update, at 43 percent, for a software upgrade. So Emily just let the update run and moved on without the program KIMMIE. As a couple of database searches were running, the detective changed her strategy to researching the suspect's technological footprint.

Having a Cathedral law enforcement member identified as the murderer by Tricia, Emily jumped onto an internal program on her workstation computer and scrambled to track that individual's technological footprint for the night of the district attorney's murder. Items like coplinks or police issued complinks, badge trackers, department wireless communicators, work issued laptops. and droid assistants like the mud tusslers' MADAD leave tracking information or digital trails on the Cathedral Police database in case a member of the CPD goes missing or is kidnapped.

The identified person's technological footprint could be used to eliminate or incriminate the suspect. After some research, Emily discovered the information incriminated the suspect and supported the accusation of murder. One of the person's departmental electronic devices was left running at the time and its tracked location put them in the vicinity of the murder at the right time frame. The detective entered this information into CaseBuilder and the program gave the accusation a favorable percentage.

Then Emily switched her attention back to the database searches. She was able to determine that the suspect was in town at the time of the murder. There were no online reports of disputes or conflicts between the district attorney and the suspect. There were a couple of articles regarding their views on private law enforcement companies, which were in opposition but nothing contentious. A pair of Cathedral precinct department captains had made accusations against the suspect for allegedly selling police work to Lawtech and manipulating departmental numbers. The district attorney's office was looking into those accusations, but there was no record of any impending charges against the suspect. The identified killer's motif, as Emily currently could assess it, was thin but there was enough here to get Eddie involved. It was time to update the lieutenant. Emily rapidly rose from her desk chair and went on the hunt for Lt. Knighton.

Emily scanned the homicide division as she moved. Eddie was not at his desk. In fact, Detective Cole was the only one currently working at his desk in the department. He looked so tired that he looked half asleep as he was slowly typing on his computer. Detective Oftenmarch hustled in his direction.

"Darius, where is the lieutenant?" she asked him.

"Still interviewing Captain Lunatic of the Mockery of Justice League." Detective Cole responded.

With that answer, Emily darted in the direction of interrogation. Full of renewed inspiration, she hurried down the corridor of interview rooms until she found the one in use by the lieutenant. After knocking with a rhythmic beat, Emily opened the interview room's door. Upon opening the door, she saw Lt. Knighton and Detective Murkendale re-interrogating Kajay Malgrave. The suspect was in the middle of a holier than thou speech when she interrupted.

"Need a quick word, lieutenant." Emily interjected.

Eddie slowly and quietly rose from his seat and walked over to her, leaving Murkendale to continue the interrogation. Emily patiently waited just outside the doorway for him. When the lieutenant exited closing the door behind him, Detective Oftenmarch shared the new discovery with him. She told Eddie the name of the person that Tricia Kawowski had identified. With little reaction, the lieutenant took the news in stride.

"Good work. Go home, Emily" Eddie commanded. Then he re-entered interrogation.

Along a dark and dreary road, the trip home was an ordeal after a long tough day of police work. Emily drove wearily with only satellite pluswave radio to keep her company. The detective listened to some sports talk chatter as she made the 25-minute drive on the too familiar streets homeward. Dull and lonely, the road stretched on in monotonous repetition.

The sportscaster was saying somewhere in this happy nation, people's spirits are bright. Joyful music plays somewhere and there are cries of delight. And somewhere fans do cheer as they merrily sing and shout. But there is no joy in Cathedral, mighty Jaye has struck out. Cathedral's power hitter Geronimo Jaye went down on strikes and the Grey Sox beat the Bishops in ten innings. That somewhere was Emily's car as she let out a hurrah for her favorite baseball team. It helped keep her awake.

The waning moon had a bright radiant reflection with wispy clouds rapidly rolling past it. The dreary rain clouds had gone but the earlier heavy rainfall had left the roads wet and slippery. A news update was playing on the radio which reminded her that this Tuesday was the start of St. Crossborns Week, celebrating the Catholic church's revival in Cathedral from years prior. David-John would have planned church events for the rest of this week, plans for which Emily was in no way prepared.

Spending so much of her time dedicated to police work, holidays and church events would sneak up quickly on Emily. One day she felt like there was plenty of time to prepare for an event and before she knew it there was little or no time to prepare for that event. And then there were times, like today, where she would miss an event entirely. Sometimes, this trend would depress Emily and add to her weariness.

Emily was so tired she was beyond tired. She was too exhausted to sleep. Her brain kept replaying the events of the day and she could not shut them off. Case facts also kept repeating in her thoughts as she mentally reviewed them without wanting to do so. Sleepiness and mental fatigue were competing to overtake her. It had been a difficult day.

Her left arm was sore again, her left shoulder continually ached. She felt some stiffness in her right knee. She also felt some slight pain in her right wrist. Emily's mouth had stopped bleeding but she had a fat lip. The collar of her borrowed shirt was stained with blood. Along with exhaustion, fatigue had set in throughout her body. The young detective was physically worn and torn. It had been a difficult day.

Emily had a throbbing headache. Long work hours, too much computer file work, being struck by a wannabe werewolf in the head, and banging her head against the floor after falling all contributed to Emily's aching cranium. Bouts of dizziness would come and go, each one a little shorter than the last. Emily now mostly felt woozy but she chalked that up to a lack of food and rest. It had been a difficult day.

To recap, Emily felt awful. She was too tired to even feel tired. She was overtired, far too tired to sleep. Full of aches and pains, her body was slow to respond to the smallest of movements. Her head throbbed persistently and everything felt like it was moving in slow motion. On top of all that, Emily had missed her husband's lecture entirely by many hours. It had been a horrible day.

It was well after midnight by the time Emily arrived home. The Chatham Hills house was calm, peaceful, and quiet. Her home was a sight of great relief. David-John had left some lights running for her so it was also well lit. The house was an inviting sanctuary after a most difficult day. It was a blessing to have wonderful home to return to after tough times. With solace, Emily pulled into the garage and headed into the house. She was more than ready for some recuperation.

After pulling her boots off her aching feet, Oftenmarch headed for the kitchen. Emily enjoyed a bowl of fresh fruit when she first got there. The fruit was followed by some cold leftover broccoli. Then she took a moment to drink some chilled water as she attempted to unwind. Stopping herself from falling asleep in the kitchen, Emily went to the laundry room and put two loads of laundry into the combo autowasher and dryer. Then she headed slowly upstairs and took a long warm shower. Emily savored every minute of the refreshing water of her prolonged shower as she tried to wash the day away. Both therapeutic and relaxing, the shower made her feel almost human again. After her long shower, the detective rubbed some ointment on her aches and pains. She started with the thicker more medicinal ointments then moved to the softer more fragrant creams. Then Emily brushed her teeth twice, absent mindedly repeating the task.

Moving to a spare bedroom trying to not disturb her husband at this late hour, Emily ran a blow dryer stand on her hair while she packed a pair of bags of spare clothing. Emily began reminiscing about her police career. When she was a rookie officer, she was so enthusiastic to help people. She was determined to make the city of Cathedral a better place to live. Her first year as detective, Emily was eager to learn and wanted to help people get answers and closure. She had remembered all the names of the victims on the cases she worked for the first 14 months in homicide. Then the job changed for her. It became a daily battle to catch violent killers and crazy misguided psychopaths. She used to come home at a reasonable hour in a good mood. Now Emily was capturing murderers and conspirators dressed up like werewolves who turned out to be law enforcement members. Furthermore, she was coming home after midnight. She was going to be glad to close the lycan masquerade killers case and ecstatic to put the whole troubling investigation behind her.

As the dryer distributed soothing warm air in her direction, Emily began to feel extremely tired. She was getting extremely drowsy as the warmth of the calming dryer air felt wonderful. Sleepiness and weariness were gaining on her faster that Emily's hair was drying. Abandoning her attempt to dry her hair, Emily switched off the dryer and quietly made her way to the master bedroom.

Emily went to bed, kissed her sleeping husband, and snuggled under the covers with her thoughts in turmoil. It was warm and inviting under the covers, even with her thoughts in turmoil.

Have a man stuck in my head. And everything he had said

The man lives inside my mind. Though his words are very kind.

Thoughts are spinning round and round. When no sanity is found.

No one is crazy like me, no one is crazy like me.

I was married to a man, who always had half a plan.

His voice inside my head, makes it tough to go to bed.

Thoughts are spinning round and round. There's no sanity rebound.

No one is crazy like me, no one is crazy like me.

I'm ready to forget, All the things that I regret

I take my shame to the LORD, sins only GOD can afford

Thoughts are focused on HIS grace, Now all sanity in place

GOD is much greater than me, GOD is much greater than me

Hallelujah in the night. Mighty GOD has won the fight.

HIS great love is wide and deep. In GOD I will find my sleep.

Thoughts of heaven cancel fears, and the crazy disappears

GOD is much greater than me, GOD is much greater than me

With these competing thoughts, both refreshing and troubling blended together, Emily began praying. As she prayed, Emily cuddled closer to David-John. As she nuzzled closer to her husband, Emily could hear his heartbeat. Next she listened to her own heartbeat and their heartbeats were in rhythm. The bed was warm and inviting but her comingled thoughts kept her awake. To change her mindset, she put her attention solely on praying. Emily continued to focus on praying and fell asleep in the middle of her bedtime prayers.

As the moonlight shone down on a hillside of pale white flowers, a dark haze drifted across the terrain intertwining with the hillside vegetation. A shadowy figure emerged from the darkness to be illuminated in the moonlight. With a cruel scowl and a menacing growl, the malus lunas roams the night with an appetite for avarice and agony. This fearsome creature is on the prowl with that appetite which cannot be quenched. Stalking the hillside with a malicious stare, the malus lunas hunts for easy prey in the dreary night. In wickedly intense determination, the beast seeks to feast.

Crossing the rolling hills of moonlit flowers, the massive brute passes through a field of fallen figures. With every step the malus lunas takes, more deceased creatures are revealed on the trodden ground. Slain werewolves, goblins, people, imps, and vampires are scattered across the heavily blood-soaked terrain. A sad sight of savage carnage, the reminisce of a recent battlefield of hostilities now dominates the night landscape. A lingering light on lost lives, the moonlight on the battlefield brings a chilly atmosphere to the night. Still motivated by hunger, the malus lunas moves away in search of fresher fodder for feasting.

As the malus lunas vanishes into the night, a clash of swords grows louder in the distance. The sounds of battle intensify as the pace of the fight escalates. A pair of armored knights come into sight on the hills of bright white flowers and blood red corpses. One knight carries a broad shield with the crest of a crowned lycan. The other knight carries a broad shield with the crest of a vampirical bat. Hordes of werewolves fight beside the lycan knight while swarms of vampires fight beside the undead knight. When one shieldbearer would strike with might, their army would surge forth. When the other shieldbearer would strike back in kind, their forces would rally with vigor. The moon grew bigger and the light off the moon got brighter.

The two armies of wicked intents were in a no effort spared, no mercy given combat of might and will. Each side had their fangs of fury tearing into their evil opposition. Wrestling and wrangling, the cruel combatants kept the relentless bloodbath raging in the blackened night. These two sides of opposing forces battled fiercely fueled by an obvious hatred of each other. Their scrum of hatred consumed the hillside as they fought tooth, claw, and battle sickle. They fought with desire; they fought with fear. Neither side wanting to yield; neither side wanting to fail. The moon grew bigger and the light off the moon got brighter.

From the forces of the undead came forth an elder vampire with wings of lightning. From the forces of the werewolves came forth the alpha lycan with a roar of thunder. Both juggernauts moved to the front of the warring armies to come face to face with each other. Neither of them spoke a word of worldly known language but both made foul guttural noises of an unspeakable and nasty tongue. Whatever they said to each other, it was not friendly because they began to fight. Hostilities ensued between the two horrid powerhouses; hostilities with intentions to inflict demonstrative damage.

The elder vampire struck swiftly with elongated claws that scraped across the alpha wolf's broad chest. In quick response, the alpha wolf sank its sharp claws viciously into the elder vampire's left shoulder. Striking back, the elder vampire landed a hard blow to the side of the alpha wolf's head. In a counterstrike, the alpha wolf hammered a fist into the face of the elder vampire. In rapid succession, the pair of combatants traded another pair of punishing punches in an attempt to pummel their angered adversary. With a mighty backhand, the elder vampire thumped the alpha wolf's abdomen. With a forceful uppercut, the alpha wolf slammed the elder vampire's ribs. Neither foe wanted to yield; neither nemesis wanted to fail.

Their exchanging of blows switched to a close quarters grappling encounter as the pair of powerhouses began to wrestle one another. As the two combatants tussled, a third wrestler suddenly joined the fray. It was an impish creature who was hindering both wrestlers. The trio of terrifying tusslers struggled and strained to outwrestle one another. The wrestlers were a jumble of intertwining limbs and a fury of force. It was difficult to discern which wrestler was winning or who was wrestling who as the trio was one enwrapped entanglement. They were a scramble of tugging and pulling for dominate position.

The impish creature exited the wrestling pile and began dancing. It started doing the old Arden three-step in a circle around the wrestling elder vampire and alpha werewolf. The harder the pair of enemies wrestled, the faster the impish creature danced. As the impish creature danced around the wrestling juggernauts, the hillside shifted into a city landscape. All the fighting and dancing was now being done in the middle of a major metropolis which looked like Cathedral. Midscrapers of Cathedral surrounded the fervent wrestlers and jolly dancer. The fight for dominance raged onward in the middle of the city.

Both prominent villains began causing damage to the city as they fought for superiority. They both were suddenly the size of giant monsters. The elder vampire shoved the alpha wolf into a towering midscraper. The werewolf smashed violently into the building, causing it to toppled. The alpha wolf retaliated by knocking the vampire backwards into another statuesque midscraper. As the vampire crashed forcefully into the structure, the building sustained heavy damage, causing it to crumble to the ground. The wolf slammed a fist into the vampire's abdomen. In retaliation for the gut punch, the vampire punched the wolf squarely in the face. After taking a fist to the snout, the wolf howled in rage. Continuing their rage filled clash, the combatants caused more destruction. In the spiteful skirmish, three more buildings were reduced to rubble. Their tussle was destroying the city of Cathedral. The more the pair of juggernauts fought, the worse things became for the city around them. As the vampire and werewolf destroyed the city in their cruel clash, the dancing impish creature laughed wickedly with devilish delight.

Faster and faster the pair of rivals fought, causing more and more destruction to the mega city. More and more the hostile juggernauts battled, causing the damage to the grand city to come greater and greater. The wicked fight was massively wrecking Cathedral. It was the city that was paying for this gruesome feud. In the middle of the struggle, a bright light shone down from the sky and a thunderous sound could be heard.

"How can you fight when you're family!" a strong voice spoke boomingly.

Emily woke up abruptly, she was muddled and confused for a moment, but then realized it was all a strange dream. She sifted through the strangeness to realize the warning. The villainous criminals were fighting amongst themselves and the city of Cathedral was suffering as a result. Still groggy, Emily heard her work complink chime. Emily endeavored to shake herself from dreaminess and focused back on reality. After a moment of waking up, she looked at the beckoning electronic device. It was a message from the lieutenant and it was time to return to work. Only getting nearly three hours of sleep, it was cruel to be time to work again.

Chapter 22

The Best Arrest for Last

Reversing her drive from earlier that morning, Detective Oftenmarch drove back into work through first light rain and then heavy traffic. She made the commute back to work way earlier than she had either planned or expected. Half asleep, Emily drove to work mostly on fumes and instinct. It was only Tuesday but it felt much later in the work week to her. Such was the life of a Cathedral homicide detective sometimes.

Somehow, the detective was able to arrive at her home police precinct just before her normal day shift was to commence. First to arrive, Emily entered an absolutely silent office and atmosphere. In the wee hours of the morning, the 271st homicide department had been bustling with activity. Now, with minutes to go before the normal work day started, the area was a ghost town. Emily was the only member of the homicide division present in the eerily quiet department. Wearily taking a seat at her desk, the detective observed that the lieutenant had put paperwork on her desk to review.

Lt. Knighton had put some statistics regarding private law enforcement usage on Emily's desk. The percentage of cases turned over to private law enforcement companies by the Cathedral police department was staggering. Nearly 48 percent of all CPD cases were outsourced. The percentage of jobs in which private law enforcement companies assigned robots or robotic assistance, particularly ones made by Lawtech, was also staggering. Most incredible was the estimated amount of money that the Cathedral police department had spent on private law enforcement over the past year. This practice of hiring private law enforcement companies with robotic technology had become so prevalent that, among most Cathedral press members, the phrase to farm out work had changed to be to robot out work. The duty of serving and protecting the citizens of Cathedral was not so slowly going to the droids. People were no longer helping people. The Cathedral Police Department used so many private law enforcement organizations with robotics and used them so often that this new term to robot out the work had become popular when the media reported on the department.

The next note Eddie had left on Emily's desk was regarding new revelations from after midnight interrogations at the 271st precinct. Both Zack Ryerson and Kajay Malgrave had claimed to be at the district attorney's suite the night of the man's murder. Now that Tricia had identified the district attorney's murderer, both men were confessing to be present at the time of the murder. Now that the murdered had been revealed, both men were willing to inform on their fellow intruder in order to save themselves from longer prison sentences. With the secret exposed, the villains were getting in line to betray the murderer in order to help themselves avoid harsher punishments.

And then there was the lieutenant's final note and it was potentially the best news to receive in this sorted investigation. Murkendale and Knighton had discovered in a post midnight interview that the murderer had allegedly given the murder weapon to Zack Ryerson for disposal. Instead of getting rid of the incriminating evidence, Zack Ryerson kept the weapon as an insurance policy. According to Zack Ryerson, the murderer wanted him eliminated, thinking the weapon had been destroyed. The logic was to make the destroyer disappear or dead men tell no tales. Being the murderer's latest target is the reason Zack claimed to pretend to be his own brother. Zeke Ryerson would only be the victim of a werewolf scare, Zack Ryerson would be the victim of a brutal homicide. Eddie had dispatched Detectives Beuhalaurr and Joppers to retrieve the hidden weapon and take it to the House of Higher Learning for analysis.

With that piece of encouraging news, Emily booted up her desk computer and loaded CaseBuilder. As the CaseBuilder loaded, the detective was seriously considering a cup of coffee. Somebody in the squad would have usually had a pot of coffee going at this hour. But since Emily was alone this morning, there had been no coffee brewing yet. CaseBuilder came ready before Emily decided on coffee so she opted to start updating cases in the system instead.

As Emily worked in CaseBuilder at her computer, she was interrupted by Captain Bronzesmith who had quietly crept into the bullpen. With incredible stealth, he had moved next to her desk. The captain was watching the detective closely when he spoke. Emily noticed him intently observing what she was working on just before he spoke. It took restraint on her part to suppress the fact that she had been startled. Normally, the detective would notice somebody approaching but the captain had passed undetected this morning.

"Is Lt. Knighton overclocking cases again? This department is not prepared to start the work day. We have to manage our workloads tighter and more efficiently." Captain Bronzesmith expressed.

"We are working as best we can to solves cases, Captain." Emily replied.

"It is not a concern over how hard everyone is working; it is a concern over how wisely everyone is working." Bronzesmith indicated.

"We are working as intelligently as we can to solve cases, Captain." Emily corrected herself. She was starting to crave strong coffee again.

"Next topic to discuss is that Lt. Knighton and yourself have won the Hawthorne award for this month. Congratulations on that achievement. I would like to remind you that this award is being sunsetted at the end of the year. There is currently a major paradigm shift in the process of policework for the Cathedral Police Department. The metrics used to award the Hawthorne award will be antiquated." Bronzesmith congratulated and reminded. The Hawthorne award took into account factors like hours worked, arrests made, cases update in CaseBuilder, and confrontations won.

"Thank you, Captain. The work of a detective stays the same, sir." Emily thanked.

"What cases are Lt. Knighton and you currently working?" Bronzesmith inquired.

"The murder of the district attorney." Oftenmarch answered.

"That's another case outside our jurisdiction. Emily, you are going to have to decide if your loyalty is with Lt. Knighton or the 271st precinct. Since Friday, the pair of you have worked in Granthum, investigated a murder in the western border of Cathedral in another precinct, went back to working the murders in New Terranceville after I asked you not to do that, investigated a company break-in for midtown Cathedral, closed a burglary case for the 269th precinct, closed a homicide case for the 275th precinct, and were involved in a war zone in the Flockman and Bellweather building in the Grand Cathedral district last night." Bronzesmith stated with annoyance.

It took a moment for Emily to realize the two closed cases were the ones they received from private detective Mercury Bryphos. "When you state it like that, Captain, the list sounds really bad. But all that work, except for Granthum, was tied to the High Commissioner's request. Eddie and I are trying to solve a problem for High Commissioner Harden and the Cathedral Police department. We are trying to stop the lycan masquerade killers. But that doesn't mean we are disloyal to this precinct." Emily defended.

"I have received no notification from the High Commissioner's office. Chief Thigby is away from his desk this morning and not available to confirm this request. Anything with such a high priority should have gone through me first. As far as I am aware, the werewolf dressed killers are not the 271st precinct's concern." Bronzesmith protested.

"The urgency of the assignment given to us may have delayed the notice to you. The check is in the mail so to speak. Maybe, the High Commissioner's office assumed the lieutenant reporting this information to you would suffice as being informed. Or maybe things have just been so chaotic that proper channels were an oversight. I can only speculate as to why you weren't told." Emily tried to solve police bureaucracy.

"Stop working on the district attorney's murder and start working on 271st precinct cases. That's an order, detective." Bronzesmith dictated.

"Belay that order, we have important work that takes priority. We need to give the FBI our full cooperation in this matter." Chief Thigby declared loudly as he entered the homicide department. The 271st precinct chief was accompanied by Lt. Knighton and three FBI agents, one of which was escorting an arrested Anton Chinchinnocippi. Lt. Knighton looked like he had not slept all night and he was still wearing the same outfit. Anton Chinchinnocippi appeared worse, looking defeated and deflated, totally the opposite of how he had appeared the night before at the poker game.

"It's the FBI's show now." Eddie announced.

"We prefer to be just considered the feature act of show. Although we may be a prominent player, there is plenty of crime for everyone to get in on the act." one of the FBI agents responded.

"Sorry, I could not communicate with you sooner, Archibald. Events started unfolding very quickly this morning and I never had a chance to update you. Lt. Knighton and I have been working ferociously this morning as the secrets of this criminal plot unraveled. The FBI reached out to the Cathedral PD very early this morning and things have been hectic since then, so I did not get a chance to get you in the loop." Chief Thigby informed the captain.

"It seems I owe you an apology, Detective Oftenmarch. I am sorry I spoke too soon with my criticism. Sorry." the captain apologized.

"I understand, Captain. Apology accepted." Emily graciously received.

"Communication within the Cathedral PD could have been better all around on this one. This whole sad situation needed less cloak and more dagger. Both the crimes and investigations regarding this situation have not been the best of looks for the Cathedral PD." the chief gave his opinion.

"I have seen worse. The Cathedral Police Department is at least trying to stop the shenanigans within its own ranks." the other FBI agent shared.

"I reviewed your copcam video from last night, Detective Oftenmarch, and I have never seen anything like it in all my years in the police force. In over 35 years of working as a cop filled with unusual experiences, I still have never seen anything remotely like what I saw on that video. It was like watching a scene from an action horror show, not police footage. The whole thing was unbelievable." Chief Thigby expressed with emphasis.

"I watched the lieutenant's copcam video and your copcam video from last night's events three times each and still can't believe what I saw." one of the FBI agents admitted.

The second FBI agent pointed at Emily's Granthum Grey Sox mug and Grey Sox flag hanging on her electronics' charging station then gave her a thumbs up gesture. "Love, your taste in baseball teams, detective." that agent commented. The first agent gave her a thumbs down gesture for the same sports memorabilia.

"Where do we stand at the moment?" Captain Bronzesmith inquired.

"The FBI has been working with the 271st precinct this morning in a number of inquiries and in the conducting of three interviews with suspects, including Cathedral Police chief Anton Chinchinocippi. This work is our main priority and it will take precedence over any other ongoing homicides." Chief Thigby indicated.

"Working since 5am with the lieutenant here this lovely morning, we have established a strong connection between your homicide case and our corruption, bribery, and fraud cases. We now believe your murder suspect is the person the FBI most wants to give evidence against corruption within private law enforcement companies." the first FBI agent disclosed.

"We have to take back law enforcement from companies like Lawtech and their rogue robots. Your prime suspect and our person of greatest interest are one in the same. The FBI is of the opinion that this person can greatly help us with our case against the leadership of Lawtech Corporation." the second FBI agent added.

"So you get a strong witness and we catch a killer. Then the FBI goes back its federal duties and we can get back to solving homicides in our favorite city precinct. No Christmas cards required come the holidays" the chief summarized.

"We arrest our target this morning. Everybody but the criminal wins. Then we go our separate ways to return to business as usual." the other FBI agent determined.

"What about any 271st precinct homicides that need to be investigated today?" the captain wondered.

"If the 271st needs help today, then I will get some help from the 270th and 269th precincts. Both of them owe us favors anyway so there should be no problem." Chief Thigby shared his plan.

"Then we are off to arrest a villain." both FBI agents stated at the same time.

"Let's get this done." Chief Thigby concluded. And with that said the mission to arrest the district attorney's killer began.

Following the FBI agents' macrocruiser, the mud tusslers drove their PSUV back into the interior of the city of Cathedral. It was Emily's turn to drive in the nightmarish mess of Cathedral's morning traffic. They were making too many trips into the heart of Cathedral lately. As they struggled through the tough Tuesday morning traffic, Detective

Oftenmarch toiled to stay with the federal agents' vehicle. Impatient commuters kept barging into any space Emily left between the PSUV and the macro-cruiser. By the time they reached North 9th Avenue, three cars were between the FBI's vehicle and their PSUV.

Emily knew they were getting close to the Cathedral Police Plaza when she saw the Studor Building. The Studor Building, formerly the Adams Building, was a 72-story, 740-foot mid-tier skyscraper rather well known and recognizable by its rounded building corners, predominantly wide horizontal windows, and golden painted vertical strips. Next to the Studor Building were the twin domes of the Powercore Unlimited Corporation headquarters, a building with which Emily was very familiar. Her late husband still had a parking spot in the building's underground garage which Emily still used from time to time.

Behind the headquarters of the Powercore Unlimited Corporation, Two Police Plaza was visible in the city skyline. Emily continued to trail the FBI agents as they crawled through the brutal city traffic. Electronic advertisement boards shone brightly along their route but were outshone by the brilliant morning sunshine radiating in the sky about Cathedral. To Emily, there seemed to be more car horn blowing this morning than most other days, but she was not this far into the city on most days. Enduring the traffic congestion and loud car horns, the group of law enforcement eventually made it to the Police Plaza.

The group was delayed again at the Police Plaza itself. You would think that the last place people would park in a restricted yellow no parking zone would be in front of the city's police headquarters. However, dozens of vehicles were parked on the restricted parking curbside in front of both One Police Plaza and Two Police Plaza. People either were taunting the police or it was the police themselves breaking the rules. In addition, there was a large group of protesters gathered around Police Plaza. None of them were very happy with the city's police. They were carrying signs that said Defund the Police, Werewolves are Fiction, and Taxpayers want More Lettuce, Less Bacon. Several of them were blocking the main driveway into the plaza. After this additional delay, the group found parking for both vehicles, albeit in separate locations, and gathered outside One Police Plaza ready to execute the planned arrest.

There was a Tuesday morning High Commissioner's meeting in progress when Lt. Knighton, Detective Oftenmarch, and federal company arrived on the 40th floor of One Police Plaza. To get access to the building, a pass to the High Commissioner's floor, and past the High Commissioner's lead admin, typically takes multiple forms of authorization, a pre-approved sanctioned appointment, or an act of congress. This morning all Eddie had to say was "Lt. Knighton, it's important." and he had to say no more. Perhaps, the FBI had something to do with this, or Chief Thigby had called ahead, or High Commissioner Harden had given them special short-term permission. Whatever the reason, the mud tusslers were admitted an audience with the High Commissioner without preamble.

Emily and the lieutenant had the pair of FBI agents accompanying them, agents Mikulasikova and Kovslovski. Emily barely got a chance to get acquainted with either agent as Eddie only had time for the briefest of introductions this morning. The group somberly rode the elevator to the 40th floor and walked to the High Commissioner's conference room in absolute silence. There was nothing to say; the time had come for action.

The 40th floor of One Police Plaza was a tidy, well furnished level. It was a plush and comfortable environment, very different from the no frills work facilities at the 271st police precinct. Full of framed wall photographs of Old Arden city and early Cathedral Police departments and stations combined with old city plaques, this floor was rich in historical decorations. Spotless, nicely furnished, and well decorated, the whole floor looked like it was a model for an online furniture catalog. This was a floor definitely designed, decorated, and decluttered for very important people.

Directly across the elevator, between adjoining waiting areas, was the floor's main hallway. Security Chief Brown was standing guard outside a conference room door at the far end of the main hallway. He appeared to be waiting for them like he knew they were coming. Without having to be told, Lt. Knighton immediately headed in that direction. Along the length of the main hallway were well spaced microsecurity cameras continually monitoring the passageway. It was clear that this hallway led to very important people, people who were protected. Maintaining their silence, the foursome dutifully marched down the hallway keeping their focus on the job at hand. Wordlessly, Security Chief Brown opened the door for them as they approached. Without scrutiny or small talk, the group was permitted to pass into the conference room.

Seven people were sitting around a large ornate conference table, the kind you would imagine to find at a major corporation, as the law enforcement group entered the room. An autoassistant was moving around the ornate table and serving warm beverages to the conferring group. The robotic servant hummed away as it served its masters their delicious drinks. The conference room occupants had been engrossed in conversation and refreshments prior to this interruption. Everyone around the table looked at the arriving group with a mixture of curiosity and startled puzzlement, with one exception.

High Commissioner Harden was seated at the head of the large table; the expression on his face was stoically unreadable, but he did not appear to be surprised at their arrival. With his focus held on the arriving group, the High Commissioner maintained his unreadable authoritative expression on his stoic face. Offering no greeting, Harden waited calmly and patiently, allowing the detectives to accomplish the task they had come to perform.

Seated to the right of the High Commissioner was his personal assistant, Lisa Maria. Those who were good friends with the friendly woman called her by her nickname Lima, short for Lisa Maria. The young ambitious, and valuable assistant was neatly and smartly dressed, befitting a successful woman in the workforce. Lisa Maria had multiple stacks of paperwork laid out orderly in front of her. Unlike the High Commissioner, her face displayed surprise, then confusion which was extremely expressive.

Seated to the left of the High Commissioner was police commissioner Zahlen Sopellento. Commissioner Sopellento had his work laptop running in front of him and next to him was a Mercury Gen 17 etableau. The midtown police commissioner had a 3D holographic personal projector connected to his etableau. It was currently projecting an image of the indigo screen of death. Sopellento was busy working back and forth from his laptop to his etableau when the group of four entered. Upon their arrival, he stopped what he was busily doing and stared expectantly at them.

Next to Lisa Maria was seated the police department's press spokeswoman, Alicabeth Buchanan. Both articulate and beautiful, Alicabeth was perfect for the job of CPD's police spokeswoman. She was also a gifted spin doctor who almost always was well received and liked by the tough Cathedral media. Her glamorous looks and bright smile could charm a room of people before she even spoke a word. It was Alicabeth to whom the servicebot was serving breakfast tea when the group of four entered the room. Like Lisa Maria, she appeared to be at first surprised then confused by the group's entrance.

Next to Sopellento was seated police commissioner-at-large Harold Chinchinocippi. The well dressed commissioner wore a nice black suit and an attractive striped silk necktie. Neither a laptop computer nor any paperwork lay on the table in front of the commissioner-at-large. The only items in front of Chinchinocippi were a warm beverage served by the autoassistant and a local deli bought bagel. He was in the middle of an animated conversation with the people at the end of the table when the group of four walked into the room. As the group entered, he paused mid-sentence in his conversation and gave them a quizzical look.

At the end of the table speaking with Chinchinocippi were a pair of police lieutenant commissioners. Both lieutenant commissioners looked like they were off to a sleepy start on this Tuesday morning. One of them had a half unbuttoned shirt with ketchup stains down its front and the other one had disheveled hair and an upside down photo security badge pinned to their shirt. Both of them had two cups of coffee in front of them, one from the autoassistant and one they had brought with them.

Neither of the lieutenant commissioners seemed overly eager to begin work. Both looked dumbfounded when the group of four entered the conference room.

If Hedra Shippendarrow had been with them, then chances are he would have said something like, 'oh look, all the king's horses and all the king's men are here'. But Shippendarrow was no longer with them and Emily had never experienced anything like this situation. There was no memorable moment where Hedra made an arrest in the High Commissioner's conference room. Deciding not to grandstand or make a long oratory, the detective used a tactic from her lieutenant's play-book and went for a direct no nonsense approach.

Without hesitation or preamble, Detective Oftenmarch strode over to where police commissioner-at-large Harold Chinchinocippi was seated. Emily walked up to him businesslike and gave her declaration confidently as she approached him. "Harold Chinchinocippi, you are under arrest for the murder of the district attorney." Emily informed him then began to read him his re-revised Miranda rights.

"Are you insane? Or is this some kind of sick joke?" Chinchinocippi asked incredulously.

Detective Oftenmarch did not answer his interrupting questions but finished reading the man his rights then concluded with the question, "Do you understand these rights as I have stated them to you?"

"Rights you swore to uphold." Eddie coldly added.

Chinchinocippi ignored the detectives and directed a question to the High Commissioner. "Did you know about this, Benson?" he queried.

"Yes, I did." Harden acknowledged calmly.

"And you let it happen? You allowed this farce to occur?" Harold posed in disbelief.

"I wanted to see how it played out. I wanted to hear the accusations and evidence. More importantly, I wanted to observe your response to the charges." High Commissioner Harden still calmly answered.

"This is neither a joke nor a farce, Commissioner Chinchinocippi. You are seriously under arrest." Oftenmarch confirmed.

"Ridiculous. This is outrageous. Do you know who I am?" Harold Chinchinocippi proudly protested.

"Yes, the man being arrested." Eddie responded.

"We have an eyewitness who positively identified you and we have the testimony of two known criminals, both of whom have confirmed their correspondences with you, to corroborate. CaseBuilder scores the case against you at 85.7 conviction percentage. If the witness holds reliable or a third criminal associate turns on you, then the conviction percentage skyrockets substantially." Emily revealed.

"Your witness must be sadly mistaken. How could they possibly think it's me?" Chinchinocippi pleaded innocent.

"The lycan masquerade killers were not arrogant or foolish enough to remove their masks while committing crimes. However, for reasons only known by you, you decided to remove your mask in the act of murder. The eyewitness saw you clearly without a mask and both criminals confirmed you removed your mask mid-crime." Emily shared.

"You have the testimony of criminals, surely you jest. The case you have against me is built upon criminals." Chinchinocippi scoffed.

"There's no loyalty in villainy." Eddie replied.

"Those criminals you worked with now tell tales in detail. Did you think there would be loyalty among the disloyal? Did you think there would be discretion among the indiscreet? Those criminals, now caught, are testifying against you; they are telling on you to save themselves." Emily continued.

"Then there's your security droid." Lt. Knighton contributed.

"You left the GPS tracker running on your droid security unit the night of the murder, Commissioner Chinchinocippi. That droid recorded your location at the crime scene. It video recorded you as being in the area during the district attorney's estimated time of death. That video has a valid and CPD certified time stamp. This places you in the perfect proximity to commit murder. It was the piece of your technological footprint you forgot to deactivate. This was a small oversight that significantly contributed to the 85.7 percent." Emily expounded.

"Finally, there is the weapon." Eddie interjected.

"We were told by your associates where to find the murder weapon. Instead of disposing the weapon as instructed, they stashed it away as an insurance policy to protect themselves. The CPD is currently somewhere in the process of retrieving, logging, and analyzing that weapon." Detective Oftenmarch added.

"Unfortunately, there is a strong well documented case against you here in CaseBuilder. This is solid Cathedral police work." Soppatellenti admitted as he was studying the information displayed on his work laptop in front of him.

"Do you honestly think I am capable of committing an act so vile as homicide?" Chinchinocippi protested.

"You were a desperate man, Commissioner. Your crimes to fabricate a false narrative of needing private law enforcement were catching up with you. You were perverting justice for many people for personal profit. You were manipulating the legal system for personal gain. You were propagating lies and fraudulent information. You were dealing out death and judgment as you saw fit. The insurmountable amount of illegal activity you were perpetrating became so immense and egregious that your own uncle and partner in crime was beginning to argue with you. The pair of you began to feud at the city's expense. Then you attracted the unwanted attention of the district attorney. You could have felt trapped and afraid it was all falling down on you. So you committed a terrible act of murder. Possibly, you found it to be a quick and convenient solution to an impending and mounting problem. Whatever the reason, the evidence shows that you were capable of committing homicide." Emily rebutted in detail.

"You seem convinced of the worst of me. Are you going to handcuff me, detective? Are you going to march me away like a common criminal?" Commissioner Chinchinocippi challenged.

"No, the FBI agents are here to do that honor. There are multiple federal charges you will now be arrested for committing. The lieutenant and I are now just here to watch that happen." Emily replied.

"Albeit with enjoyment." Eddie confessed.

It was now FBI agent Mikulasikova's turn to step forward. Moving next to the detectives, the FBI agent addressed the accused commissioner with the next declaration of apprehension. "Harold Chinchinocippi, you are under arrest for criminal misconduct, falsifying documentation, perverting the course of justice, aiding and abetting, embezzlement, bribery, tampering with evidence, seditious conspiracy, conspiracy to commit fraud, and conspiracy to defraud the United States of America." Mikulasikova informed the commissioner. The agent then began to read Chinchinocippi his re-revised Miranda rights.

"This is more absurd than the last accusation." Chinchinocippi shouted angrily.

"Harold, what have you done?" Lisa Maria asked with concern.

"Unfortunately, what he was doing was systematically ruining the Cathedral Police Department in order to promote the privatization of police work. He could personally capitalize on and control private law enforcement once he had succeeded with destroying government run law enforcement." Mikulasikova explained.

"Let me guess, you have found another lying witness to testify against me." Chinchinocippi mocked in disgust.

"Could you really expect people who are willing to be disloyal to their duties and departments to be loyal to their corrupt leader? A group of people untrustworthy enough to give into temptations are not going to remain loyal to their wicked ring leader. Again now that they are caught, they are testifying against you; they are informing on you to rescue themselves." Emily reiterated.

"The FBI has spoken with seven Cathedral police captains and three Cathedral police chiefs, including your own uncle, who have testified your plotting and execution of deliberately mishandling or misfiling criminal cases. They all testify those same criminal cases are then auctioned off to private companies, often companies in which you have ownership, for personal profit. Their testimonies are detailed and consistent." agent Kovslovski contributed.

"The commissioner was using any means necessary, legal or illegal, to undermine the current Cathedral Police Department and to make private law enforcement companies, particularly his own, more profitable. The FBI also interviewed dozens of private law enforcement company investors, who all tell a similar tale incriminating the commissioner-at-large." agent Mikulasikova added solemnly.

"That would suggest several weeks of detective work. Why is this all just now being disclosed?" one of the puzzled lieutenant commissioners inquired.

"We have been working on this case for months. When Cathedral law enforcement began doing database searches regarding the Cathedral Commissioner-at-large late last night, we suspected that he had become the focus of an investigation. When Lt. Knighton continued to make inquiries regarding the Cathedral Commissioner-at-large, we were concerned he might jeopardize our ongoing investigation. When the FBI reached out to Chief Thigby and then the lieutenant, we discovered the commissioner's crimes now include murder. It was at that moment the FBI decided it was time to make an arrest." agent Mikulasikova disclosed.

"The FBI had a stronger case against your uncle, Commissioner, so he was arrested first earlier this morning. Along with Lt. Knighton, we questioned your uncle and now have a much stronger case against you, Commissioner Chinchinocippi. In speaking with your uncle it became clear he preferred using the lycan masqueraders as a scare tactic and opposed the idea of having them kill. He painted a picture which shows you as the person in charge." agent Kovslovski appended.

"What makes you so suspicious of my uncle and myself?" Chinchinocippi asked offendedly. He turned a cold gaze directly at Detective Oftenmarch.

"It was the abnormality of your precinct and your uncle's precinct which looked suspicious. All the other city precincts had rising rates of convictions overturned or dismissed cases. Only your uncle's precinct and your precinct kept those rates down. Digging deeper into that anomaly, it appeared like in order to avoid suspicion you and your uncle recruited detectives, cops, and supervisors from other precincts to turn corrupt. Corruption in their precincts would cast doubt on others and not yourselves. In the end, it was your precinct and your uncle's precinct that were suspicious because they were uniquely different from the rest. They were the abnormality." Emily logically shared.

"You and your uncle are suspicious, Commissioner, because both of you are guilty. The FBI is confident you will be found as guilty as you are in a court of law." Kovslovski commented.

"Benson, you know me. Do you believe I could possibly do any of what they are accusing me of doing? How long are you going to allow them to indulge in this gross slandering? Please come to my defense." Chinchinocippi pleaded with the High Commissioner.

"I believe in the legal system I represent. I believe in due process and that you will have your day in court. By the laws of the city, state, and country, you will get a defense. It is not my job to judge. It is not my right to interfere with the course of justice." the High Commissioner replied somberly.

"So, you will do nothing." screamed Chinchinocippi, losing his composure.

"Allowing law enforcement to do its job and allowing the legal system to proceed as it was designed is not the same thing as doing nothing," High Commissioner Harden retorted calmly, keeping his composure.

"I am the victim here. This is just another example of how broken this city and nation's legal systems are. This is the thanks I get for all my hard work for this department and the city of Cathedral." complained Chinchinocippi.

"You are not the victim here, Harold. You can drop the pretenses. We now know all about the Lycan program." Mikulasikova replied.

"Last year's criminal activity numbers." Eddie revealed.

"You have no idea how much damage you are doing, Lt. Knighton. Look at how much the Cathedral Police has improved. There are advancements like the Quad P program, increases in efficiency, and decreases in payroll expenses. Work is flowing to private law enforcement which has better technology and superior personnel structure for effective police work. The Lycan program has launched a new revolution for a better police department, a better system of serving and protecting the citizens of the city of Cathedral. Not to mention the competition between government run police and privately run police is improving both of them." Harold Chinchinocippi proudly declared.

"Cathedral's crime rate is up six percent since private law enforcement has been legalized and instituted and nine percent over the last year. Complaints and misconducts against private law enforcement is double that of public law enforcement. Public expenditures have sky-rocketed to pay companies like Crimestoppers and Lawtech. Jurisdiction disputes between private and public police are ongoing while criminal activity goes unchecked. None of this sounds like improvement." Kovslovski argued.

"More lies and distortions. Law enforcement is on an upward trajectory none of you could fathom. Bold measures had to be taken to make big progress." Chinchinocippi stated.

"Murders, break-ins, hacking, extortion, murders" listed Lt. Knighton.

"Unfortunate necessary measures to achieve better policing for the future. Difficult choices sometimes have to be made for a better tomorrow. This is something the High Commissioner is unwilling to face." Chinchinocippi again proudly stated.

"Think you're justified for all those who died? You stomp the lowly, to act all holy. And the killers did what you told them. And the cheaters did what you told them. And the demented did what you told them. And the killers did what you told them." Emily challenged.

"Time to pay the Bramble." Eddie told the commissioner-at-large.

This was in reference to a gambling term that originated in Cathedral. Instead of paying for a bet, a bettor could take out a loan to place a bet. The loan was called a bet recovery account mitigating beats loan easement, or Bramble for short. If the bettor won, they could repay the loan from the winnings or keep the entire winnings and repay the loan, plus interest, at the end of the month. If the bettor lost on the bet, then they would owe the money plus interest on the loan at the end of the month. Like a credit card, the debtor was only required to pay a minimum, or the interest on the loan, and was allowed to leave the bulk of the loan payment pending while still accruing interest. State law put restrictions on the duration of such loans to prevent bankruptcies. Gamblers were allowed to carry this type of loan for up to nine months.

At the end of the ninth month, the entire loan, plus interest, was due. The Bramble had come due; it was time to pay the Bramble.

"Things are worse than advertised because you are trying to sell the illusion that private law enforcement works so that you may profit. You cheated, killed, and gambled big to achieve your goals. You have made bad bets, Commissioner Chinchinocippi. You have dug yourself into a deeper and deeper hole. Now the Bramble has come due." Emily agreed with her partner.

"You are under arrest, Harold Chinchinocippi." Mikulasikova repeated.

"I don't know which two detectives people would have picked to catch you but I do know which two detectives have caught you. That says it all, Harold." Soppatellenti expressed.

"Today can be a day of forgiveness; today can be a day of repentance and grace. GOD loves you, Commissioner. Confess your sins and ask for forgiveness...." Emily started to caringly explain.

"Don't you dare speak to me like that, you stupid little..." Chinchinocippi began to spew nastily as his face turned red.

Lt. Knighton quickly moved in front of Emily and stood up close to the Commissioner-at-large and defiantly interrupted. "You're done huffing and puffing." he flatly stated to Harry Chinchinocippi.

The FBI agents moved forward to arrest Chinchinocippi. They attempted to peaceably detain the man in a respectful manner but Harold Chinchinocippi was not having any of that. He was determined to put up a fight; he was going to struggle to the end. The commissioner-at-large squirmed, fought, and resisted, but he was no match for agents Mikulasikova and Kovslovski. In less than thirty seconds they had the hostile suspect restrained. As a result of the struggle, Chinchinocippi had dropped his identification security badge. As the enraged man was marched away in handcuffs by the FBI agents, Lt. Knighton reached down and picked up the security badge. Eddie prompted threw it away in the nearest wastebasket. It was about twenty feet away but the lieutenant's shot found nothing but the bottom of the basket.

As Chinchinocippi was half escorted half dragged from the conference room, his cursing grew fainter and fainter. After the man was removed from the room and the door closed in his wake, the room was quiet for a long moment. Something unthinkable had just occurred, the arrest of a city police commissioner, and the reality of that sobering fact had left the room in a moment of silence. Eddie and Emily began their discreet departure to follow the FBI agents when the High Commissioner broke the silence to address them.

"One moment please, detectives. My sincere thanks to the pair of you. Your dedication and devotion are appreciated and will not be forgotten. The amazing work the both of you have done over the past two days has been immensely helpful to both myself and the entire Cathedral Police Department. The role both of you played in this chess match to restore order in the great city of Cathedral was more valuable than any other. Chess pieces that get good value or accomplish a lot on the chess board, called depasser le bon pion, cannot compare to your excellent contributions. Your tireless work was so amazing I have a new nickname for the pair of you. You are the guardians of Cathedral. You have protected both the reputation of the department and the city of Cathedral from maniac masqueraders. The pair of you have also been the silver lining to this whole hellish nightmare of police corruption and murder. The pair of you have restored my faith in the hardworking members of the Cathedral Police Department. Years ago in the fallen city of Arden, the first city sheriff created a service award called the Distinguished Golden Badge of Gallantry. This award was given only a handful of times before the Arden city sheriff's office was decommissioned. In the early years of the city of Cathedral, its police department reinstituted this award. However, in all the years of serving and protecting the citizens of Cathedral, not one member of the Cathedral PD has been given this award. That changes this week because both of you will receive a monetary reward and the Distinguished Golden Badge of Gallantry award. In addition, I am awarding you both the more well known Cathedral Police

High Commissioner's Medal of Distinction. I believe these awards have been more than earned and I am happy to bestow these accolades upon you. Again, you have my deepest thanks and appreciation. Thank you." High Commissioner Harden expressed his gratitude. He then stood up, walked over to the pair of detectives, and gratefully shook their hands.

"Thank you, boss." Lt. Knighton stated as he shook the high commissioner's hand.

"Thank you, High Commissioner Harden." Detective Oftenmarch thanked as she shook his hand.

"Take the rest of the day off with pay. You have most definitely earned it. Now if you will excuse us, we have much to discuss at this meeting, starting with what to publicly disclose regarding the events at the Flockman and Bellweather Building last night and culminating with damage control from criminal activity committed within the Cathedral Police Commissioners' office. Good day to you both." High Commissioner Harden bid them farewell.

Chapter 23

Epilogue

The sun seemed to shine brighter in the sky over the city of Cathedral on this day. Fewer clouds than normal hung over the city. The atmosphere in the city seemed to be less polluted than most days. For on this day, the acts of wicked men did not go unchallenged. For on this day, those who speak for the aggrieved persevered to overcome the adversities of evil. Their noble actions did their talking. This was a good day, the lycan masquerade killers terrorize the city of Cathedral no more. No more running for the suburbs. No more running for safety. Now you could run for your happiness, run for your lover. The werewolf days were over. The werewolf nights were over. The werewolf nights in Cathedral were over.

This was also the day where a supermanga hero movie, called The League of Captains and Queens, was being filmed in downtown Cathedral in the afternoon. Thousands of people were heading down-town for a chance to become extras in the movie. Even the beloved top rookie prospect for the Cathedral Bishops was rumored to have a cameo in the major entertainment production. The mood in the city streets seemed to be cheerier on this day. Their cares had been averted from crime and the people of Cathedral were now focused on the distraction of movie entertainment. No more dark news of werewolves hunting people in the city. The lycan masqueraders did not pass go, they did not collect two hundred dollars, but went directly to jail.

Breaking news on Central Nexus News, WXLT Cathedral: There was an altercation last night in the Flockman and Bellweather Building. According to local officials, LawTech Patrollers defended citizens and engaged in fighting against intruders dressed as werewolves. These intruders are believed to be the masked killers who have been causing havoc in the city. Witnesses to the event said the Patrollers came to the aid of city police. Several arrests were made after multiple confrontations broke out inside the midscraper, causing tens of thousands of dollars of damage. The Cathedral Police Department declined to disclose any details regarding the nature of the fights or the names of those arrested.

It was a much deserved rarely given weekday off from work for Emily and Eddie. As they were leaving the precinct, the lieutenant had silently given Emily a big bear hug before departing. For a moment, Emily thought she had imagined the whole thing. But it was real and she knew it was Eddie's way of saying thank you from the bottom of his heart. Despite all his peculiarities, the man was a good lieutenant and a great partner.

It was a great day. Emily did not hear deceased detectives, she did not see wild werewolves, but went directly to jubilation. No longer did she question her own sanity. Emily could see clearly now the storm had gone. She could see all life's obstacles in her way. Here was the miracle Emily had been praying for. It was going to be a bright sunshiny day. She could see clearly now the wolves were gone. All dark and gloomy entrances were now okay. Here was the sanity she had been hoping for. It was going to be a bright sunshiny day.

Having the rest of the day off, Emily left the congestion and busy-ness of the city of Cathedral. Deciding to make the most of her time off by surprising her husband, the detective decided to pick-up a hearty lunch for David-John and take him to his favorite park for a picnic. Hoping to atone for missing last night's speech and genuinely wanting to surprise her husband, Emily thought this to be a great inspiration. Emily drove to Chatham where David-John worked Tuesday mornings at the Greater Cathedral Evangelical Library until noon. Making three stops along her route, Emily was attempting to time her arrival just before David-John's shift was done. The first stop was at a Chatham Hills bakery where Emily purchased some cupcakes. Her second stop was on the outskirts of Chatham at Super Feasters Deli and Tavern where she bought a couple of warm sub sandwiches, fruit sticks, and spring rolls. Emily's final stop was at a TwentyBucks two blocks from the Greater Cathedral Evangelical Library where she purchased a couple of deluxe lattes.

This day continued to be a day of good fortune because Emily was able to make all three stops efficiently and arrived at the library at five minutes to noon. She was able to make it without having to spoil the surprise with a text of tardiness. As Emily pulled into the parking lot of the Greater Cathedral Evangelical Library with her Jaycox Motors car, David-John was speaking with Father Ulbermann just outside the main entrance on the front walkway. He did not have his cane with him, so he was doing better on this day. Seeing Emily arrive, David-John did look both pleased and surprised at the same time. The expression on his face made Emily delighted; it made her day. Without delay, Emily exited her car and hustled up the walkway to give her husband a big hug and the picnic invitation. Recognizing the happy moment for the married couple, Father Ulbermann kindly let David-John depart a few minutes early to enjoy a nice picnic with his wife.

Given permission to leave, David-John followed Emily as she drove to the Monroe Meadow metro park located in Chatham Hills not far from their home. In the center of David-John's favorite park was a pleasant man-made lake with a pair of picturesque water fountains. Each water fountain satisfyingly sprayed a cascade of water about fifteen feet upward and roughly twenty feet outward. The pair of happy lovers selected a picnic table in a pleasant section of the park lawn with a good view of the water fountains. As the sun shone down brilliantly, it was a beautiful day for a pleasant picnic.

Their meals were almost as good as their company because their free time together was rare and always amazing. After a delicious meal, they held each other close. There was something intoxicating about their togetherness. Just the two of them, holding each other tightly and tuning out their surroundings. Warm and fuzzy feelings held in their embrace. His love for her was as strong as her love was powerful for him. As the sunshine lit up the park, it was a beautiful day for a tender hug.

They shared a kiss like a loving couple should. They shared a kiss like in the fairy tales of old. It was a kiss that renewed passions and rekindled desires. It was a kiss that should never fade. Kisses for a love cherished, they had a romance of shame perished. Their kiss was a precious treasure which could never be sold; their kiss was a treasured outpouring of love to behold. They shared a kiss like true lovers steadfast in love.

No longer did the detective have a case of the lycans. Emily had a new case; she had a case of the I love yous. Over and over, she told David-John she loved him and in reply he repeated the same to her. Happily together, the couple took a walk through the pleasant park. Around the water fountains they circled twice before moving further into the park. They had a peaceful stroll until they decided to kiss again. This was a long kiss that was meant to be remembered.

Emily and David-John had to enjoy the moment while it lasted. Unfortunately, he would soon have to leave to work his shift at the Chatham Hills Public Library at the information desk. As for Emily, she would have to head to church to help cook spaghetti dinners for roughly a hundred people. Life would move onward but for the moment, they enjoyed their time together.

Breaking news on Cathedral 24/7 MegaNews: A brand new private law enforcement company called Greater Safety Corporation has opened its doors today. This company offers a bright new future to a suffering public after the many shortcomings of the public police department. The Greater Safety Corporation will begin its operations in the city of Cathedral. With recently rising crime rates, the city of Cathedral will benefit from the arrival of this ambitious new private law enforcement company.

In a modest sized eatery, called the Whistlestop Tavern, on the outskirts of Cathedral there was a lull between the breakfast rush and the lunch crowd. Seventh walked through the front door of the tidy establishment and searched for his friend. The tavern was full of railroad themed memorabilia to enhance its locomotive themed decor. At a hightop table on the left side of the tavern next to window, Seventh spotted his friend Travis seated next to another man. The pair of them were enjoying some hot wings. Seventh waved to his friend as he made his way over to the table.

"We missed you on Friday night, Seventh." his friend Travis said as Seventh approached the hightop table.

"Sorry, I howl at the moon sometimes. Had myself a night last Friday." Seventh shared as he sat down at the table.

"Seventh, this is Jameson Burkess. Mr. Burkess, this is my friend Seventh Day." his friend Travis gave the introductions.

"Thank you for this opportunity to speak with you, Mr. Burkess." Seventh greeted.

"Nice to meet you, Mr. Day. Travis has been telling me you are quite the athlete." Jameson counter greeted.

"I was telling Jameson how well you played football back in your younger days." Travis confessed.

"Played well in high school but once I got into college the level of competition surpassed me. Went from all state status to all done status." Seventh admitted modestly.

"So what makes you want to join the Cathedral Fire Department, Mr. Day?" Jameson asked quizzically.

"I have a younger sister who is a detective for the Cathedral Police Department. She inspired me to work a job where I can help people." Seventh disclosed.

"Interesting. Who is your sister?" Jameson inquired.

"Detective Emily Oftenmarch." Seventh answered with a hint of pride.

"I know, Emily. You're hired. Report to the station tomorrow morning at 8am. We will need you to fill out some paperwork on your first day. Congratulations." Jameson gave Seventh a job in the fire department.

"Thank you, Mr. Burkess." Seventh thanked the man. He was surprised but pleased. That was both the shortest and the best interview Seventh had ever had and he had been on a ton of interviews in his lifetime. Today was turning out to be a good day.

Breaking news on NNC, Network News Channel: Federal authorities have verified they are investigating a pair of private law enforcement companies. Both SuperSafe and Lawtech are being investigated for interfering with criminal cases and obstruction of justice. There are speculations that charges may be filed in the next couple of days. A spokesperson for SuperSafe stated that the company is cooperating with federal investigators and is confident this misunderstanding will soon be resolved. They claim SuperSafe will be found innocent of any wrongdoing. The company of Lawtech declined to comment on the allegations.

Lt. Eddie Knighton was exhausted. He had been awake for over twenty-seven of the last twenty-nine or thirty hours. He had taken a sad nap in an awkward position at the 271st precinct earlier that morning, but it had done little to quench his current sleepiness. For as tired as he was, Eddie was more relieved than anything else to have concluded the lycan masquerade killers case. He no longer had a case of the lycans. Too tired to drive, the lieutenant caught an air shuttle bus to Granthum Heights. During the air bus ride, the lieutenant took a second nap despite his best efforts to stay awake. He drifted off to sleep in the first few minutes of the journey and only awoke in time to get off at his intended stop because of the loud air horn of a double-decker truck. This normally irritating noise was actually accommodating this time. Wordlessly, Eddie sleepily stumbled out of the air shuttle bus and onto the streets of Granthum Heights.

Quietly, the lieutenant walked eight city blocks repeatedly trying to quit thinking about case facts and CaseBuilder notes that should be made. It was peaceful and serene in Granthum Heights. He silently made his hike in warm sunshine to a senior living retirement home called Grathum Heights Superannuation Society senior center. The senior center consisted of a dozen well kept buildings which formed a semicircle on a tidy immaculate grounds. Making his way to the main building of the Superannuation Society, Eddie inaudibly admired the scenic grounds of the senior center. The main building of the retirement home had a short squat clocktower which was running five minutes fast. Once at the main building, Eddie, with few words, logged into the guestbook and registered with the establishment as a visitor.

Now in compliance with the facility's rules, the lieutenant stealthily strolled through the retirement home buildings to the Parker Hall of building E. Eddie passed two ladies dressed in choir robes having an animated chat, an elderly man in his underpants looking for an ashtray, a clown carrying a dozen colorful balloons, a service droid repeatedly running into the same wall, a moose mascot for a local high school, three members of a mariachi band, and a man wearing a long billboard sign that read 'When does it end?'. Nothing unusual for this retirement home. He continued his mellow march until he came to a residence door labeled Room E216, Eleanor Knighton. The door was left wide open. Inside the room was an elderly lady walking around the room listening to symphonic music, waving a conducting wand through the air, and talking away to seemingly nobody. Under closer observation, it became more apparent that the elegantly dressed lady was talking to her cat and a pair of large house plants. If a person listened long enough they would hear her address each by name. Eddie knew the names well. Their names were Flora, Blossom, and Mischievous. He often stood silently in the doorway listening to his mother as he was doing now.

"Hear the lovely tune, Flora. Oh, the lovely robust sound. Hear the sweet accompaniment, Blossom. The notes coming together at the correct time and measure. Well done. Can you hear the depth of the sound, Flora and Blossom? The pleasant wafts of musical delight. Please sit still, Mischievous. Just enjoy the music, silly. Hear the lovely tones of treasured treble. Very nice, now please don't rush these measures. Keep with the flow of the melody. Let it be pleasing. Keep with the ebb of the melody. Now fortissimo, fortissimo. Finish with a flourish. Oh how wonderful, oh how marvelous is the music. Let there be a big finish and then take a bow." Eleanor Knighton spoke aloud as she conducted along with the music.

"Good morning, Mother." Eddie greeted her as he entered her room.

"My son Edward is here" Mrs. Knighton said to herself. Then she rushed past Eddie and to the door where she called to her next door neighbor, "My son Edward is here, Martha!".

As his mother left the room to call her neighbor, the lieutenant stood in her room alone. "Nice to see you, too." Eddie said to himself as he suspiciously watched the cat, Mischievous. Making itself comfortable on his mother's nice davenport, the cat returned his gaze with one of indifference.

Still watching the cat, Eddie's focus had switched to the furniture. His mother's favorite davenport, which she took with her everywhere she moved, could qualify as an antique. His mother had the davenport since before he was born. It had been reupholstered fifteen times in his lifetime and probably more before his birth. His mother had kept this piece of furniture in excellent condition throughout the years. Sensing that Eddie was still watching them intently, the cat decided to jump off the davenport and hide under a nearby dresser. The cat knew that Eddie knew that the cat was up to no good, mischief if you will.

After about a minute of Eddie being left on his own, Eleanor came back with company. His mother returned with her neighbor, who was carrying an electronic knitter and multiple spools of yarn. The poor lady had obviously been uprooted from what she was doing and brought here to meet the lieutenant. She kept a friendly smile on her face which reminded Eddie of Oftenmarch.

"Martha, this is my son, Edward." Eleanor introduced her son to her friend.

"Nice to meet you, Martha." Eddie greeted.

"Hello, young man. Eleanor tells me that you're a policeman." Martha replied.

"A police detective for Cathedral." Eddie clarified.

"My son is a crimefighter in the streets of Cathedral, a city full of trouble and hooligans. He fights the terror that lurks in the night so people in the city can sleep tight." Eleanor bragged with embellishment.

"It's nice to meet a policeman. My uncle Sedwick was a policeman. He worked for the Granthum Police for decades before he had to retire due to poor health." Martha shared.

"There is no better profession than being a police officer. They keep the citizens safe and send the baddies to jail." Eleanor gave her opinion.

"I thought robots were now doing the work of the police." Martha offered.

"Robots do not protect people, people protect people." Eleanor responded.

"Well, that does make sense." Martha admitted.

"There are so many stories from being a policeman. My son is full of wonderful stories. He is quite the storyteller. Please tell us one of your interesting tales from your work, Eddie. You could tell your splendid story to Martha, Flora, Blossom, Mischievous, and me." Eleanor encouraged her son.

"Oh, goodie. This sounds exciting." Martha exclaimed as she sat in a chair in the corner of the room and began to use the electronic knitter while anticipating a story.

Releasing a small sigh, Eddie knew he had no choice. Taking a seat on the old dependable davenport, Eddie calmly began to tell a tale, "The lesson for today's story comes from Proverbs 14:12. *There is a way which seems right to a man, But its end is the way of death.* Once upon a time there was a group of foolish men who thought they knew better than GOD."

The End

Made in United States
Orlando, FL
21 December 2024

56328353R10290